*Pamela,
Hope you fall as much in love
with Jackson as I did
Jamie Farrell*

Southern Fried Blues

JAMIE FARRELL

ISBN-13: 978-1-940517-00-1

SOUTHERN FRIED BLUES

Copyright © 2013 by Jamie Farrell
2nd Edition

All rights reserved. This book or any portion thereof may not be reproduced or used in any manner whatsoever without the express written permission of the publisher except for the use of brief quotations in a book review.

This is a work of fiction. Names, characters, businesses, places, events and incidents are either the products of the author's imagination or used in a fictitious manner. Any resemblance to actual persons, living or dead, or actual events is purely coincidental.

Cover design by Sweet 'N Spicy Designs
Cover photo by Deposit Photos/natika, saje, and real_texelart
Edited by Penny's Copy Sense

*To Shannon, for everything.
And because our marriage is fine.*

Acknowledgements

Special thanks to my amazing critique partners, Maria Geraci and Kelsey Browning, for being fabulous at everything they do. Thanks, too, to Pam Trader and Lisa Stone Hardt for brainstorming and sanity checks.

Thanks to my husband and kids for the inspiration, for letting me have my precious writing time, and for understanding my gone-to-LaLaLand stares. A special thanks to the boys for the "Go Mama" dance. That's my favorite. For real.

And thanks to all my extended family and friends for believing in me. Your faith and support has gotten me where I am today.

Chapter One

She was lovable in her own way, which sometimes meant she was not loved at all.
—The Temptress of Pecan Lane, *by Mae Daniels*

THE ONLY THING better than watching a handsome man in uniform was taking him home at the end of the night to strip him out of it. With his fresh haircut and tailored Air Force mess dress, Anna Martin's husband complemented the elegant southern grandiosity of The Harrington's ballroom better than the faux marble floor and the towering magnolia arrangements.

This wedding reception couldn't end soon enough.

Anna slid up beside Neil at the open bar and nudged him with her hip. "I always feel bad for the bride at these things."

"Why?" Neil took two beers from the bartender. He tucked a few dollars into the tip jar.

"Because you're already taken so they had to settle for second best."

His face twisted into the same pained expression he'd worn the last half-dozen times she'd used that line, but she gave him a *you-know-you-love-me* grin anyway.

Because he'd still been happy to let her take him home and strip him out of his uniform after the last half-dozen weddings.

She shoved the gift she'd snuck from the pile at the bride's request at him. "Oh, wait." His National Defense Service Medal was crooked.

Before she could straighten it, he handed the gift back. "It's fine, Anna. C'mon."

He strode past tables of wedding guests finishing their chicken and cheese grits. Anna tagged along, enjoying the view from behind.

"Jules mention what's in that?" Neil asked over his shoulder, his gaze shifting to the present.

"She said it's from Rodney and they want to open it in private. So probably something with fur and spikes."

She waited for Neil to laugh. Instead, his gaze went unfocused. Anna steered him around a chair she didn't think he'd seen.

Jules, almost as resplendent in her ivory satin gown as Neil was in his mess dress, dove for the box as soon as Anna was within arm's reach. Her thick dark hair was tucked and tamed into her tiara, but her wedding day hadn't entirely cured her sardonic lip curl. She stashed the gift under the table.

Neil handed the groom one of the beers.

"That box has some giggidy written all over it," Brad said. He and Neil shared a man-grin and a fist bump. Rodney leaned around the newlyweds for a high five.

"Your giggidy's gonna give your grandmother a heart attack." Jules snagged the beer Neil was passing to Rodney, then gave Neil a fist bump of her own. "Hope you have something nice to say," she said to him. She jerked a thumb to Rodney. "I almost let Anna smack a *dangerous when speaking* label on his forehead."

"I'm dangerous all the time, baby," Rodney said.

Anna had spent a total of five minutes with him, but she'd agree with that. The groom and his best man shared the same bulky build, bushy blond hair, and lewd grin that, when flashed over their uniforms, had inspired half the women at the wedding to check that their dresses were still buttoned.

Anna only checked when Neil flashed her that grin.

The DJ worked his way behind the table to hand Rodney a mic.

"Does that thing have a profanity delay?" Jules asked the DJ.

He shook his head. She took a hit from her beer.

Anna settled into her seat and adjusted her fork and knife on her plate so they were parallel, then did the same for Neil's. "Ready?" Anna murmured to him.

"Of course."

Rodney clinked his glass to get the room's attention. The hum of voices and clink of silverware dropped off. "Evening, y'all." His voice boomed around the massive room. "Want to thank you for coming out to watch my little bro give up his manhood for a woman." Amidst a smattering of chuckles, he raised his glass. "Unlike these Air Force weenies, us Marines don't waste our words, so I'll make this short and sweet. To Brad and Jules. May the mountains in your lives be peaked with pleasure, and the valleys between show you the way to heaven." He wiggled his eyebrows. "And may you still be getting it up when you're eighty-three."

"Giggidy," Brad said with a brow wiggle of his own.

Jules gave him a playful shove. A few more people laughed. Brad's mother's long-suffering sigh made her jowls droop further. Anna assumed the suffering was more habitual than forced after a lifetime of raising those two boys.

Anna and Neil had put off discussing raising kids of their own until they paid off some debts and Neil made it through the latest round of force reductions, but Anna had been drawing a steady paycheck for a year—a new record—and Neil's job was safe. She hoped tonight, with their busy schedules finally slowing down, they'd talk about their future. Their beautiful, baby-filled future.

Maybe they'd do some practicing too.

Rodney handed Neil the mic. As the only married member

of the wedding party, he'd been asked to give a toast as well. Neil stood and gave his jacket a tug, then surveyed the room. Anna smiled up at him. A light behind his head illuminated his sandy hair and his hazel eyes took on a deeper hue over his Air Force blue mess dress. He didn't fly planes for the Air Force, but instead worked behind the scenes making sure the next generation of airmen would have the best training and equipment in the world.

She loved him for his higher purpose.

He flexed his left hand, but otherwise appeared perfectly at ease. "Good evening," he said into the microphone. "I'm Neil Martin, and I've known Brad since he made me eat dirt in field training."

A few chuckles came up from the crowd, mostly the uniformed contingent. Neil paused, and a muscle in his cheek spasmed. He clapped Brad on the shoulder. "Well, buddy, yesterday you asked my advice about making marriage work. It's pretty simple. Put your dishes in the dishwasher, wipe out the sink after you shave, and for God's sake, man, learn to use the hamper."

Brad shook his head and pointed at Jules, which the crowd loved.

"Well, then, I guess the best I can do is to tell you what I was told all those decades ago, when I took up my old ball and chain. You can be right, or you can be happy." Neil leaned closer to Brad and dropped his voice in the mic. "But trust me, sometimes you can't be either one."

Hoots of laughter erupted around the room. *All those decades* were six and a half years. Neil knew how to work a crowd. The bride gave him a wonky eyebrow.

"Remember today," Neil said to Brad. "Remember right now, this moment. Remember how happy you are. Because someday, you're going to look at her and it will finally sink in that her face is the only one you're going to see every single morning of the rest of your life."

A couple people *aawed*, but Anna's shoulders went back.

That hadn't sounded entirely complimentary.

Brad raised his champagne flute. "Ain't just her face, bro. Giggidy."

Jules elbowed him.

"Yeah, well, that drops off too," Neil said.

The male guests roared. Anna's face flamed. Jules shot her a *what the hell?* look.

Anna tried an *I don't know, they're guys* look back, but she suspected it came across more like *would anyone notice if I ducked under the table?*

Neil's skin was splotchy above his collar. A fine sheen of perspiration glistened on his forehead. He nodded toward Jules. "And with her job, forget those dreams of a hot meal waiting every night when you get home. Got some takeout numbers for you. Hope one of those presents is a grill. Gonna need it, man, gonna need it."

"They're ordering a maid and a cook," Rodney said loudly.

"That'll go nice with the moving companies," Neil said. "But if she ever buys a label maker, watch out. When PCS time comes around, she'll be so busy using *it* for packing, she won't have time for *you*. Guess which one she'd rather sleep with?"

Over yet another round of laughter, Jules shot Anna another look and made the drinky-drinky gesture.

Anna couldn't even shake her head. She was too busy pretending her husband hadn't insulted her and their marriage in front of everyone they knew at Gellings Air Force Base.

He didn't *really* think she would've rather slept with her label maker, did he?

"Might come a day," Neil said, his voice getting thick, "when you're better off not telling her you've got those moving orders so you don't have to deal with all that shit."

Cold spikes of alarm scratched like fingernails over Anna's skin. Her lungs shuddered. Silence stretched over the room. She latched onto Neil's sleeve. He blinked at her like he'd forgotten she was there. Something dark flashed through his eyes.

Something guilty.
Something honest.
Something terrifying.

He cleared his throat again, his face so red Anna was perspiring for him. He broke eye contact with her and focused on Brad. "But you're one of the lucky ones, man. You got Jules, and you two are going to have the time of your lives. To you, man. To both of you."

Except Neil choked over the words, and when he raised his glass, he couldn't seem to gulp the champagne fast enough.

A few people clapped. Rodney rescued the microphone and handed it to the DJ, who prodded the happy couple to do some kissy-kissy before they got to their first dance.

Neil stumbled around the table toward the door.

Anna scrambled after him, forcing smiles at her coworkers, making herself stay upright and moving forward so they wouldn't know the champagne was roiling in her stomach like grade-A wedding poison. With his long stride and frantic pace, he was gone when she stepped out of the ballroom.

The door at the end of the hallway clicked shut.

She tripped over her heels dashing after him. Her feet moved in time to the rapid firing of her heart. Her strappy sandals cut into her feet, and her legs had all the flexibility of a freeze-dried Twinkie, but she kept moving as if her existence depended on it.

Because she had a horrible, ants-marching-over-her-grave suspicion it did.

She burst through the exit and found him hunched over next to a garbage can at the edge of the parking lot. She wanted to reach out to him, but the distant wariness in his gaze held her back.

She slowly licked her lips and tried to keep her voice steady. "Neil? Are you okay?"

He swiped his forearm over his brow, still staring at the concrete. "It's over, Anna."

"What's over?" She barely recognized her own voice. Her arms hung like wet dishrags at her sides, and a roaring she didn't recognize crashed through her head.

"Us. We're over. I want a divorce."

A gigantic *No!* welled up in her throat, but it got stuck somewhere between her tongue and her ears. There was *no* possible way she'd heard him right.

He didn't mean it.

He couldn't mean it.

"I got orders to San Antonio. Leave in two weeks." He looked at her then, the truth of every word written in the crooked dip of his mouth. "I've been trying to tell you."

Anna's teeth chattered in the sudden chill of the evening. "No." She'd put all the strength she had into the word, but it was barely loud enough to get past her mouth. "No. You haven't."

He tugged at his cuffs. A faint scent of cigarette ash wafted from the trash can, and the fading evening light made it difficult to catch all the nuances of his expression. "I was working up to it."

Her legs suddenly wobbled like a meringue that hadn't been beaten enough. She opened her mouth again but it took too much brain power to understand his words and form her own in response.

She'd been busy lately, but she would've known if there were a problem.

Wouldn't she?

"Why?" Her voice wavered, the single syllable stretching between them.

"We were too young," he finally said. He rolled his neck, then looked past her shoulder. "I got love and lust confused, and now that one's faded, I've realized the other one was never really there. We're just not right, Anna."

She tried to take a breath, but she was pretty sure there wasn't enough oxygen to fill the black hole sucking her heart out. "We'll go see a counselor."

He hung his head again. His breathing was ragged, completely out of sync with hers. "I'll treat you fair, okay?" he said. "Send you home if you want."

"No."

"You want to stay here?"

Stay here? Was he kidding? They were still married, and they would stay married. She'd PCS with him, go to San Antonio. They could work this out. "*No.* You love me. I know you do. Even if you don't know it, I know you do. And I love you. I do, Neil. I love you. I love you enough to see us through this."

He treated her to the same saggy-jowled look Brad's mother had worn minutes ago. "It's over, Anna."

"*No, it's not.*"

"Will fighting make you feel better?" He flung an arm out. "Fine. Let's fight. I want to go one goddamn day without being told I put the silverware away wrong. I want to buy a new T-shirt and not walk into the closet an hour later and find it hanging up, ironed, with a fucking *label* in it like I'm a goddamn toddler. I want to break every single goddamn label maker you've ever bought with my money so I don't have to sleep with one eye open for fear you're going to label my dick while I'm sleeping. Feel better now?"

She blinked. Then she had to blink again. Because her eyes were dripping and the pressure in her sinuses was the size of Lake Superior, and if she couldn't dam it with her eyelids, she would disintegrate into nothingness.

"You love me."

His pained expression came back. "I'll stay here tonight. Movers come Friday. If you don't want it packed up, get it marked. You're good at that."

This time when he turned away, she didn't try to follow him.

She was too afraid of falling into the vast chasm of nothingness that had splintered the earth between them.

Chapter Two

Her world had been colored in blues and yellows and greens, until it was plunged into shades of gray.
—The Temptress of Pecan Lane, by Mae Daniels

MONDAY MORNING, Anna drove to Rockwood Mineral Corporation headquarters because it was what she always did on Monday mornings. Except she wasn't sure it was Monday, and if it hadn't been for the fact that all the clocks in her house were set to military time, she wouldn't have been sure it was morning either.

Logically she knew it had to be Monday, because she'd survived Sunday, counting minutes, then hours, baking pies and labeling them and waiting for Neil to come home or answer his phone. But this Monday didn't feel like any other Monday she'd ever met.

And when she pulled into the RMC headquarters parking lot and looked at the two-story brown building and the parking lots around it, the clusters of smaller buildings and giant fuel storage tanks in the distance, she wasn't sure she was in the right spot, because Friday, the building's brown walls had been warm and comforting, the windows had had souls, and the parking lots had been solid ground instead of a sheet of glass that could give at any moment, letting the earth swallow her whole.

Anna wasn't just a thousand miles from home.

She was in a completely different life.

But going to work had been normal Friday, so she'd make it normal today. And then maybe Neil would be normal again, then their marriage could be normal again, and they could get back to their regularly scheduled life.

She snagged her pie carrier and made her way into the lab. She couldn't have told anyone her passcode for the door if they'd held a gun to her favorite label maker, but her fingers punched in the right numbers in the right order anyway. Her shoes echoed in the eerily quiet room. Once the pies were safe on the clean surface of a seventies-issue metal desk inside a cubicle clearly labeled *Anna Martin*, she hit the button on a nineties-issue desktop computer.

And found one more bit of normal. Her voice was froggy, but her Monday companion wouldn't care. "Morning, Rex."

The computer sputtered and whirred a response.

She unhooked her white cardigan from its perch on the cube wall and wrapped it around herself, buffering her skin from the meat locker setting on the air conditioner, then took the pies to the office snack kitchen around the corner while she waited for Rex to finish his Monday morning grumblings.

Like normal.

Except for the ring choking her left finger.

In the kitchen, Anna found Shirley, her program manager, sipping from a "World's Best Mom" mug and listening to Todd, RMC's contracts guy, talk about something that was probably normal too.

Anna forced a *nothing-wrong-here* smile and a spring in her step.

Because that was normal. "Good morning."

Todd's eyes zeroed in on the pies. "Aw, Anna, you know how to make a guy happy on a Monday morning."

Her eyelids went stingy, but she held on to her fake happy and slid the pies onto the counter. "I do my best." Todd, obviously, hadn't been to Jules's wedding.

"Man, I wish Mindy's best was half this good." Todd snagged a plate out of a cabinet. "But don't tell her I said that."

"Of course not." Even if Anna had wanted to use her pies to poison other people's healthy relationships, she couldn't remember what Mindy looked like or if she even existed.

Shirley surveyed first Anna, then the pies. On a real Monday morning, Anna would've expected the obligatory *How was your weekend?* Today, she hoped that glittery angel pin on Shirley's blazer would work a small miracle and keep either of them from unconsciously uttering the words.

"You okay, kid?" Shirley asked.

Anna's legs wobbled so hard her heels jackhammered the linoleum.

But she *wanted* to be okay, so she jutted her chin out. "Just peachy." She reached for the coffee.

The pot was empty.

Sort of like her life.

A shudder slinked through her body. She yanked open the cabinet where the coffee grounds and filters were stored. The door hinges squeaked. Todd mumbled something about a contract and scurried out of the kitchen, clutching the pie as if it could shield against PMS.

If only monthly hormones were the problem.

Shirley deposited her dirty mug in the sink. Her still-within-regs, Clairoled-within-a-millimeter-of-her-roots hairdo tilted toward the pie. "Your latticework's crooked."

"I—it—" It *was*. On the middle pie.

Had Anna really made that pie?

She squeezed the coffee packet so hard it let out a *pop!* Coffee dust billowed into the air.

Shirley headed toward the door. "Need the RR-40s from last week so we can get the trucks moving this morning."

Normal. "They're on Jules's desk."

Shirley pursed her lips and stuck a hand on her hip. Shirley-speak for *I don't enter toxic waste zones*. And she wasn't talking about the hazardous waste disposal bins."

Anna winced. "I'll get it in a minute."

After Shirley left, Anna started the coffee, cleaned up the dust, and then sliced the middle pie so no one else would notice the lattice problem. She poured herself a fresh cup, then retreated to the lab. Samples were due to arrive from three trucks and four monthly tank checks this morning, and she had to dig through the mess on Jules's desk to find last week's jet biofuels release authorizations.

Normal was good.

In addition to their roles as a fuels distributor and specialty engine modifier for the civilian world, RMC was the primary government contractor for fuel supplies for all the military bases in Georgia. Since the military had turned to biofuels in so many of their planes, RMC's operations had expanded significantly. Which was why Anna had a job at all. She'd been temping around town when Jules found out Anna had somewhat of a technical background and gave her a recommendation for the lab assistant position that was created about a year ago.

Rex had finished his Monday morning sputtering, so she logged on and fired up her email. While Rex processed her request, she went into Jules's cube.

To call it a mess would've been like calling Minnesota a state with a couple of lakes. But Anna didn't have the nerve to take her label maker to Jules's Leaning Towers of Important Crap. Instead, she rummaged around the top layers until she found last week's documentation. She popped back into her own cube, which had to be hers since it was neatly organized, and she checked her email, which also had to be hers since her fingers knew the password.

Her heart gave a sputter that matched Rex's Monday morning grumblings.

Finally, Neil was talking to her.

She leaned in and clicked the message.

Wanted to let you know my attorney will be in touch. Don't want to make this difficult, but probably best if you get your own. Want to make sure we do this fair. Neil.

P.S. I'd like my grandmother's ring back.

Her heart writhed in her chest as if someone had doused it in gasoline and ignited it, and her throat clogged up from the fumes. She stared at the screen, unable to blink or breathe.

But then her lungs moved, air tickled her nose on its way in and out, in and out, and she felt something else growing inside her.

Something hot and dark and ugly.

She yanked the ring off her finger and slammed it on her desk.

She'd sacrificed her education. Moved three times. Kept his house organized, stocked, and cleaned, all while working the same hours as he had for over half their marriage.

So he could throw her away.

The *bastard*.

She hit the monitor's power button. The screen went black and empty and useless as Neil's fickle heart.

She snatched the RR-40s and marched to Shirley's office.

"They're not signed," Shirley said. And the look she shot Anna added, *So what are you going to do about it?*

If the releases weren't signed, the fuel wasn't officially QA certified and couldn't be delivered to base, which meant a potential for unplanned aircraft downtime for lack of fuel. Which was expensive. Which meant the government might look for another distributor when RMC's contract was up for renewal. *That*, Anna could fix. And being able to fix *something* felt good. "I watched Jules test it. It's fine. I'll sign for her."

Shirley's jaw settled into that stubborn tilt. "Has to be the analyst. She's qualified. You're not."

Oh, good. A fight. Anna set her jaw to match Shirley's. "I have a year of experience and I'm highly educated."

"But you don't have a degree."

No, she didn't. Because she'd left college two semesters short to marry Neil when he convinced her she could finish up at a school close to his first assignment.

He'd been wrong.

About more than she could've imagined.

She'd had to retake a few classes that hadn't transferred in order to get into senior design, and had one semester to go *there* when Neil got orders early because of his program moving to a different base. Wash, rinse, repeat.

Shirley's gaze landed on Anna's hands. Anna curled them into balls and thrust them into the pockets of her cardigan. "Jules said they were good to go."

"Jules was preoccupied," Shirley said. "What happens if you sign off on our delivery and the plane goes down because something wasn't right on our end? Then your butt's on the line, and more important, *my* butt's on the line for letting a tech aide certify our analyses. You want to sign that dotted line, go back to school."

A lump of hysterical laughter popped and fizzled around Anna's larynx. She was still paying student loans from three different institutions and had her doubts Neil would consider signing over his GI bill to her as part of a divorce settlement.

Oh, *God*. She was getting divorced. "Right."

"Right's exactly right." Shirley plucked a couple of brochures from an uneven stack of papers that made Anna twitch. "The job's always come second for you."

"I—"

"I don't fault you for that," Shirley interrupted. "You came here as an officer's wife looking for an outlet and a paycheck. The team's appreciated your work. But you've been lax with continuing education and certifications. You're organized, but are you ambitious? Do you want a job, or are you going to start watching the men around here like they're your next meal ticket?"

Anna couldn't even manage a squawk of protest. She was

too busy figuring out if she was angry, sad, or suddenly living someone else's life.

Shirley pointedly gestured to Anna's hidden left hand. "You're a pretty girl. They'll start circling soon enough. Just make sure it doesn't mess with the work."

Oh, God. She was right. Men would think she was *available*. More like physically ill.

Shirley leaned forward and shoved the brochures at her. "Take a breather. Look these over. Nice week to take an afternoon off, what with Jules out." She gestured to her clock. "I have to go placate a client who's not going to be happy about that late delivery."

Anna shuffled out of Shirley's office. Halfway down the hall, she risked a glance at her ringless hand to inspect the brochures.

Three were about RMC's internal fuels expert certification programs. The last one outlined RMC's tuition assistance policy.

And in three more days, Anna would qualify.

She stopped in the hallway. Her lungs seemed to be battling one another. One side of her chest felt panic, the other hope, with her heart caught in the crossfire.

Neil could change his mind.

Or she could put herself first for once in her grown life.

She wrapped her arms around her chest and squeezed to dispel the internal fighting. Divorce wasn't on her calendar, but neither was living with a man who didn't love her.

It was time for a new plan.

Chapter Three

Not every man could appreciate the beauty of an alphabetized medicine chest, but he was not just any man.
—The Temptress of Pecan Lane, *by Mae Daniels*

ANNA FLEW DOWN the hallway to the lab. She was late. Her first class of her new life, and the samples were late. Which meant the documentation was late. Which meant she was late checking it all into the system. Which meant she would be *that* student in class tonight when she walked in fifteen minutes after the first roll call of the semester.

She'd never been that student.

She hit her passcode wrong on the lab door and had to enter it twice before she finally got through. Rex had fallen asleep. She jiggled his mouse. "Come on, come on, *come on*." She should've been halfway to James Robert College by now.

Jules leaned into the cube and tapped her stubby fingernails on the doorframe. Her normally poufy brown hair was even bigger today, apparently still recovering from all the humidity of her tropical honeymoon. And seeing her smile so much was plain weird. But other than having to listen to her tell the story about Brad and the horny dolphin half a dozen times, the wedding and honeymoon talk had been minimal.

The familiar box Jules carried on her hip didn't look promising for the trend to continue.

"I'm hurrying," Anna said.

"Eh. It'll wait until tomorrow. Got a minute?"

Work, waiting until tomorrow?

She eyed the box again. Oh, jeez. Not now. "Actually, I'm late."

Jules set the box by the door, then propped herself on a corner of the desk and grabbed Anna's silver letter opener out of the desk organizer. "Meeting with the lawyer?" She casually flicked the letter opener beneath her fingernail.

"Class." Despite her mother's insistence that Anna could still save her marriage if she tried, Anna's sister had come through as the voice of reason. *If he doesn't love you, screw him. You deserve better.* Judging by how fast Neil had accepted Anna's lawyer's proposed settlement, Anna figured Beth had been right.

Even if it still stung a bit. Like losing an arm in a paper shredder.

Rex finally came to life. Anna pounded in her password. The dinosaur thought about accepting it.

Jules slid further onto the desk. Her rump scooted Anna's desktop calendar crooked. "They have divorce classes?"

"Thermo," Anna said. "I enrolled last week."

Jules glanced up sharply. She dropped the letter opener into the organizer in the midst of all the highlighters. "Didn't you take that in college?"

"Too long ago. James Robert College wants me to take it fresh." Anna plunked the letter opener into its slot beside her ruler. "And I'm late. Really, really late." She told Rex to close her mail program, then tabbed over to the database and told Rex to close that too.

"Listen, about your scene at my wedding."

Anna cringed. "Really?"

"Dude. Bad juju. You don't think I'm going to forget that shit, do you? Now listen. Rodney's coming through on leave this weekend before he ships out, and I promised the big lug we'd do karaoke at Taps. He wants a Sandy to his Danny. You come be his date, or I'll tell my Aunt Bernie that Brad's holding back on sex and I think it's your fault. She'll come up with some crazy-ass juju-washing ritual involving that gift right there and dancing naked in the moonlight, and then you'll wish singing in public was all you'd done. 'Kay?"

A date. She was late for class. She could still barely process that she was about to become the first Jensen in the history of Jensens to get divorced. Her closest local friend was returning the wedding gift Anna and Neil had given her. And she was supposed to go on a date.

She gulped back the diamond-sized lump lodged in her esophagus. "If I say yes, can I go now?"

Jules slid off the desk and gestured to the cube door. "Of course. But if you're just saying it, you *will* pay. I told Brad you get us in the divorce, but that's negotiable if you act like you don't want us."

God. It wasn't enough to split their belongings, they had to split their *friends* now too?

She was never, *ever* doing this again. "Thanks."

"You're welcome. Go on, get going. I'll shut this down for you. And take that present with you. I don't want it."

Anna grabbed her purse and the label maker she'd gotten the newlyweds, and she made a mad dash out the door. Pop Rocks fizzled in her belly. Probably a good thing she didn't have time for food. She wasn't sure she could keep it down.

Outside, she stumbled into a wall of air as hot as a cheese curd–frying vat back home at the state fair. Her steps slowed. Maybe it would be easier to swim to her car. At least she'd thought to park beneath a tree.

An extra burst of heat spilled out of her car when she swung the door open. This weather was defying the laws of thermodynamics. At least, what she remembered of it. Thank goodness she didn't have to smell pretty to be smart. But it was *June*. Nowhere should've been this hot in June.

She tossed the label maker in the back seat. She braced herself, scooted into the car, and cranked the engine. Steam flowed out of the air vents. She tilted them away while the AC system caught up. After buckling in, she gave her rearview mirrors a quick check. The gearshift seared her palm, but she gritted her teeth and put the car in reverse anyway.

Something tickled her finger. She absently scratched it and gave the car a little gas. Something else tickled the back of her hand.

She frowned.

Sweat didn't usually tickle. Not like that.

She moved to shift the car into drive and something dark scurried over her windshield. "What the—"

A line of fire ants marched across her steering wheel.

Anna shrieked. She threw the car into park and tumbled out of it. "Get off! *Get off!*" She raked her hands over her arms and hopped on her clogs to shake the little buggers off. The prickles moved to her back, up her neck, into her hair. She knew the ants couldn't be up there, there'd only been one or two, but she scrubbed at her scalp anyway.

"Ma'am? You okay?" A guy leaned out the side of a red car behind her. She was blocking one of the exits.

"Oh, yeah, sure, you betcha." She wiggled her itching toes. "Sorry. It'll just take me a minute to get out of your way."

Her car's engine whined. Heat radiated off the hood and wrinkled the air. The backs of her knees tingled as if a hundred ants had gathered there for an impromptu Riverdance.

A car door shut behind her. "Need a hand?" he drawled in a local-boy kind of way.

"Everything's fine. Thanks." Because she carried insect-killer in her car all the time in case her car came down with a case of the ants.

It took some effort to not reach for her phone. This was the kind of thing Neil would've taken care of for her. And it pissed her off that she wanted to let the man approaching solve her problem.

She was an independent woman, dammit. She'd fix this herself. She squared her shoulders, marched to the edge of her door, and hit her trunk release. She scooted around the car to survey the potential ant weapons in her trunk. She had to have *something* useful. Maybe she could club them one by one with her jumper cables. Shoot her emergency flares at them. Drop the box of Neil's junk on them. Label them to death with the label maker.

It'd worked on her marriage.

And there was that stingy feeling behind her eyeballs again.

Long runner's legs ending in flip-flop-clad feet entered her blurred vision. "You got some friends there."

If Neil had to leave her, he should've done it somewhere else. Somewhere without fire ants, somewhere more hospitable to her Norwegian coloring, somewhere with halfway intelligent locals. She shot her audience a look she should've tried on the ants. "Where I come from, they're called a nuisance."

Instead of shriveling up and dying, he flashed her a goofy grin. His dark-lashed eyes creased in the corners.

Those lashes and the mass of just-long-enough-to-be-curly hair on his head were proof positive a man could have brains or looks, but not both.

And that tingly sensation along her breastbone was proof positive she had no business being single. First she agreed to a date with Rodney, now she was getting hot over a redneck.

She was supposed to be worrying about the ants. Class. Her *life*.

He scratched his curly hair and surveyed her neatly organized trunk.

As if he could wield her jumper cables better than she could against an army of fire ants.

Instead, he swung her Windex out of the trunk like a gunslinger preparing for a showdown, then tucked her paper towels under his arm.

"My car is very—" she started, but then it hit her.

He wasn't going to clean it.

Carbon-based ants, meet ammonia.

Forgetting simple chemistry principles was not a good omen for her degree.

Wanting to watch her unexpected helper go to battle against the ants wasn't a good omen for her sanity.

Her skin flushed as if she were standing inside Hell's boiler room. She reached for the Windex, but something stopped her before she could get close enough to grab it.

Something that tasted suspiciously like fear.

Not of him.

Of herself.

"I'll do it," she bit out. She flicked her fingers up, gesturing for him to hand over the Windex.

"Ain't no trouble." His gaze wandered down her body, and she felt a whomp in her chest beneath the tingles spreading to her rib cage.

"Be a shame to mess up them pretty clothes," he said.

"I can handle this," she said firmly. She gestured to his car. "There's another exit two rows down. I've taken enough of your time."

His eyes were big and blue as her wounded heart, but when he squinted at her like that, they went a shade darker to cobalt. "Now I'm sure it don't matter none to you, but my momma'd have my hide if she heard I abandoned a lady with critters in her car."

Anna stifled a whimper of frustration. She swiped at her forehead. She'd probably drown in her own sweat before she managed to wrestle the Windex out of his hands.

If she could get brave enough to get within touching distance of him. "I don't know your momma, so you don't have anything to worry about."

He scratched his hair again, and she felt an intense desire to claw out that part of her that wanted to know how it would feel between her fingers.

Rebound, her brain yelled.

Something more primitive was still clamoring about his hair.

"Reckon you might be right on that one," he finally said. "But she'd still know. Scares me more'n that mound you parked over, that's for sure."

"I didn't—" She stopped herself. Red ants swarmed around a huge ant mound beneath where her front bumper had been. "That wasn't there this morning."

"Be doing me a real big favor if you let me take care of this for you." The solemnity of his expression was refreshingly innocent compared with what she expected out of Rodney Friday night. "Besides, killing bugs ain't no work for a lady. Even a Yankee lady."

An unexpected snort of amusement lodged in her nostrils. This one was either Southern chivalry at its finest or a few tomatoes short of a ketchup bottle. "This Yankee lady takes care of herself, thank you."

But she still couldn't propel herself close enough to grab the bottle.

He propped himself into the drivers seat and squirted a trail of ants. A whole row of the little buggers curled up in the fetal position. He took a leisurely swipe at them with a paper towel, then sprayed again. He shot Anna a sly look out of the corner of his eye.

Like he was looking to see if she were watching him.

She quickly dropped her gaze and made a show of checking the time. Her heart thumped again, but this time it was pure panic. If she left now and ran once she got to campus, she'd only be seven minutes late. Plus heatstroke recovery time after the dash to the classroom. She tapped a foot. "We could be done in two minutes if you'd let me help."

Squirt. Squirt. Squirt. "Getting the ones you can see don't mean you're getting the ones you can't."

Anna shivered. "Still, you've done enough. Would it help if I wrote your momma a thank you note?"

Oh, *God*, and he had dimples. Of course he had dimples. This fiasco wouldn't be complete if he *didn't* have dimples.

"It sure would make her day," he said.

"Then if you'll hand me my purse, we can both be on our way."

"Reckon I could do that, but then I'd have to find some other excuse to stay here and coax that pretty smile."

Oh.

It was one thing for her body to go renegade on her. It was something completely different for her mind to contemplate skipping class so she could listen to Momma's Boy drawl out Southern platitudes.

Neil never talked to her like that.

Of course, Neil had left. Packed up while she was at work. Sent his attorney to pick up her wedding ring. Avoided her like she was some kind of freak with a communicable label maker disease.

"Now, see, that's supposed to make you smile *more*," he said.

Anna blinked, but her eyes still burned. "Sorry. Bad timing."

He squirted a few more ants. "Shoulda got him with the Windex."

Anna inadvertently pictured herself chasing Neil out of their house with her label maker and a bottle of Windex, and she was surprised to find she still had a laugh in her. "Now what would your momma say to that?"

"That I should buy you dinner for making you sad." He took another swipe at her steering column. "I'm Jackson."

All she had to do was tell him her name. She didn't have to go to dinner, didn't have to ever see him again. Tell him her name, and she'd move back into the ranks of the mostly-single-and-attractive-to-somebody ranks, questionable though his mental state might be. But she'd still be late for class.

She sucked in a breath. She could do this. Just say her

name. "I'm—I'm late. For class. And I don't do late, and I don't want to start off on the wrong foot. And I need this class, I really do, because—well, I just do, so I need to take the ant-mobile and go. But thank you. It was nice of you to help."

"Darlin', you ain't gonna get outta this parking lot without getting all bit up. They're still crawling out your vents."

She wouldn't cry again. She wouldn't. "Then will you *please* let me help?" Nine minutes late. Did professors lock the classroom doors when class started? She couldn't remember.

He gave the dash a couple of quick squirts, then handed her the paper towels. "Keep on going. I'll go on and get 'em from the other side."

Anna heaved a sigh of relief and sank into the car. She attacked the melting ants with an efficiency that apparently hadn't made it this far south yet. Between the semi-cool air blowing on her, the faint scent of Old Spice lingering in her seat, and the feeling of being useful once again, things looked less dire.

Jackson climbed into her passenger seat and kept squirting. "You taking classes out on base?"

She suppressed a shudder and tore off another paper towel. These ants were going down faster than her marriage. "James Robert." A beautiful, private campus without any military presence.

"Ol' Jim-Bob, eh? What kinda class you taking?"

"Heat Transfer in Hell." She lunged for an errant ant.

"Thermo?"

She stopped wiping to stare at him. "You've heard of thermodynamics?"

He blinked, almost like he was offended, then nodded solemnly. "Yes, ma'am. I grew up Baptist. I know all about them temperatures in hell."

Another shadow of a laugh eased a bit more pressure in her airways. "Guess your momma raised you right then."

"Yes, ma'am."

Together, it took five more minutes to wipe out the worst

of the ants. If she sped on the roads and ran from the parking lot, she'd be only thirteen and a half minutes late, assuming a quick heatstroke recovery time. She tucked her Windex and depleted paper towel roll back into her trunk organizer, and she found a genuine smile for her unexpected helper. "Thank you."

"My pleasure." He took her hand into his, his grip warm and smooth and flutter-inducing, and pressed something against her palm. "In case you need help with any more critters." He stepped back, amusement evident in the quirk of his lips. "Hope you know more about hell than you look like you do."

He'd written his name and number on a paper towel.

It was almost sweet enough to make being fourteen minutes late for her first class worth it. Even if he was a big ol' redneck, he thought she was cute.

Ants and all.

Or maybe he owned an exterminator company.

She sighed. Given her track record of being lovable, she was betting on the latter.

JACKSON IDLY scratched at the red bumps popping up on his right hand while he watched the Honda Civic pull out of the parking lot. Never would've guessed Kaci was doing him a favor making him and Lance watch that old crappy girly movie about that Greek wedding last night, but he wished he'd squirted his itchy hand with the Windex before he let Miss Late Yankee peel out of here.

Should've told her to change the label on it too: *Windex, Ant Killer, and Bite Spray*. He opened the Jetta, chuckling about the labels on her trunk organizer and boxes. His favorite had been the one labeled *Jerkface's Stuff*.

Northern folk weren't so bad. He knew that after spending a spell or two up past the Mason-Dixon line, but he hadn't met many who would offer to write his momma a note excusing him from being a gentleman. Between that and her sad doe eyes, he reckoned he didn't have much choice but to leave her his number. She wouldn't use it, hoity-toity Yankee who stared down her nose like that when his accent hit her, but she looked like she needed some reminding she was pretty.

Especially when she let loose a smile, even if it was because she thought he was some dumb redneck. He grinned bigger. Would've played dumb to put her at ease, gentleman that he was, but he did love playing mind games with Northerners.

The sound of his phone hollering out "Sweet Home Alabama" in the cup holder killed his amusement real quick.

Momma liked to say God made man for practice and woman for perfection, but Jackson reckoned that was before Momma and Daddy made Louisa. Didn't mean he could ignore her call, though. He settled into the driver's seat and picked up the phone. "Yes, ma'am?"

"Jackson Beauregard Davis, where is my car?"

Maybe he'd take the long way up to Auburn. Reconsider this whole moving-back-close-to-home idea, if Uncle Sam and his new landlord would let him. He gave the Jetta's wheel a tap. "Right here."

He didn't remember girls huffing at him like that back when he was in college. Thought they all gave it up by then. But not Louisa. Must've been a generation thing.

"You said you'd be home an hour ago," she said.

"Car wasn't done yet. You got somewhere to be?"

"No, you're just slower'n an elephant chasing a tiger with a football."

Jackson dropped his head back against the seat. "Pretty strong fighting words. Bit early, isn't it?"

"Never too early to remind a traitor where he stands."

And here they went. "You want your car, or you want your car running?"

"Both."

He scratched the back of his hand again. Now what else

had he expected from a female? Perfection indeed. Girl didn't know how good she had it, having a stepdad with the connections for a vegetable oil engine retrofit and a brother with the time to come all the way across the country and bring it over to Georgia for the work.

Or maybe he had it good, getting that excuse to leave Auburn early last week and stay here a couple extra nights while he took care of what he told them all was military business.

"Don't you have some studying to be doing?" he said.

Wasn't every woman that could narrow her eyes out loud, but Louisa could. "You're not late because you've been playing kissy-face with some girl are you?"

"You wanting your car so you can play kissy-face with some boy in it?" Sweet Lord, when had she gotten old enough for that? And what was worse, thinking of his baby sister making out with some yahoo, or suddenly picturing himself showing Miss Late Yankee how a man did things in the South?

"She know she's toast soon as hunting season rolls around?" Louisa said.

"He know I've added to Daddy's old shotgun collection?"

Louisa snickered. "How dumb do you think I am to go flirting with boys who'd be scared of the likes of you?"

He opened his mouth, but since he didn't have as much of a clue as he should've as to what kind of boys Louisa brought home, he reckoned he'd better not jump into that one without thinking it through first. Wasn't sure which one of them would look dumber if he did, and he wasn't keen on him being the one.

"Huh," she said. "Gotcha there, don't I?"

"You ever park on top of an ant hill?" he asked finally.

"Are you for real?" Louisa scoffed. "Even your dog's smarter than that."

Sure, his dog was, but that didn't mean Louisa was. Not that he had any intention of pointing *that* out, since she currently had possession of both his dog and his truck. "You keep any Windex in this car?"

A girly cackle was his only answer. Figured she thought she was above cleaning her own car now too. Wasn't like she had to pay for the thing herself.

That had him rubbed wrong, but he couldn't finger why that was. Russ had offered Jackson a car and free ride to college when he graduated high school. Just because Jackson wouldn't get within sniffing distance of their stepfather's money didn't mean Louisa had to join him on the high road. She'd been too young to understand back then, and nobody talked about it now.

Not her fault.

He strapped himself in and gave the seatbelt a tug for good measure. Then he cranked the engine. "Need to make a stop, but then I'm heading up. See you in a couple hours."

And a lot more often after that, but he wasn't ready to tell her his road trip was about something more permanent.

Not when he was wondering what Miss Late Yankee would be doing about the time he rolled into town for good. She might be going to Kaci's school, but the physics and chemistry departments didn't mingle. Or so he'd heard her say. Might've been perfection in that too.

A familiar chuckle he hadn't heard in too many years echoed between his ears, and he could almost hear his daddy's voice again too. *Have your fun while you can, son. One day it's gonna have you.* He looked around, but other than a couple women walking to their cars, there weren't any people in the parking lot. He rolled his shoulders back. The leaves on the old oaks fluttered, but the wind couldn't have made that sound. Nothing could've made that sound, and he would've given his right arm to go back to the last time he heard it.

But Daddy had been gone sixteen years now, and Jackson had learned to let the memories be enough. He still had Momma, and he still had Louisa. It was time to get on with getting on. He shifted the Jetta into gear and settled in for the long road home.

Chapter Four

Failure was not a shortcoming she suffered lightly, but as she'd had little practice getting back on the horse, she suddenly found she didn't even know where the horse was.
—The Temptress of Pecan Lane, by Mae Daniels

ANNA SHOULD'VE taken the date with the exterminator.

She sat in a corner of the Jimmy Beans Coffee Shop a block off campus, rubbing at the uneven tiles in mosaic tabletop as if she could force them into symmetrical lines. The instrumental music coming out of the ceiling was probably supposed to be soothing, but it reminded Anna of funeral hymns. Not even the aroma of fresh roasted beans could make this better.

She should've gone home to study, but she still shuddered at calling her new, affordable-on-a-single-income apartment *home*. So instead, she'd walked into Jimmy Beans to grab a latte. Wasn't as if her fish would notice if she were five minutes late. A line of kids who hardly looked old enough to vote had filed in after her, and instead of pushing back through them, she'd used the human wall as an excuse to claim a table in the back corner and feel sorry for herself.

The coeds were apparently part of some campus group, and *not* the officers' ex-wives club that she'd seen advertised on the bulletin board outside her thermo classroom. If she were being honest with herself, she would've admitted she'd come here looking to make a friend or two who might tell her life would go on.

But it was easier to scowl at the table and pretend she hadn't been rejected by a group of bitter divorcees. The kids gathered at the front of the room took papers from skewed stacks that made Anna's fingers itch. They gradually filtered out into the night. The door's bells jingled, and warm air wafted over Anna's skin. A blonde stayed behind by herself, her back to Anna, but she called out in a Dolly Parton-ish drawl, asking the barista for another espresso.

Anna's finger burned from the friction it was creating on the tiles, so she switched hands. Stupid South. Stupid Neil. Stupid, arrogant James Robert College professors.

"Sugar, it's too early in the term to be letting the classes get to you."

Anna blinked up. The blonde peered down at her. She'd seen the girl shopping in the bookstore yesterday. Her perky attitude and infectious grin had made her stand out.

But it was the massive rock on her left hand that Anna remembered more. If love were measured in carats, she must've gotten the ring from God.

Also definitely not the ex-wives crowd.

Without waiting for an invitation, the blonde plunked her petite frame into the wire-backed chair across the table. "I'm Kaci. You got a name, sugar?"

Anna blew out a slow breath. She fisted her hands and put them in her lap. Sure, she had a name. It started with an *F* and ended in an *—ailure*. But since Minnesotans prided themselves on their "nice" the way Southerners prided themselves on their manners, Anna nodded. "Anna Mar—somebody."

One hour. She wanted to get through one hour without that damn burning behind her eyes.

Kaci gave her a smile laced with sympathy and encouragement. "How long's it been since you took classes?"

Great. Now Anna was an *old* failure. She dabbed at her eyes with the back of her hand. "A few years."

"It'll come on back soon enough." Kaci leaned back in the chair and gave her hair a fluff. "What're you studying?"

"Chemical engineering." *How to Make Your Life Implode* wasn't formally offered at James Robert.

The other girl's nose twitched. "Military bring you here?"

No, she always wanted to be underemployed in a place that didn't recognize ketchup as its own food group. But the words got stuck under the lump in her throat.

"Aw, sugar. You're gonna be just fine. Look at you taking classes. That's something. That's something real big."

She wanted to tell Kaci the lie that had become so easy the last week—that she was already fine—but the girl *had* sat down. Anna could've called Jules, but she didn't want this spreading around the office. "I'm already failing," she whispered, because she was afraid if she said it any louder, she wouldn't be able to recover. She'd walked into class sixteen minutes late, right as Dr. Kelly was collecting the pop quiz he'd started the semester with.

Timeliness, according to Dr. Kelly, was the sign of a strong mind, and only strong minds would survive.

"Aw, sugar, you can't be—" Kaci started, but her encouraging smile dropped off almost as fast as Anna's marriage had. "What class?"

"Thermo."

Kaci whipped a smart phone out of her messenger bag. "I swear to sweet baby Jesus, if I told that man once, I told him a billion times, teaching ain't about being an ass."

That sinking sensation in Anna's gut was becoming all too familiar as well. "You know Dr. Kelly?"

"Oh, I know him." Her drawl flared. "Know him all too well. Pompous old windbag. Never did care about people needing to make a living first and educating themselves second. I've got half a mind to go on over there and give him what for."

Her thumbs flew so fast Anna saw smoke. She lunged for the phone. "No. Please, please don't say anything. I was the only one. He'll know it was me. I need this class." Her voice cracked. "I really do. Please."

Kaci regarded Anna with a mix of curiosity and sympathy. "Don't you worry about that pop quiz. Tell you a little secret, sugar. Jim-Bob's great-great-great grandson sitting over there in the chancellor's office is making the old bag of bones curve since he flunked his whole last class. Ol' grandpappy, he likes to feel all important."

Anna's breathing evened out, but her pulse was still hammering faster than a hummingbird's wings. He couldn't flunk the whole class. That was a good thing. But she would still have to study her brains out to earn tuition assistance from work.

"Dr. Kelly's your grandfather?" She wouldn't have thought he was old enough to have grandbabies, much less a grown granddaughter. Maybe life was doing her a favor to even out all the bad lately.

Kaci grinned. "No, sugar, he's my ex-husband."

"Your *what?*" Anna sputtered. No way Kaci was old enough to have been married. Not with those baby cheeks and flawless skin. And to *Dr. Kelly?*

Oh, God. Dr. Kelly was a retired colonel. Kaci *was* the officers' ex-wives club.

Kaci winked. "Chaps his knickers when I call him that." She fluttered her left hand. Her diamond sent rainbows dancing over the mocha walls. "But it taught me a darn good lesson. I'm going for a younger man this time around."

"Is that legal?" The words were barely out before Anna clapped her hand to her mouth. That was rude. Minnesota had minimum age restrictions, but—

"Sugar, this here's Georgia," Kaci said. "Everything's legal when you're marrying your cousin."

Anna's lips twitched. Then her chest heaved. Not the pathetic, *Titanic*-watching, broken label maker kind of heave.

More like an amused, my-best-friend-told-a-dirty-joke kind of heave.

But if Anna wanted to pass thermo, dawdling here tonight probably wasn't in her best interest.

The twinkle in Kaci's eye outshone her diamond. "Just joshin' ya, sugar. Lance isn't my cousin. But he *is* one of them Bama boys. They do things even worse over there. Now listen to me. Here I am scaring your poor Yankee sensibilities."

Anna sank back into the chair, fascinated and mildly besotted. She hadn't made a friend outside the military or work since college. "I don't think being from Minnesota makes me a Yankee."

Kaci cocked her head. "Whatcha call that war the States fought back in the 1860s?"

"The Civil War?"

"See right there? Yankee. But don't worry. I won't hold it against you."

Anna's smile grew. "Thanks."

"So. What'd he do to you?"

"Dr. Kelly?"

"No, sugar. Your man."

And there went her momentary happy. "What man?"

Kaci pointed to Anna's ring finger. The indentation from six years of wearing a wedding ring had completely faded already, but the spot burned under Kaci's scrutiny. "That man," Kaci said. "You got the look, sugar."

Anna slouched. "I'm fine."

Kaci pursed her lips, then nodded. "You bet your britches you are."

Anna could've made an excuse and left. Gone back to her apartment, pulled out her label maker and used it until she felt better about having to downsize in the first place. But there was something perceptive about Kaci's gaze. Something that told Anna Kaci *got* it in a way her family and her friends couldn't.

So Anna took a sip of her chai latte, then went for the

distraction. "What are you studying?"

"Efficient combustion physics."

Anna stifled a hiccup of surprise. "Grad student?"

Kaci grinned. "Professor." She gave her own baby cheeks a pat. "Good genes, sugar. Still working on my tenure." She gestured to the scattered papers on her table. "Means I get to babysit the high school programs too, but that's the most fun part. Still got some influence over those minds. You need any physics classes?"

Anna shook her head. "Those transferred."

"Perfect. You got plans Friday night? Some of us girls are having a pinot and pedicures night. You come on over, and I guarantee you'll be happier than a goose on tequila come Saturday morning. Most of the rest of 'em are busy tonight."

A girls' night.

With real girls.

Longing welled in her chest and almost choked her. "I can't."

"Kids?"

Anna shook her head.

"Well, you've got my blessing to slug the first person who says that's a good thing."

"They don't really say that, do they?"

"Sugar, they say all kinds of crap. That kid question, it's barely the start. Hope you got some good family to back you up."

Anna's chai latte got stuck between her throat and her stomach right about where her heart used to be.

It wasn't that they didn't support her. They were simply disappointed.

"He did you good, didn't he?" Kaci said.

And there was that damn stinging in her eyeballs again.

"Don't you worry," Kaci said. "Whenever you're ready, I got just the thing for you."

Anna leaned into the table, a real smile threatening to show. "I hid his electric toothbrush so he'd have to ask me where it was."

"Good on you, sugar. Good on you."

"And—some other things."

"He notice they're missing yet?"

Anna's shoulders sagged.

"Then you're better off without him. You really busy Friday, or you telling me that so you can slink away without giving me your number?"

There was a time she would've slunk home and gossiped with Neil about the crazy chick who married her grandfather, but Kaci was growing on her. "I promised a friend we'd go do karaoke."

"Y'all aren't planning on doing Aretha, are you? Gloria Gaynor? Sugar, you can do better than that."

"*Grease*. With her new brother-in-law. I kind of owe her a favor." And between the high schoolers filtering in to report on their progress with the physics-themed scavenger hunt Kaci had sent them on while she waited for losers like Anna looking for friends, Anna's story came tumbling out.

An hour later, Anna had her second phone number of the night, but this one she intended to use. Kaci had anointed herself Anna's guardian divorce angel, and Anna was smart enough not to argue with a woman who kept instructions for a divorce survival kit in her purse at all times.

Plus, as Kaci said, a friend who made you laugh was worth ten ex-husbands, and Anna needed all the laughter she could get.

AFTER JACKSON GAVE Louisa an earful about how to use the Jetta's new vegetable oil engine and made sure Radish, his old spaniel, was fed and watered and happy, he made himself scarce before Momma got hold of him and made him stay for dinner. He had a date at the bowling alley. Didn't take long to find Mamie and her crew. Only had to look for the gray-hairs with the highest scores.

"Gimme a minute to get this here strike, sugarplum," Mamie called as he approached. "I got me a game to win."

When she grinned big like that, her face exploded in wrinkles, but she was still near about the prettiest thing he'd seen today. Near about. "Go on and make me proud, Mamie."

He settled in with her normal crowd, asking after Miss Flo's great-grandbabies and Miss Dolly's poodle while Mamie cleaned up the lane. Miss Ophelia must've seen him coming, because she walked into the pit with a big old cup of root beer like she used to when he was shoulder-high to an armadillo. "You're sweet as ever, Miss O. How're them boyfriends treating you?"

"Ain't you a sugar-pie, worrying over little old me," she said with a pinch to his cheek.

"Aw, shucks, ma'am, it ain't nothing. Just making sure you're keeping Mamie stocked with ideas for those books of hers."

The ladies tittered. Down the lane, ten pins exploded against the back wall. Mamie pumped her fist in the air. "Eat my ashes, you old biddies," she called.

Jackson gave her a high five, then helped her off the lane. Not that she needed it. She'd probably be handing him his own cane some day, rate she was going. "Ain't you a little young to be trash-talking like that?" he said.

She gave him a squeeze. "Such a charmer, you. Go on and fetch me my phone. I gotta Tweet the score."

"Yes, ma'am."

After Mamie updated her Twitter and Facebook accounts, and after Miss Dolly and Miss Flo got on their phones and fired back some gently bred insults of their own, Jackson followed the ladies up to the snack bar and treated them to a pizza party.

"You planning on sticking around a while this time?" Mamie asked over the normal din of the bowling alley. "Us girls could use a strong handsome man to fetch our balls."

"What's wrong with my Cletus?" Miss Ophelia said. "I

thought he done a right good job of ball-fetching."

"But he ain't the looker Jackson here is." Miss Dolly wiggled her penciled-in eyebrows. "He grew up right pretty, he did."

"Right perfect," Mamie corrected.

Jackson grinned. These sweet old gals could show a Yankee girl how to flatter a man. "I ain't got nothing on you fine ladies, and you know it."

"You keep sweet-talking, I'm gonna start thinking you're here looking for something," Mamie said.

"Just looking for time with my favorite gals," he said.

"Uh-huh," Miss Dolly said. Miss Flo stretched her neck out and peered at him over her glasses.

Miss Ophelia adjusted her hair. "What's her name, and how far along is she?"

Jackson choked on his root beer.

"Now why would you think that about my sweet Jackson?" Mamie demanded. "He might could have a couple other things bothering him." She dropped her voice and leaned into him. "It ain't a girl, is it, sugarplum?"

Jackson wiped his mouth. "No girl," he assured her.

She pinned him with the same stare his daddy'd always used. "You getting out of the service?"

He'd be getting out about as soon as he'd be planning on being a daddy himself, and Mamie knew it. "Got orders."

All four women sucked in a breath as one. Miss Flo gave herself the sign of the cross.

"You be careful over there, y'hear?" Miss Ophelia said.

"Moving orders," Jackson clarified.

Their breaths whooshed out as one too.

"To Gellings."

Mamie let out a whoop, and Miss Ophelia gave his cheek another pinch. "Don't you be scaring us like that, y'hear?"

"Yes, ma'am," he said with a chuckle.

"You looking to settle down while you're here?" Miss Flo wanted to know. "I got a granddaughter about your age. She's real nice. Bakes good biscuits too."

"That means she ain't got the looks God gave a porcupine, bless her heart," Miss Ophelia said.

"She's a real sweet girl," Miss Flo insisted.

"That she is," Miss Dolly agreed. Miss Ophelia added an "Mm-hmm," but Mamie rapped a knuckle on the table. "Y'all leave my grandbaby alone. Just 'cuz he's back here in God's country with all these nice Southern girls don't mean he's gonna pick the first one what comes along. He's gonna be trying biscuits all over half the state when the mommas find out he's come home, you mark my words. How long you gonna be here, sugarplum?"

"Couple years." But he wouldn't be sampling just any biscuits. A few assignments ago he would've, but he'd learned the hard way when he sampled the biscuits, the biscuit baker expected him to bring home the butter, and he sure wasn't planning on doing that.

Mamie might write those nice books with happy endings, but he knew firsthand the biscuits went stale and the butter spoiled. He'd rather not have the biscuits at all.

Milk, though, that'd be hard to give up all together.

Mamie was looking at him like his daddy used to whenever Jackson would get a notion to head out with Craig for some no-good fun. Like she could read his brain cells. "Ain't you a little young to be talkin' smack about forever?" she said softly.

He reckoned she was in a position to think so. But it wouldn't change his mind. "You go on and write me a happy ending, Mamie."

'Cuz that was the only forever he'd be buttering in this lifetime.

Chapter Five

When she first made a splash in the world, she rippled out of her comfort zone in small waves. When the world made a splash in her life, she discovered in her possession a tidal wave of sparks with which to splash back.
—The Temptress of Pecan Lane, *by Mae Daniels*

FRIDAY NIGHT, ANNA climbed off the stage at Taps, hot and sweaty and laughing after a rusty rendition of "Summer Nights." She sucked as Sandy, but Rodney was worse as Danny. And he'd reveled in his badness for every last horrific second.

They made their way through the crowd to their table. Brad jumped up on his chair and gave a whistle. "More! More!"

Jules yanked at his belt loops. "God, how can you still hear after that? Get down."

"You kidding, babe? That was like angels. *Angels*. If I'd been up there—"

"My eardrums would still work," Jules said.

He hopped down and bumped into their waitress. Her tray flew out of her hands. Full soda cups went flying. People at the next table skittered for cover. Anna shrieked and ducked, but she got splattered with half a Sprite.

"Smooth, bro." Rodney held out a fist, and Brad bumped it.

"You okay, Anna?"

Jules handed her a wad of napkins. They disintegrated on the sugary liquid on Anna's arms. "Just wet," she said.

"So to speak," Rodney and Brad said together. They shared another fist bump and a "Giggidy."

"Could you quit acting like Neanderthals?" Jules said.

"Sorry, babe." Brad grinned at her like, well, a Neanderthal. He and Rodney went down on all fours to help the waitress, and he gave her a grin too. "Sorry, ma'am. You can add 'em to my tab."

Jules rubbed her forehead. "He is such a doofus. But he's my doofus."

"I'll let you have him." Anna gestured toward the ladies' room. Jules followed her.

Anna had dressed for a night in a bar. Jeans, sparkly top, and boots that made squeaky noises on the restroom floor once the noise of the bar and karaoke were shut out by the door. "Rodney's totally checking you out," Jules said.

Anna went straight for the sink. "Technically still married here."

"Don't be like that." Jules leaned into the mirror and checked her mascara.

"Like what?"

"Bitter about me getting the better brother."

Anna was up to her elbows in pink bathroom soap and chlorine water, with jeans that were stuck to her legs, and she was laughing for the second time in five minutes. "No offense, Jules, but I wouldn't have picked either of them."

"Yeah, well look what you pick—erm, what you're missing out on." Jules pulled a lipstick out of her back pocket.

Look what you picked. Right. But Jules using her verbal filter for once made up for the near insult. "Yeah, can you picture the in-law Christmases? Imagine the toys Rodney and I could come up with to give you in front of their parents."

Jules gave her a withering look. "Dude. Did I tell you what he gave us for the wedding?"

Southern Fried Blues

Soapy hands or not, Anna clamped her hands over her ears. "La la la, not listening."

"Exactly," Jules said with a smirk. "You'd totally tame him. Nothing else with spikes for us."

Anna shuddered. Sex was great exactly the way it was meant to be. With two bodies, on a bed, in the dark. Maybe next to the bed, but that had to be planned in advance in case things got messy.

Jules fussed with her hair while Anna finished cleaning up as best she could. "Ready?" she asked Jules a minute later. She reached for the door. Jules grabbed her arm.

"Hey, listen. Rodney's not really into commitment, but I've never heard a complaint about his *skills* from any of his girlfriends, so if you wanted to" —Jules cleared her throat— "with him, to, you know, get experience with someone else, maybe take the edge off, I'm cool with that."

Good thing they were in the restroom, because Anna wanted to wash her hands again. Maybe a few other parts too. Moving on was one thing. A pity screw with Rodney—no. Just no.

"Or not." Jules shrugged. "Your call. Thought you should know he'd be up for that." She tilted her head. "So to speak."

The restroom door opened, and two drunk coeds staggered in. Jules's eyebrows went wonky. "But then, that might be more his speed. God, I am the best sister-in-law *ever.*"

If she said so. They left the restroom. "You gonna sing tonight?" Anna asked. Brad and Rodney had fresh drinks at the table.

"There isn't enough alcohol on the planet," Jules replied.

She slid into the seat beside Brad, who put his arm around her shoulders and tipped a bottle into her mouth.

Anna took her own seat and averted her gaze.

"Disgusting, isn't it?" Rodney said. He dropped his arm over the back of her chair. A familiar scent overcame the lingering Sprite on her clothes.

Rodney used the same body wash Neil had. Anna crossed her legs. She leaned left, far enough to get the odor out of her nose, which, unfortunately, put her closer to Brad and Jules, who were now rubbing noses and doing something borderline obscene with their tongues. She tried to smile at Rodney. "Like watching my parents make out."

Rodney guffawed. His eyes dropped to her chest. His tongue darted out of his mouth. "I like funny girls."

Anna caught sight of the two coeds. She nodded toward them. "The redhead over there was in the bathroom telling blonde jokes."

His eyebrows looked like two fuzzy caterpillars hooding his eyes. He contorted one in his *giggidy* pose, but never once looked toward the redhead. "You're a funny girl."

Anna instinctively reached for her ring. Long gone, but she could still feel it there. Rodney, apparently, couldn't. "I'm technically still married," she said.

The other eyebrow went all giggidy too. "Got an idea to help with that."

He leaned in closer. Anna lunged for her iced tea. "So. Another song?"

"I got a song for you, baby." His lids were half-lowered. "Wanna see the eighth wonder of the world? Give you a hint. It put the *Rod* in *Rodney*."

Anna's facial muscles contorted. She took a big gulp of tea to hide the worst of the twitches, but the tea hit her stomach like a one-two punch of reality.

Men actually said things like that to single women.

Rodney slipped the tea out of her grasp and put it back on the table. No more shield. Lots more body wash odor. "I'm trying not to think about it, but I'm headed off to war next week. Never know if you're coming back or not. Got to take every last opportunity to live to the fullest, you know? Do things I've never done before, with people I've never done them with."

"Technically still married," Anna squeaked again.

Southern Fried Blues

That only upped the giggidy in his eyebrows. "Never done that before. Come on, baby. Grease my lightning."

He was so close she could see every blond follicle on his chin and cheeks.

"Ask not what you can do for your country, ask what you can do to service your country's servicemen." His tongue rolled over his bottom lip. "Us Marines are better at *everything* than those Air Force weenies. *Ooh*-rah, baby."

His lips loomed in her face like two gigantic garden slugs. There was definite movement in the Rodney, Jr. area.

Her heart triple-timed it. Adrenaline pinged through her veins. Her thighs clamped shut on their own, and her lungs felt as if they were filled with cement.

Sex was *totally* out of the question. As for the garden slugs, she hadn't kissed anyone but Neil in over eight years. It was inevitable she'd kiss someone eventually, but she didn't know where Rodney's lips had been.

An involuntary whimper slipped out of her frozen mouth. She lunged for her drink. Her clumsy fingers connected with the glass. Tea went everywhere. All over the table, all over Anna's jeans, all over her broken life. She jumped to her feet with a shriek.

Rodney jumped up too. "Dude. Really?"

She opened her mouth to apologize, but her throat was thick with tears.

Rodney got the panicked expression of a guy who'd rather park his car over fire ants than deal with a soggy female. He gestured helplessly at Brad, who was probably only acting stoic for Jules's sake.

Jules heaved a sigh and disentangled herself from her husband. "More napkins?"

Anna waved a hand to the door, but then tucked it into her soggy pocket when she remembered what that hand was capable of. "Paper towels. In my car. I'll be okay. Thanks. Fun times."

Jules cut her eyes to Rodney, then back at Anna. "Need a

ride?"

"No!" Anna fumbled with her purse, also dripping. She'd had a tea and fries. Easy math. "No. Thanks. I'm okay."

Brad gave her foot a nudge. "We got you, Anna."

"No, really, I can pay for myself." She slipped a ten out of her wallet and set it on the table. She could barely make eye contact with Jules. "See you Monday. I need to go. Get cleaned up. You know."

But as soon as she was out the door, safely headed to her car, she dug into her purse for a phone number.

And two minutes later, she headed to her first officers' ex-wives club meeting.

"SUGAR, WHOSE ASS do I have to kick?" Kaci asked as soon as she opened the door.

She lived in a neighborhood like Anna used to. Oversize cookie-cutter houses, high ceilings, bedrooms as big as Anna's whole apartment, twenty-five minute commute to base, ten-minute ride to James Robert, five to Taps.

Anna had wanted to go home, but she was soaked, her hands shook so bad she could hardly steer, and she was so, so tired of feeling lonely.

The ominous sounds of quiet from inside the house didn't bode well for her choice in how to deal with her humdinger of a mess of life. "Did I miss the party?"

Kaci's nose twitched. "Oh, no, sugar, it's a small one tonight." Her smile was part hesitant, part hopeful. "Really, it's just me. Sarah's kids got sick, so her new friend cancelled too. But I got what it takes to be a club all by myself. You get on in here and relax. I'll go open up a bottle."

Anna hesitated. She wasn't good at this. Neil had always made her friends for her. He'd take her to Company Grade Officers Association functions, introduce her to a few guys who'd introduce her to their wives or girlfriends, then they'd invite her over to their houses for candle and basket and kitchen gadget parties. They'd ask her to join the officers' wives club, which she'd politely decline since they held all their meetings during school or working hours, and Anna would be that wife that showed up at picnics and cookouts and sort of knew people, but didn't really.

She'd gotten good at only sort-of knowing people.

That's why she'd liked Jules so much. Jules seemed good with the sort-of knowing people thing too.

But Kaci didn't strike her as the sort-of type.

"First step's remembering who you are without him, sugar," Kaci said. "It's a doozy, but it gets better after that."

That explained why Anna's knees didn't want to move. But her brain and her heart and her soul did, so she picked up her feet and crossed into the cool foyer.

Kaci's baby cheeks split into a grin. "You up for some peach cobbler, or is chocolate more your speed tonight? Got a big old box of Godiva in here too."

Godiva. Probably from the BX with the BX discount.

Anna needed to stock up before she turned in her dependent ID and lost base shopping privileges. They weren't in her budget right now, but a chocolate emergency was a chocolate emergency.

Tonight was bigger than a chocolate emergency.

"Tequila shots?" Kaci said.

"God, yes."

"You and me, sugar, we're gonna be good friends."

The living room was tiled in oversize beige porcelain tile and furnished in warm browns. Ole Miss memorabilia hung on one side, while Bama souvenirs dominated the other. In between, on a mantel of a fireplace that was probably used only a half-dozen times a year, was a picture of Kaci and her tall, dark, handsome fiancé. Tall, dark, and handsome was in a flight suit.

Good for Kaci, but Anna wasn't *ever* doing a military guy again.

She looked away from the picture and found herself

staring out the back door to twinkling pool lights.

This was what she thought she'd have the rest of her life.

Instead, she had an apartment in a lower tax bracket, and she was standing in the middle of a one-woman party.

Her legs threatened to do their freeze-dried Twinkie impression again.

Kaci trotted in from the semi-open kitchen and handed her a shot glass. "Lime?"

"Ketchup."

"*Ketchup?*"

"I'm a lightweight." Anna's nose gave a telltale crinkle. Her eyes followed. The lake was building in her sinuses again, her eyelids preparing to be dams. Her voice cracked. "And ketchup makes me think of home."

"Well, sugar, you named your poison. Sit on down. I'll bring you the whole bottle."

"But—" Anna gestured to her clothes. They were half-dry, and her top had developed a few weird wrinkles.

Kaci sprinted to the kitchen, then huffed back with a ketchup bottle. She snagged Anna's elbow and pulled her into the master bedroom.

The walls were a lovely mocha, the crown molding blinding white beneath a tray ceiling. Clothes and books and fireworks were strewn across the four-poster king-size bed.

Fireworks?

Oh, God. Neil really *had* stranded her in the South. The deep South, all pretty on the outside, all backwoods on the inside, without the buffer of the base.

He'd up and left her in Redneckville.

"I hate him," Anna blurted.

Kaci looked up from a drawer. "Got every right, sugar."

"Not *hate*-hate," Anna said, and she felt another case of the sniffles coming on. "I mean, I *loved* him. It was what I did. And I was good at it. I really was."

Kaci came up with a pair of sweatpants. "I know you were, sugar. Here. See if these fit."

Anna shot her tequila and killed the fire-throat with a squirt of ketchup straight from the bottle. She slammed both the glass and the ketchup down on the nightstand. "All I ever did was love him."

"How long?"

"Long enough to think we'd have forever." She kicked off her shoes, dropped her pants, and pulled on the sweatpants. They were too long, obviously Kaci's fiancè's, but Anna only had to tighten the string in the waist a little. "One of my sorority sisters introduced us. She was dating one of his friends, and they were all older so they graduated first. Then they got sent to Oklahoma together, and Neil kept calling and saying he *needed* me. So we got married and I transferred schools, and I needed more classes because not everything transferred. But the four of us were together, except then Neil's program moved a year later, then our friends got divorced, and then the only thing I had going for me was being a military wife."

"Aw, sugar, it ain't easy to resist a man in uniform. Look at me, going after my second one. And my daddy was Air Force too. Gets in your blood."

"No. Not me. I'm not *ever* dating a military man again. Hell, I'm not ever *dating* again." Because the thought of dating made her stomach dip as it did on a roller coaster, and her heart felt as if it were stabbing itself with one of her ribs.

"I swore off academics after ol' grandpappy," Kaci said with a knowing nod. "Wouldn't have given my Lance another look if he'd been any brighter than a dumb cargo jock."

Anna reached for the ketchup bottle again.

"Gets easier, sugar, but it's okay to take your time. Went three years myself without dating anybody after I welded ol' grandpappy's car doors shut and hid his uniforms on Air Force Academy graduation day."

Anna choked on the ketchup, but it felt good to laugh at something again.

"Tell you what," Kaci said with a nod, "that man realized

who *he* needed that day."

"I don't think anybody's ever going to need me again."

"Aw, sugar, *somebody's* gonna need you. Bet you got a lot of somebodies who already do."

"No, they really don't." Anna swiped her nose with the back of her hand. "Beth's boys are too old for babysitters. Gram has all the help she needs rolling pie crusts at the shop. Dad hires high schoolers to reorganize the bookstore. I thought they needed me, but they replaced me as soon as I left for college. So when Neil needed me, I thought he was the only one. And I needed him to need me, so it was perfect."

"Sounds like how I felt the first time I saw ol' grandpappy's potato gun. Didn't know why, but I knew I had to have him."

"His *potato gun?*" Anna lunged for the ketchup and took another hit straight out of the bottle.

"It was a beaut," Kaci said on a sigh. "Shot potatoes three miles if they went an inch. But that man knew as much about being a husband as a crocodile knows about knitting a sweater. Nothing worth keeping there. I didn't need to be anybody's trophy wife. Especially not after he kept all the trophies. I *earned* him those trophies."

"Jerk."

"Well, trust me on this one, if he doesn't want you, he doesn't deserve you. Marriage is give and take. If he can't give you what *you* need, and sugar, he has to give you more than needing you, then good riddance."

Anna took another hit of ketchup. "You know what he *needed* me for? Sex. Just sex. And now my friends are trying to set me up with guys who want me for sex." Her eyes were leaking, but for the first time since Neil had said the D-word, they weren't sad tears.

They were freaking *furious* tears.

She yanked off her shirt and took the Ole Miss t-shirt Kaci handed her, then pointed to the firecrackers. "You know what I think about being used for sex? I think I'd like to strap *their* potato guns to those firecrackers. *That's* what I'd like to do for my country."

Kaci tilted her head, a thoughtful gleam in her eye. "We could do the next best thing."

Anna stopped mid-ketchup shot. She gulped the Hunts down in a painful lump that settled right over her heart. "What's that?"

"You still got any of his stuff?"

The ketchup bottle wobbled in Anna's hand.

She had a whole boxful in the trunk, neatly labeled *Jerkface's Stuff*, that she was planning on delivering to her attorney next week.

And Neil could pay for shipping, since he was covering her attorney's fees as part of the settlement.

The fireworks on the bed whispered sweet nothings. *Do it for your country, baby. We might not live to see tomorrow.*

They were technically illegal in Georgia.

But when was the next time she'd get a chance to blow Neil the hell out of her life?

"Damn straight I've got something."

It didn't take much more than an encouraging grin from Kaci to propel Anna out to her car. Moments later, they were sprawled out in front of the pool, strapping Neil's belongings to firecrackers, and moments after that, Kaci handed Anna a lighter.

"Which one you gonna do first, sugar?"

Anna took another hit from the ketchup bottle. "His favorite boxers."

They positioned the firecracker in the middle of the yard. Anna lit the fuse, and the two of them stepped back. The rocket shot into the air with a squeal.

Ka-BOOM!

A shower of red and yellow sparks exploded in the night sky. Kaci let out a whoop.

Anna saluted the sky with her ketchup bottle. "I'll miss that dust rag."

She positioned the next firework, then lit it and darted

back to Kaci's side. When that one exploded, goo splattered down on them. "What is that *smell?*" Kaci asked.

"His favorite body wash."

"It smells worse than a wet hog in a trough of rotten peaches."

"Smells worse on." On all of them.

Two weeks ago, she wouldn't have believed she could send the ashes of her marriage up on firecrackers.

But it felt good.

Necessary.

Freeing.

Anna laughed. She scampered forward and lit another firecracker.

"Which one?" Kaci asked.

"His iPod. I never have to listen to the very best of the Neils again." She'd spent so many hours listening to Neil Young and Neil Diamond on car trips, she'd taken to offering to drive so her Neil could use his iPod's earbuds.

In retrospect, Diamond's *Red Red Wine* and Young's *Birds* on repeat were more prophetic than annoying.

A rainbow-colored burst of sparks spread out in a sphere over the sound of the firecracker's boom. Something whistled then splashed into the pool with a heavy *kerplunk!*

Bye-bye, Neils.

"Don't ever doubt terminal velocity," Kaci said. Anna turned to the pool, but Kaci stopped her. "Lance'll get it, sugar. He's used to this. What's next?"

The *pièce de résistance*. "His retainer."

"His *what?*" Kaci said. "Like for his teeth?"

"Uh-huh."

"Sugar, tell me he didn't kiss you with that thing in."

Anna snuck forward and bent to light it.

"Anna, sugar?" Kaci said. "You didn't let him do that, did you?"

"We were *married*. You do a lot of weird stuff when you're married."

"Don't light it!" Kaci suddenly shrieked.

"What? Why? What's wrong?" Anna blew on the fuse, but it only sped the fire.

"That there's date repellant, and you're blowing it up." Kaci dropped next to Anna, then blew out a breath. "Hoo boy." She grabbed Anna's arm and dragged her back. The fuse stopped. A second later, the firecracker and the retainer shot into the sky.

"Now look what you gone and did. Ain't no reason for any girls *not* to be dating him now," Kaci said.

Sparks showered down. "Well, damn," Anna said. "I didn't think about that."

"Sugar, I got lots to teach you."

Anna grabbed her ketchup bottle and squeezed in another shot, more for fun than necessity. "Is it enough if I wish his first new girlfriend gives him herpes?"

"That'll do. Feeling better?"

Anna inhaled sulfur and hints of smoke. She caught sight of a wispy trail from the last firecracker floating through the sky, and she realized her shoulders weren't bunched, her teeth not clenched, her muscles not spun tight.

She was free.

Not alone, but free.

She smiled at Kaci. "Yeah. A *lot* better."

Kaci gave her arm a squeeze. "Good on you."

On impulse, Anna snagged Kaci in a hug. "Thank you."

"That's what your ex-wife friends are for." Kaci squeezed her back hard. "You stick with me, sugar, and everything's gonna be fine."

Chapter Six

His body was a temple, well-fed, well-slept, well-exercised, but upon taking her hand a second time, he realized his heart had been sorely neglected.
—The Temptress of Pecan Lane, *by Mae Daniels*

FRIDAY NIGHT, JACKSON put his phone on silent, gave Radish a big old belly rub and a bowl of fresh water, then left the piles of boxes in his new house to deal with next week. Lance and his old lady were having a Fourth of July cookout, and Jackson was curious enough about their friends to call Auburn and let the family know he wasn't coming up until tomorrow.

His new place was closer to base than Lance and Kaci's house. Homier, too, in his opinion, but that was probably the Radish effect. Still, he and Radish had appreciated a few meals in Lance's mini-mansion while they were getting settled. Made it easy to walk through the door, greet his hostess in the kitchen with a kiss on the cheek, and navigate through the growing crowd to head straight for the grill.

"Hey, Bubba," Lance called from the man spot on the patio.

"Thumper." Jackson snagged a cola out of a cooler and sauntered over to shake his buddy's hand. "Big crowd."

Easy to pick out Kaci's friends from Lance's. The Jim-Bob

crowd all had long hair and were fanning themselves, while the Company Grade Officers Association folks were close-trimmed and dressed for the weather.

"Hey, if Kaci mentions redneck golf, tell her you pulled a hamstring or something." Lance's lovestruck moon-eyes ruined his shudder. "Girl can't throw a bola for shit. Takes forever to let her win."

"Should've told me before I got here. Already promised her a game."

"Hell, Bubba."

Jackson grinned. "You pull a hamstring."

"Not a bad idea. Probably get a rubdown out of it."

"More power to you, man."

Lance flipped the lid up on the grill and started poking at the burgers. "Still avoiding the war eagle crowd?" he asked.

"Heading up that way tomorrow." Louisa's birthday wasn't until Sunday, but the girl did birthdays like New Orleans did Mardi Gras. Wouldn't have surprised him to pull up to a parade. But it was her twenty-first, and he'd missed more of her birthdays than he'd made, so he owed her.

They stood there shooting the breeze and grilling until Kaci showed up with a plateful of cheese slices lined up so straight Momma's Junior League friends would've been impressed. "You boys about done with the burgers? We got a hungry crowd."

"First round's coming off now," Lance said. "Hey, Bubba, you mind grabbing the rest out of the fridge?"

"Oh!" Kaci spun at him so fast, the cheese almost flew right off the plate. She had a look in her eyes that made the hairs on the back of his neck stand up. Like Miss Flo before she got to talking about her single granddaughter.

"Yes, ma'am?" Jackson ventured.

Kaci's face went all innocent. "While you're in there, go on and ask Anna for the hot dogs, would you, sugar?"

"Yes, ma'am." No need wasting words asking who Anna was. She'd be the sweet one with questionable biscuits.

Probably he should tell Kaci about his thoughts on butter, but she was already gone, flitting about among her guests.

He strolled to the door, tossing his cola can in the recycling bin on the way.

The back door opened into the living room, which was one of the things he didn't like so much about all these newer houses. The kitchen was off to the right, partly open into the living room. Two women were in there talking. Rather, one was talking. The other was cutting the most uniform tomato slices he'd ever seen.

It wasn't the tomatoes that stopped him.

It was the doe eyes.

So that's who Anna was. He'd lay odds the cheese plate had been her doing too.

She looked like she could've used some fried chicken and biscuits to put some meat back in her cheeks, and her straight light hair was longer than when he saw her last time.

Prettier than he remembered, and he'd remembered her awful darn pretty.

There was that chuckle in his head again. Combined with the unusual thumping in his chest, he took a second to pull himself together.

"Thought you went home after Neil left," the other one was saying. Jackson recognized her from outside. She had railroad tracks knitted on the shoulders of her blouse to match her CGOA president husband's rank of captain.

If it weren't for the way Anna's nose wrinkled whenever one of her slices was thicker than the others, he wouldn't have thought the first girl's yammering bothered her. "Nope. Still here." And she sounded as happy as if she were facing fire ants again.

He'd been raised better than to listen to two ladies gossip, but he reckoned this was the only way he'd ever find out anything about her.

Besides, it was entertaining.

"If it weren't for Tom there's no way I'd stay here." The

other woman gave a high-pitched giggle that made Jackson's ears hurt. "So are you working or something?"

Tomato juice flew off the end of the knife. "I've always worked."

"Oh, right, right. You're a receptionist somewhere?"

"Analytical technical support." She grabbed a paper towel and wiped the tomato juice off the counter, a big old fake smile shining away.

At least there weren't any tears this time. He might work up some of his own if that other girl didn't quit that shrill giggle though. "That's all over my head," she said. "So are you here with somebody tonight?"

Jackson cared about that answer more than he should've. That chuckling in his head and pounding in his chest got louder too.

"I'm with the school crowd."

"Oh, good. An education is so important for a single woman these days. What are you studying?"

"Chemical engineering at James Robert."

The other girl's eyes went big as Jackson guessed his own were. He'd known she had some brains, but didn't know she had that many. "Oh, wow. Wouldn't it have been easier to take the alimony?"

Just when things were getting interesting, Anna stood up about fourteen feet tall and glared down her nose like she'd been born and bred a Southern lady herself. "A friend of mine at school mentioned she got one of the scholarships the officers' wives club sponsored this year. She was really grateful. You'll have to let me know when the next fundraiser is. If ex-wives can contribute, that is."

Jackson didn't know how the girl had missed that duck-and-cover sign. It should've thwacked her upside the head a second time, it swung down so hard, but the girl kept on talking. Good time to get those burgers and hot dogs. "'Scuse me, ladies. Anna, Kaci's wanting the rest of them burgers and those hot dogs for the kids."

Anna looked at him, then looked again, and her cheeks went all dark. Her jaw hung like a door with broken hinges, and her eyes darted this way and that as if avoiding him meant he wouldn't be there.

But he kept on walking into the kitchen as if he didn't notice. Partly because his momma had taught him better than to embarrass a lady, but more because he was glad she recognized him.

He'd never been good with being forgettable.

The back door opened, and the base commander's wife walked in behind him. Lance had pointed out the higher-ups, and Jackson was glad he had. Lance had also told him Kaci and the commander's missus were tight over their officers' ex-wives club thing, the commander being his missus's second husband, and it didn't take a rocket scientist to know Kaci was up to something.

Even if it did take a rocket scientist, he had that covered too.

"Wendy, there you are," Sarah Sheridan said. "Do you have a minute? Rosa and I need a little help on a thrift store problem."

"Absolutely, Mrs. Sheridan," Wendy chirped. She gave Anna a bright, "See you around!" then smiled at Jackson on her way past.

Before the door shut behind them, Anna had herself buried in the fridge. When she finally pulled her head back out, her cheeks were pale again, and she almost made eye contact. She handed over a platter of hamburgers, then dove back into the fridge.

Good thing Mamie and Miss Flo weren't here to see this. Might hurt his reputation.

Or get Anna in trouble for insulting their sugarplum.

She came back up with a bowl of hot dogs and some of that spine she'd shown Wendy the Windy. "That's the last of it," she said, and she even looked him straight on.

"Much obliged, ma'am."

She must've gotten her fill of his pretty face, because she looked away right quick. Her gaze fell on the window, and her face went screwy.

Mrs. Sheridan and Wendy were on the other side.

"You handled her right good for a Yankee," he said.

That earned him a hint of a smile, which earned him another big old wallop right about where his heart sat.

And because he wasn't a fool about knowing what wanting to see a bigger smile out of her might mean, he took himself and the meat outside.

ANNA COULD'VE USED about half a lifetime to recover from the triple-whammy of signing her divorce papers yesterday, Wendy's inquisition about her failures tonight, and the exterminator's appearance in the middle of it, but the cookout had just started. Before she could straighten the ceramic utensil crocks on the counter, Lance brought in the first batch of burgers. Behind him, a crowd filtered inside looking for food and cooler temperatures.

When all the extra bodies made the house feel hotter than boiling oil, Anna ducked outside in search of a dark, quiet corner. The sun hadn't set, and too many people were still playing in the pool for her to succeed in either goal. Instead, she settled for a semi-hidden spot near a fan where she could arrange the bin of pool toys by size and color. If she'd known how many CGOA people would be here tonight, she would've bailed. Which was probably why Kaci hadn't mentioned it. She wondered if the CGOA was the exterminator's crowd.

Jackson, she reminded herself.

And there he was again, squatting next to the pool in his board shorts and faded Alabama T-shirt, showing a kid how to hold a Nerf football. Jackson didn't seem to mind the occasional splash the kid caused. He glanced up and met Anna's eyes and gave her a friendly smile. She quickly looked away, realizing she'd dropped a pair of water balls where the pool noodles would've fit better. But a minute later she found herself focusing on Jackson again.

He was still watching her.

"Good gravy, sugar, you haven't changed into your swimsuit yet."

Anna gave Kaci a weak smile. "Pool's a little crowded."

"Never mind that, then. You hungry? Lance's got the second batch of burgers all hot and ready."

Anna glanced back at the pool, but Jackson had moved on.

Kaci squinted at her. "You looking for someone?"

"No, I—sort of." She dropped her voice. "You remember the ants in my car? And the guy who helped me?"

"The dumb old redneck?"

Anna darted furtive glances around until she spotted him with Lance. "He's here." She nodded at the grill.

Kaci followed her line of sight, then let out a whoop of laughter.

"Sshh!" Anna hadn't thought her body could generate more heat in the summer evening, but her cheeks were flaming again.

"Aw, sugar, Jackson's good folk. He taught Lance how to throw rifles in ROTC at Bama. Just PCS'd here for good last week. If it makes you feel any better, he never mentioned the ants to us. That boy's momma raised him right." Her ring flashed when she gestured to the kitchen. "Heard you got rescued from an inquisition. You doing okay?"

"I'm fine." Aside from realizing her love life was prone to suicidal attractions, that was. Of course he was military. "She was trying to be nice."

Kaci humphed. "That girl doesn't have the sense God gave a gnat. You give one of us a signal if she tries to corner you again."

"Thanks, but I'm good."

Kaci flitted off to play hostess. Anna snagged a margarita inside, then a burger and chips. The air conditioner was no match for the crowd, so she found a spot by a fan in a shady corner of the yard with Sarah and a couple of other girls. Occasionally, she spotted Jackson wandering around the party, and she found the nerve to smile back at him once or twice.

She didn't have to follow through on a smile. Probably wouldn't, with him being military. But the last few weeks, Kaci kept insisting Anna would eventually want something more than the battery-operated devices in her divorce kit. Anna was almost ready to admit she might be right.

About the "eventually" part.

Eventually wasn't today.

She was just practicing. She *was*, after all, legally single now.

Hints of dusk filtered in. Fluffy piles of Georgia clouds took on pink and orange hues. The crowd in the backyard thinned, with the families leaving first, then the couples dropping next. Wendy bid her an overly friendly good-bye, and Anna was happy to discover the encounter didn't leave her needing to straighten the pool toys again. Someone turned on the patio lights and lit a few tiki torches for bug control. She hadn't meant to be among the last guests tonight, but she was still happily nursing a slight buzz from the margarita.

She'd fed her fish before she left for work this morning. No one expected her anywhere. And the night air was warm enough to be cozy without the oppression that made it hard to breathe. She treated herself to another margarita, only half full this time, and took her pick of the empty lawn chairs near the pool. She curled her legs up and settled in, and Kaci appeared at her side. "You up for some redneck golf? Lance is betting me the dishes he'll beat the pants off us."

Anna smiled fondly. "Don't think so. He always lets you win."

"You bet your britches. That's how it's supposed to be."

"But it's not *fun*."

Kaci huffed. "Lance, get over here and talk some sense into this girl."

Lance dropped his grill brush to cross the patio. "What's

wrong, babe?"

"She says it's not any fun when you let us win." Kaci stuck her lip out. Anna stifled a snort in her margarita.

"Make you feel better if I pretend I'm trying?" Lance said to Anna.

"Nope." She had enjoyed the evening too much to ruin it watching Lance help Kaci score points and toss his bolas way off mark. She was happy Kaci had found someone to take a second chance with, but tonight, she wanted to be happy and single with no reminders of the kind of romance she'd probably never have again.

Someone sat on her other side. She glanced over and found Jackson studying her. "I won't let you win," he said.

She studied him right back. Her heart gave a jolt. She shivered against the tart taste flooding her mouth. His hair was within regs, barely a hint of the curl she'd seen on him last time. His cheeks showed a five o'clock shadow. "How would you explain that to your momma?"

A big grin lit his face. "Well now, I reckon that'd be my problem."

Anna reclined in the chair. "Sorry. Don't believe you." She took another sip.

"Aw, c'mon, sugar," Kaci said.

"We might could make it interesting," Jackson said. "Got a lot of boxes sitting around my house and not much mind to put 'em away. How about when us guys win, you come on over and set up my kitchen for me?"

Anna pulled herself upright. That should've sounded paternalistic and condescending, but instead it made her nipples tingle. This was the closest she'd come to having someone talk dirty to her in, well, a lot longer than it should've been. She licked her lips. "And if we women win?"

He scratched his head. "Suppose I could come on over next time you need a man to stomp out a spider. You still got my number?"

"Spiders don't bother me."

The glint in his eyes told her he didn't buy her bluff. "I hear tell some ladies like fancy chocolates. Might could pick up a box or two."

Oh, yeah. Definitely dirty.

"That's a pretty darn good deal, sugar." Kaci stood. "So we playing or not?"

Anna set her margarita aside and stood too. "Yeah. We're playing."

But only redneck golf.

Or so she told herself.

Chapter Seven

She partook of ladylike games in a ladylike manner, but when called upon to participate in gentlemanly endeavors, she executed her role regimentally as if she'd been a general in a previous life.
—The Temptress of Pecan Lane, by Mae Daniels

A FEW MINUTES LATER, Lance carried two PVC ladders out of the garage. Jackson followed with the bolas, which were thin ropes anchored with golf balls on either end. Bama colors for Lance, Ole Miss for Kaci.

The guys set up the ladders about twenty feet apart. There were three rungs on each. One point for wrapping a bola around the bottom rung, two points for the middle rung, three points for the top. Lance and Kaci took their positions at one ladder, while Anna and Jackson stationed themselves at the other. Kaci was up to toss first, so Anna scooted as close to the pool and far away from the ladder as possible. After Kaci's first toss went wild, Jackson joined her. "Guess this might could take a while."

"Mm-hmm." His drawl was growing on her. If he talked to his commanding officers like that, she doubted he'd be in the Air Force long, but that didn't matter to Anna.

Nope, not at all.

But he was watching her like he thought she was worth watching.

And it couldn't be bad for her to feel attractive for one night, could it?

Nothing wrong with feeling good.

She snapped her attention back to the game. Kaci wound up to toss her second bola at the ladder. It didn't matter how Jackson looked at Anna, because that zinging thing in her chest that kept happening when he looked at her was margarita chemistry, not commitment.

He was like a practice date. A Kaci-approved, nondangerous, practice date.

He tucked his hands into his pockets and rocked back on his heels, vigilantly watching Kaci. "So how's the old ant-mobile?"

"Ant-free for over a month now, thank you."

Kaci's toss came up short. Lance wrapped an arm around her waist and guided her through the proper tossing technique.

Jackson tucked his hands under his arms. "You ever get to wondering if she's tossing bad on purpose?"

"Used to, but I don't anymore."

In the sparse light, his eyes looked like midnight. "So is she acting?"

"That's a three-point question."

"Gonna be like that, is it?" He rubbed his chin. "All right then."

The grin he gave her made her nether regions quiver.

They were practicing being on a date too.

Kaci's last bola, thrown with Lance's assistance, neatly wrapped the two-point rung. Lance stepped up for his turn. "No cheating," Anna called.

Lance gave her a mock salute.

Then he hooked the top rung.

"Three points," Jackson said. "So is she acting?"

Anna shook her head. "She understands the principles, but she's the reason people talk about throwing like a girl. She can't quantify the force in her arms."

"You might could think about taking statistics instead of thermo. Your odds here ain't looking good."

It was Anna's turn to grin at him.

After Lance's last toss, the guys were up four to two. Anna scampered around the yard grabbing her bolas while Jackson unwrapped two of his and snagged the third one at his feet. When she stepped back into the game, he gestured for her to go. "Ladies first."

"Nuh-uh. Whoever's partner scored most last round goes first. You're up."

"House rules?" Jackson called to Lance.

Lance hid a laugh behind a cough. "Go on and let her go last."

Jackson tested the weight of his bola. "You play dirty?"

"Three-point question."

It took him all three tosses, but he draped a bola over the three-point rung. Anna stepped up and stared down the target.

"You gonna tell me if you play dirty?" he said.

"Maybe." She lined up, gave her bola a tentative swing, and let it fly.

It wrapped around Jackson's bola and pulled it off the ladder.

She flashed a triumphant grin. "Don't think I need to answer that now, do I?"

"That's just one kind of dirty."

"You go, sugar," Kaci called. "How about you rustle us up some points now?"

At the end of Anna's turn, the guys were still ahead, four to three. Anna scooted close to the pool again when Lance handed Kaci her bolas. Jackson stepped up next to her. "So how's a Yankee girl get to be a redneck golf shark?"

"Raw talent combined with a little bit of a buzz." Once the

margarita wore off all the way, she'd probably get so tense from being this close to him that she'd start throwing worse than Kaci usually did.

Kaci's first toss sailed clear over the ladder and hit the fence. Jackson chuckled. "Sure hope she ain't planning on tossing her bouquet."

She scored two points on her next toss, but her last throw went wild. Anna tried to skitter out of the way. Jackson ducked the same way, and they bumped shoulders. The bola plopped into the pool beside them. He reached a steadying hand to her, and a shiver slinked down her arm and straight to a couple of other parts that hadn't had any attention in a long while. "Okay?" he asked.

Anna sprung away and brushed her hair out of her face. "Oh, sure. You betcha. Just peachy. At least I'm not wet."

So to speak.

He glanced at the pool. She did too. The bola floated to the bottom in a slow circle. Waves rippled out on the surface of the water, shimmering in the floodlights. If she could see her own panic level, it would probably look something similar.

"Oopsies," Kaci said.

Jackson gave Anna an amused once-over. "Darlin', this one's gonna cost you."

"I'll go get the pool skimmer."

That made him grin bigger. "You afraid of the water, or you afraid of having fun?"

She was afraid of what seeing *him* wet might do to the funny thumping in her chest.

He snagged his shirt behind his neck and stripped it off in one smooth motion. "Mind holding that for me?"

Reflex made her accept the warm fabric. She caught a flash of solid chest, a tiger paw tattoo and a sprinkling of dark hair. Her mouth went dry. He hopped into the pool, then dove down in one fluid stroke to snag the bola off the bottom.

Anna gulped. Her thighs quivered and her heart banged her chest so hard she checked to make sure her breasts weren't bouncing.

He surfaced and held the bola up.

She reached for it and fumbled it twice before she had a solid grip on it, and even then, she almost dropped it back into the pool.

He pushed up out of the water and grabbed a towel. He gave his head a quick rub-down, making the muscles in his arms flex and stretch. Droplets sluiced down his chest and abdomen toward his waistband.

He tossed the towel aside, then pinned her with an amused look while he held out his hand for the shirt.

Caught. She nodded at his tattoo, which had the number 33 in the middle of the paw. "Huh. Thought that'd be your momma's name." Her voice almost sounded normal. She surrendered the shirt, praying it didn't have any sweat marks from her clammy hands, and turned her back on him. She waved to Lance. "Ready when you are."

Jackson stepped up beside her, his shirt on again *thank God*, and quietly watched Lance score a couple more points.

But once they'd gathered the bolas to take their turns, that ornery spark returned. "Sure you don't want to go first?"

"I'm good. Thanks."

"Starting to think you're fixing to throw the game so you can get into my kitchen."

If he'd promise to help with his shirt off... "Interesting. How big is it?"

"What you really gotta be thinking about is how I plan to use it." He lined up for his first throw. "You watch this right here. I'm gonna show you the right way to ring a three-pointer."

Anna suppressed a smile. "Uh-huh."

"What? You think I can't do it?"

She rolled her shoulders back. She'd forgotten the thrill that came with flirting. "Everybody gets lucky now and then."

He chuckled. "Tell you what. I hit this one, you tell me how late you were to class that day we met."

She hoped Kaci was right about his momma raising him right, or she'd be answering too many personal questions tonight. "And when you miss?" she said with more composure than she felt.

"*If* I miss. Whatcha wanna know?"

The heat must've melted what was left of her brain, because she couldn't think of a single decent question. "Why you thought of the Windex," she finally said.

"Deal." He let the bola fly. It circled through the air, then hit the three-point rung and wrapped itself neatly around.

That one would be impossible to knock off. "Sixteen minutes. My professor gave a pop quiz to start the semester, and I flunked it because I wasn't there."

He winced. "Aw, jeez, I'm sorry."

Anna shrugged. "I was already late before I saw the ants. My fault. Bet you can't hit another three-pointer."

"Been late since?" he prompted.

"Two-pointer. I still want to know about the Windex."

He tossed his second bola and ringed the one-point rung. He glanced at her, then grinned an unabashed grin. "Saw it in a movie."

"Which movie?"

He gestured toward the ladder. "Two-pointer."

His toss fell short.

"Movie?" Anna prompted.

He raked a hand over his short hair, and she noticed a hint of curl at the ends. "Can't remember the name. Some girly flick with big hair and ugly dresses."

What did Windex have to do with big hair and— "And a wedding?"

"Sounds about right. Kaci hog-tied me and Lance and glued our eyeballs open so we had to watch it all. Didn't mind the hog-tying part, but that glue gunked up my eyes for weeks."

He'd used *My Big Fat Greek Wedding* to make himself look good.

And then he'd admitted to it. Wasn't something most guys she knew would've done. "Your eyes looked fine to me."

"Shucks, ma'am, your eyes look real fine too."

So did his smile. But despite the weird flippy-do in her belly, she had to laugh. "I walked right into that."

"Sure did."

"C'mon, Anna," Kaci called. "Get us back in the running."

Now *that,* she could handle. She stared down the target and tested the weight of her bola. She swung it back and forth. She was about to let go when Jackson murmured, "'Course, your trunk's real fine too. Nice 'n clean."

The bola slipped out of her hand and almost beaned Lance. "Sorry," she called to him.

He waved it off. "Suppose you owed me for Kaci here."

Anna turned on Jackson, hands on hips, bolas dangling against her knee. "Are we playing dirtier now?"

"Sure wouldn't mind, but my momma'd have my hide if she heard I cheated. Betcha your last name you can't hit that there two-pointer."

Anna faltered. She hadn't decided yet what she wanted her last name to be.

He seemed to realize he'd goofed, because he started to say something, but she cut him off before she let her brain process the words. "Middle name if you still have four points when I'm done. But if I knock you off, I want to meet this momma of yours."

He glanced over at the ladder, then back at her, his eyes getting all squinty. "Big fighting words for a Yankee."

"Chicken?"

"That'd be like being afraid of winning. You go on and take your turn, then go on and whisper that little name right here in my ear."

As if. Anna got into good bola-swinging stance and let it swing like a pendulum. No way could she take his three-pointer off. But she might be able to do something about that one-pointer. She brushed her thumb over the divots on the golf ball. Yeah, she could take his one-pointer off.

"Got a lot of equipment to squeeze into my drawers," Jackson murmured.

Anna burst out laughing. She almost dropped the bola. "Stop. Just stop."

"Starting to think I shoulda offered something better than chocolate."

Two tosses later, Jackson was down a point, and Anna's competitive nature had stepped in a pile of something that reeked of relationship stink.

She'd asked to meet his *mother*.

"Huh," he said. "Looks like I'm gonna be needing your phone number." He rocked back on his heels. "'Course, you're gonna be needing my address before this is over so you can fix up my kitchen right good."

On her next turn, Kaci managed to avoid hitting anything major, including the ladder. Lance did too, but Anna suspected that was on purpose. She and Jackson lined up for their turns. He gestured to the ladder. "Two-pointer for your middle name."

"Three-pointer."

He cast a sideways glance at her.

She gave him a saucy grin. "I might be a Yankee, but I'm not easy. Your last name if you miss."

He hit all three rungs with his three bolas. After his last toss, he looked at her expectantly. She gaped at him. "Who's calling who a shark now?"

"You still got a chance to knock me off the board."

At the end of the round, the guys were winning by a landslide.

"Grace," she said.

"That's a right pretty name for a Yankee."

"I'll be sure to pass your compliments on to my parents." She signaled Kaci. "Your dishes are on the line here," she called.

"Don't I know it, sugar. You had to go and ask 'em to mop

the yard with us, now didn't you?"

"So start scoring some points."

By sheer miracle, or more likely pity from the men, ten minutes later the guys' score was steady at twenty to the women's eighteen. One point, and the Bama boys would win.

Jackson lined up for his first toss.

"I was kidding about meeting your mother," Anna confessed.

"Now who's chicken?" he teased.

"Come on, you introduce the woman who sets up your kitchen to your mother, she's gonna start hearing wedding bells."

His toss went wild.

Anna giggled.

"You're learning, Anna Grace."

Hearing her name rolled out in his Southern drawl gave her a glimpse into a world that gave her the shivers. She shut them down and put her game face back on. "If you miss, you owe me your middle name."

He ringed the two-point rung.

"You're over points," Kaci called. "Doesn't count. Has to be exact."

"Your middle name?" Anna prompted.

"Now that's cheating. Didn't miss. Just didn't hit the right one."

"Semantics. One-pointer, or your middle name."

"Gonna make me break a sweat here."

She doubted he ever sweat over anything. But he wrapped the one-point line. Anna was up.

"Need a three-pointer, sugar," Kaci called. She bounced on her feet. "Let's show these boys what for."

Three points. No pressure. She could do it.

And then she'd let Jackson off the hook on the chocolates, and tonight would be all fun, no consequences.

She'd keep hanging out with Kaci and the rest of the girls, and things would be cool and comfortable whenever she happened to run into Jackson. No pressure. Just some fun.

She lined up her shot. She swung the bola back and forth. Three points. She could hit a three-pointer.

She started to let go.

"It's a real big kitchen," Jackson said.

The bola slipped out of her hand and whipped across the yard to the ladder. It wrapped around Jackson's two-pointer and knocked it to the ground.

"Twenty-one," Lance called.

Kaci swatted his arm. "Nuh-uh. She's got two tosses left. Don't you be counting your balls before Anna's done with 'em."

Jackson's chuckle rumbled low and deep. "Beautiful."

Anna gritted her teeth. Two tosses. She could tie the score, or she could try to knock his other bola off.

Or she could completely miss and end up owing Jackson a clean, organized kitchen.

On the one hand, she didn't need to get any more attached to him.

On the other, she did love putting a big mess away.

Were there Hail Mary passes in redneck golf?

She tossed her second bola, and it draped itself neatly over the two-point line. Twenty-one to twenty. If she knocked Jackson's bola off and hung hers on the one-point line at the same time, she and Kaci won.

If not—the kitchen.

"Long shot there," Jackson said.

Anna wiped her hands on her shorts. "Mm-hmm." Staring down that ladder was like staring down thermo.

"You can do it, sugar," Kaci called.

The night insects chirped happily, completely oblivious to the stakes riding on Anna's toss. A few stars had popped out overhead. The ladder glowed eerily in the yard lights. With a long, slow exhale, she wound up her toss, and let the bola go.

The middle of the rope smacked the one-point rung. Jackson's bola wobbled there, but didn't fall off. Anna's two-pointer, though, slid off its rung and plopped to the ground, followed neatly by the bola she'd just tossed.

She'd knocked herself off the board. Lost the toss. Lost the game. Lost the bet. She owed him. And owing him sent various parts of her a-tingling that no longer a-tingled for any man. Her a-tingle meter had to be off, because she was quite certain it'd never tingled that high.

Maybe he'd go shirtless while she paid up.

Lost the bet? More like lost her mind.

She squared her shoulders and faced Jackson. "Looks like I'll be needing your address."

His slow, triumphant grin sent another wave of a-tingles down her spine.

"Wouldn't be right gentlemanly of me not to offer to let you off the hook, seeing how I didn't know you got a broken partner," he said.

"Afraid of letting me and my label maker into your kitchen?"

"No, ma'am. Looking forward to it. You know how to use a kitchen, or just put stuff away in one?"

He *so* wasn't in the plan, but a little bit of fun never hurt anybody. So long as she kept him only for fun, she'd be fine. "Three-point question."

"You're on."

Chapter Eight

To his way of thinking, if a man had a good shotgun, football season, and a dog, he had all the love he needed.
—The Temptress of Pecan Lane, by Mae Daniels

JACKSON HADN'T PLANNED on staying late enough to help with the clean up, but on his way through the kitchen to say good-night, Kaci shoved a piece of apple pie at him and offered him a second to take home if he made himself useful. He took one bite and offered to marry her instead.

Pretty safe bet considering she was already taken. But it earned him a smack upside the head, and not from Lance. "Anna made that pie."

"She bake biscuits this good?"

He thought that was a safe question too, since Anna was outside gathering trash, but Kaci smacked him again. "Don't you play games with her, you hear me?"

Well, tarnation. "She looking for number two?" If that was the case, he'd make himself scarce quick. Anna was some fun when she loosened up, but like Mamie said, he had some choices when it came to his biscuits.

"It's not what she's looking for that has me worried. It's what she's not looking for but still needs."

Jackson looked to Lance for a translation, but his buddy gave a shrug. Man-speak for *I don't talk woman. You got her going. You figure it out.*

Jackson took another bite of pie and waited.

Kaci checked Anna's progress through the window, then hopped her backside onto the counter Lance had cleared. "Her ex didn't treat her the way a man should."

Now that was clearer, but still not straight enough. "He hit her?"

"Pshaw. Anna wouldn't have stood for that."

"Cheat on her?"

"Nope."

Well what else was there? "Didn't let her have new clothes and get her hair done?"

"No, sugar, he didn't love her."

Lance shook his head like Miss Flo and Mamie did whenever Miss Ophelia started yapping about her boyfriends leaving the toilet seat up.

It was always *love*, wasn't it?

Man could work his rear end off, treat his woman right, respect her, give her everything she ever asked for, but if she decided she didn't love him anymore, then he was done for.

Jackson never had made up his mind if his daddy was lucky he'd passed on before he figured out Momma was in love with his best friend, or if his life would've changed enough that he wouldn't have been on that road that night. If he would've moved out, stopped for dinner on his way home instead of heading for Momma's cooking, anything to put him on a different street or milliseconds to one side or another of his drive home.

Mamie said a person's time was a person's time, and God would've gotten him anyway, but Jackson still wondered.

Still, Jackson was glad he wasn't in a lifestyle that lent itself to settling down. Nobody to please but himself and Radish, and if he got run over by a truck tomorrow, nobody left waiting for the news that he wasn't coming home.

Except Radish.

Poor pup.

He polished off his last bite. "Good pie. Y'all recycle?"

He didn't avoid Anna and her picking up on purpose. It was more of an on-purpose-accidental thing she was out in the backyard while he cleaned the living room. He should've been thinking about getting home to let Radish out, but his brain kept puzzling over why sane folks bothered with love. His daddy and Lance and Kaci included.

He reckoned Mamie might be able to explain it to him, what with her writing all those books about love, but he made a point of not using the L-word in front of her.

Didn't take him too long to put the living room to rights, so he went in to help dry dishes. The ladies were outside talking. Anna was laughing. The sound made something in his chest go all soft.

"Appreciate the help," Lance said. He handed over the last of the grill tools for drying. "Know what's good for you, you'll knock off before the girls get back in."

Right smart guy, Lance was. Would've made a good wingman except for the settling down part.

"Pass on my thanks to Kaci," Jackson said.

But Lance got a grin a guy didn't usually like to see on his wingman. "Anna's gonna want your address."

"Just a trick to get her to play."

That chuckle didn't go so good on a wingman either. "Girl likes to settle her bets."

Smart thing to do was walk away and not look back. But a few minutes later, walking past her Civic, Jackson tucked his number and address under her wipers anyway.

He'd never met a woman who'd pay that bet. Wasn't fair, and they all knew it.

Still, she'd had a look.

And she'd offered to write his momma a thank-you once upon a time.

Might be some perfection in this after all. Didn't much

matter to his kitchen one way or another if she paid up, but he liked watching her try to figure what to make of him.

Wouldn't mind seeing if he could figure out what to make of her.

PAYING UP ON A BET wasn't usually so nerve-racking. There was nothing personal about forks and knives and mixing bowls, so why did the idea of organizing Jackson's kitchen feel so intimate? She wouldn't be rummaging through his underwear drawer or his toolbox.

There went that pesky heart again. She hadn't had an adrenaline rush like this around a guy since, well, the first time she saw Neil. And all she'd done was think about Jackson's tools.

And underwear.

Damn heart. This was only a dumb bet with a goofy guy who was friends with her friends, and that muscle in her chest could stay out of it. This was *practice* flirting.

Nothing real.

She adjusted her left hand on the wheel so it was at exactly ten, in line with her right hand's two o'clock, and felt marginally better. She'd organize his kitchen, keep out of his more personal belongings, and scurry back home before she got any more ideas.

This was *practice*, and he was military. She had plans. Get her degree, combine that with her experience at RMC to find a good job back home, buy a cute little cottage, adopt a couple of kids, and live happily ever after.

That pang of regret that she couldn't have her first choice in life would probably always be there, but she'd make the most of her life yet.

Jackson lived in a yellow-sided, two-story house in an older but still respectable neighborhood a mile or so from her old home. An ancient Chevy truck sat in the driveway. The rear window featured two decals, an Alabama logo and Calvin peeing on a Ford logo.

Her heart gave another thump at the shadow passing in front of the door.

She wanted to give it a thump right back.

Instead, she climbed out of her car, armed with her purse, label maker inside, and headed up the driveway to the curved walkway.

She took the wooden stairs to the wide porch, then rang the doorbell. It echoed softly inside the house. She heard a muffled bark. A green lawn chair sat off to the side next to an upside-down moving box with a bottle of Bud in the middle of concentric water rings.

The door clicked open. Her heart *ka-thudded* a couple of times at the sight of another old Alabama T-shirt and board shorts. She didn't want to know what it would do if she looked high enough to see if he'd shaved this morning.

Novelty, she told herself. She faked a bright, sunny smile, and risked a look at those dark-lashed eyes. "Good morning."

Jackson stared at her for half a second like he couldn't figure out why she'd be at his house, but then he gave her a pained smile.

And it was too late to pretend she was looking for directions.

An old spaniel poked her nose into Anna's hand. Anna gave her head a little scratch, and she wagged her tail. "Well, hi, there, you sweet thing." Anna knelt to gather her composure and love on the dog, who ate it up like she'd never had a belly scratch in her life. "Is this a bad time?"

Jackson's relaxed grin came back in full force. "Well shucks, Anna Grace, you're starting to give Yankees a good name. Didn't think you'd pay up."

The way he said her name made her feel all warm and Southern inside. "Just Anna's fine. If you didn't want me to come, you wouldn't have left your address. Your momma not up for the job?"

He coughed into his hand. No mistaking the laugh lines around his eyes. "Right sure it'd make her keel over with a heart attack."

No mistaking the unrepentant grin he sent her either. The one that said *I'd rather have you here than her anyway.*

Or so Anna hoped.

She gave the dog a final love pat and stood. She could do this. She could handle being a single woman with a single man in his house with his dog. Doing domestic things. With no commitment.

Just... doing something. "Then it's your lucky day. Or your momma's lucky day."

"You sure you got the time today? Don't want to keep you from your studying."

Some of her glow dimmed. "You're not afraid of my label maker, are you?"

"No, ma'am. Just offering to be a gentleman."

She pinned him with her best *oh, please* look.

He did that coughing thing again, but this time, he stepped back and held the door open for her. "C'mon in then."

A tinny rendition of "Sweet Home Alabama" erupted from his pocket. His shoulders twitched, but he led her through the house as if he didn't hear it.

She followed him through a small foyer and into a living room that made her palms itch. She fought to keep walking behind him, his dog at her heels, as she took stock of the mess. More paperbacks than she would've expected leaned in haphazard stacks about the room amid toppled piles of action-adventure and military DVDs. Two pressed-wood bookcases stood at odd angles beyond a staircase, their shelves propped up against the wall. The wide-screen television was dark. Anna would've bet her label maker it was hooked up and tweaked perfectly for the room though. Mismatched orange and navy throw pillows decorated an L-shaped tan sofa. Jackson's phone continued to sing, but he didn't reach for it.

"Aren't you going to answer that?"

He shrugged and turned the corner. "If it's important, they'll call back."

Anna followed him into the kitchen and instantly felt another zing at the glorious disaster.

They would be here for hours.

His phone stopped ringing. He tucked his arms over his chest and stood wide-legged in the space between the kitchen and the breakfast area. "Haven't had much time to do anything with it."

The room looked like a giant had picked it up, shook out the cabinets and drawers, then put the house on spin cycle. The counters and floor were heaped with pots, dry goods, assorted tools, and a bronze armadillo.

Wait. A bronze armadillo? Nope, not going to ask.

Out of the corner of her eye, she caught Jackson watching her. Her heart tripped. The taste of tart strawberries flooded her mouth. "Rent or buy?"

His eyes crinkled. "We getting personal, Anna Grace?"

"Just Anna's fine." She pulled her label maker out. "Temporary or permanent?"

He sucked his cheeks in, but his eyes were still laughing. "Rent."

"See, now, wasn't that easy? Any preference on what goes where?"

"Nah. Figure you know more about kitchens than I do. But don't be taking off with my armadillo. I've been guarding that from you Northern types for years."

"Don't worry. Your armadillo's safe from me."

Her cheeks went hot, but like last night, he ignored the accidental innuendo.

"Sweet Home Alabama" erupted from his pocket again. He gave a sigh and stepped toward the living room. "'Scuse me a minute, Anna Grace."

"Just Ann—never mind."

He disappeared around the corner with a chuckle.

The kitchen felt bigger without him in it. Anna studied the room's layout. Pots and pans would go in the cabinets by the stove. Pantry items near the fridge. Silverware, plates, and cups closer to the dining area. She'd fill everything else in where it fit. She turned her label maker on, listening to the easy cadence of Jackson's speech. She couldn't make out his words, but his voice sounded strained.

Was that even possible?

Paws clicked across the wood floor. The dog plodded into the dining area, then plopped on her haunches. She sniffed in Anna's direction, her chocolate eyes soft and lovable. "Such a sweet thing," Anna murmured.

Jackson appeared in the doorway. He gave the dog's ears an affectionate rub. "I got some stuff going on, so I gotta get going," he said to Anna. "You okay here?"

Get *going*? He was leaving her *alone* to put away his kitchen? Was she *okay* here? *No, you dumb redneck, I thought the stupid bet was a ploy to hang out with me.* She floundered for her fake happy face. Bad enough she'd misunderstood his intentions and thought all the teasing meant he *liked* her. She would be mortified if he realized it too.

"Sure," she said. "Absolutely. I've organized a kitchen or two. I think I can handle this one. Besides, you'd be in my way if you stayed." Or make her like him more.

She was *so* bad at this.

He dug a set of keys out of a heap on the counter. "Got a couple of pizzas in the freezer. You know how to use the oven?"

Was that guy-speak for *So, can you cook? I'll be back for lunch at noon.* "Frozen pizzas. Right. I'm on to you. The bet didn't include a hot meal."

Bad move. Now she had to watch that killer smile again. "A hot meal. I like those stakes. Might could be up for a redneck golf game when I get home Monday."

Monday. He wasn't leaving because of the phone call. He'd planned to go all along. "Sorry, I have plans Monday." If planning not to see him counted as having plans. "You want me to lock up when I'm done?"

"That'd be right decent of you." He tapped his leg. The dog

went to his side. "Don't be messing up your whole day here if you got other stuff to do. Appreciate the help. You're a peach, Anna Grace."

She twitched but kept smiling. "My pleasure."

He took the dog out the front door, and then she was alone in a near-stranger's kitchen, doing his damn momma's work. He was a thoughtless, ignorant redneck who flirted and teased and asked girls out to dinner so he could get a clean house or a hot meal.

She stormed around the kitchen. She should put his silverware in the drawer near the stove, far, far away from the dining area. That's what she *should* do.

But then he might think she was mad about his leaving.

Or worse, that she was too dumb to organize a kitchen. Wouldn't that be the redneck calling the Yankee a hick?

At least things were straightforward with her label maker. It might've been made in China, but they understood each other perfectly.

"YOU TRIED DAISY'S biscuits yet?" Miss Flo asked Jackson Sunday afternoon.

They sat at a rented table on the lawn behind Russ's Confederate mausoleum. Louisa and her girlfriends squealed and giggled and gossiped two tables down. Jackson's head ached like his stomach had after he'd sampled Miss Flo's granddaughter's biscuits this morning.

"Light and fluffy," Jackson said.

Miss Flo beamed. "She's coming bowling with us tonight if you got a notion to hide out from all the fireworks."

"Now you hold on there, Flo," Mamie said. "You know Gertie asked if Jackson could sit with Scarlett at the show already, and Ophelia claimed his other side for Cletus's great-niece."

Jackson spotted his momma carrying out a couple of pies. He leapt to his feet.

All unhurried and manly and graceful-like, of course.

"'Scuse me, ladies, looks like Momma needs some help."

She didn't, of course, but Jackson had been over in the desert and missed sweet potato pie last Christmas.

"Bring us back a couple pieces," Mamie said.

"But make mine small." Miss Flo adjusted her librarian glasses over a saggy pout. "Doctor says I have to watch my girlish figure."

"Looking good to me, Miss Flo."

And while the ladies tittered away, Jackson went off hunting some sweet potato pie.

But five minutes later, when he'd finished delivering the ladies their after-fried-chicken desserts, he sat down to enjoy his first sweet potato pie in over a year and a half, and found it wasn't the right mix of sweet and potato.

Maybe it was the conversation.

"Is Daisy the one with the mole?" Louisa was asking. She'd joined the ladies when her girlfriends went off in search of refills. Looked like Momma and Russ would be hosting a sorority party at the mausoleum tonight. Jackson said another silent thanks for Mamie's couch. He'd logged a lot of hours on it already this summer.

"No, no, sugarplum, that's Scarlett," Mamie said.

"Daisy's the one with the" —Miss Ophelia shot Jackson a look and dipped her voice to funeral parlor soft while rubbing her upper lip— "hormone imbalance."

A chorus of "Ooohhs," accompanied a round of heart blessings.

Jackson shoveled another bite of pie in his mouth.

It was the crust, he decided. Not as flaky as he remembered.

A creeping sensation went down his back, like he was being watched by a rabid armadillo.

Wasn't Momma's crust that'd ever been so flaky.

It was Anna Grace's.

"Pie okay, sugarplum?" Mamie asked. "You look like you swallowed a frog."

Pie was great.

But it wasn't that apple stuff he'd had two nights ago. "Pales in comparison to the company," he told Mamie with as much of a charming grin as he could muster when he was getting ideas about sneaking out of Louisa's post-birthday breakfast tomorrow to head on back to Georgia for some apple pie for breakfast.

He hoped leaving Anna Grace in his kitchen hadn't screwed up his chances of getting some more of that pie.

He eyed Mamie. She eyed him right back.

Hoped she didn't figure out he'd left a lady alone in his house to put his kitchen together. He'd been raised better than that.

But the way Anna Grace had salivated at the mess, he reckoned it would've been right cold of him to tell her to come back another day. He'd lay odds the girl had more issues than her ex-husband not loving her.

Wasn't ready to lay odds more of that apple pie would be worth it though.

Still, he'd take apple pie over Daisy's and Scarlett's biscuits.

He broke eye contact with Mamie and turned to his baby sister. Her eyes were crawling with an afternoon hangover, but she was grinning big, Daddy's dimple popping out, telling Miss Ophelia about that engine Russ had arranged for her. "Smells like french fries," she said. "You wouldn't believe the guys *that* attracts. Not the kind I'd give my biscuits to, don't you worry, Mamie."

"Get anything else good?" Jackson asked.

"Craig and Maura got me *textbooks*. For my twenty-first birthday. You believe that?"

"Good for your brain," Jackson said.

Louisa's nose crinkled up all girly-like.

"I'm sure they meant well, sugarplum." Mamie patted Louisa's hand. "And what did you get the birthday girl?" she asked Jackson.

"Daddy's old twenty-two," Louisa said. "And he's gonna

take me hunting."

The Misses went wide-eyed and pale-faced. "Well," Miss O said. "Bless his heart."

Yeah, he was thinking that move was about as smart as setting off a firecracker in the only outhouse for miles, but Louisa didn't have much of Daddy's.

Jackson didn't either, come right down to it, but he had memories.

Louisa had Russ.

Mamie gave his arm a squeeze. "Right nice of you," she said. He felt an unfamiliar prickle in his eyes at the shiny gloss in hers. "He'd be right proud."

He planted a kiss on her weathered cheek. "Thanks, Mamie."

He stayed the rest of the weekend, even though it meant sitting through the fireworks with his dates.

They weren't bad to talk to or look at, but they were both sporting that look girls got when they started thinking about big white dresses and diamond rings.

Made him right twitchy. But he treated them gentlemanly all the way through handing them back to the Misses.

Louisa was more than hung over for her post-birthday breakfast, so Jackson made sure she was going to live, gave his excuses to Momma and Russ, loaded Radish up, and headed home.

He had some apple pie waiting for him.

But the closer he got to home, the closer he got to crossing that line to nervous. Wouldn't have surprised him to walk into his kitchen and find his armadillo missing.

He could hope, anyway. But he still found himself smiling over the way Anna had slung that label maker out of her bag like Miss Dolly whipped out her knitting needles. She'd looked downright adorable swinging that thing around, and the way her eyes went all dark had given him a few ideas he was best not having.

Still, he found himself wondering how a guy fell out of love with something like that, if he was dumb enough to fall into it in the first place.

Not his problem, though.

Not like his kitchen was.

If she'd left it a mess, wasn't like he'd notice. Had a woman or two do a lot worse than he reckoned Anna Grace had the nerve to try.

So when he and Radish got home, her giving him a look Mamie liked to call the stink-eye for making her endure both the noise at Louisa's party and the drive, he gave his dog a rub behind the ears and strolled all casual through his mud room and into the kitchen.

Whatever he was expecting, it wasn't sparkly clean countertops and neat little piles of screwdrivers and mismatched socks Anna probably thought didn't belong in the kitchen. His cabinets and drawers were all labeled with surgically centered labels.

Radish sat back on her haunches in front of the table, stink-eye getting stinkier. He rubbed a hand over his head. "Think I got the better end of this one, huh, girl?"

He had half a mind to call up Anna and invite her to dinner to thank her, but once he talked the number out of Kaci, he'd probably have a heck of a time convincing Anna to let him pay.

Crazy woman.

He slid open the drawer next to the oven and found his hot mitts, just like the label said. It peeled off easy, no damage to the drawer. He added a bottle of wine to that dinner he'd probably have to play her another round of redneck golf for.

She'd labeled every drawer and cabinet with exactly what he found in them. Except for one little surprise in the cabinet next to the fridge. He opened it up, expecting mixing bowls and small appliances, and came face-to-snout with his armadillo.

Only scared him a little.

Good thing Radish couldn't tell anybody otherwise.

He made to shove the armadillo in a corner, but then he

got a better idea.

Radish gave a sigh and padded into the living room. His dog's way of claiming innocence. Pretty sure she threw a *you're too old for that, dummy* in for good measure.

Louisa was coming next weekend. She'd given him the armadillo for his twenty-first birthday. Didn't matter where he was in the world, first thing she did when she came to visit was check on it. Once or twice she put a dress on it. The armadillo, he'd keep. The dresses went to the shop for grease rags.

A note on the table caught his eye. Curious, he tucked the armadillo under his arm like a football and went to check out Anna Grace's parting shot.

The handwriting was about as symmetrical as he'd ever seen, and the note wasn't half-bad either.

Jackson –

Your movers lost your silverware organizer. Also, it's difficult to dry dishes with towels that are made of holes instead of cotton. I only mention it because I didn't see any paper plates.

Anna
(JUST Anna)

She'd probably stood about fourteen feet high and looked down her nose at that paper while she was writing the note, too.

The lady might be strung tight, but she sure amused him.

He crossed the kitchen to the fridge and deposited the armadillo in it front and center, right where it'd make Louisa scream like a girl the first time she went digging for his beer.

That's when he realized something was missing.

Son of a biscuit. His apple pie was gone.

Still, he felt his grin go a little wider. "Good for you, Anna Grace," he murmured to himself. "Good for you."

Chapter Nine

She made plans, and life changed her plans. So she planned to change her plans in anticipation of life, until the day she surrendered her plans to change her life.
    —The Temptress of Pecan Lane, by Mae Daniels

THWACK!

A gust of cool air swept across Anna's nose. She bolted upright in her desk chair. "Entropy at absolute zero is impossible."

"Can you leave that crap in the classroom?" Jules tapped her fingers on the blue binder she'd dropped on Anna's desk. "Quarterly review. Customer. Need a slide flipper. For God's sake, wipe your chin."

Anna swiped at her mouth. She worked her jaw around, wincing at an unfamiliar pain on her cheek. She gingerly fingered the abnormally smooth grooved skin. "Oh, no."

"Oh, yes." Jules smirked. "You got some shift and caps lock on your face."

Anna rubbed at her cheek where she'd been laying on her keyboard. Thermodynamics would kill her yet. "Three more weeks," she grumbled. Then finals, but at least she'd be done. She stood and had to grab her desk when her left leg refused to work. Apparently sleeping at her desk was bad for her face *and* her circulation. "I have a test tonight." She fingered her skin again. "How bad is it for real?"

"Pretty sure you don't have to worry about anyone hitting on you today."

Like anybody in the office would try. Jules was the only one who still treated her mostly the same as she had before the divorce. Anna tested her weight on her leg. Getting better. "Is everybody else already there?"

Jules leaned out the door. "Shirley's not—no, wait, there she is. Yep, everybody else is ready."

Anna limped out of her cube, using the walls for support. Her leg tingled. "I seriously hate thermo."

"It doesn't like you much either." Jules grabbed the binder and stalked out of the lab.

Anna gimped along behind her. "Some days I wonder how Brad puts up with you."

"Are you serious? Somebody has to kill those bloody rays of sunshine he's always crapping out." She grinned, still riding the newlywed high. It was like a happiness record for her. "But they do make him kinda cute, don't they?"

Anna winced. "If you say so."

"Hey, Brad Skyped with Rodney the other night. He said to tell you even covered in Sprite, you're still better looking than the goats over there. But he thinks they might sing better."

That wasn't nearly as embarrassing as it should've been.

They'd almost reached the conference room when Brad himself barreled around the corner, the receptionist jogging after him, insisting he didn't have clearance to be in the building. His blouse was unbuttoned, and he hadn't taken his hat off. His skin matched the gray camouflage of his uniform. The sheen of grief in his eyes and his uneven stagger sucked every bit of rightness from the hallway.

Anna's heart dipped to her toes then ricocheted up like it was on a bungee cord.

Jules went pale. "Ohmigod," she breathed. "Rodney?"

He crushed her against him, raw pain twisting his face. He blinked rapidly over shiny eyes, and when he spoke, his voice

was husky and cracked. "Fuckers got him with an IED."
"Is he—"
"Gone."
Anna's limbs turned to silly putty. She choked on the *No!* in her throat.
Jules pounded a fist on Brad's chest. "Shut up," she said, her tone weak and watery.
She needed to give them their privacy, but she couldn't move. Any moment now, Brad would say *Never mind, gotcha.*
Except he didn't.
He stood clutching his wife, trembling and shaking and gasping.
Anna's throat clogged and her chest ached. For Brad. For Jules. For Rodney. She tried to swallow, but her mouth had gone dry and her jaw was clenched too tight for her tongue to work right.
Shirley stepped outside the conference room. She surveyed the lot of them, dismissed the receptionist with a flick of her finger, then gave Anna's elbow a tug. Anna's joints flexed, and soon she was inside the conference room, the door closed against Brad's and Jules's grief. "His brother," Anna said. The words rolled past her lips, becoming more real as they lingered in the air.
"Goddamned war." Shirley's eyes took on a gloss that disappeared in a blink. "You okay?"
Anna wasn't, but she nodded anyway.
Shirley seemed to get it. "Good. We might not be out in the trenches ourselves, but they count on us to get 'em in and out of there. You know enough to brief the customer today?"
Anna took a shaky breath. "Yes, ma'am."
Giving the quarterly briefing wouldn't change Rodney's fate, but this was something small she could do for Jules. And the presentation was *normal*, organized and color-coded, something tenuous and logical.
Inconsequential in the grand scheme of life, but normal.
When it was finally over, Jules and Brad were gone. Anna

slipped outside for a hit of fresh air. The stench of boiled asphalt smacked her in the face instead. She took refuge at a picnic table beneath an umbrella in a small grassy area behind the building, then pulled out her phone. Three clicks later, it rang on the other end. "Dr. Vaughn's office," a cheery voice with a familiar Northern drawl said.

"Hey, Trina, it's Anna. Is Beth busy?"

"I think she's finishing up a filling. You want me to have her call you back?"

"Yeah, that—" A lump clogged Anna's throat. "No, actually, I need to talk to her now."

"Okay, hon, hold on one sec, okay?"

"'Kay."

Anna tried deep breathing, but the humidity on top of the lump made her feel like gagging. Beth came on the line quickly, thank God. "Hey. What's wrong?"

"I love you."

Beth's surprised laugh rang through the phone. "You called me out of a filling for *that*? Can you give my kids lessons?"

Anna pinched the bridge of her nose. "A friend of mine at work just lost her brother-in-law."

"Aw, honey. I'm sorry. That bites."

"So even though you're not fighting a war, I want you to know I love you. You know. In case you get hit by a bus or something."

"I'll watch out for buses. Promise."

"And falling space junk."

"Anna," Beth sighed.

"I'm serious. You never know when your time's up, and I might never get another chance to tell you I'm glad you're my sister."

"I'm glad you're my sister too, but Tony's not falling-space-debris lucky," Beth said. "And if it makes you feel any better, you're in my will."

Anna blinked at the woven metal tabletop, all neat and even and insignificant. If she'd let Rodney kiss her that night, would it have changed anything?

"I'm joking, Anna-banana. Nothing's going to happen."

She blew out a slow breath. She could do this. She could fake normal. "Take me out of the will. I don't want your gerbil."

"You are such a dweeb. I really need to finish up this filling, but I can call you back in fifteen."

"I'm okay. Really. I just needed to hear your voice."

"I'll come visit soon. I need a day without sniffing testosterone. Keep your chin up, okay?"

She'd had enough practice lately.

So she said good-bye to Beth and went on with her day. Because while the world had lost Rodney, Anna still had a schedule to keep.

"HOW'D IT GO, SUGAR?"

Anna dropped into the seat across from Kaci at Jimmy Beans that night as if her butt was carrying around the weight of the entire last week. Considering all the thermo knowledge that had evaporated out her ears during her test the last two hours, she should've weighed less than the chai latte Kaci had waiting for her.

"It's over." She gestured to the cup. "What do I owe you?"

Kaci sniffed and ignored the question. "I've got half a mind to march into ol' grandpappy's office and give him what for. Giving a test first class after a long weekend. Humph. I don't know what I ever saw in that man."

Anna had a couple ideas. There were the potato guns and his penchant for discussing the ignition point of various substances, both turn-ons to Kaci. Plus, he'd retired from the service earlier than he'd wanted, to move across the country and try to win her back. But Kaci had Lance, and Lance had not only voluntarily gone into the training squadron to avoid deployments for Kaci, he'd also stood up to her mother. Considering Kaci's stories of ol' grandpappy flirting with her mother, Anna thought Kaci was better off with number two.

Good for her, but Anna wasn't *ever* doing a number two.

Not given the way her post-divorce love life had gone.

"You okay, sugar?"

Kaci's tone had that sympathetic note that tended to provoke lumpy throats and stingy eyes. But Anna swallowed both with her chai and met her friend's eyes. "Thermo didn't beat me the first time, it won't beat me now."

Not what Kaci was asking, and Anna knew it.

Kaci didn't push. She simply waited while Anna let herself process what she'd been hiding from most of the day. Shirley had come through with a few details, the most comforting being that Rodney probably hadn't felt a thing, but for the most part, Anna had shut Rodney and Brad and Jules out and coped by focusing on her test.

But her test was over now.

"He asked me for pre-war sex," she finally said. "In case he never came back. And I shot him down. And now I keep thinking, what if he never found his last lay? He *loved* women. What if I was his last chance? What if he was flirting with me to make me feel better? What if I'd done the same for him? What if I'd stayed and kissed him and that changed everything in the rest of his life by the right number of milliseconds it would've taken to change his destiny? I don't want to *marry* the guy, but I don't want him dead either."

"Anna, if you kissed him, those little puffs of air missing from when you flew out of that parking lot might've been the ones settling out the pressure in the jet stream and keeping a tornado from exploding over New York City next week."

Right. And marriage was forever.

Kaci reached over and squeezed her hand. "Sugar, you can't butterfly-effect him back."

"But what if it all means I'm supposed to get hit by a bus tomorrow and never kiss another man in *my* life?"

"You got a man you wanna be kissing?"

Anna slunk back in her seat. "I don't want to get married again."

"Kissing isn't marrying."

"This is hardly appropriate. Look what happened to the last guy who tried."

Kaci clucked her tongue. "You're sitting here telling me a man who loved women wouldn't want us talking about you and men? Sugar, those uptight sensibilities of yours are about as right as a rainbow without the rain. You still got some time on this here earth. You gonna live it, or you gonna let it live you?"

"I need to finish my classes and get my degree so I—"

"Pshaw. You keep putting off living a full life during your todays, you won't know fun tomorrows if they smacked you in the butt and called you honey-pie."

"English?" Anna sputtered.

"Gotta find your balance, sugar." Kaci slid an envelope across the table then plunked a small gold box of Godiva on top of it. That sly sparkle was back. "Speaking of, somebody thinks I'm nothing but your messenger girl."

Anna's heart pittered in an unsteady rhythm. Bold, masculine handwriting spelled out *Anna Grace* on the back of the envelope.

Kaci reached for her coffee mug. "What I hear, he ain't so big on getting married either," she said over-innocently.

Anna fingered the ivory envelope. It was thick and soft. High quality. The pen marks were clear, no streaks or smudges. No obvious indents in the letters either.

These days when Anna scribbled her name, she nearly went through the whole paper.

"You gonna open that?"

"What's it say?"

Kaci's eyes went big, and she clasped a hand over her heart. "That there's *your* mail."

"What's it say?" Anna repeated with a smile at her friend's feigned innocence.

Kaci took a sip of coffee. "Can't do your living for you, sugar. 'Sides, Lance wouldn't let me have it till I left to come up here to meet you, and that didn't leave any time to steam it open. Couldn't tell you if I wanted to."

"I'll look at it when I get home."

Anna moved to slide the note and the box into her purse, but Kaci dropped her coffee and lunged across the table. "Now that's no fun. How'm I supposed to giggle over it with you if you're not gonna open it with me?"

Anna wasn't sure there would be any giggling. But she slid a finger under the envelope flap anyway.

The note was written in the same bold handwriting on a linen note card. Not what she expected of a guy whose hand mixer had only one beater. His momma must've kept him stocked in stationery.

But she was pretty sure his momma wouldn't have approved of the message.

Anna Grace,

Thanks for making my kitchen right nice-looking. Next time you come over, you bring a pie, and I'll play you for my living room. Might even toss in another box of chocolates if you throw one of those smiles my way.

Your friend,
Jackson

P.S. Radish says Hi.

Kaci smacked Anna in the arm. "*You cleaned his kitchen?*"

"I lost the bet."

"Sugar, that heat fried your brain. Ain't a Southern gentleman in the world who would've expected you to pay up on that." Kaci fluffed her hair. "Lord-a-mercy, girl, still so much to teach you."

And that's exactly why Anna hadn't told her she'd done it. She gestured to the note. "Okay, then, oh wise one, what am I supposed to do about *this*?"

Kaci stopped mid-fluff and eyed Anna as if she'd stolen the

answer key for a test. "You like him?"

"He's not my type," she said, but she could feel her cheeks betraying her.

Kaci gave her eyebrows a waggle. "Thinking of trying on an old redneck for size?"

"He doesn't like me."

"Lordy, sugar, there's not enough coffee in the world for this tonight." Kaci sucked in what Anna assumed to be a Southern woman's fortifying breath. "He likes you. He hasn't come to terms with it yet, but you mark my words, he knows that note to you is the same as talking dirty to other women. Sorta like you like him but you're not sure about letting a military man back in your life."

Anna shook her head. "Not in the plan."

Kaci gave her a knowing smile. "You'd do him if he was just a dumb old redneck."

"Not the point."

"You got some practicing to do before you settle, and he's a good one to practice with. Good Southern gentleman. Might show you how a man's supposed to treat a woman."

"And that's good *why?*" Sounded like an excellent way to get started on the L-word.

"Shoot, sugar, dating the military's exactly what you need. Got an expiration date. Perfect for a woman not looking to settle down, don't you think?"

"An *expiration date?*" Yeah, her last date had an expiration date too. It was with an IED in Afghanistan, and he didn't live to tell about it.

Kaci flitted a hand. "That didn't come out right. Let's get back to the living part. You like him, he likes you, you two should have some fun." She winked. "Call it stress relief."

"Your brand of stress relief is going to give me a heart attack," Anna said. She stared at the uneven mosaic tiles, and her fingers itched to rub them.

Kaci gripped Anna's cold fingers in her warm ones. "Lots of stress relief in keeping them girly bits as fine tuned as that brain."

Their favorite male barista suddenly had a coughing fit behind the counter.

"My girly bits are fine," Anna hissed, but she suspected Kaci would believe her cheeks over her words.

"Of course they are, sugar." Kaci's wicked grin lingered. "But you ask yourself, what's the last thing you want touching your girly bits before you get hit by that bus, and I got a feeling that good ol' military redneck won't look so bad after all."

Later that night, Anna tossed and turned in her bed. In the midst of trying to forget thermo and Rodney and work, she acknowledged to herself Kaci had a point.

Anna sighed and flopped over, then reached for the light. She crept out into her living room, whispered, "It's okay, Walker, go back to sleep," to her betta fish, and pulled a piece of paper and an envelope out of her desk.

She tapped a pen against her lip for a minute, and started writing.

Then she shredded it and started again.

Fifteen minutes and eight sheets of paper later, she was pleased with the result.

Jackson,

The kitchen was my pleasure. Especially since I got to meet Enrique. I hope he's enjoying his new home and that he gives you your other beater back soon. I've never met a more well-behaved armadillo.

As for our rematch, when I win, I'd like to borrow your pole and go fishing. The pie will depend on how gentlemanly you are about losing.

Cordially,
Anna

P.S. Please give my condolences to Radish on her name.

And when she went back to bed, she slept like a baby.

Chapter Ten

He'd never been a man to want what he couldn't have, until he found appreciation in having the smallest thing he'd thought beyond his charm.
—The Temptress of Pecan Lane, *by Mae Daniels*

BETWEEN THE FUNERAL and a sustainable fuels conference, Jules was out of the office almost two weeks. Her first morning back, she'd overdone the makeup, but it wasn't enough to hide the puffiness around her eyes. She sped past Anna's cube with a brief wave.

Since she'd ignored Anna's texts and calls, Anna got up and followed her. "Hey."

Jules held up a hand. "Not ready for Ms. Sunshine yet, okay? You didn't come in here and organize my shit while I was out, did you?"

"Only the important parts." Anna leaned into the doorway, since she couldn't go much farther in without tripping over Air Force Instruction manuals and professional magazines. "One of our suppliers dropped off the face of the earth, so we're short a few samples this week." Which meant they were backlogged only six test days instead of seven. But since Anna had caught up on studying and sleep while Jules was out, she was managing her panic over the workload fairly decently.

Even if she was starting to think that managing her girly bits might help too. She had become pretty adept at convincing herself that there was no correlation at all between the notes Kaci kept delivering and those moments when she felt that she could handle what life was tossing at her. But she wasn't delusional enough to think the notes had nothing to do with her girly bits humming during those same moments.

Jules tossed her bag behind her desk and flopped in her chair. "Idiots."

Anna shook her head. "I worked with Shirley and Todd to try to find a new one. We have a couple of leads."

"Better than letting you loose with that damn label maker again." Jules reached for the button on her computer, but suddenly stopped and looked straight at Anna, though her eyes weren't really focused.

"Yes?"

Jules blinked twice. "Nothing."

Anna took a step out of the cube. It always took Jules a little bit to get settled, but grief obviously wasn't helping. "Holler whenever you're ready."

"I'm ready. Still gotta make a living." Her eyes went shiny, but she blinked it back and stood. "Where's the paperwork?"

Anna snagged a clipboard from the mail holder between their cubes.

"Samples?" Jules asked.

"Lined up and waiting."

Jules curled a lip. "You didn't try to do anything else helpful and efficient while I was gone, did you?"

"I set up a new color-coding system for the samples, and I studied."

"That's nice, but you're not getting my job."

The air conditioner kicked on, but the draft coming from the ceiling vent was warm compared with the chill in the lab. Anna straightened and tugged on her blouse. "Jules? I'm really sorry."

"Yeah, well, life sucks."

"But it still goes on."

Five hours later, Anna wasn't sure how much more going on she could do with Jules's snarls. When Jules ordered Anna to leave for lunch, she was more than happy to take her thermo book and her normal Monday ham sandwich and fruit cup to the break room on the second floor.

Because the kitchen next to the lab was too close.

Anna cracked her thermo notes, and Shirley walked in.

"Morning okay?" Shirley asked.

"Work's getting done."

"Not what I asked."

Anna held up her hands. "I don't know what to do."

Shirley poured herself a cup of coffee and sat. "There's never a right thing to do. You do the best you can." She poked Anna's book. "How's class?"

"I'm learning a lot." Whether her grade would reflect it was another matter. Even if Kaci was right about Dr. Kelly using a grading curve, a couple of smarty-pants teenagers in Anna's class would probably blow it for her.

Brats.

"Must enjoy it for how much you're studying," Shirley said dryly.

Anna cringed. "The semester started out rough, but I really am learning a lot."

"You registered for classes for next semester yet?"

"I sign up next week."

Shirley leaned back in her seat and crossed her legs. "There's no degree requirement to take the first fuels certification here."

Anna's sandwich sat on her tongue like sawdust. She worked it around a bit, then swallowed it and followed it with a gulp of water. She'd been putting off the certifications while she concentrated on her degree, but Shirley had a look. "Would that allow me to more actively participate in the lab?"

"Since you're working on your degree and have a year of experience, it's highly likely. HR would have to clear it, as would safety and the base contracting officer, but I don't think that would be a problem."

"Are we expanding operations?"

"Possibly in the civil sector, but it's a distant possibility. I'm not counting on it."

Anna's pulse bumped. "Jules is very good at her job."

"Technically, yes." Shirley's pale eyes didn't waver. "But she's a military wife now."

Anna's breathing evened out. Brad *would* eventually move, and Jules would go with him. "What happens if they PCS before I'm done with my degree?"

"Contract world, kid. Everything's negotiable."

Sounded pretty win-win to Anna. Especially with the experience she'd have on her resume when she was finally done with her degree. "Where do I sign up, and who do I need to talk to?"

"Check your email. It's all there." Shirley stood and took her coffee with her. "Good luck this afternoon."

Anna had no doubt she'd need it. But diving back into thermo wasn't nearly the chore it had felt like a few minutes ago. Her life was finally turning around.

A WEEK LATER, Anna was so frustrated at work, she actually enjoyed the break of taking her thermo final. At the very least, it turned her brain to jelly so she couldn't remember how Shirley kept popping into the lab and how Jules kept sniping at Shirley. Anna kept doing her best to stay out of everyone's way while she started on her fuels specialist level one certification. She scheduled a vacation day for the Friday after finals, and she intended to use every minute of it to sit around and remind herself that she could do this.

Then she'd spend Saturday and Sunday studying certification materials.

But by eighty-thirty Friday morning, Anna was right back into the books.

Because she didn't do bored well.

Kaci called at noon. "What're you doing, sugar?"

"Nothing," Anna said.

"You're studying, aren't you?"

"No?"

Kaci blew out a breath Anna could almost feel over the phone. "Get on over here. Lance and I both took the afternoon off. Pool's perfect and we're fixin' to slap some ribs on the grill later. We've got lots."

Anna glanced at her book. Her eyes crossed. "What can I bring?"

"Shoot, sugar, you don't have to—oh, wait. Lance says he'd take one of your pies if you've got one lying around."

Anna stretched her hands up toward the cracked ceiling and smiled. "None lying around, but if you don't mind me using your oven, I can have one done before dinner. I'll stop and pick up some fruit on my way."

"Huh." Kaci's voice grew far away. "Lance, stop by the fruit stand for peaches, and you'll get your pie." She came back. "That work, sugar? You need anything else?"

"I'll stop at the store. It's on the way."

Anna could picture Kaci tugging her hair out. "Sugar, I'm starting to think you're hopeless. Now listen up. Sometimes we need to let the men think we need 'em for something, and today's Lance's day to be needed. Now are you getting your rear end over here, or do I need to send him over to pick you up too?"

Anna flipped her book closed. Arguing would take more time than leaving a few dollars to pay for the peaches. "Give me fifteen to put a crust together, and I'll head over."

When she arrived at Kaci's house, her friend had on a short swimsuit cover-up. She ushered Anna in the front door. The house was still and cool and comfortable. "C'mon in, sugar. Here, let me have the crust. You go get changed. We've got some time for a dip before the peaches get here."

Anna slipped into the bathroom, changed into her

swimsuit, and slathered on sunscreen to compensate for her Norwegian genes. She met Kaci out at the pool, where she slid into the shallow end and sighed. "Thanks. I needed this."

"You bet your britches."

Anna slipped under the water and let the coolness envelope her. The August heat was far from livable, but the pool was perfect. She came up, swiped her hair out of her eyes, and the two of them soaked and gossiped until Anna's fingers were pruny.

Kaci's ring caught Anna's eye. "How are the wedding plans coming?"

The wedding wasn't until Columbus Day weekend. They would've had it over the school break—*not* during football season—but Lance's sister wasn't due home from Afghanistan for another month, and they didn't want her to miss it.

"I haven't felt like shoving a firecracker up my momma's rear end in at least a week, so that's good," Kaci said. "I'm telling you, eloping's the way to go. Can't believe I'm letting him insist on treating me like a princess. Might near kill me." She grinned. "But he's worth it. This one's gonna stick."

"You bet your britches, baby," Lance said from the door. "Got a whole load of peaches for you, Anna. You want us to slice 'em up?"

She moved toward the stairs. "No, no, I'll do it."

"You sure? I got a big pocket knife."

Anna scrambled out of the pool. He'd probably lose half the peaches in the skin, or—Gram would have a heart attack—not peel them at all, and the pie wouldn't bake even if the peaches weren't peeled and sliced uniformly.

"You quit teasing her or you won't be getting any," Kaci chided.

"Pie, or...?"

"Sugar, it's all pie."

"Put a sock on the door if you decide to go skinny-dipping," Anna said.

"You bet, sugar." Kaci winked.

Anna wrapped a towel around herself and barely made it to the door before Lance cannon-balled into the deep end, sending water splashing across half the yard and the windows.

Inside, she shuffled through the drawers, looking for the knives that she was certain had been next to the sink last time she was here, but she couldn't find them. When she straightened, Jackson was watching her from behind the small counter between the kitchen and the living room.

Her heart gave a big *thud*, but she wasn't sure if it was surprise or excitement. She hadn't seen him since he'd left her in his kitchen.

But they'd traded plenty of notes through Kaci. His momma must've kept him well-stocked with that paper.

Today he wore a different pair of board shorts but the same faded Alabama T-shirt and the same big, crinkly eyed smile. His hair was shorn so tight she wouldn't have suspected curls, and his face was clean-shaven. "Hey, there, Anna Grace."

Something fluttered in her chest at the way her name rolled off his tongue. Something suspiciously similar to a pheromone-induced adrenaline rush. "Do you have to call me that?" she asked, though it was impossible not to smile back.

"Well, now, it's pretty, and it fits you, so I reckon I do." He settled on a barstool on the other side of the counter, propping up his tan forearms. He grabbed a peach and shifted it between his hands. "Brought some extra peaches so you can make one of those just for me after our rematch tonight."

Another frisson of awareness prickled her wet skin. She bent over and, out of desperation, peeked in the dishwasher to hide her reaction. *Bingo*. There were the knives. She plucked a paring knife out of the silverware section, then gave one of the peaches a sniff. Peach season was winding down, but these smelled sweet and yummy.

He looked yummy. In an *I'm only in it for the lust* kind of way.

Maybe Kaci was onto something with that expiration-date

thing. "Nobody told me you were coming, so I only brought one crust," she said, and she gave him a wink Kaci would've been proud of. Her cheeks warmed, but she didn't care.

Because he'd leaned closer. His gaze dropped to her mouth.

And she had a suspicion he wasn't as dumb as he wanted her to believe.

"No problem," he said. "Kaci probably has flour and bacon grease somewhere in here."

She almost dropped the peach. "Bacon grease? In *pie crust?*"

"Ain't that how your momma taught you to make it?"

"My *momma* taught me to make pie taste like pie and pig taste like pig."

"Then what do you do with your bacon grease?"

In the middle of her shudder, she caught the look. The *I'm playing games with the uptight Yankee* look.

She'd be damned.

She'd been rednecked.

This one was a *lot* smarter than he let on.

She jutted her chin until her nose was high enough for her to stare him down. "I donate it to our annual *Hicks Without Hogs* drive at work."

"Right decent of you." But if that ornery spark was any indication, his coughing fit had nothing to do with the pollen count.

She took the paring knife to the first peach. The skin slid off in even, curving strips. "Somebody has to give us Northern folk a good name."

He rolled a peach out of the neat line Anna had arranged them in. "Baking pies like that, all you need to do is loosen your tongue up a little, and nobody's gonna notice the Northern part. You make biscuits too?"

Anna snatched his peach away and put it back in place, but only to distract her from thinking about him thinking about her tongue. "Three-point question." She sliced her peeled peach and dropped the slices into the bowl, then grabbed another peach.

"How about a trade instead?"

And there was that tart strawberry flavor sitting on the back of her tongue again. "What kind of trade?"

He shifted her last three peaches, putting the smallest in the middle. "You tell me all about your biscuits, and I'll tell you where I went while you were putting my kitchen together."

The way he asked about her biscuits inspired thoughts that had nothing to do with baking. "Oh, I think I'm going to need something better than that."

"Huh." He scratched his chin. "What're you doing tomorrow night?"

That sparked a big old *ka-thump!* in her chest. Her hand wobbled. The peach skin slid off with a jagged edge. "Studying."

"Thought finals were over."

"Need a certification at work."

"Gotta eat though."

She started to tell him about her Sunday baking system that allowed her to eat labeled leftovers the rest of the week, then realized he was grinning at her like he already knew.

She'd way underestimated him.

And she didn't like that she couldn't decide if she liked smart Jackson or dumb Jackson better. She knew one thing for sure. She liked smart Anna, and smart Anna took care of herself first.

While she was deciding if she could take care of herself and let him in a little further, she conjured up a Southern smile of her own. "That's so sweet of you to worry about little old me. But I'm in a real busy spot at work right now, and I need to keep my focus so I can keep eating. I'm sure you understand, being such a busy, important man yourself." If he was worth her time, he'd fight for it.

Instead, he coughed into his hand again, his eyes going all crinkly, and then he had to turn away and cough again.

She sighed in her peaches. She couldn't even politely stall for time without getting laughed at.

He eventually recovered, though his straight face seemed to be a struggle. "Reckon I should feel special you're taking the time today to make me a pie."

And suddenly she didn't care if he was laughing at her, because he probably had issues of his own if he had to hide who he was behind that goofy redneck act. And if he could spend the time flirting with her, then she could be nice back.

"Well." She grabbed another peach and took her knife to it. "I don't make pies for just anybody."

When he didn't answer right away, she cut a sideways glance at him. His smile softened. "Careful there," he said. "Next step's letting me buy you some ice cream."

He was watching her as if she were a puzzle he'd like to unravel, and the interest in his eyes was enough to make her want to be unraveled. Her knife slipped, and something sharp stung her thumb. She shifted over to the sink and flipped on the cold water to rinse off the peach juice, then grabbed a paper towel.

Jackson came around the counter. "Okay there, Anna Grace?"

"Fine. Really. It's a little knick. I do this all the time."

He set one hand at the small of her back and cradled her injured hand with the other. She caught a whiff of Old Spice. Something tingled low in her belly.

"Might could be you're working too hard."

She'd never believed in kissing boo-boos. A mini-panic attack seized her chest, but his touch dulled the throbbing in her thumb. When she tried to brush off his concern, she instead leaned closer to his warm, solid body. "Baking isn't work."

His rumbly chuckle sent delicious shivers over her skin. "It's putting all those peaches and sugar where they're supposed to be, hm?"

"Exactly." She pulled the paper towel away from her

thumb and inspected the injury. Very little bleeding, barely a tiny knick. The bigger injury would come from the electric shock when she broke contact with him before grounding herself.

Jackson brushed his thumb over the wound. "Looks like you're gonna make it."

"It's no big deal." She forced herself to look up at him. "I've got a Band-Aid in my purse."

His eyes were warm and smoky over his crooked grin. "Course you do." He pressed a soft kiss to her thumb. "How about I go get that for you?"

Some padding for her self-preservation would be more effective. *Lust*, she reminded herself. She was good with lust. Six and a half years of practice at it.

She slid her hand out of his grasp. "I can get it."

"As the lady wishes." He picked up her knife and the peach. "You got some particular way you been peeling and cutting these here?"

Anna snatched the peach back. "I'll just be a minute. The peaches can wait."

"You sure do know how to make a guy feel useless, Anna Grace."

"I—you—you're not useless."

"I dunno. You don't need help with your ants. Don't need help with your peaches. Probably wouldn't let me hold a door for you if it was raining a hurricane and you had your hands full. Don't matter what it is, you don't ever take help, do you?"

"Like the help you offered in your own kitchen?"

She gave herself a mental pinch. Her prissy side was coming through again.

But his slow grin told her she'd walked into that.

"Aw, now, that's different. You lost fair and square on that one." He leaned into the counter. "Besides, I reckon that pie you took was good payment for a job well done."

"*I baked that pie.*"

"And I'm right looking forward to this one. So you gonna

let me help with your peaches or not?"

She brushed an errant strand of drying hair out of her eyes. "You have to *earn* helping with my peaches."

His gaze dipped to her mouth again. Abruptly, he stepped back. "Dunno, Anna Grace. Ain't so sure you're ready for that."

The back door flung open. Kaci shuffled in with a goofy grin. She'd wrapped a sarong around her waist, and her belly button ring glinted in the light. "You get that pie in the oven yet?" she asked. "Lance is firing up the grill."

She stopped and glanced between them.

Anna turned back to the peach. "Almost."

"No hurry if you're busy," Kaci said.

"Just waiting on the all-clear to go outside for the man-work," Jackson said.

"Huh."

Out of the corner of her eye, Anna watched Kaci give them both another once-over. "Well, if that's the case, you go on out there."

"Yes, ma'am." Jackson snitched a peach slice and winked at Anna. He took the plate of ribs Kaci pulled out of the fridge, then disappeared out the back door.

Kaci fluffed her hair and tied it back into a ponytail. "He flirting with you?"

"I think so."

"Sugar, if you don't know for sure, he's not doing it right."

If the strawberry taste in her mouth and the weird thumping of her heart were any indication, whatever it was he was doing, he was definitely doing it right.

And based on the way Kaci was grinning, she knew it.

But it wasn't until after the pie was in the oven that Anna realized Jackson hadn't told her where he'd gone when he left her alone in his kitchen. But then, she hadn't told him about her biscuits either.

They'd been too busy talking about her peaches.

JACKSON DIDN'T KNOW he was a pie man until that long spell between the best pies he'd ever tasted. Those funny notes she kept sending him had him intrigued, but if he were the kind of man to fall in love, it would've been the peach pie that did him in.

Her ex-husband was a lug-head to walk away from Anna Grace's pies.

Thoughts like that made him glad he'd gotten out of the kitchen when he had. But then he'd gone and snagged the seat next to Anna when the ribs came off the grill, and with her eating that peach pie right next to him, he was getting ideas he shouldn't be having. Not with hunting season coming on.

"—And I swear on my daddy's grave," Kaci was saying, "that pumpkin landed plum smack in the middle of a pig farm. Went half a mile if it went an inch. My momma's face 'bout near turned purple when that old pig farmer showed up with half a hog carcass and a bill for the rest of it."

"Now, did *you* aim the trebuchet, or did your friend?" Anna asked.

Kaci tossed a napkin at her.

"Decent question," Jackson said.

"What about you, Bubba?" Lance said. "Seem to recall you had a few good tales."

Anna's eyes narrowed at him. He had a feeling she was onto him. And he wasn't entirely disappointed.

He did like his competition smart.

He took another bite of pie and tried to stay on the earthly plane. Damn good pie.

She was ruining him for biscuits. She really was.

"Yeah," he finally said, "I got a couple good ones."

"Which one's your favorite?" Anna asked. She had a sparkle in her eyes, like she expected him to refuse to tell it.

He wasn't one to disappoint a lady. "Dunno about that, Anna Grace. Stories like that, you gotta earn 'em."

She fiddled with the pie server, stroked a finger down the handle. He felt a familiar tightening down south.

He'd gotten a good number of biscuit offers back in Auburn this summer, but not one of them had grabbed his attention like she did.

Her voice went low and husky. "Pretty sure I've earned this one."

Kaci snickered.

"She's got a point, Bubba," Lance said.

"That's how it's gonna be, is it?" Jackson leaned back in the chair, crossed his ankle over his knee, and reached back to a few memories he held close. "Reckon I was about fifteen or so," he said. "Had a friend who liked to have some fun. Get creative. Give our mommas heart attacks. So one day we were hanging out, and we started talking about what we were gonna be when we grew up."

"What were you going to be?" Anna asked.

Jackson scratched his head. "Hadn't rightly decided yet, but Craig, he said he was gonna fly rocket ships to the moon. So I got to thinking, and I told him we could build a rocket right in our own backyard."

Kaci leaned forward. "Did you?"

"Tried real hard," Jackson said. "Tell you what, if that old Hoover of Momma's had as much suction power as those commercials said, we would've done it on the first round. Instead, we had to amp that sucker up and give her more power."

Kaci was near salivating. Lance shot him a dirty look, probably because Jackson's rocket story was bigger. Anna Grace, though, was sucking her lips in like she was afraid she'd laugh before the punch line.

"How far did it go?" Kaci breathed. "Did it blow up?"

"Made it high as my granddaddy's oak tree if it made it an inch. Would've gone further, but Craig's astronaut steered like a girl."

"Your momma," Kaci said. "You break any arms or legs?"

"Nah, but little Eunice wasn't ever the same."

"You put your *dog* in the rocket?" Lance said.

"Shucks, no. It was some old Cabbage Patch Kid. Course, Momma was madder'n a wet hen over that too. Ruined her Hoover *and* broke a good doll."

A whimpery laugh slipped out between Anna's lips.

Figured she'd like that, since she managed to make vague references to his momma every few notes.

"She blister your backside?" Kaci asked.

Jackson chuckled. "Nah. Daddy handled us instead." Sent Craig home to Russ for a whooping, then sat Jackson down, looked over that old modified engine sitting there in the backyard, and said, *Son, you owe your momma a new vacuum. Then I don't care what it costs, you're going to space camp this summer. Long as I got breath in my body, I ain't gonna let you waste those smarts you got.*

"So you fly planes now?" Anna asked.

He shook his head. "No waiver for what I've got."

Her brow wrinkled.

"Damn shame," Lance said.

Anna Grace's wrinkle got wrinklier.

Jackson flicked a mosquito off his arm. "Don't you worry none," he said to Anna. "Doctors say I got at least six months."

He was working up a little guilt for the way her eyes went wide when Kaci smacked him in the shoulder. "Don't you be falling for that old line," she said to Anna. "He ain't dying, he's color-blind."

Jackson looked at Lance, who grinned. "Sorry, Bubba."

"Your turn, Anna Grace," Jackson said. "You got any fishing stories?"

She had that devil look going again.

She did it good.

"You betcha," she said.

But she wouldn't tell, and it was getting late. They carried their dishes in and got the kitchen mostly put to rights. Anna made like she was heading for home.

Lance tilted his head toward her, but Jackson was already

on it.

"Let me get that door for you, Anna Grace."

She did that cute thing where she tried to look like she didn't want help and didn't want him to see her smile about it. "Afraid your momma's going to hear you let a lady walk to her car by herself?"

He pulled the door open. "More like wondering if you'll let me get away with it."

She puffed herself up a couple of inches and marched outside.

"Didn't hurt a bit, now did it?" He tucked his hands in his pockets and moseyed beside her.

Her lips were fighting another smile. "Thank you."

"You feel that, Anna Grace? That's progress. I'm real proud of you."

This time she smiled all the way. Between that smile and her pie, he needed to keep hunting season in mind. Didn't like it when he couldn't get away any old weekend he liked.

"Are you always this old-fashioned, or are you trying to goad me?" Anna asked.

"Shucks, ma'am, ain't nothing old-fashioned about manners."

"I suppose not."

"But if you were thinking to reward me for good behavior with your phone number, well, now, I sure wouldn't be put out."

She laughed. "You wouldn't, huh?"

"No, ma'am."

She paused beside her car and leaned into him. He smelled peaches and pool water and perfection, and he had to concentrate on breathing steady. "Yes, ma'am?"

She crooked a finger. "I need to tell you a secret."

Hell with hunting season.

"Sometimes," she whispered, her breath tickling his ear and most of the rest of his body all at the same time, "a girl appreciates a guy for who he is, instead of who he's pretending to be."

She pulled away and held out her hand while he was still puzzling out if she'd just confessed to liking him. "Let me see your phone," she said.

He handed it over and she typed away on it, tilting it so he couldn't see what she was doing. After a minute, she handed it back to him. "If you can find it, you can use it."

He coughed back a chuckle. "That a comment on my technical skills or my puzzlin' skills?"

"Do you frequently have trouble using your equipment?"

"Don't reckon you'll know unless I find that number."

Her cheeks flushed so dark they blended into the night. "That's a very good point."

"Reckon a girl with your organizational skills still has my number."

"Oh, I kept it. In case I ever needed an exterminator again."

Funny girl, that Anna Grace.

He stepped away from her car, because she'd found her flirting words tonight, but the way she kept hugging that door told him she wasn't ready for following through.

That was okay with him. He'd waited thirty-three years to find out he was a pie man. He could wait a while longer to find out what else she could teach him. "You have a nice evening, Anna Grace."

She winked at him. "You have a nice time hunting for that number."

It took some effort, but he waited all the way until her taillights disappeared before he tried. And when he finally found it, he wouldn't even tell Radish how long it took. But he did get a good laugh out of it.

My Favorite Yankee, she'd labeled herself.

He couldn't argue with that.

Chapter Eleven

He knew the pleasure of a kiss with the wrong woman, but he had yet to discover the power of a kiss with the right one.
—The Temptress of Pecan Lane, by Mae Daniels

A LITTLE OVER A WEEK later, Anna walked into the lab and found Jules sitting on the floor in khakis and a blue knit shirt amid piles of magazines and old efficiency reports, tossing things into her trash can.

Cleaning.

Anna froze. Maybe if she tiptoed back the way she came, Jules would pretend she hadn't heard Anna come in. And Anna could pretend Jules's cube still needed quality time with a backhoe and a label maker, and the world would keep spinning on its axis.

Jules shot her an *I dare you to say something* look.

Anna smiled, which probably looked as fake as it felt. "Hey, Jules. How's it going?"

"What's it look like, genius? Don't even think of bringing that chipper attitude in here. You didn't get laid or something this weekend, did you?"

No, she'd apparently hidden her phone number too well for that, because *someone* hadn't called. He had sent a very complimentary note about her pie through Kaci though. "I studied." The level one certification test wasn't for another three weeks, but after squeaking by in thermo with a grade barely high enough for tuition reimbursement, she was enrolled in two classes at Jim-Bob for the semester starting next week.

"You are so lame," Jules said.

Anna couldn't argue with that. She nodded at the garbage can. "What's going on?"

"This a crime? Because I was even thinking of asking for that label maker back." Jules flung two more magazines into the trash. Her monitor was dark. Half her drawers were open. Her wedding picture lay facedown on her desk.

Not good. "It's yours if you want it. You guys have a nice weekend?"

Two binders hit the floor. "Brad took a package."

"Took a—oh. I didn't know he wanted out." The Air Force had been offering voluntary separation packages in overstaffed career fields to cut long-term costs. Neil had mentioned it once or twice, but he'd never sounded interested in taking the offer.

Jules slumped over and buried her head between her knees. "He doesn't want his parents to lose both their sons to the war."

Anna gulped back the instinctive sympathetic noises. It would've only pissed Jules off. She gestured toward the mess instead. "Does this mean—"

"It means I'm getting my shit organized to be the primary breadwinner until he figures out what the hell he's going to do with himself."

Anna swallowed. Then swallowed again.

It meant Jules and Brad wouldn't move unless one of them took a job somewhere else. It meant certifications and working toward her degree wouldn't move Anna up the RMC chain. She blew out a slow breath. "Doesn't the base offer some career counseling?"

There was that *duh* look again. "Please. Like *Brad* needs counseling."

Considering he'd given up his career a couple of weeks after his brother's death, it couldn't hurt. "You don't have to need it for it to be helpful."

"Whatever." Jules dumped a stack of magazines into the trash. "If you're going to stand there, do something useful and take this to the Dumpster."

Anna took the can, more as an excuse to get away than because she enjoyed being garbage girl. She paused on her way out of the cube. "Jules? It'll be okay."

"Take it back to your own office. This is a sunshine-free zone on Mondays. I'm fine, okay?"

Every day with Jules was a sunshine-free zone. "Sure."

With any luck, biofuels would take off in the civilian sector, and there would be plenty of work for both of them. In the meantime, Anna still had a lot of studying to do. RMC might not do as much for her resume as she'd begun to expect, but she'd make the most of the opportunities while she was here.

ANNA'S LAST CLASS of the week let out three minutes before nine the next Thursday. She stumbled out of the classroom into the darkened hallway behind her classmates. The rough gray carpet muted their footsteps, and the few talking did so in soft tones that were sucked right into the walls. Her head swam with equations and theories that made no sense.

Her bed was a thirty-minute drive away.

Might as well have been an eternity.

She slogged out the door. Her skin went clammy in the cooler but still humid air. Nights like this, packing it up and moving in with her parents sounded nice. But then she'd have to move the stack of self-help books her dad kept mailing from his bookshop.

Or maybe she'd donate them to Kaci and the ex-wives club.

She powered her phone back on while she walked to her car. Maybe Beth would still be up to keep her company on the ride home.

Her phone beeped with two text message notifications. She checked the first one.

You in class?

She squinted at the number. Not local. Not from back home. She checked the second. It was from the same number.

I dropped by that Bean place over by Jim-Bob, and they gave me some fancy cold girly drink with my coffee. Said my favorite Yankee liked it. Yours if you want it. Stop on by.

A smile tugged at Anna's lips. He'd found her number. And she really *was* his favorite Yankee. That made her heart tingle.

She rubbed her eyes. A caffeine boost would get her home. Stopping was the smart thing to do.

Maybe not the smart thing for the *rat-a-tat*-ing in her chest, but definitely the smart thing for operating a vehicle.

Eh. Her heart could use the exercise.

She cranked the engine and buckled up. Five minutes later, she walked into Jimmy Beans. Jackson was stretched out at the far table, staring at his iPhone. Before the bells on the door finished tinkling, he'd tucked the phone into the pocket of his jeans and stood.

Jeans.

He'd dressed up.

"Hey, there, Anna Grace. You look right pretty tonight."

She lifted an eyebrow.

"For a Yankee who got into it with a possum," he amended with an ornery grin.

She dropped her purse under the table and collapsed into the chair. "What do I owe you for the drink?"

"One of them pretty smiles sure would be nice."

"I'm not sure one drink will be enough for that."

He stretched back out. "Rough day?"

She took a sip and closed her eyes. Chai latte. He was good. Or, more likely, Kaci was easy. "Yum."

She opened her eyes and found him watching her with too much interest for tonight. "I'd say I'm glad the weekend's almost here, but I have to study. Study study study. I hate studying. I already did this once. I'm tired of doing it again. I just want to be done. Finally." She thunked her head on the table. "I used to like school."

"You work full-time the first time?"

She rolled her forehead. "Nuh-uh." It took some effort, but she forced herself upright and took another sip. "Thank you."

His leg bumped hers under the table and stayed there. "My pleasure."

Anna rubbed at an uneven line in the tabletop. She slid her leg closer to his, solidifying the connection. Her body wanted to flirt, but her mouth had other ideas. "You know the worst part of all this? By the time I finally finish my bachelor's, I'll need a master's to even apply to take the professional engineer exam. It'll take me *years*."

"You still like what you're studying?"

She blinked. "Why wouldn't I?"

He slid a china plate stacked with three chocolate chip cookies back and forth with slow fingers. "People change."

"Living that, thanks. Not because I wanted to." The middle cookie should've been on the bottom. It was biggest. She fisted her hands to keep from fixing it.

Or stealing a cookie.

His leg slid against hers. A pang of longing squeezed her thighs. She'd taken the physical contact for granted when she was married. What was she supposed to do now?

"I had a family thing of sorts," he said.

She squinted at him.

"The day you fixed my kitchen." A flattering red crept up his ears. "Supposed to head over Friday night, but a cookout sounded fun."

"Your momma let you get away with being late?"

The blush in his ears faded in direct proportion to the grin dimpling his cheeks. "She was right proud I tricked a Yankee into doing what she usually does for me."

"Uh-huh." Anna decided she'd leave an extra dollar and snatched a cookie off his plate. "So how many master's degrees do you have?"

Jackson's grin dropped off again, and his ears switched course until they glowed an unnatural pink. He stacked the last two cookies, leaving the top one slightly off-center. He eyed her, but she didn't so much as twitch at the disorder.

Not that she didn't want to.

"Three," he finally said. "According to Uncle Sam, anyway. I only count one."

It took a minute to process that, until she remembered Neil had mentioned some of the Air Force continuing professional development programs counted as master's degrees when they were done in residence.

If that was the case, Jackson outranked Neil.

She wanted to laugh. How was *that* for a rebound?

Jackson stacked the two cookies evenly. "Been thinking about that night you didn't share any good fishing stories."

"I'm boring."

"I hear tell you're pretty good with firecrackers."

She looked up from watching his long fingers on the cookies. "You've been talking about me?"

"Mostly listening." His dimples seemed extra-dimply tonight.

Anna's face was hotter than Jim-Bob's parking lot, but she found a cheeky grin of her own. "So you got the briefing about getting on my bad side?"

"Yes, ma'am."

Yet he'd still asked her to coffee.

Better and better.

But just to make sure— "Do you want to get married?"

His eyes went wide and a strangled gasp escaped his lips. "No, ma'am."

Kaci must've been right about his momma raising him right, because even though Anna heard about a hundred expletives hanging in the air between them, they hadn't come from his mouth.

Better and better had just become nearly perfect. She took a nonchalant sip of her chai, then gave him a sassy smile. "Me neither."

He tugged on his collar. "You're a right funny girl, Anna Grace."

She methodically split her cookie into bite-size pieces. "Had to check. I didn't enjoy getting divorced the first time, and I don't plan to put myself in a position to go through anything like it again." And that was as serious as she wanted to get with him. "But I think you're cute."

He rewarded her with one of those grins that made her very happy to be a single woman. "So you're telling me my timing's getting better."

"It's not getting worse. And I've obviously been a good influence, because your grammar's getting better too."

The slide of his leg against hers told her he took that as encouragement.

She didn't mind a bit.

Fifteen minutes later, he walked her out to her car. "You okay to drive home?" he asked.

She nodded. "Much better now. Thanks."

"Call any night you need a pick-me-up, you hear?" He brushed a kiss to her temple.

She tilted her head back to look up at him. She couldn't resist it. Might as well indulge. Just because she wouldn't get married again didn't mean she had to stay celibate. Besides, he had an expiration date called *orders*. That would be easy enough to walk away from. "Can I call for anything else?"

"Anytime, Anna Grace. Anytime." He twirled her hair around his fingers, then dropped it and stepped back. "Drive safe."

"You too." He turned away, but she impulsively reached for his hand. "Jackson. Thank you. Again. This helped a lot."

"Yeah?" He stepped back into her personal space. "Don't

suppose you're grateful enough to tell me about your biscuits."

She licked her lips. She wasn't thinking about biscuits at all. But if she did this, there was no turning back. He was friends with Kaci. She'd see him again. A lot.

Excitement tingled her girly bits.

She grabbed his face and went up on her tiptoes, then pressed a kiss to his lips. His hands settled on her waist. After a moment's hesitation, he kissed her back.

Lordy, did he ever kiss her back.

The hint of strawberries was nothing compared with the rich flavors of coffee and caramel on his lips. He slanted his mouth over hers, his breath tickling her cheek. She slid her arms up and around his neck, pushing up higher on her toes.

Neil hadn't been this tall.

He'd always stayed in decent shape, but she didn't recall his being as solid as Jackson was.

Or as thorough.

Did a guy get this good at kissing through practice? Was it her fault Neil had been a bad kisser, because they hadn't practiced enough?

Or was Neil simply inadequate?

Jackson broke the kiss, but he kept his hands anchored around her waist. He tilted his forehead against hers. "That's some awful loud thinking, Anna Grace."

She froze. "I-I'm sorry. I—it's—crap." Kissing wasn't supposed to be this complicated.

"That bad, was it?"

She squeezed her eyes shut. "No! It was very nice."

"Nice?"

The way he said it didn't *sound* nice. "Better than nice." It was enough to make her tingle in places she'd forgotten another human being could excite, but she wasn't ready for *that* yet. Not by a long shot. "It was a lot better than nice. It was... nicer."

His body shuddered against hers. She popped one eye open and found him shaking with silent laughter. "Highest praise I've had all day."

She tried to untangle herself, but something about the cool evening made her want to huddle close for warmth, though she doubted he would appreciate it now. "I'm not very good at this," she said.

"You're good at something or we wouldn't still be here." He hooked a hand around her neck and kissed her forehead again. "Next time, Anna Grace, I'll make sure you're not thinking about anything else."

She suppressed a shiver at the promise lurking deep in his voice. If he could deliver—well, did that count as being cured of her divorce? The physical parts, anyway?

For now, she'd take heart that he was willing to try. She licked her lips. "You're on."

He released her. A wave of cool air wrapped her body. "I'll be seeing you, Anna Grace."

The look in his eyes guaranteed that was a promise.

THERE WAS NOTHING like a nice hot morning squirrel hunting with a ragamuffin crew tagging along to make a man wish it was deer season. The three pans of biscuits Mamie and Miss Ophelia had set in the front seat of Jackson's truck should've been his first clue, but while Miss Ophelia rattled on about Miss Flo's having *three* single granddaughters now, such a shame, tsk tsk, Jackson's mind had been circling back to peach pie.

But not the kind that came in a pie plate.

Even Mamie's description of the girl who'd baked his third pan of biscuits—a nice Baptist girl who did things her parents called scandalous—hadn't been enough to distract him.

He had a feeling Mamie knew it.

But then Louisa had driven up in that car that made him think of donuts, and that'd distracted everybody.

"You told 'em we were hunting, right?" Craig said. They were unloading the shotguns from the back of Jackson's truck.

Jackson took his time looking over one of Daddy's old shotguns that he was holding on to for Louisa. Beat looking at the womenfolk who were yapping loud enough to scare a bear. "Yep."

"Good thing squirrel sees about the same as you do."

Jackson gave the women another once-over. Louisa was wearing camouflage, though it was tight enough that she would've looked more appropriate in the kind of place she better never set foot in. Miss Ophelia had on a dress that even he could tell was brighter than the sunshine. Only Mamie was in sensible pants and boots, but she was talking into her phone, using some app that acted like an old-fashioned Dictaphone. Radish sat adoringly at her feet.

Or maybe snoringly. Getting hard to tell with the old girl.

"You young fellers need any help?" Miss O's boyfriend, Cletus, sauntered over to the back of the truck with the bowlegged stride of a man whose center of gravity had finally shifted below his better assets. He gave Craig a nudge. "Or care to make an old man look useful in front of his girl?"

Craig handed the old guy a shotgun.

"Loaded?" Cletus asked.

"Not yet."

Cletus went back to the women. To show 'em how to hold a gun, he said on a wink.

Louisa started to reply to that, the slant to her eyes saying more than the words she had yet to launch. Jackson shot her a look, and thank the blessed stars, she shut her trap.

Beside him, Craig chuckled. "How far is it to your place from here?"

"About an hour."

"We could give 'em a head start."

Decent idea. But far as he knew, not one of them knew first aid. Mamie'd written a couple of doctors and nurses in her books, but Jackson didn't reckon her research had given her hands-on experience. He eyed the truck bed. "Huh," he said pointedly. "Looks like I forgot the shells." Brought his dog too.

Wouldn't have done that if he thought he had any real chance of bagging squirrel today.

Craig clapped him on the shoulder. "Next time, man."

Coming home had been good for something, at least. He'd forgotten how much fun he and Craig used to have.

They both looked at the women and Cletus again. "Your mamie's gonna be disappointed," Craig said.

"She'll be happy with getting a feel for the lay of the land. Next time I'm in town, I'll take her out to the range so she can see how shooting feels."

"Can't decide if you're brave or nuts."

Jackson thought of a certain pair of doe eyes and showed a rueful smile. "Little bit of both."

They broke the unfortunate news to the ladies and Cletus that they wouldn't be taking home any squirrels unless they happened to get close enough to club 'em on the head with the butt of a shotgun. No one seemed to mind, so they went ahead and traipsed into the woods for Mamie's research.

If Jackson didn't know any better, he would've thought Louisa looked relieved. But she shook her dark curls down her back and marched up alongside him. "Awful careless of you," she said with a sidelong glance. "Guess you've been distracted."

Yeah, he'd had pie on his mind lately, but admitting that to Louisa would be akin to inviting his family over to sift through his underwear drawer. "Distracted by what?"

"That piss-poor lineup Alabama's calling a football team this year."

"Louisa Margaret, I know your momma didn't raise you to talk like that," Mamie said. "Lord-a-mercy, what your father'd say if he heard you now. Got half a mind to take you over my own knee."

"Squirrel!" Miss O flung her gun up so fast, Radish dove between Jackson's legs. She aimed at the tree straight overhead. Her hair tilted all funny. Cletus clapped a hand to it. "That's right," she said to the sky, "you go on and run, you little furry rascal. If I had some bullets, you'd be going in my soup pot tonight."

"Ophelia, that's not how hunters talk," Mamie said. "They get all quiet-like and creep along until they've got a good shot."

"I had him in my sights."

"But squirrel's got ears, you know."

Jackson squeezed Mamie's shoulder. "We'll find another one." He dropped his voice to a whisper. "And we'll do it quiet-like. What we need to do now is find us a good tree all full of nuts to sit under."

Craig grinned and shook his head.

Didn't take a rocket scientist to figure out what he was thinking.

"Should've brought them biscuits Flo's younger granddaughter baked," Mamie murmured.

"Now you hush," Miss Ophelia whispered back. "She's the prettier one."

"Shows in her baking, bless her heart."

"Don't matter none," Louisa said. "Jackson don't like any of their biscuits."

Miss Ophelia gasped. Cletus patted her shoulder. "I like your biscuits," he said.

"Did he tell you that?" Mamie demanded of Louisa.

"Didn't see him eating any of them, did you?"

All five of them turned to look at him. "Had a big breakfast," he said.

Mamie peered over her spectacles. "You getting a taste for something other than biscuits?"

Danged if his ears weren't getting all hot like when Anna Grace called him out on being more than a dumb old redneck the other night. "PFT coming up."

Her lips pursed. "You ain't telling me you're getting too old to run a couple miles and do a few push-ups and sit-ups, now, are you?"

"He is getting a few gray hairs," Louisa said.

Jackson tucked her into a headlock. He pointed down the path. "Y'all want to hunt squirrels or not?"

"We should get going," Miss Ophelia said. "Flo and Dolly are setting out lunch over the pass. And Dolly's bringing that girl from her church who fries chicken so nice."

"That means she's got buckteeth and birthing hips," Louisa said.

"Bless her heart," Mamie agreed on a sigh. She patted Jackson's arm. "Don't you worry none, sugarplum. Still lots of nice young ladies out there for you."

But nice young ladies got ideas. And there wasn't one of them who could touch Anna Grace's pies. Hunting season or not, that suited him fine. He had a feeling some milk would go good with her pie, and he was patient enough to wait for it.

Chapter Twelve

There were things she wanted to do and things she had to do, and she was stubborn enough to do it all alone.
—The Temptress of Pecan Lane, by Mae Daniels

ANNA FLEXED HER fingers over Rex's keyboard and stifled a yawn. She'd been up studying past midnight every night this week. But she'd finished her first certification this morning, and tonight was her last class night of the week. She could catch up on sleep this weekend.

When she wasn't studying.

Still, she had reason to smile. She planned to stop at Jimmy Beans after class and drop Jackson a note about joining her.

She wiped the yawn-induced tears from her eyes, then squinted at the documentation from the new supplier. It didn't look right. Or maybe her brain had finally hit overload.

Jules sauntered into her office. "Are you always this useless after a test? I've been emailing you all morning."

"You're in the next cube."

Jules grabbed the ruler out of Anna's desk organizer and tapped it on the desk. "Didn't feel like yelling. You have that tech report done yet?"

"Tomorrow," she said. Maybe she'd locate a few extra

brain cells by then.

Jules slid the ruler over her fingers like a bow on a violin. "You busy tonight?"

Anna hadn't been out with Jules since karaoke. "Class. Maybe tomorrow?" She was supposed to hang out with Kaci while Lance was gone TDY, but she could cancel.

Jules dropped the ruler into Anna's in-basket. "No trivia at Taps tomorrow."

Anna moved the ruler back into place. "We could go somewhere else."

"Afraid of karaoke night?"

Sensitive subject, meet land mine. "We can do whatever you guys want."

"Never mind. I get it. We're not as cool as your post-divorce friends." Jules stood. Her pantsuit hung limp and her cheeks seemed extra hollow.

But *How are you doing* wasn't a question Jules took kindly to. Anna ignored the barb. "Have you heard how Brad's interview went this morning?"

"He skipped it." She leaned into the desk and plucked a pen out of the pen holder, then dropped it back in with a *plink*.

"He did?" Anna eyed Jules, but her friend focused on the pen. *Plink. Plink. Plink.* "Did he say why?"

Plink. Plink. "Apparently their corporate office in Virginia installed some fancy glass that birds can't see. He found pictures on the Internet of all these dead birds on the sidewalk around the building, and he says he won't work for bird killers."

"Oh."

"So trivia runs until nine or so if you get out of class early."

"I'll cross my fingers."

But two hours later, when the email arrived announcing class was cancelled, Anna bit back a curse. If Jules hadn't made a point of inviting her to trivia, Anna would've texted Jackson to see if he was up for something more than coffee. After three coffee dates in the last two weeks, it was obvious he was letting her call the shots.

And she liked that.

A lot.

But aside from one awkward lunch shortly after Rodney died, Anna hadn't seen Brad since the last karaoke night. And they'd been good friends before Neil left. So that evening, when she would've headed to class, she pulled into the Taps parking lot instead.

Inside, she found Jules and Brad sitting with two of Brad's old friends at a table littered with peanut shells in the middle of the loud, crowded bar. Jules was wearing a strained smile, and Brad was deep into a heated debate with the beefier of the two guys. Mitch, if Anna remembered right. And the guy with the receding hairline was Cookie. He probably had a real name, but Anna had never heard it. She snagged the chair next to Jules. "Hey."

Jules lifted a sardonic eyebrow. "Didn't think you'd make it."

"Going to bed an hour ago was tempting." Anna smiled at Cookie and nodded to Brad and Mitch. "You guys order yet? Or are more people coming?"

Jules slid her a menu. "Just us. The waitress is slacking tonight. You've got time."

"Hope she's not counting on a good tip," Brad said.

Jules *shush*-ed him. He rolled his eyes like Anna used to at her mother, then settled his attention on Anna. "How's school? You smart yet?"

"Getting there."

Brad grunted. He spun his silverware in circles. His knee bounced under the table. Jules snatched the silverware away. He glared at her, then turned back to Mitch. "Purdue's new quarterback is a pussy. They're fucking losing everything this year."

Their waitress, a bubbly college-aged girl, slid up to the table. "Hey, folks! Thanks for waiting. I'm—"

"Slow." Brad glared at her. His cheeks were puffier than

they'd been the last time Anna saw him, and the buttons on his shirt strained. "We need another pitcher. And some wings. Might as well bring the check now if you want us to pay before tomorrow."

"God, Brad." Jules pinched the bridge of her nose.

Anna tried to smile at the waitress. "Can I have a small salad please?"

Cookie and Mitch ordered. Jules waved off food, asking for a rum and Coke instead. Brad added fries and onion rings to his demands. The waitress tucked her order pad into her apron and scurried away.

Anna glanced at Jules.

"Stop looking at me like that." Jules snatched her glass and took a huge gulp. Ice cascaded down inside the glass. Water splashed over Jules's jaw and down her red blouse. "Dammit!"

Anna lunged for the extra napkins at the center of the table.

"Jesus, Jules," Brad sneered. "Wet much? God, can't take you anywhere."

Jules's face crumpled. Anna grabbed her arm and flashed a feral smile at the men. "Excuse us. We need to go to the ladies' room."

"I don't—" Jules started.

Anna cut her off. "Yes, you do." She tugged harder. Jules stood. She wobbled beside Anna through the tables of raucous patrons who were waiting for the start of trivia night.

In the bathroom, Jules glared at Anna. "What the hell?"

"That's what I'd like to know." Anna pointed toward the door. "Jules. You're hurting. He's hurting. Worse, he's turning into an ass. That's not Brad. You two need help."

"Fuck off."

"I don't want you to end up like me."

"I'm *not* you." Jules snatched a fistful of paper towels and shoved them across the wet spots on her chest. She swiped with a ferocity that matched the scowl on her face but was ruined by her wobbling chin and the splotchy cheeks. "Thank

God. Are you done?"

Anna swallowed hard. "No. I'm trying to be your friend."

Tears clung to Jules's lashes. Fury emanated out of her body. "Go be all touchy-feely with someone else. You don't know anything about this."

"I know you don't cry."

"My eyes are leaking in sympathy over your ignorance of the realities of married life."

Anna sucked in a breath. "I also know you bite, but you're usually not cruel."

The door swung open. A mother with her toddler walked in. Jules squeezed her eyes shut. When she opened them, the intentional blankness was scarier than mean Jules. "Whatever. Just don't make us lose trivia." She thrust the paper towels in the trash and marched out the door.

Anna let out a shuddery breath. She could leave. Corner the waitress, cancel her order, and go. But this wasn't about her. It was about helping people who'd been her friends.

What was she supposed to do when she didn't know which was the better of two bad options?

She unclenched her hands. Her nails had cut into her palms and her skin felt clammy. She washed her hands, dried them thoroughly, then headed back out to the table.

By the time trivia ended at nine, Anna felt like an emotional punching bag, and her cheeks hurt from forcing smiles all night long. Their table came in second in trivia, first in biggest drunkard in the room, dead last in the race for an enjoyable evening.

Anna didn't wait around for the prize. She put cash on her receipt and pleaded homework. No one tried to stop her, and no one argued with her paying for herself.

She drove home on autopilot, half wanting to call Kaci and ask advice, more wanting to test out her theory that Jackson had nice shoulders to cry on. But in the end, she tumbled into bed and had a fitful night of sleep.

The next morning, she was tucking her phone into her

purse on her way out the door for work when she realized she'd missed a text message the night before.

The only thing prettier than this coffee would be your smile right over it.

Anna winced. Her thumbs hovered over her phone.

Sorry, just got this, she typed out quickly. *Hope you didn't wait long. I'll make it up to you later.*

She hit send before she overthought it. Then she dropped her phone into its pocket in her purse, sprinkled food into Walker's oversize brandy snifter, and headed for work.

Because today had to get better.

ANNA DIDN'T SEE Jules until lunchtime. And she was getting paranoid about their paths not crossing. Shortly before noon, though, Jules stepped blank-faced into Anna's cube. "Samples are coming in from the new supplier this afternoon. Make sure you file them right. I'm working this weekend to make up for all these damn meetings."

"Sure." Anna eased back. "You need help?"

"Last I checked, I was qualified to run the tests myself."

Her face choked on a benign smile. "Sure are."

"Damn right."

Anna expected Jules to storm back out. Instead, she loitered in the cube entrance, but she kept her hands off Anna's desk organizer. "So," Anna ventured, "are we okay?"

Jules's blank mask didn't waver. "Were we not okay?" She folded her arms. "You know, being a professional means not taking everything personally. If you have a problem with separating work and fun, then we shouldn't fraternize after office hours."

"Last night wasn't fun."

The wonky eyebrow made an appearance. "Sorry to hear that. Probably a good thing you're always in class. How's that going, by the way? Passing this time?"

Anna bit the inside of her cheek. "Doing fine, thanks." She

rolled her chair closer to her desk. "Last month's reports will be ready after one more spell check."

"Good plan." Jules stalked out and didn't look back.

The rest of the afternoon dragged by. Jules left shortly after four. Anna shut the dinosaur down, grabbed her purse, and headed to Shirley's office.

Her program manager was still in, hammering at her laptop between gulps of her afternoon coffee in her *World's Best Mom* mug. "Yes?"

It was as much of an invitation as Anna expected. She sank into Shirley's faux-leather sitting chair. "I'm worried about Jules."

Shirley finally swiveled away from her computer. "How so?"

"I think she's having some personal problems, but I don't know what to do to help."

"Sometimes you can't help."

"Somebody needs to."

Shirley's hard-ass face dropped. Her skin sagged beneath her eyes, and she was overdue for a touch-up on her gray. She set her glasses aside. "Things get messy at work when you interfere with coworkers' private lives."

"It'll be messy here no matter what if they don't get the help they need at home." Stories about trivia tumbled out. Anna finally held her hands up. "Her family's out West, his is in Texas. I don't know if she has any other friends here besides us at work, and it's not right for her and Brad to go through this alone."

Shirley's lips were turned down so far they hit her jaw line. "Until it interferes with her work, there's nothing I can do."

"You could have a heart."

Shirley's frown went icy. "There are plenty of resources on base to help them deal with their problems. You want to help, go ask them what to do."

"She spends forty to fifty hours a week with us. She'd spend, what, thirty minutes with a base counselor, *if* they'd see her since Brad's out now? I might not be married to the military anymore, but I know the culture. We *are* her family. You know it too. She. Needs. Help."

"And what exactly do you think we can do?"

"If I knew, I wouldn't be in here asking for your expertise. What would your commander have done?"

"Training," Shirley sighed. "Fine. I'll do a touchy-feely briefing at the monthly staff meeting next Thursday. Happy?"

Shirley briefing Jules on touchy-feely would be like the devil's briefing angels on how to use their wings. "Guest speakers are always a nice touch."

"You want one, you find one. Talk to HR. Are we done?"

"Yes, ma'am." Anna stood. "Thank you."

"Get out of here," Shirley said gruffly. "It's the weekend."

She didn't need to be told twice.

Chapter Thirteen

The grace of a woman was evident in her arrival.
—The Temptress of Pecan Lane, by Mae Daniels

NOTHING SAID *SORRY I missed your call* like a fresh-baked pie.

Or so Anna hoped. Was a pie too much? She didn't want to give him the wrong impression. Like that she was *too* attached. Gram had always said the way to a man's heart was through his stomach, but she wasn't looking for his heart.

She should put a note on the pie.

And say what? *I like you, can we be friends? Maybe with benefits?*

Right. She liked him, he liked her. She felt bad for missing coffee so she'd take him a pie. Because she wanted to.

So Sunday afternoon, after she'd studied until her brain resembled molten roadkill, she baked a pie. She studied a few more brain cells out while it cooled, then packed it up.

She thought about calling first, but she was afraid he'd tell her not to come, or worse, get gentlemanly and make her wonder if he was only being polite about inviting her over.

Or if he was just in it for the pie. Not that she'd completely mind, since his kisses had progressed to where she couldn't remember her own name, let alone her ex's, but she hoped he liked her for *something* other than her pie.

When she pulled up in front of his house, the garage door was down. No one answered her knock. No barking either.

Anna had triple-wrapped the pie, so the local critters probably wouldn't bother it if she left it on his porch.

Probably.

He did have a screened-in porch in back. And he was fairly laid back. He wouldn't mind if she left a note telling him it was there, and he'd probably appreciate the pie so much, he wouldn't care if she broke all the way into his house to leave it.

Not that she'd go *that* far. But leaving it on his back porch was reasonable. She rang the doorbell and knocked once more for good measure. Definitely no one home.

She scanned the street. Despite the finally bearable temperatures, no one was out and about. She went off the porch and across the driveway. She'd leave the pie, then go back to her purse for a pen and paper to write the note.

A wooden privacy fence surrounded Jackson's backyard. She crunched over the dying grass and had to step around an ant hill. She shuddered. He'd *definitely* appreciate her leaving this on his back porch. She was two steps from the gate when she spotted an armadillo that wasn't Enrique at the corner of the fence.

It eyed her.

She eyed it right back.

Wait. Was it staring at her *pie?*

She'd thought the only thing armadillos did was to lie on the side of the road with their legs in the air. But this one was very much alive, and it was snuffling toward her.

Her Yankee upbringing was moderately disturbed by this new turn of events.

She hustled the last two steps to the gate handle and tugged. The door didn't budge. The armadillo came closer. She didn't like the semi-crazy look in its eyes.

Were armadillos friendly? This whole it-being-alive thing was disconcerting.

She yanked harder on the door. It caught on something up top. Stupid thing locked from the inside, and not only was she too short to reach over the fence and unhook the latch, the armadillo was sniffing closer.

And those weird dots all over its shell weren't symmetrical.

She took a hesitant step back.

The armadillo took a bold three steps forward.

She scrambled farther back. Her heel banged into an old railroad tie. It bordered the small alcove where Jackson kept his garbage cans. Maybe she could flip one onto the armadillo. She eased up onto the railroad tie, then slid the lid off the closest can, grateful to find it empty and smelling of grass clippings. Jackson *was* a bachelor, after all. Balancing the pie in one hand, she reached for the handle on the garbage bin with the other.

Barking exploded on the driveway. Anna turned with a gasp. She teetered on the railroad tie. The pie tilted. She spun back, reached to steady it. The armadillo jumped straight in the air. Anna shrieked and tried to retreat. Radish bore down on the armadillo. Anna's heel slipped, she lost her balance, and suddenly she was tumbling backward, fighting to keep the pie from flying out of her hands.

She had a moment to process one thought—*This is going to hurt*—when her rear end thumped into a hard object and instead of falling, she was sliding, butt-first, into something round and plastic and grassy-smelling.

It wobbled, then everything stopped. Her feet stuck out of the garbage can. The rim of it dug into her back. Her arms were cocked at a weird angle.

But by God, she'd saved the pie.

A shrill whistle broke the stillness. Radish growled, but she didn't seem to be eating the armadillo. It gave a sniff, then backed away. Radish stalked it until it was out of sight.

Anna gave a heave with her arms and legs, but instead of leveraging herself out of the garbage can, she sank deeper into it, legs akimbo, still clutching the damn pie.

Too bad she hadn't baked her dignity into it.

Jackson ambled into view. He wore running shorts and a ratty Bama T-shirt that dripped with sweat. His face shone with perspiration, and his chest heaved.

Anna squeezed her thighs and tried to pump her legs for momentum to get out. No dice. She was stuck. Stuck and bent in half. "*Urg!*"

Jackson peered at her over the pie. His lips twitched once, then settled into a serene, gentlemanly expression as if he pulled women out of his trash cans every day. "Need some help there, Anna Grace?"

"Oh, I've got it. Thanks." Her cheeks flamed. She was an idiot. An idiot holding a pie in his garbage can. He probably thought she was a stalker. Or crazy. She tried to leverage out with her legs again, but she couldn't move.

With the dangerous armadillo gone, Radish wandered over and sniffed at the pie.

"Back, girl," Jackson said. Radish whined, then thumped onto her haunches. Jackson folded his arms. His eyes went cobalt and crinkly. "Wouldn't be any trouble if you needed a hand."

"I'm good," she insisted. Or she would be, if he'd take the damn pie and leave her alone. She threw her weight back and forth, to get the can rocking so it would fall over and she could scoot out.

Because really, did she *need* to add *pulling me out of a trash can* to his list of things he'd done for her?

"How about I take this here from you." He lifted the pie away. She tried to lower her arms, but she was past armpit-deep. Instead, she flapped, shimmying left and right. She hadn't thought she could sink deeper, but she did. The angle was compressing her lungs.

Crap. She had to ask for help.

He peeled back the aluminum foil and sniffed the pie. "Mmm, cherry. You do a pie proud, Anna Grace." A muscle in his cheek twitched. "Sure I can't give you a hand?"

She tried rocking the can again. Because if she could get out, then she could crawl into a hole and hide until he went inside.

She swung her upper body right, then left, then right again.

The trash can didn't move.

Jackson seemed to choke on something. Despite the ornery gleam in his eyes, she hadn't caught a glimmer of a smile. He set the pie on another can, then gripped her under the armpits and hauled her out in one smooth motion.

Her heart gave one of those weird thumps she was getting used to, and suddenly she was nose-first in hard, sweaty Jackson chest.

She hadn't been near a sweaty male in months.

She hadn't *liked* it for longer.

The testosterone evaporating out of his pores was raw and potent. Her primal nature missed that.

A lot.

Trepidation warred with excitement in her chest. She tilted her chin up and stared at his nose. She hadn't noticed the little bump in it before. Had he played sports? Been in a fight? Or maybe he'd been born that way.

His nostrils flared. She took a fortifying breath, then raised her gaze another inch. His dark lashes were so low, they brushed his cheeks.

It wasn't fair for a man to have lashes that long and thick.

It wasn't fair that he seemed to be waiting for her to make the first move either. She'd taken charge every other time. It was his turn.

Because if he'd kiss her already, she wouldn't have to worry if she was doing it right, if he wanted to kiss her, or if he was only holding her to make sure she was steady. Which would've been nice of him since she wasn't sure there was ground under her feet.

He *did* want to kiss her, didn't he? Or was there another

reason for him to be caressing her waist with his thumbs?

"Okay, Anna Grace?"

That low, husky voice sent a shiver down her spine. "Peachy." Except for the part where every nerve ending in her body had a couple of loose electrons.

"Next time, I'm gonna make you ask for help."

He dropped his hold on her. Those electrons skittered off into the ether. Radish sniffed at the pie, but Jackson snapped his fingers, and she sank onto her haunches again.

Was the dog *pouting?* Anna could sympathize. She swallowed her disappointment and tried to put on her happy face. Maybe she smelled too bad to be kissed. His momma'd probably warned him about trashy girls. She gestured to the pie. "Sorry I missed your message Thursday night. I wanted to make it up to you."

That big, goofy grin sent her heart pitter-pattering again.

"Darlin', you just did, and it didn't have anything to do with the pie."

She shifted from one foot to the next. Her back was cramping in a weird place. "I didn't want to leave it out where bugs might get it."

He reached over the fence and clicked the lock open. His dog trotted through. "Come on in."

That sounded like a very bad idea. A very good, very bad idea.

"You got supper plans?" he said.

Her plans hadn't included wondering half the night if he wanted to kiss her. She had too few brain cells left to figure out that puzzle. "I have some leftover hot dish I should eat before it goes bad."

"Hot dish?"

"The original Minnesota casserole."

"I've got homemade fried chicken and biscuits."

"You make it?"

Did her heart *always* have to do that pitter-patter thing when he grinned at her?

"My momma sent it home with me."

She *did* have a freezer, and hot dish froze well. She hadn't had real Southern fried chicken in—well, longer than it had been since she'd been turned on by a hot, sweaty man. "I wouldn't want to—"

"Of course you wouldn't. But you brought dessert, so let's call it even."

"You really think a pie makes dinner and coffee even?"

His lips were twitching again. He shot a glance at the garbage can. "Maybe, maybe not. But you look like you could use a good meal, and I never object to pretty company."

"As long as you're sure it's not a bother."

The gate clanged shut behind them. "Anna Grace, you're a lot of things, but you're never a bother."

Like he'd tell her if she were.

He let them into the house through the screened-in porch. Radish moseyed along next to her. Anna scratched the dog behind her ears. "How'd Radish get her name?"

He slid his phone and the pie onto the counter and flashed another of those ornery grins. "Aw, now, that ain't a right proper story for a lady. You go on and make yourself at home. Won't take but a minute to get cleaned up."

He disappeared around the corner toward what she assumed to be the bedroom, and she found herself as disappointed as Radish when Jackson wouldn't let her sniff the pie.

Because she wouldn't have minded getting cleaned up with him.

IF JACKSON HADN'T thought Anna would've gotten derailed putting his bedroom to rights, he would've invited her to join him. Instead, he hopped about, tossed off his dirty clothes and then dug for a clean pair of jeans and a shirt in the laundry basket. One of these days, he'd burn some leave to finish putting the house in order. But between all the time he'd been spending up in Auburn or hunting, and then TDYs and training and getting up to speed at work, sorting out the house hadn't taken priority. He'd done what he needed to live in it and put the rest off for when he had more time.

Seeing as he had a woman who'd brought him pie here now, getting his bedroom put to rights was fast moving up his list of priorities.

But first, a shower.

He was back out in the kitchen in less than five minutes. Anna wasn't there. He poked his head around the corner and found her sitting in a pile of books and movies, label maker out beside her, nose buried in a Mae Daniels book.

She caught him watching her and pointed to her label maker. "They're temporary."

He flashed her an easy grin. "Think you're missing your calling, Anna Grace."

She ignored that and held the book up, and he caught the laughter dancing in her eyes. "One of your favorites?"

Summerswept. He'd liked it the first time around, but it was an older Mae Daniels. She'd gotten better and better since then. He dug into the pile and came up with *Southern Honey.* "Try this one."

The smile on her face slid into an O. "Does Lance know about this?"

"Shoot, Anna Grace, who do you think gave 'em to me?" He snagged *Hero Nurse* out of the pile too. "Don't let the title fool you. You can bring it back next time you're over. Might could learn a thing or two from Bernice in there. You like okra?"

She snapped out of her surprise to give the same kind of nose wrinkle he expected out of someone who hadn't grown up on the good stuff.

"That's okay, I got potato chips too," he said.

She moved to stand.

"Sit," he said. "You go on and keep having fun." He snagged the remote off the counter and handed it over. "Don't reckon you'll need this, but if you do, hope you like football or hunting shows. I disabled all the girly channels."

"Of course you did." She tucked the three books into her purse, and she was smiling when she went back to his mess.

Nice symbiotic relationship they had.

As it turned out, even though Anna insisted an undying love for the unfortunately named Golden Gophers, she was pretty smart about football. She didn't seem to mind watching the Bama game he'd recorded while he was taking Mamie out to the shooting range. And though he'd been sure it would rankle Anna to eat greasy, cold fried chicken on the couch, she helped herself to a few extra paper towels and dug in beside him.

She even opened up that bottle of ketchup he'd bought after Kaci mentioned Anna thought it was its own food group. Long as he didn't watch her dipping Momma's fried chicken in it, he was fine.

She skipped the biscuit, which he couldn't fault her for, since Miss Dolly's niece's cousin's biscuits were light and flaky as a brick, but she liked her chips well enough to sort them into piles. Broken chips, whole chips, and it took him a minute to puzzle out that the third pile was folded-over chips. Looked like she was saving them for last, so he slid a couple of his own over onto her plate, making sure he accidentally-on-purpose brushed his arm over hers.

She blinked a couple times quick. "Thank you."

He got a notion it'd been a while since anybody noticed the little things. Probably longer than since her moron of an ex took himself out of her life.

"Leaving more room for pie," he said.

She rolled her eyes, but she smiled. And then she ate all of her chips—without ketchup, even—and helped herself to a couple more off his plate while they watched the game. Alabama kicked off after their field goal. Anna gestured to the screen with her chips. "Is it hard to tell the difference between the teams?" she asked.

He'd taken enough ribbing in his life over not seeing colors right, but she seemed honestly curious. And for once, he found himself on the laughing side. "Nah, I just root for whoever doesn't have *North Texas* scrawled over their helmets."

"Oh. That makes sense."

"I'm a right smart one."

She crunched into another chip, and he didn't mind listening to that at all. Play continued in the game, and he leaned close enough to her to smell her hair. Smelled pretty.

And a bit like grass.

"So," Anna said, "how's a guy who grew up in Auburn end up going to school in Alabama and getting a tiger paw tattoo, but live to tell the tale?"

She was a right smart one too, sneaking that in there. "You learn not to talk about it."

She tilted her head back and peered up at him. A commercial came on. He paused the game and took the plates into the kitchen, wondering if it was his imagination or if she was giving him a dirty look for avoiding the question.

He decided it was his imagination, because that had this evening ending better than her giving him dirty looks. Once he slid the plates into the sink, he went digging in his drawer for a spatula to serve the pie with, but came up empty. "Anna Grace, you know where my pie server is?"

"When's the last time you used it?" She popped into the kitchen and leaned against the counter. Her shorts had a few stains he guessed had come from her tumble earlier, but he didn't reckon he needed to point that out. Still, she didn't seem bothered at all, so that was a good sign their symbiotic relationship could survive his avoiding a question or two.

He scratched his head. "Don't remember."

"If it's not in the drawer, I'd check your dishwasher."

She seemed to get a kick out of knowing his kitchen better than he knew it himself. He pulled the dishwasher door open and about jumped out of his skin.

His bronze armadillo stared up at him from the depths of his dishwasher.

"Oh, hey, Enrique," Anna said. Her lips quivered like she was barely keeping it in, but since she crossed the kitchen to bend over and pat his armadillo, putting her that much closer to him, he'd give her this one. "How's it going? Oh, look. Pie server."

She lifted it out and smiled at him with all the innocence of a woman. He took the utensil, set it on the counter, and kicked the dishwasher shut. He closed the small gap between them. "You having fun, Anna Grace?" he asked, slipping his hands to those hips that were getting some curve back.

Speaking of curves, there went her lips too, all full of sass and some intentions he could get on board with. "I am, thank you." Her fingers slid up his arms and her bare calf brushed his, leaving him wondering how he managed to find near about the perfect woman.

Watched football, ate cold chicken, didn't want commitment.

"But that was awful mean of you to leave Enrique in the dishwasher," she said.

"You want an audience?"

She shivered against him, but since she leaned closer, he took the shiver as a mark in his favor. "Maybe not."

Her lashes flirted with her cheeks. Her fingers had walked up his arm and shoulder to do something to the back of his neck that he was enjoying in other parts of his body too. He ran his fingers through that soft, pretty hair, then nudged her head closer to his. A hint of a smile teased at those soft lips. He brushed them with his own.

She angled closer. He took his time enjoying all that soft skin and warm mouth. He did love a good long kiss with a kissable woman. He liked those little noises she made too, the way her leg crept up his, how she pressed closer and closer even though his body had gone past gentlemanly about the time he'd started looking at her lips.

He found himself mighty glad she didn't like biscuits. Mighty glad she was willing to share her pie with him too.

He was thinking about giving in to those little hints she was dropping about where she wanted his hands to go when AC/DC exploded out of his phone on the counter.

Wasn't often Mamie irritated him, but either her timing was bad, or she knew he was sampling a Yankee's biscuits. Frustrated the heck out of him to pull away. "Sorry, Anna Grace. This one's important."

She took a shaky breath. "Okay. But I'll be here. You know. When you're done."

Just like that, she had him smiling again. "Pretty sure I can find you."

He snagged the phone and took himself into his bedroom. If he could get the bed cleared off and keep Anna focused on kissing him until they got there, he figured he had a sixty-five-percent chance. "Yes, ma'am?"

"Sugarplum, I've been—you got a girl over there?"

He tucked the phone under his chin so he could shovel underwear into a box. "Yes, ma'am."

"She bake biscuits?"

"Dunno." He pushed his guns under the bed then shoved his travel bag under too, listening to Mamie think as loud as a few other women he knew.

"You ain't asked her," she said.

"Already got a freezer chock full of 'em. Didn't see any reason to."

"Interesting."

Stick his head on a platter and call him toast. Mamie had that tone again. That Mamie-on-a-mission tone.

"Thought you'd be bowling tonight," he said. He dumped a stack of *Air Force* magazines in the closet.

"Me and the girls are taking a night off," she said.

Jackson straightened. "Everything okay, Mamie?"

"Nothing you need to be worrying over. Got a little bit of a sore shoulder after all that firing yesterday. I'll put some ice on it and be better right quick."

"You sure that's all?"

"Had a few more hunting questions, but I can call you back later. You go on and have some fun now. And don't forget protection."

Didn't matter how many times she used that phrase over his lifetime, still made him wince knowing Mamie knew what was going on in his head. "Yes, ma'am."

They disconnected. There was still too much junk piled on his dresser, but he'd made a clean path to the bed and it was made. He sucked in a breath, double-checked he had unexpired protection, then headed back to the kitchen.

He turned the corner, and Anna's phone beeped. She was still propped against the counter. A sweet smile curved her lips up. She noticed him and treated him to a *you silly guy* look. "Cute," she said.

"Wasn't me," he started, but she'd apparently already figured that out.

Because when she looked down at her phone, her smile dropped away, her eyebrows knit tighter than a sweater, and her whole body went rigid as an armadillo's armor.

He had a feeling he wouldn't be needing that protection now. He approached her slow, as he would a wounded deer. "Okay, Anna Grace?"

"Yeah." She sucked her lips into her mouth, staring at the floor.

"Rain check?" Being the gentlemanly thing to say didn't make it what he wanted to say.

Her eyes squeezed shut. "Sorry." But she lifted her head and looked straight at him, and he saw something else he wasn't used to seeing in Anna Grace.

Whatever that message was about, it had her spitting mad.

Only two things he knew of that caused a woman to look like that, and since she didn't have any babies to protect, he was betting it was a man. But she wasn't railing at Jackson, so he took that as a good sign she might bake him another pie sometime.

Might give him a gander at her peaches one of these days

too.

He gestured to the cabinet under his sink. "Got some Windex if it'd help."

A smile broke through her anger, but she was still simmering. "Don't think it'll squirt that far, but thank you." She crossed the room, went up on her tiptoes to brush his cheek with a sweet little peck, then stepped away. "Thanks for dinner too."

"You going to Lance and Kaci's wedding?" he asked, and then wanted to kick himself.

Both because taking a girl to a wedding went against his religion, and because he wanted her to go with him anyway.

She bent to pet Radish. Her doe-eyes were headlight wary. "I—I suppose I'll see you there."

He should've been relieved. Wasn't like he wanted the expectations of having a date at a wedding. Still, long after he'd walked her out to her car and seen her off, he was puzzling over how he was going to handle finding the perfect woman.

Because despite how long Momma'd been saying women were perfection, this was the first time in his life he'd ever found evidence she might be right.

Chapter Fourteen

The perfection he found in one woman made the imperfections in the rest all the more obvious.
—The Temptress of Pecan Lane, by Mae Daniels

ANNA CREDITED NEIL'S text message Sunday night to drunken texting. Because why else would he send her a message asking how she'd been since they hadn't talked in a while?

But when she got a second one Thursday afternoon at work, in the middle of the day, followed by an email to the same effect, she couldn't deny he was talking to *her*. On purpose.

So she deleted the messages and called Beth.

"Molar extraction going on here, Anna-banana," her sister said. "Make it quick."

"Neil texted me."

"*You still have his number in your phone?*"

"Well, yeah. How else am I supposed to avoid his phone calls?"

Beth's sigh echoed through the lab. Jules was at a staff meeting, and Anna was supposed to be proofreading more reports.

"Who's that friend you keep talking about? Kaci? I need her number," Beth said.

"Why?"

"So she can steal your phone and delete Neil."

"But the next time he texts, I won't know it's him, and I won't know to not answer."

"Good! Say *who the fuck is this?*—sorry Trina, I'll get a quarter—and let him get the hint that you've moved on with your life."

A loud crash boomed behind Anna. Heart leaping, she spun in her chair. Jules was in the doorway. A stack of binders were scattered on the floor.

"I'm getting back to this extraction, and you're deleting him," Beth said. "Delete. Him. Understand?"

"Yes, ma'am."

"God, you need to get out of the South." The line clicked off.

"Hey, Jules," Anna said, her pulse thinking about settling back into a normal rhythm. "What's up?"

Other than the guest speaker—on the topics depression and spousal abuse—at the staff meeting. Anna wasn't invited to staff meetings, so she had no idea how it had gone over.

Her optimism only went so far, and Jules's lip-curl didn't look positive.

"Your new sample-tracking color-coding system was the toast of the town." Jules nudged the binders. "Shirley wants the last two years of data synced to match. Preferably by next week. Corporate's coming."

Anna whimpered. Someone wanted to sink her happy boat. Not that she didn't appreciate color-coding. Like Jackson said, it was her calling. But her first round of tests were soon, and she'd signed up to get officially certified on all the lab equipment.

The fun kept coming.

"Hope you didn't have any weekend plans," Jules said.

None that she was excited about. "Not really. How about you guys?"

Jules gave her the wary eye. "We're getting out of town."

"Oh. Nice."

Southern Fried Blues

"Yep." Jules hitched a shoulder. "Enjoy your weekend."

Shirley stopped in shortly after Jules left. "Nice speaker," she said unconvincingly.

"It was short notice. Did Jules even listen?"

"Couldn't tell." Shirley gestured to the binders. "Redoing the old stuff to match?"

"Jules said—" Anna buried her head in her hands and groaned. "Is Corporate really coming in for a visit next week?"

"Yep."

"But you didn't ask me to make the old data match the new system before they get here."

"Nope. Not a bad idea though. Eventually." Shirley tapped her pack of cigarettes against the cube door. "Well, kid, at least now you know she was listening."

But it didn't mean she heard.

THERE WASN'T MUCH of anything moving in the trees today, not in the right direction anyway. Jackson had a notion that had something to do with his hunting buddy.

She hadn't clamped her trap for more than the millisecond it took her to suck in a breath since they left his truck this morning. Radish hadn't been happy to be left home this morning, but right now, Jackson was jealous of the old girl. Least she had some peace.

"How many times did it take you to pass economics?" Louisa was saying.

He swiveled his head away from the tree he'd been scanning to look his baby sister up and down. "You failed economics?"

"My teacher was a real dickhead."

An explosion the likes of which he'd never heard from his daddy's mouth erupted in his head, accompanied by a couple of tirades he *had* endured from his momma. "You talk to Mamie with that mouth?"

She rolled her eyes heavenward, though if she thought

Daddy would've been on her side, she was flat wrong. "He was. It's like he thought we all wanted to be *economists*." She spat the word like it meant the same thing as *murderers*. "Plus we *all* had other classes."

"Some teachers are tough. Means you gotta be tougher."

Her lower lip curved. Barely a smidge, but he noticed.

"Not everybody's tough as a big old military officer," she said.

"An economics class isn't war." He scanned the trees again. A branch rustled. A squirrel paused on it. He lifted his shotgun and aimed at the furry little thing.

"You got one?" Louisa yanked out her shotgun and bumped Jackson's arm. "Where? I wanna get it."

The squirrel jumped branches, and Jackson watched its path disappear in a zig-zag line of rustling leaves. "Louisa. Ain't gonna get a thing if you don't pipe down."

Didn't need to look close to see the lip now.

Jackson stifled a sigh. That no-women-during-hunting-season rule apparently applied to girl hunting buddies too. He slouched against a tree. "We hunting or jabbering?"

The lip got bigger in direct proportion to her narrowing eyes. If it wasn't for her having Daddy's eyes and dimple, he would've wondered if they were full siblings, but she had 'em all right.

Used 'em like Momma did though. "Some people can do *both*. Guess the big old Air Force didn't teach you that yet."

"Air Force taught me to keep my trap shut if I didn't want to draw attention to myself."

"Yeah, well, the squirrel won't shoot back at you."

Sweet baby Jesus, he'd brought a pacifist hunting. "You ever go hunting with Craig?"

That was a silent snarl if he ever saw one. Her face got so scrunchy even her hair curled up tighter.

He put the safety on his shotgun and tucked it down at his side. "What's wrong with Craig?"

"Mr. Daddy's Favorite? Like *he* had to work in college. He

knew Russ would hire him. But he's always picking on me because I'm a girl."

Jackson's throat muscles worked. He'd herded lieutenants who left him wondering about the future of the Air Force, but not one of them, not even the LT who had his momma write him an excuse for his PFT, had left him unable to form a coherent response.

Louisa had that stubborn debutante pose going on, so he eventually snapped his own trap shut and went back to scanning the trees.

Louisa slouched beside him. "I'm just glad Uncle Sam sent you back here close enough for me to go hunting with someone who can handle a gun."

He slid his eyes to her. Girl was all talk. He was sure of that.

But he couldn't figure out why.

"We doing this again next Saturday?" she asked.

Never thought he'd be grateful for a buddy tying the knot, but Lance and Kaci's wedding suddenly seemed like a vacation. "Busy next Saturday."

Louisa made a girly snort. "It's always something, isn't it? Sunday then."

"Sunday's not looking too good either." For Louisa. It was looking mighty good for Jackson. Anna Grace didn't have classes Saturday *or* Sunday, and he hadn't missed that internal war she'd been fighting between getting sleep and going home with him after coffee two nights ago.

Louisa gave him the psychic eye. "You're not giving up hunting for a whole weekend because of a girl, are you?"

"Nope." Far as he was concerned, he was giving up a whole hunting weekend to suffer through and recover from a wedding.

But when they headed their separate ways after Louisa had talked his ears deaf and scared all the squirrels away, she insisted he'd meet her Sunday. So he sent Craig a message asking him to watch out for her, then went home to Radish.

Empty-handed and a little empty-headed too.

Chapter Fifteen

Life went on, except when it went backward.
—The Temptress of Pecan Lane, *by Mae Daniels*

BY THE TIME KACI'S wedding rolled around, Anna was waffling between utter sexual frustration and the giddy feeling that came from being thoroughly courted.

She mostly got why things with Jackson hadn't progressed much since she fell in his trash can. He'd gone TDY and then hunting a couple of times. The one night they'd met for coffee, she'd been so exhausted that if she'd taken him up on his offer of a place to crash, she wouldn't have made it past his front door, much less all the way to his bedroom. He'd seemed to understand when she insisted she'd stay at Kaci's instead.

But he'd texted. And she'd texted back. And he'd arranged to have Kaci deliver a few more notes and another box of chocolates, so when she put Kaci and Lance's wedding gift in her car, she put an overnight bag next to it.

She was wearing her favorite aubergine chiffon dress. The cut was borderline unfashionable, but no one would notice. Not with the bridesmaid dresses that Kaci's mom had picked out. Besides, she loved the way the smooth fabric brushed over her legs.

And she already knew it went well with Air Force mess

dress.

Kaci had not only refused Anna's offers of last-minute assistance, she'd forbidden Anna from arriving at The Harrington any earlier than twenty minutes before the ceremony. Something about her mother, Yankee interference, and everyone's constitution. After the fallout of the last wedding Anna had attended at The Harrington, she was more afraid of infecting Kaci's wedding with bad juju.

She arrived thirteen minutes before the ceremony. The parking spot she found two places down from Jackson's truck had to be a good omen. Some of the tension that had popped up at the sight of the grandiose hotel melted away.

More tension dissipated when Jackson swung out of his truck the same time she stepped out of her car.

But then she spied someone who wouldn't have been included on the guest list even if the wedding was in hell.

"Oh, shit," she whispered.

He leaned against the building, well out of sight of the entrance around the corner, fidgeting with his phone. His tie was crooked and despite the pleasant seventy-two-degree weather, he'd already mopped his brow three times with a handkerchief.

She left the gift in her car but snagged her small purse so she'd have somewhere to stash her keys and phone, then gave Jackson two seconds to catch up. "Anna Grace?"

She latched onto his arm, ignoring the flutter in her heart from touching him, and pulled him toward Dr. Kelly. "How are you with distracting retired colonels who are crashing their ex-wives' wedding?" she murmured, looking anywhere but at him and the bronze oak leaves on his shoulders.

She hoped like hell after *this* wedding she'd be stripping a man out of uniform.

Especially since Neil had nothing on Jackson. The uniform had made Neil look good, but Jackson made the uniform look good.

"I, ah, he—what?"

Anna nodded toward Dr. Kelly. "Kaci's ex," she whispered.

Jackson's face twisted into an expression that made her wonder if his momma knew he knew those ungentlemanly words. His lips settled into a resigned line. "Gonna owe me for this one, Anna Grace."

"Got an overnight bag in my car."

He didn't twitch a single muscle, but his eyes turned to midnight. "Got a pie in it?"

She laughed. "Something better."

Dr. Kelly looked at both of them, and his eyes narrowed.

Jackson nudged Anna forward. "Works for me."

Kaci's ex looked ready to bolt, and not toward the parking lot, so Anna stepped up her pace. "Hi, Dr. Kelly," she called. "Beautiful day, isn't it?"

Jackson gave a soft snort. "Smooth, Anna Grace."

She elbowed him. Dr. Kelly angled closer to the corner.

"Whew, this place is crawling with military guys today," Anna said. "Weren't you—"

"Evening, sir," Jackson interrupted, sticking his hand out. "Been a while."

Dr. Kelly clasped Jackson's hand. "Stuck it out this long, have you?" the older man said. He spared another eyeball toward Anna before focusing on Jackson again. "Thought after AFIT, you'd hook up with Boeing."

Anna stifled a surprised squeak. Neil always said it was a small Air Force. Guess it was true.

"Not in it for the money." Jackson nudged Anna.

"Nice to see you," she murmured, and slunk around the side of the building to let Jackson handle it.

She thought *Kaci* probably owed him for that one, but Anna was willing to take one for the team and pay her friend's debt.

She was a giver like that.

She pushed through the revolving door and into the reception area. Clumps of people in fancy attire milled about the room in a disorganized line to the ballroom.

The ballroom where her marriage had evaporated.

Hoo-boy.

"Anna?" A somewhat familiar, lanky brunette captain approached. She flashed a smile at Anna, her brown eyes keenly observant. The wings on her mess dress flashed.

Anna didn't know much about Lance's sister beyond her call sign and that she flew fighters—and that Jackson had once asked her out—but if anyone fit the bill as a relative of Lance's, this woman did. "Lightning?"

She tipped her head up when she laughed. "Cheri, please. Kaci's asking for you."

"Everything okay?"

"Mostly." She leaned in and lowered her voice while they picked through the crowd. "Kaci's momma insisted on doing everyone's makeup. You seen the bridesmaids? Her momma's turning this wedding into *Gone with the Wind* meets *That Seventies Show*."

Instead of heading toward the ballroom, Cheri led Anna up the back stairs to the second floor. She slid a key-card into the door slot, then pushed in. "Kaci? Found her."

"Thanks, sugar." Kaci poked her head out of the bathroom, looking like an albino raccoon with purple lips. She shooed Cheri away. "Go on and make sure our mommas aren't fighting over that big flower to-do, will you?"

Cheri inclined her head, her brown eyes flashing in easy amusement. "Yes, ma'am." The door clicked shut behind her.

Kaci yanked Anna into the bathroom. "Ol' grandpappy's here, isn't he?" Her pulse fluttered in her neck. She grabbed onto the yards of lace enveloping her, twitched it between her fingers, dropped it, then grabbed it again. "I swear I saw his car drive up when I was looking to see if Lance was here yet."

"Did you invite him?"

Kaci cocked her head and planted a fist on her hip. "Do I *look* like I need more wedding drama?"

She looked like she needed a tequila shot and a ticket to Vegas. "Kaci. Forget your mother. Forget your ex-husband.

Forget the flowers. You're here today to marry Lance, and that's what matters, right?"

Kaci's hands wobbled. Her lips crumpled. "Sugar, you'd tell me if I was making a mistake, right?" She flitted her hand at the door. Her engagement ring caught the light and sparkled in the mirror. "My momma, she says she ain't doing this so I can ditch another one. I didn't ask her to do it at all, but what if I'm not really the marrying kind? Or what if I *am* the marrying kind, but I'm not the *being* married kind?"

Her eyes shone with unshed tears. Anna's heart squeezed for her friend. "What's the first thing you do every morning?"

Kaci visibly swallowed. She nodded. "Go on."

"Who's the first person you call with good or bad news?"

"Keep talking, sugar."

"Who do you trust more than anyone to understand what you need, when you need it?"

A crocodile tear rolled down Kaci's overly rouged cheek. "Ol' grandpappy never got it."

"If you saw them side-by-side, would you still take Lance, or would you walk away from both of them?"

Kaci smacked her. "Quit talking stupid, sugar. Of course I'd marry Lance."

Anna smiled. "Then what's the problem?"

"No problem." Kaci yanked her skirt and adjusted the girls. "You go on and get lined up for your seat. I've got a man to get hitched to."

Anna gestured to Kaci's face. "You want some help with that first?"

"Lordy, yes."

Anna pulled a small stash of makeup wipes from her purse, and the two of them went to work making Kaci look like Kaci again. "So, if ol' grandpappy did show up," Anna said nonchalantly, "it wouldn't bother you?"

Kaci's brow furrowed. "You know what, sugar? I don't think it would."

"Even if he made a scene?"

Kaci dropped her eyeliner. "Did that man make a scene at my wedding before it even started?"

"Not yet." Anna glanced at her phone. "At least, not that I'm aware of."

"*Hmph.*" Kaci grabbed the liner again and leaned into the mirror. "It'd be a story for the grandkids if he did."

"You *are* one-hundred-percent certain you're divorced from him, right?"

Kaci smacked her in the arm again. "Someday I'm gonna be asking you the same question. Won't be so funny then."

"Go ahead and keep telling yourself that."

Kaci leaned back, blinked at her reflection, and then grinned so big the subtle lines that spoke her age popped out. The door to the room clicked, and stale air filtered in.

"Ready, Kaci?" Cheri asked. "Your momma's having a conniption down there about the music going on too long. And Lance is starting to look nervous."

"Go on and tell Lance he doesn't have a thing to worry about," Kaci said. "He's gonna be stuck with me soon enough. He can wait another three minutes. And ignore my momma. She's hell-bent on not being happy enough with this since we wouldn't take it back to Mississippi, so there's no sense in even trying."

"Yes, ma'am." She looked at Anna. "But can I borrow you for a minute?"

"Go on and take her," Kaci said. "I got one last thing to do." She blinked rapidly and gestured up to the ceiling. "Promised my daddy I'd give him a minute on my day."

Cheri led Anna back downstairs. They snagged a bridesmaid who was made up to look more like a victim in a virgin horror flick than an attendant in a military wedding. "Kaci's in Room 254," Cheri said with the same inflection she might've given to a weather report. "She'll be down in a minute."

The girl scurried off toward Kaci's momma. Even though the matriarch wasn't in sight, Anna knew she was that direction because of the flood of teary-eyed girls heading away from her. Cheri flashed a dimple. "Still gotta watch out for my little brother." She led Anna into the ballroom, where most of the chairs were occupied for the ceremony.

Exactly the same as they had been for Jules and Brad's wedding.

She sent a silent prayer to Kaci's daddy that this one ended better for all involved.

Cheri gestured behind the door. "Here you go."

Jackson stood at ease, waiting. He cocked a brow at Anna. "Any other problems?" His lips did their telltale twitching in the corners.

"Nope. You?"

"Let Lance have a go with him. The good professor's promised to be civilized."

Anna felt her jaw hang.

Jackson chuckled and offered her his arm. "Sometimes, Anna Grace, us menfolk know what we're doing."

"But only sometimes."

"Nah." His eyes crinkled. "Most of the time."

THE WEDDING WENT off without a hitch, thanks, Anna was sure, to Jackson's insistence that they flank Dr. Kelly while he watched his ex-wife marry her new love. And as far as Anna could tell, it took only one little throat-clearing from Jackson to keep Dr. Kelly in his seat when the justice of the peace asked if anyone objected. When the bride and groom finished their vows, Dr. Kelly headed for the door. Jackson followed, but was back beside Anna before the couple finished their first kiss.

Anna lifted an eyebrow.

Jackson nodded.

So that was that. No more ex-husband wedding crashers.

Once the wedding party departed the room, the guests were ushered out into the hallway for the open bar while the hotel staff set up the ballroom for dinner. Jackson got sucked into a discussion with a couple of captains who worked for him, but he gave Anna a smile that promised she'd have his attention soon enough. She wandered through the crowd talking with friends. Lance had invited everyone in the CGOA, and Kaci had invited the entire physics department and half of the other departments on campus. Because, she'd said, if her mother was paying for a party, then by golly, they were having a party.

And it was definitely a party. By the time dinner was announced, Anna had relaxed enough to have forgotten her bad memories of The Harrington.

But then she sat down at her assigned seat.

And found a face from her own past smiling hesitantly at her. Slightly crooked teeth, medals just this side of off-center, wary guilt in his eyes.

She couldn't stifle a surprised gasp. Her heart pounded, then spun as though her chest were in a centrifuge. Her fingers and toes iced as if they'd been dipped in liquid nitrogen. Her breathing went shallow and rapid.

He wasn't supposed to text her.

He wasn't supposed to email her.

And he sure as hell wasn't supposed to show up here, where he'd publicly dumped her then left her, and sit there smiling at her like he was stupid enough to think she'd consider smiling back.

Her blood pulsed in her head, thrumming and swirling and crashing through her veins until it was louder than the din of the wedding guests around them.

If he ruined *this* wedding, she'd dip his extremities in liquid nitrogen, chop them off, and shoot *them* up on a firecracker.

She leaned back and folded her arms to block the view of her rapidly rising and falling chest.

Not all his extremities.

Just one.

Neil's smile faltered faster than his iPod had sunk in Kaci's pool. "Hey, Anna."

As if he were supposed to be here.

As if they were friends.

As if he was an idiot.

Anna could've asked him a million things. Why he was here? Who helped him get in? How had he arranged to be at her assigned table? What in *hell* did he hope to accomplish?

Instead, she pointed to the door. "Leave."

The hairs on the back of her neck stood up. She looked to her left, and found Jackson watching her two tables over. His gaze flicked to Neil, then back to Anna. "Okay?" he mouthed. He looked as disappointed as Radish did upon being denied fried chicken.

The spinning in her chest stopped and a fire licked up in its place. She glared at Neil again. "What would your mother say if she knew you'd crashed a wedding?" she hissed.

Neil's cheek twitched. "My mother? What does she have to do with anything?"

Anna stood so fast her chair tipped. She snatched her place tag and pointed at Neil with it. "Southern hospitality might dictate you're welcome to stay, but I'm not Southern, and you need to get the hell out of here. You are *not* ruining this wedding too."

"Maybe we could—"

"Excuse me, Anna Grace." Jackson was suddenly beside her, his drawl bordering on dumb redneck. "Wondering if you might do me a favor and switch places."

Her eyes darted between her ex-husband and the man she'd hoped to strip out of his uniform tonight. Neil's brows dipped in the pouty-disappointed look he used to get when it was her turn to pick the movie for date night. Jackson stayed cool and calm and Jacksonlike. She finally settled her gaze on him. "I—"

"Don't need any help," he finished. He put his hand at the small of her back and nudged. *Go on*, his gaze said. *Cool your jets and take it outside later.*

Great. Now he'd do the man thing with *her* ex-husband.

Jackson's lips quirked up. Just a smidge, right there in the corner.

The room was growing quieter and people were starting to notice. Anna lifted her chin and headed for Jackson's seat. Kaci and Lance were laughing with Cheri. Kaci's momma was adjusting the straps on the dress of a junior bridesmaid. They hadn't noticed. Maybe this reception was salvageable.

If Jackson and Neil both survived sharing a meal.

Anna's new seat was between two of Lance's cousins. They had almost as many stories about their misspent youths as Kaci did about hers. Still, it wasn't enough to distract Anna. And when dinner ended and the cake was cut and the toasts done—without any overtly awkward moments this time—Neil dropped into the seat Lance's cousin abandoned.

"Listen, Anna, can we talk?"

She stood. "Nope." Jackson was still at the other table, nodding politely to one of Kaci's older female relatives, but she knew he was watching.

Waiting to be asked to help, she supposed.

And she couldn't decide if she appreciated it or not.

"I'm sorry you're upset," Neil said. "If you'd give me a minute—"

She didn't let him finish. She was too busy walking away.

Kaci and Lance were on the dance floor, happy and blissful. Anna hoped they stayed that way for many, many years.

She herself would've been satisfied with just being happy. But Neil was following her, so she went the one place he wouldn't follow.

Not in uniform, anyway.

Five minutes later, Cheri joined her in the bathroom. "From Jackson." She handed Anna a margarita. "And I introduced your friend to three of the bridesmaids, so he's currently occupied if you want to come out."

"I'm not hiding," Anna said. "I'm avoiding making a scene."

Cheri laughed. "Too bad. C'mon. I've got lots of practice being a wingman. You've earned a nice time tonight."

She and Cheri returned to the ballroom. On one corner of the dance floor, Neil had his own fan club. He was slow-dancing with two women while three more giggled and watched. He looked as happy as if he were being pecked to death by a couple of loons. "You're good," Anna said.

"Have to be." Cheri flashed a cheeky grin. "*Now* let's have a party."

Chapter Sixteen

She had no fears of becoming too comfortable. Not when life was all too willing to smack her upside the head.
—The Temptress of Pecan Lane, by Mae Daniels

IF JACKSON HADN'T been in uniform, he would've handled this ex-husband business differently. Good-old-boy style. But he *was* in uniform, and he'd been raised to have better manners than wedding crashers.

Besides, he didn't reckon he'd get any pie if he got in Anna Grace's way.

How hiding out in the bathroom was winning, he couldn't quite figure, but he'd never claimed to understand a woman's *why*. Just her *what*. And Anna's *what* was akin to Craig's baby girl's *I do it myself*.

One of the bridesmaids eyed him. She had enough looks going for her underneath all that poufed fabric and big old hair bow that he was willing to bet her biscuits suffered for it. She gave him a coy smile. Miss Flo and Miss Ophelia would've liked this one. The girl put the right amount of swing in her hip when she took that tentative step toward him.

But he had better plans for tonight, so he pulled Anna Grace's cake plate closer to him. The girl's eyes shifted to the plate, then back up at him. Her nose got a crease up top, and she swung her hips right around the other way.

Jackson coughed back a chuckle.

"You are my hero," Anna Grace suddenly said next to him. She set the margarita down and flopped into her seat. All that soft material in her dress rippled around her legs as he hoped his sheets would before the end of the night. She snatched the cake plate—sans cake—and went to work sorting the mints he'd piled up as high as he could.

He leaned in close to her. She hadn't said *thank you* exactly, so he didn't offer up that it was his pleasure. Instead, he took a sniff of her hair. "Still hoping for some pie."

"Your odds are definitely improving." She flashed some tooth with her smile.

Cheri sat on his other side, moving sedately in her mess dress. He had a good feeling she would've rather spun the chair around and straddled it as she would've in a flight suit, but that ornery spark told him she was having fun in her own right. "She won't let me take care of him."

"I didn't say anything about after the reception," Anna said. She had five piles of mints going, lightest to darkest. She flicked a glance at Jackson. "What? No *that ain't right fit talk for ladies?*"

Funny girl, his Anna Grace. "No, ma'am. I trust she'll do what needs doing."

"That's right forward thinking of you."

"Forward thinking my ass." Cheri leaned around him. "He got on my bad side once."

Anna mirrored her, talking around Jackson like he was a decoration.

Not that he didn't think he could be. Mamie liked to tell him he was handsomer than a June bug in uniform, and she swore on her collard greens she wasn't just saying that.

"What happened?" Anna asked.

"He tried to hold a door for me."

"Now don't go getting any ideas that I was playing favorites or think anybody's weaker," Jackson told Anna. "I held the door for all of 'em."

"All the ladies?"

Cheri laughed. "They looked like ladies, didn't they?"

"That they did," Jackson agreed. The whole lot of the freshmen on the drill team that year had been a sorry bunch after Hell Night. But Cheri and Lance, twins determined to one-up each other, had come through standing.

Anna rolled her eyes. "Same story, different detachment."

"I don't think I damaged anything vital," Cheri said. "If that helps at all."

"I'll let you know tomorrow."

If he was still getting pie, they could make as much fun as they wanted. Since Anna had slowed down on her sorting with half the plate still to go, his odds were looking better. At least sixty-forty now.

He glanced back at the dance floor.

The ladies were still dancing, but Anna's ex had disappeared. Jackson gave the room a casual perusal. Wasn't really his business why the yahoo was here, and Jackson enjoyed weddings little enough without sitting across from the hoity-toity captain through dinner. But Anna Grace deserved a nice night, and instead of being giggly and girly over her friend's big day like females liked to do, she was letting Jackson do her favors.

"Hey, Anna Grace," her ex said behind Jackson.

Anna's pretty little nose scrunched up like she'd bitten into a rancid grapefruit. Her fingers vibrated over the mints. Fire flashed in her rapidly narrowing eyes.

"Don't call me that." She had the tone of a wounded tiger stalking her hunter.

The captain's light gaze snapped to Jackson, then back at Anna. He rolled one shoulder and slid a plate to her. "Brought you some cake."

Jackson might've been insulted that his manners were in question over the lack of cake on the plate *he* had brought

Anna, but the captain's lack of knowledge of his ex-wife was pitiful. She eyed him like she wanted to smush that cake over the front of his mess dress and then stick the fork where his sun didn't shine. Wasn't a doubt in Jackson's mind Louisa would've done it, but Anna Grace had the restraint of a proper Southern gentlewoman.

She touched the plate only as much as she had to and scooted it in front of Jackson. "Cake?" she said.

If it hadn't been for the *keep your trap shut and eat the damn cake* message her eyes were broadcasting, he might've taken that as a hint that she'd let him into this battle with her.

But he couldn't deny some curiosity as to how deep that spark of wounded mischief went in her, so he murmured, "Thank you, ma'am," and picked up the fork.

Cheri caught his eye. She nodded at the idiot. *Dumbass,* she mouthed.

"You want to dance?" Anna's ex asked.

Anna crossed her arms and her legs and stared him down like she triple-dog-dared him to repeat the question. But her pulse fluttered in her neck as fast as Jackson's plans for tonight were tanking.

He didn't sleep with women who were looking long-term.

He didn't sleep with women he didn't trust.

And he didn't sleep with a woman who was looking to use him after a bad breakup.

Same went for a woman whose ex rattled her up. Wasn't often Jackson had the urge to punch a guy, but this one's face looked like it needed some rearranging.

"C'mon, Anna," the captain wheedled. "It's just a dance."

"And this is just a wedding, and it was just a toast." Her foot jiggled, showing off pretty toes. "If I dance with you, will you leave?"

Jackson twitched.

"Cross my heart."

Jackson would've rather danced with her ex himself than let the yahoo get within touching distance of her, but Anna

Grace was broadcasting stubborn again.

He bit down on a forkful of cake.

Darn good cake. Not as good as pie though.

"I'll pick the song," Anna said.

If that gleam in her eye didn't scare the S-O-B, he had no business calling himself a man. "Save my mints, okay?" She said. She pecked Jackson on the cheek.

The captain's cheeks sprouted thunderclouds. Jackson swallowed a grin. "Yes, ma'am."

The DJ broke into the music. "All y'all ready for a bouquet toss?"

Something passed between Anna and the captain. A flock of bow-headed bridesmaids and an army of normal-dressed single women rushed the dance floor. So did a couple of ladies who looked fit to take on Mamie and her friends at the bowling alley. Anna's shoulders drooped like they were being tugged down from hell. She flicked a glance at Cheri. "I'm going to go freshen up."

"I'll join you."

The captain reached out to Anna. She cut him off with a look hot enough to slice frozen butter. He shifted into an at-ease stance. "I'll wait here."

Anna and Cheri waded into the crowd. A bunch of women flashing rings gathered around the dance floor. Kaci peered around, then pointed to the four flower girls. They squealed and ran to join the single women.

"You sleeping with my wife?" the captain asked Jackson.

Jackson held his gaze for what felt like a good five minutes longer than necessary before he answered. "Your momma raise you to talk like that?"

He let that hang between them while he watched for the girls. Anna and Cheri got caught in the throng of men waiting for the garter toss, slowing down to weave between the crowds.

The DJ started his countdown. Kaci did a mock toss-back on three. Then two. Anna and Cheri paused between the crowd wanting the bouquet and the crowd waiting to see who caught it.

Then Jackson realized Kaci's bouquet wasn't made out of flowers.

He shot out of his chair. "Stop!" The DJ reached one. Kaci squeezed her eyes shut and flung the lollipops, and Jackson muttered something his own momma would've preferred he didn't say in polite company.

The bouquet sailed over the single ladies who rose and jumped and crashed into each other with all the grace of Auburn fans doing the wave, but the bouquet kept on flying over all of them.

The men all skittered back, leaving a clear view of where the bouquet was headed.

"Anna!" Jackson hollered. "Duck!"

In the span of two heartbeats, she twisted her shoulders toward him, then back toward the bouquet. Her shriek split the air. The crowd gasped. Her knees bent. She flung her arms up, but it was too late.

The glob of lollipops smacked her upside the head.

She teetered. In the span of his next two heartbeats, Jackson made a whole host of promises to God if she'd be okay.

It took him an eternity too long to get to her through the crowd. Somebody had shoved a chair beneath her. Cheri was talking to her. Jackson squatted in front of her. "Anna Grace? You okay?"

She blinked at him, eyes not quite focused. A red welt was already forming on her temple. He brushed his thumb over it, then down her soft cheek. "Anna Grace?"

She blinked a couple more times, her chest evening out into a more normal rhythm. Finally, she looked straight into his eyes. "I need some Windex," she said.

He crushed her against him, breathing in the soft scent of her shampoo. "You got it, darlin'."

"Jesus, Anna, are you all right?" Her ex elbowed in.

"I got this one." Cheri stood and faced the captain. "You sit there and work on feeling better."

"Oh, Lordy, sugar." Kaci finally made it through the crowd herself. Lance was right behind her.

Anna pushed herself straight, then blinked at the bouquet in her hands. "Shit."

"We'll strap that to a firecracker too," Kaci said. "You okay? I'm so sorry, sugar. I practiced and everything, but then the flowers got all messed up, and somebody handed that to me, and my momma's driving me so nuts I wasn't thinking."

"My wife needs a doctor," Anna's ex said to Cheri.

Kaci twisted her head. Then she blinked. Then she stood and looked Anna's ex up and down.

"Oh, shit," Anna said again. She looked at Jackson and winced. "Sorry."

He winked at her. "Don't worry. My momma didn't hear."

"Who are you?" Kaci said to the idiot.

"I—"

"You crashing my wedding?" She stomped a slipper that took her four feet closer to the captain. "'Cuz I've heard what *you* do at weddings, and I ain't got no use for that."

"Kaci," Anna said.

"She needs a doctor," the captain tried again, but under Kaci's stare, the yahoo went green.

Kaci glanced at Jackson, then back to the captain. "You ever see combat?" she asked. She flicked at his four medals that clearly stated he hadn't. "I reckon she's in about the best hands she could be right now, so you go on and fix yourself a plate, then go on and sit in the corner and eat it, then you go on and get out of here before I tell my momma about what you like to do at weddings. You seen my momma yet? You ain't seen a Southern woman mad 'til you seen my momma dealing with wedding crashers who make the kind of toasts you do, and that ain't a sight I reckon the likes of you will live through."

"Anna?" the captain said. "Look, sweetheart—"

"My wife was polite about it," Lance said, "but I won't be."

"Won't look good when this gets back to your commander," Cheri said. The steel in her eyes belied her easy posture.

Jackson almost felt sorry for the guy.

"I'm only letting you all handle him because my head hurts," Anna said.

He laughed out an exasperated sigh. "Darlin', it's being handled because you picked the right friends. Same as doing it yourself in my book. You getting sleepy?"

Worry lines branched from the corners of her eyes, but her pupils were fine. Even had some spark to them again. "Adrenaline crash," she said. Her gaze followed her ex disappearing into the crowd. "I've got half a mind to ask your momma to have a go at him."

"I swear to sweet baby Jesus, if one more ex-husband shows up at this wedding, I'm strapping *him* to a firecracker," Kaci said. "Anna, sugar, you all right? For real?"

Forming that pretty smile seemed to perk Anna up. Did wonders for Jackson too, truth be told.

"I have three nephews. Not my first bump on the head. I'll be fine."

And Jackson found that Anna's being okay meant more to him than getting pie tonight.

ANNA WAS A MESS. Her temple throbbed, she was beyond embarrassed, and she'd run through at least three cycles of being furious with Neil, then furious with herself, and then back to furious with Neil.

All this Southern gentility had gone to her head. In retrospect, it was clear she should've asked him to step outside before dinner, racked him, and dumped him in the bathroom for a janitor to find.

Much less messy.

And on top of it all, she was afraid Jackson had stuck around only because his momma would've had his hide if she had heard he abandoned a lady in distress.

She obviously wouldn't be stripping him out of anything tonight.

There went her fury again.

Jackson returned to his seat beside her. If he noticed she'd moved from sorting the rainbow mints to lining up the random wedding-shaped silver confetti sprinkled around the candle centerpieces, he didn't comment. He plunked another cake plate in front of her, this one with actual cake on it. Three ketchup packets too. "Kaci's orders," he said. "She threatened to tell my momma some very uncomplimentary stories if I didn't bring it over for you."

Anna managed a small smile. "Thank you."

"I'm right proud of you, Anna Grace. Using your manners and everything." The sparkle in his eyes wasn't as bright, and he couldn't seem to look away from the spot on her temple that was currently throbbing. "Sure you don't want anything for that?"

She shook her head. The motion sent a stabbing sensation through her brain. "I'll take something when I get home."

So much for her overnight bag.

Jackson's eyes narrowed. His shoulders shifted back.

Man-mode. *Southern gentleman* mode. She stifled a sigh and squeezed her eyes shut.

"My daddy died in a car accident," he said. "I'd rather you didn't drive tonight."

Oh.

Vulnerable wouldn't have made her top-fifty list of things she knew about Jackson, but it was etched across his face clear as a Minnesota winter sky. She touched a shaky hand to his cheek. "You're a good man."

"Not always." He pulled her fingers to his lips for a gentle kiss, then tucked her hand back down onto the table.

Right. Moment over. Because they weren't about moments.

They had an expiration date. Not that it mattered if they never *started* something.

"I'll get a room here tonight," she said.

He blew out a heavy breath. His lips thinned and he tucked his hands under his arms.

Anna fought the smile, but it felt too good that she wanted to smile, so she gave up and let it through. "Does your momma know you cuss like that in your head?"

"Eat your cake and take your ketchup."

It wasn't pie, but The Harrington made a mean cake. The cake part was as fluffy as cotton candy, but not nearly as sweet, which balanced nicely with the berry filling and buttercream frosting. It made the ketchup shots unnecessary. She was licking the last of the frosting off her fork when she saw one of the older bridesmaids making eyes at Jackson.

He didn't seem to notice, but she suspected he didn't miss much. "You don't have to sit here with me if you want to go enjoy yourself."

"She's eyeing your bouquet." His gaze didn't waver from the crowd on the dance floor.

"Actually," Anna said, "I think she's looking for a different kind of lollipop."

She'd made him blush. That didn't happen often.

"No more cake for you." A dimple peeked through. "How's your head?"

"Pretty much still aches like a mother." She pushed her plate back. It wasn't quite eight o'clock yet, and Kaci and Lance showed no inclination to leave their party anytime soon. They were leading a conga line around the room, probably because the suggestion had made her mother turn purple.

"Think they'd mind if I bailed?"

"Anna Grace."

Right. They'd mind if she stayed here nursing a headache on a sugar rush in a loud room.

Jackson stood. "You gonna let me help?"

"No."

"You're a right stubborn woman, you know that?"

"I have a headache and a credit card. You'll have more fun

out there."

But she accepted his help out of her seat. Not because she needed it but because he offered, and she appreciated his patience with her.

She also would've appreciated knowing when she could offer him pie again. Maybe it wasn't supposed to happen.

He insisted on walking her out. When he'd confirmed for himself that Neil wasn't lurking in any corners—not that she asked or he confessed—he let her go by herself to the reception desk.

"I'm sorry, ma'am," the honey-voiced desk clerk said four minutes later, "we're all sold out tonight." She flicked a hand toward a group of wedding guests. "The wedding and parents' weekend on campus have us booked."

Anna propped her elbow on the marble countertop and pinched the bridge of her nose. "Not even one room? Don't you always hold one or two back for special circumstances? I got beaned with the bridal bouquet and shouldn't drive home."

"Yes, ma'am, usually, but the college president came in an hour ago with some distinguished guests." She dropped her voice. "I'm not supposed to talk about it."

"How about a broom closet?"

"I'd be happy to call the Camp Inn down the road for you."

"Maybe I can help."

Neil's voice made Anna's shoulders bunch. "I've got it, thanks."

Slick shoes shuffled against the tile floor beside her. "Look, Anna, I've handled today poorly."

"Just today?"

The hotel clerk cleared her throat and slid away. Neil tugged on his cuffs. "Let me make it up to you." He slid a flat key-card onto the counter. "Take my room."

Anna's neck muscles hurt from holding her head upright. A haze of exhaustion crept into her vision. "No, thank you."

"It's my fault you got hit. You should take my room."

The normal cocky tilt to his head was gone, replaced with a

humbler straight-on hazel plea for something she didn't have the stamina to interpret. She signaled the clerk. "Do you have a number for a taxi service?"

"That's not necessary." Neil shifted again, but his lips settled into an unfortunately familiar rigid board, his voice tight. "If you won't take my room, let me drive you home."

More familiar. In a car. In the dark. With Neil. Driving home from a celebration. Unwelcome nostalgia made her nauseous. "I can take care of myself."

"You always could. That's one of the things I love about you."

He *what?*

"Look, I know you're tired, but I'd really like to talk."

Oh, Lordy, he'd pulled out the earnest puppy face. And aimed it at *her*.

As he had on the night he proposed.

He took her by the elbow. She gulped back something that tasted like diseased strawberries. "Neil. Stop."

He stepped close enough for the mingled odors of wet hog and rotten peaches to seep into her nose. She covered her mouth, but still found her face squished into the front of his tuxedo shirt. "Anna, I was wrong. I miss you so much. Baby, I'm falling apart without you."

Voices lingered somewhere nearby, but whoever it was either didn't notice or didn't care that Anna was suffocating in the scent of Neil's body wash. She wrenched away from him. Her head teetered on her neck. Her temper teetered on something significantly less solid. "Take it back."

"I can't. I screwed up, and I'll do whatever it takes to get you back. You want kids? You want me to get out? Anything. You name it."

Her voice wasn't as steady as her knees, and those were about to buckle. "I want to go home, *by myself*, to my label maker."

A woman who hadn't been married to him for six years might've missed it, but she caught the way his right nostril flared at the mention of her label maker. The slight movement set loose a fresh volcano of anger. She pointed a shaky hand at the door. "Get out."

"I love you."

"If you love me, you will turn around, walk out that door, and never, ever bother me again."

"Anna—"

"No. Don't *Anna* me. You don't get to say my name. You don't get to be in my life. You gave me up. You left me here. My world does not revolve around you and what you want. Not anymore." Her voice was high and unstable, and she hated that she had to swipe at her eyes. "I had plans for tonight. I was going to go home with a really funny, decent, honorable guy, and instead, I'm stuck here talking to *you*. We're not even married anymore, and you're *still* ruining my sex life."

Eyes wide, he worked his jaw up and down.

Exactly like the first pet they'd picked out together.

She slugged him in the arm. "And you haven't asked about Walker. You want to have kids? You can't even remember your *fish*. Grow up, Neil. Grow up, and get out of my life."

She stalked past him. He made another grab for her arm. "Where are you going?"

"To get a ride home from someone I trust."

His grip tightened. "You think you know enough about him to trust him?"

"Of the two men who've offered me rides home tonight, he's the one who's never broken a promise to me."

The weariness in Neil's sigh combined with the tremble of his chin almost broke her indignation. "Let go," she said.

He loosened his grip finger by finger. "Maybe this was a bad time."

She flung her purse over her shoulder. "There was never a good time."

Anna blinked back the stinging in her eyes and stalked back toward the party. Alone.

She rounded the corner onto velvety carpet, and the click

of her heels on marble faded away. The catering staff were cleaning the tables around the makeshift bar. Further, by the ballroom door, Jackson and Cheri were laughing at something.

Anna slowed.

Maybe he'd found something better to do after all.

But then he glanced her way. The smile slid right off his face. He moved toward her, and all she saw was six solid feet of highly intelligent, well-trained intimidation.

Her steps faltered. The normal strawberry taste in her mouth morphed into something richer. Internal suction pulled her ribs into her chest. Maybe a cab was a better idea.

But then he grabbed her into a fierce hug, cupped the back of her neck, and between the hint of Old Spice and the feel of his heart hammering through his uniform, she discovered she could take a real breath again.

"Okay, Anna Grace?"

Not yet. "Take me home?"

"Be my pleasure."

Chapter Seventeen

A woman didn't always know why she wanted a man, but when she had him, she knew she had what she needed.
—The Temptress of Pecan Lane, by Mae Daniels

ANNA'S VISION WAS hazy around the edges, from exhaustion, from stress, from tight neck muscles restricting blood flow to her head. She absently reached across her body and kneaded into her shoulder while Jackson steered the truck out of the parking lot. He'd been mostly quiet, but she hadn't missed that he'd snagged her overnight bag from her car. When he spoke, his quiet voice rumbled right along with the engine. "Notice you didn't mention whose home."

"All I need is a bed."

And his was closer.

A lot closer.

Neither of them talked much. When Jackson pulled off the main drag fifteen miles too early to be taking Anna to her apartment, her breathing hitched.

"This okay with you?" he asked.

"Mm-hmm." More than okay.

A couple minutes later, he killed the engine in his

driveway. Her mouth was dry, her legs wobbly. Being on heels all day, she suspected, had nothing to do with it.

She followed him into the front door. He greeted Radish with an affectionate ear scratch, then led Anna up the stairs. She didn't want to sleep in the guest bed, but she couldn't share his bed with him tonight.

Not when she couldn't guarantee Neil wouldn't sneak into her head.

The guest room was sparsely furnished but comfortable. A simple maroon comforter covered the double bed. The small bookcase held an assortment of science fiction novels with the occasional Mae Daniels novel tucked in between.

Good. Switching out the three she'd borrowed had been in her plans too. *That*, at least, she'd follow through on. Jackson had good taste in romance novels.

Also not something she would've guessed about him.

"Bathroom's down the hall," he said. "Anything else I can get you?"

Some good old-fashioned comforting sounded nice. "I'm okay."

He pulled two more packets of ketchup from inside his jacket and put them on the small bookshelf beside the bed. "Need anything else, I'll be downstairs."

She dropped her hands before she could reach for him. He cupped the back of her head and pressed a kiss to her temple. "You go on and get some sleep. Gonna need it to fix me up that big old breakfast you promised."

"I didn't—"

He flashed a *gotcha* grin. She sighed, but her lips curved up.

Being in his house made the pressure in her head ease. Made *all* of her pressure ease.

He was a good friend.

"'Night, Anna Grace."

Then he was gone.

She perched on the edge of the bed and peeled off her

shoes. The bed creaked beneath her, the smell of Jackson's laundry detergent wafting up from the sheets. She wondered if the noise carried downstairs.

She retrieved her bag from beside the door. A door shut downstairs. Outside, Radish gave a single happy bark. Anna was intruding on their quality time, man and dog, their own little family unit.

Kaci and Lance were like family, and Jules and Brad were akin to dysfunctional cousins who happened to live nearby, but Anna missed the quiet home family time. Reading a book on the couch while someone else flipped channels on the TV. Sharing meals.

Not being alone.

She dug into her bag for her Tylenol, then slipped down the hall for water.

Jackson's bathroom, like the rest of the house, was sparsely decorated. Anna suspected the green paint was original from when he'd moved in. Two navy towels dangled from the towel rack, and a navy hand towel was crinkled on a hook next to the sink.

The image in the mirror wasn't something she was prepared for. Her eyes were bloodshot, her mascara gooped. Her lipstick had worn off but for a single dark ring around her lips, and her cheeks were pale. Except, of course, for a baseball-sized peppering of round, purple bruises rising on her left temple.

She gulped down the pills, then rummaged in the drawers of the vanity for a washcloth. She scrubbed her face clean and let her hair down, then rinsed with some mouthwash she'd found.

Back in the bedroom, she dug into her overnight bag again for the T-shirt she'd intended to wear tomorrow. She lifted her arm and gave the side zipper on her dress a tug.

It didn't budge.

She twisted her head, holding her arm aloft, and peeked inside the dress. Nothing seemed stuck, so she gave the zipper another tug.

The zipper's pull tab snapped off between her fingers.

A strangled moan slipped from her lips. "Are you kidding me?"

She glared at the zipper. It was too tiny for her fingers to grasp, but she tried anyway.

She tried and she tried, but all she got for her effort were sore fingertips and enough frustration to heat a tincture to boiling.

She needed to ask for help.

The pit of her stomach twisted until it resembled the knotted rawhide bone Radish liked to carry around. Asking for a place to stay was one thing.

Asking for help taking her clothes off...

Scissors.

She'd ask for scissors.

She poked her head out the door. Nothing moved, nothing creaked. She couldn't even hear the refrigerator running. A small bit of light drifted up the stairs, but no shadows. If Jackson and Radish were down there, they were being awful quiet.

She went back to the bathroom and dug into the drawers again. No razors. No scissors. She had fingernail clippers in her purse, but they weren't strong enough to split the fabric of her dress. It would take all night to trim her hem one stitch at a time with nail clippers. Who knew she needed to carry a seam ripper in her emergency kit?

The dress was too fitted to pull over her head, but she tried.

No luck.

Something flashed downstairs. The TV.

Jackson was still up.

She took a big gulp of courage and tiptoed to the stairs. A male voice spoke over a crowd.

Football game.

Radish stepped onto the small landing two steps up from

the ground floor and sniffed in Anna's direction.

Jackson said something softly. The dog looked toward his voice, then crawled another step toward Anna.

The TV went silent.

Radish stared up the stairs. Her soft brown eyes seemed to say, "I only wanted to make sure you're okay, and now I'm in trouble." Anna stood between dog and master.

She took one step down, then another, until she reached the landing. Jackson paused, his hand on Radish's collar. His gaze traveled up the length of her body until his ever-darkening eyes stared right into hers.

She licked her lips and tightened her fingers around the banister. He was barefoot, in navy sweat pants and the military-issue white cotton undershirt that accentuated the olive tones in his skin. "Anna?"

Scissors. She needed scissors. But her arm went up as if someone was up on the second floor, pulling her strings. She pointed at her zipper. "I need help."

His adam's apple bobbed. Despite the quiver in his lips that told her he was trying, there was no hint of humor in his strained voice. "Not so hard to say, now, is it?"

Her own voice wavered. "The zipper broke."

He stepped up to the landing and leaned in close enough for her to remember she hadn't showered in hours. His fingers grazed her between the dress and her raised arm. At his touch, a tremor rippled from her skin all the way to her bones, then bounced back again.

"Hold tight," he said. "Got something that'll work."

He stepped off the stairs and headed toward the kitchen. Anna scrubbed her hands over the goose bumps that popped up in the absence of his presence.

She should've had a ketchup shot before she came down here.

Radish sprawled on the landing. Her snout rested on Anna's foot. If it hadn't, Anna might've run back upstairs and slept in the damn dress.

Jackson returned. His loose-limbed, measured stride was completely at odds with his darkened eyes and pinched lips. Her neck and shoulders were so tight they probably had their own frequency. She tried to swallow but her mouth was too dry. Her voice came out a husky croak. "Scissors?"

Even scornful looked hot right now. "No reason to cut up your pretty dress." He gently pried her fingers off her arm. "Trust me?"

More than she trusted herself. She bit down on her lip and nodded, then raised her arm, determined not to think about the fact that he'd more than likely seen his fair share of naked women.

He flipped open pliers on his multi-tool. His fingers slid between her dress and the skin beneath her arm, warm and sure and steady. He could've copped a feel, but after she'd arrived on the landing, his eyes didn't stray beyond her face or the zipper.

The zipper he was separating tooth by tooth, millimeter by millimeter. His breathing hitched. Anna's own lungs couldn't find a steady rhythm. When she inhaled, she noted something spicier, richer, about his scent. She'd never noticed the few strands of silver among the subtle swirls that hinted at the curls in his close-cropped hair, or the way his ears crinkled tightly at the edges.

Jackson slid the zipper farther down. Cool air drifted between the panels of her dress. His lashes were lowered to his task, his lips taut in concentration.

Unzipping a zipper wasn't that hard, not with tools.

Her heart thudded like a gong announcing dinnertime. Jackson pulled back. His eyes were black as the night outside, his nostrils flaring unsteadily. "That far enough?"

With him on the step below her, they were at eye level. Anna clumsily felt her dress, unable to tear her gaze from his. She licked her lips again. "Should be."

He gave a brief nod. "Need anything else, give a holler."

Before he could step down, Anna put her hands to his

shoulders. "Jackson."

His eyes flickered. His chest rose and fell as rapidly as hers. "Yes, ma'am?"

She felt his breath everywhere on her skin. Her head still ached, her feet wanted rest, but her body, her femininity, everything else about her didn't want to break the chemical bonds holding them in this weird equilibrium.

"This is where I wanted to be," she said.

His unsteady hands settled on her hips. "Here now, Anna Grace."

She tilted her head and leaned into him. The friction between their bodies held her against him stronger than the zipper had sealed her dress shut.

His eyes flicked over her face, his gaze searching for something. "You sure?"

She brushed her lips over his. His fingers tightened into her hips, his eyes slipped shut, and then he was kissing her back, slow and steady, soft and smooth. His lips tasted like skin and cake. His stubbled jaw was the right bit of scratchy.

Anna slid all the way into the kiss. The day, her head, everything but Jackson faded away behind the way their mouths fit together. His hand, so courteous and respectful moments ago, slid into the opening in her dress. The other wrapped around her neck, his fingers magically easing away her tension and replacing it with a primal excitement so long forgotten, her body felt as if it were coming to life for the first time.

But her thighs remembered this tune. Between his skilled mouth and capable hands, soon her breasts were humming along as well. She deepened the kiss, pressed closer to him, and scraped her fingers down his back. She felt a bulge against her pelvis, and another zing of excitement surged over her skin.

He didn't owe her anything. No obligation, no responsibility, no commitment.

His tongue flicked over her lower lip. The heat that

erupted in her veins *had* to be against the laws of thermodynamics.

She wanted to feel his skin, and she wanted another peek at that tattoo, but she couldn't bear the thought of his hands not on her skin for a single second.

Especially not when he had his fingers splayed across her back, slowly, slowly, slowly sinking lower, lower, lower until his fingertips brushed the silk of her panties.

And stopped.

She whimpered.

He threaded his other hand through her hair, her scalp tingling beneath his fingers, and let his tongue leisurely explore her mouth. She rocked her body harder against his, felt his erection jerk against her, while his other hand stayed firmly planted on the border between *that's good* and *ohmigod*.

She pushed up on her tiptoes.

He shifted with her.

Her whimpers turned into a groan. She snaked her hand down his arm to his hand, and pushed it down.

Right onto her ass.

He pulled out of the kiss, his voice the smoke to the fire in his eyes. "Anna Grace, quit being so bossy."

"I—"

He silenced her with his mouth, slipped a finger beneath her panties, and all rational thought fled her mind. Another finger caressed her hidden skin. Then a third.

She wrapped her leg around his waist, pressing his erection as intimately close as she could while they were both still clothed. She tugged at his shirt. He broke the kiss again, this time with a chuckle. He dropped his hands long enough to pull his shirt off, then stepped onto the landing with her, dislodging her leg. "You going somewhere tonight?"

To the top of Mount Orgasm if he'd stop dawdling in the foothills. "N-no."

He crinkled her dress in his fists, pulling it up with his signature slowness. He backed her up another step and brushed his jaw against hers on his way to nibbling at her collarbone. "Feeling better?"

Her words slipped out on a satisfyingly frustrated sigh. "Oh, yeah."

Something furry brushed her calf. They had an audience. Jackson's fists lifted past her hips. Cool air rushed between her thighs. "Radish," he said into her shoulder. "Get."

The dog huffed. She left the stairs, tags jingling. Jackson's hands grazed Anna's waist. More cool air swirled around her skin. Everywhere his hands went, though, she felt branded by fire.

"Bedroom?" she said on a gasp.

He chuckled.

His fists inched higher. And higher. Until the backs of his fingers brushed the sides of her breasts. Anna lifted her arms. He pulled the fabric over her head and tossed it up the stairs, then gazed down at her. "Better?"

"Getting there." She pushed up on her toes, claimed his mouth, let her hands roam free over his solid body. He traced the lace of her bra, dipped his fingers under her panties again, and backed her against the wall. She waved a hand toward the walls between the stairwell and his bedroom. "Should we—"

"You just enjoy yourself, Anna Grace."

She was definitely enjoying herself. In fact, she wasn't sure she'd *ever* had quite this much ecstasy out of being nearly naked. It had to have happened sometime, but his body, his movements, his mannerisms, they were all uniquely Jackson. All perfect, all thrilling.

For tonight, they were all hers.

She tugged at the waistband of his sweatpants, and felt his smile against her lips. "You sure you wanna do that?"

"Not planning on waiting for you to get to it."

He pulled a foil packet out of his pocket, making her thank God he was optimistic. Then he nuzzled her neck beneath her ear. "All right then." He pressed a trail of kisses along her jawbone while she pushed his pants down, slowly, but not as slowly as he would've.

Just slowly enough to listen to his breathing accelerate when her fingers came into contact with the skin on his hips.

Just slowly enough to feel his heart pound faster against her chest.

Just slowly enough to realize he wasn't wearing anything beneath.

"Oh," she breathed. Her thighs clenched. Her fingers wavered.

She suddenly felt overdressed. And they really needed to get to the bedroom.

"Taking your sweet time, darlin'?"

Her bra released with a flick of his fingers. She gave his sweatpants one more tug, and they fell to the floor. Her hands roamed over his hot skin. Her hips thrust against his. Her body remembered the rhythms, but this tune was different.

In a good way.

She slipped out of her bra, and Jackson's eyes went darker, ringed by blue fire. Her unhurried, savoring lover slipped away in a tangle of hot, eager kisses. Slow perusals became heated, impatient strokes until Anna found herself seated on the stairs, legs spread wide sans panties, while Jackson showed her *exactly* how much he liked her girly parts.

With his tongue.

And after he'd helped her to the top of Mount O once, he eased her down to the landing, where she rolled on top of him.

She hovered with her hips above his. She wanted him to feel as right as she did, but she suddenly felt shy. Inexperienced. Almost virginal.

He brushed his thumb over her cheek. "Okay, Anna Grace?"

Oh, yes. Very okay. Except—

"I don't know what you like," she whispered.

She caught a hint of a dimple. His warm hand left a trail of hypersensitive, happy-tingly skin down her back.

"You," he said, and he didn't need to say more.

The affection in his gaze, the timbre of his voice, the feel of his body beneath her, foreign and familiar at the same time, the rightness of it all swirled around her insecurities and swept them away. She lowered herself onto him, taking his solid length into her already swollen, satisfied body...all the way in...feeling him, enjoying him, watching his eyelashes flutter as she pleasured him, pleasured herself. And nothing else mattered, because they were right.

Maybe not forever, but for now, they were oh, so right.

So right, and so easy to make love to him, to come with him again, until she collapsed against him, the two of them a pile of rubbery limbs, satisfied down to their bones.

At least, Anna assumed Jackson was satisfied. She snuggled onto his chest, feeling the rise and fall even out while his fingers tangled in her hair. His lips pressed into her ear.

He didn't say it, but she heard it all the same. *Real good progress there, Anna Grace.*

Real good, indeed. He was a perfect new first.

"Thank you," she whispered.

"My pleasure, Anna Grace."

"Let's not wait so long to do it again."

His answering chuckle sent a happy after-shiver through her. "Yes, ma'am."

And because he was the obliging kind of gentleman, they didn't.

Chapter Eighteen

*Her baby steps had become leaps that burst
beyond the tethers of her old life.*
—The Temptress of Pecan Lane, *by Mae Daniels*

ANNA AWOKE SUNDAY morning to the soft pitter of rain. Someone was snoring, but when she rolled over to give Jackson a shove, he was watching her.

Not wide awake, but awake enough that the continued snoring couldn't be his. "Your dog sleeps loud."

Beneath the sheet, he ran a hand over her bare hip. "She's not the only one."

She did give him a playful shove then.

"Rested yet?" he said. "I'm real good in the shower."

His gray sheet was draped across his stomach. She reached out and traced the 33 in the middle of the Auburn tiger paw on his chest. "Showers are cold."

He screwed his eyes up all crinkly and his lips did that thing like he was holding back a laugh. "Anna Grace, you been showering with the wrong people." He rolled up and over her with a speed she still found uncharacteristic of him, but the grin was all Jackson. He dipped his head and pressed a kiss to the hollow of her neck. "You go on and head to the bathroom, and I'll show you how two people are meant to shower together."

That sounded promising.

Radish snorted. Her tags jingled. Jackson's hand slid up to caress Anna's breast, but when the dog let out a low growl, he stopped and cocked his ear toward the door.

Something that sounded suspiciously like a lock clicked somewhere beyond the bedroom.

Jackson was out of bed, reaching for one of the random pairs of pants scattered about the room, when the hollering started.

"Jackson Beauregard Davis, you've got some explaining to do!"

Whoever she was, she was spitting mad.

And Anna couldn't help but silently echo the mystery woman's sentiment. Mad and all.

Jackson and Radish disappeared outside the bedroom door. "Pipe down," she heard him say. "The neighbors might still be sleeping."

"You wanna tell me why in tarnation *Craig* was out there this morning instead of you?" The woman made an outraged squeak. "You stood me up for a *girl*, didn't you?"

Anna's pulse ricocheted through her veins like an unstable electron. Jackson *was* a decent guy, wasn't he? There had to be a reasonable explanation for a woman having a key to his house. A woman who thought she'd been stood up. For what? *Church?*

Lordy, what had she gotten herself into?

Anna scrambled out of the bed. She pulled the sheet off and wrapped it around herself. Twice.

Whoever the woman was, Anna wasn't taking a chance of meeting her naked.

Though a meeting *would* take place and explanations *would* be given.

Jackson talked softer now, too quiet or too far away for Anna to hear more than the measured cadence of his voice. Her overnight bag was still upstairs and her dress was somewhere close to there, so she stomped over to his dresser. She located a T-shirt in the first drawer, then grabbed a pair of pants off the floor.

Clean or dirty, she didn't care.

She cared only that she was in something more than her birthday suit.

She was trying to hop into the jeans without dropping the sheet when the door clicked shut behind her. Jackson set her overnight bag on the bed. He eyed her, and a grin split his cheeks. "Don't reckon you need any help getting untangled from that sheet."

Her face twisted disbelief. *There was another woman in his house.* "Maybe five minutes ago."

He ambled up to her, still eyeing the sheet. "You got yourself wrapped up good in there."

She arched an eyebrow. A very angry eyebrow.

"You thinking about homework, or you waiting for me to explain the crazy girl making us breakfast in my kitchen?"

He reached for the sheet. She swatted at his hand. "You'll have better luck with her than you will with me right now."

That wiped his grin off. "Darlin', not even in Arkansas. Tell you what. You take your time in the shower. Louisa's gonna be a while out there."

Her eyes narrowed. He was playing with her again.

Too bad for him she wasn't feeling like being played with. "I'm locking the door."

"Go on and do what you need to." He plucked the Bama shirt out of her hands, murmured, "Thank you, ma'am," slid it over his head, and sauntered back out of the bedroom.

Leaving her mighty glad she was in this only for the sex.

LOUISA PROBABLY DIDN'T know it, but when she glared at Jackson like that, eyes flashing, nose flaring, she looked like Daddy used to whenever Auburn was losing a football game. "So it *was* a girl," she said.

"It was a wedding."

She morphed into pure Momma mode quick, eyes narrowing to little pinpricks while she tried to find something to do with her hands. She settled on flinging a spatula at him. "*You got married?*"

Radish growled. Jackson flipped the spatula in his hand and headed to the refrigerator. He was glad Anna Grace looked angrier than a herd of rabid termites, because she was gonna need that mad to handle Louisa. Little sister had some territorial issues. "Mamie said it was a right pretty service."

Didn't have to turn to know when to duck this time. Little sister was also predictable.

"I'm calling Momma."

He was thinking eggs weren't all that great of an idea for breakfast. Likely to wear more of 'em than he'd get in the pan, the way Louisa looked. But he had all the fixings for biscuits and gravy and grits, and he had a mighty big appetite this morning.

The bedroom door clicked open.

Jackson stuck his head back out of the fridge. Louisa watched the kitchen entrance with undisguised interest.

Considering he'd made sure she'd never met any of his girlfriends, he couldn't blame her. And he had to check his grin knowing what she was about to see.

But he was more curious how quick Anna Grace would put it together.

Pretty fast, turned out. She took two blinks at Louisa, then raised a brow at Jackson. "Kissing cousins? Kinky." She swatted his butt. "Quit rednecking me."

"Didn't mind last night," he murmured.

She blew out a girly huff.

Louisa, for once, was speechless. Anna walked up to her, crazy hair, big purple bruise spilling over her temple and all, and stuck her hand out. "Hi. I'm Anna."

"She's a *Yankee*? Does Momma know about this?" Louisa looked her up and down. "You bake biscuits? 'Cuz Jackson don't need any more of those."

"Don't pay Louisa no mind," Jackson told Anna. "She thinks being old enough to vote means she doesn't have to use her manners anymore."

Something flashed across Anna's face, but those worry marks on her forehead faded as quick as they'd appeared.

Louisa glared at him, then gestured to her own temple. "He do that to you?"

Before Jackson could defend himself, there Anna Grace went being fourteen feet tall again. "I'm sorry, have you *met* your brother?"

"Thought so, but he told me y'all got married yesterday, and you better believe *my* brother ain't the marrying kind."

"He does like a good joke though, doesn't he?"

Jackson hid his grin in the freezer while he went digging for Miss Dolly's mailman's girlfriend's niece's biscuits to toss in the oven. He came home thinking he'd learn something about his family. Hadn't struck him they might learn a thing or two about him too.

Louisa was still eyeing Anna. "You bake him any biscuits?"

"I don't like to talk about my biscuits," Anna said as though she were sharing a secret.

Jackson wasn't so keen on the two of them having any secrets. He pulled a gallon of milk and some sausage out of the fridge. "Louisa. Grab me a skillet down there."

Her eyes rolled all the way up to her forehead, but she but bent down and yanked the cabinet open.

Then shrieked like a girl.

Anna leaned over and peeked in, then gave Jackson another girly look. "And you wanted *me* to make breakfast?" She pulled out his armadillo. "How you doing, Enrique? Kinda dark in there, isn't it?" She checked to make sure his label was still on his bottom, then plopped him up on the counter. "So much better for all of us, isn't it?"

"She named the armadillo?" Louisa hissed.

Jackson grabbed his own skillet and set about making

breakfast. "Yep."

"She name anything else?"

He worked up an old look of Daddy's and stared at her. She shrunk a couple inches. He gestured to the pantry. "Momma teach you to make grits?"

"What can I do?" Anna asked.

"Sit down and look pretty."

She crossed her arms. But her fingers fidgeted, and he didn't miss the glance she shot up to his clock.

"Or you can go take a real shower before I feed you and take you home."

Surprised the heck out of him when she did just that.

"She might be okay for a Yankee," Louisa said. She dumped water in a pot and brought it over the stove. "But you didn't really marry her, did you?"

"Nope."

"Gonna let Momma meet her?"

He scratched his head. Momma and Anna in the same room would be a mite bit more interesting than Louisa and Anna. Long as neither of them got any ideas. Much as he liked Anna Grace, he wasn't interested in staying in anything long enough to watch it go sour.

He reckoned she wasn't either.

They matched up nice that way. Plus, she was smart, she amused the dickens out of him, and last night had been worth the wait.

Thought he might've even seen a few colors beyond shades of blue and green sometime in there.

If she could handle his putting up emotional road blocks, he could handle her sticking around a while.

Maybe not long enough to have to meet his momma, but awhile.

Still, Louisa didn't have to know that. "Ain't decided yet."

About the time breakfast was ready, Anna came back out, her straight hair darker and dripping on the ends. Jackson slid her a cup of coffee. She went to the silverware drawer.

And laughed.

Prettiest thing he'd heard all morning. "What?" he said.

"It's organized."

"Nice try, but I have homework."

"Next time then." He'd found some sticky notes to label parts of the drawer. Silverware slid all over tarnation every time he opened it, but he could mostly find a fork when he wanted a fork and a spoon when he wanted a spoon. And now Anna Grace had a good reason to come back and visit him again. He'd just have to make mention that he found a drawer organizer.

"Homework?" Louisa asked.

"Mm-hmm." Anna moved to the table to set three places. "Trying to finish my degree and get a few certifications at work. What do you do?"

"Little as possible."

Jackson's ear twitched at the truth of *that* statement.

"I tried that once." Anna plunked a fork down, then a spoon and knife on the other side, and pushed up the bottoms until they were even. "Didn't last long. I got bored."

Jackson pulled the biscuits out of the oven and dished up. Louisa took a plate for herself and moved to the table. "I don't have that problem."

"Gonna have other problems real soon," Jackson said.

He felt her scowling at him. "Guess maybe if I wasn't a girl, then I might've been good enough for the family business. But seeing how I am, it doesn't do me much good to fight it, does it?"

Jackson started a second plate. He kept his hands steady, but he was getting mighty annoyed. "Getting your grades up might do you some good."

"If you talked in plain English when I ask you a question, I might could."

Anna snorted into her coffee.

Louisa flung herself back in her chair. "You ever listen to a rocket scientist try to explain algebra?" Her nose wrinkled.

"Probably not."

"I liked algebra. Calculus too."

"*You* can do calculus?" Louisa's incredulous tone made Jackson's gentlemanly side want to offer Anna Grace another apology.

But Anna took it in stride. "I can do anything I want to do." She snagged the ketchup out of the fridge before she took the plate Jackson handed her, then went up on tiptoe to kiss his cheek. "Including let someone else make me breakfast once in a while. Thank you."

"My pleasure, Anna Grace."

He helped himself to his own plate, then joined the ladies at the table. He'd barely sat down before Louisa got that look again.

The brewing trouble look.

"You know," she said, "Jackson was supposed to go hunting with me this weekend. He couldn't go last year because he was over in the stupid desert, and now this year, he's bailing on his family again. He tell you that?"

Anna smiled blandly. "What're you hunting?"

"Snipe."

"A little early for snipe season, isn't it?"

"About a month," Jackson said. Louisa looked disappointed that Anna was smarter than she looked about hunting. Jackson, though, was intrigued. "Rabbit and squirrel season now."

Louisa's interest was obviously piqued. "You hunt?"

Anna shook her head. "My dad and brother-in-law go every year. I fish though."

"Huh." There was something too calculated in the tilt of Louisa's head. "I might could give up a hunting weekend for a good camping trip."

Jackson stopped eating. If she was looking to interfere in his love life, she was looking in the wrong place. "Thought you didn't like sleeping with spiders."

"Aw, shoot, if Anna Grace can do it, I can too."

"It's just Anna."

"You sleep with spiders?"

"Yep, and I bait my own hooks when I'm fishing too."

Jackson laughed softly. "Of course you do."

Didn't matter what Louisa threw at her, Anna Grace handled it like a champ.

That made Jackson happier than it should've.

And when he dropped her off at the hotel, he was right glad for a few minutes of privacy. Especially since she was looking at that big old hotel like she had plans to go inside.

If she was going inside for what he thought she was going inside for, he didn't like it.

Not that he should've cared.

Still, he didn't feel the least bit bad about pulling her across the seat and giving her a good reminder of what he could do for her.

Didn't mind that she gave it right back either. Girl could kiss like sweet rain on a hot Alabama afternoon. "You ever take that overnight bag to class?" he asked.

Her hand slid somewhere it should've been physically impossible for her to reach, and he found himself mighty frustrated there wouldn't be any follow-through.

"You asking me for another sleepover?" she said.

"Yes, ma'am."

"How's Thursday?"

"Long time away."

She laughed again. The sound suckered him deep in the gut, right in the place that used to ache after his daddy died.

If he weren't careful, she was going to do him good.

She cupped his cheek and grinned a sweet little grin that made him think of peaches and pool parties. "Two tests Thursday."

"Two?"

"Work and school. But I'll be out of class early." She pressed one more kiss to his lips. "Hope you and Louisa have a nice day."

He snorted.

"Not easy being the baby sister. Especially when you have so much to live up to." She said it lightly, but the way her eyes flicked down, he didn't know if she was talking about Louisa or herself. She nodded toward the hotel. "I have some business I need to finish up in there."

"Want help?"

"No."

"Had to ask."

"And I had to say no."

"Make sure you get all those no's out before you come over Thursday night."

Her saucy grin promised all he'd be hearing out of that mouth would be yeses.

Now if he could figure out how to handle having the perfect woman.

ANNA KNOCKED ON the door of Room 416 in The Harrington. After a minute, Neil opened it and blinked bloodshot eyes at her. He was still in his white linen mess dress shirt and whatever liquor he'd steeped himself in last night.

He stood straighter and winced. "Hey." His voice was froggy. "Wanna come in?"

She'd seen him drunk enough to know the next step. He wasn't a mean drunk.

He was a sorry drunk.

And she was about to make him wish a hangover was all he had. "You have ten minutes to get yourself cleaned up and meet me downstairs. After that, I'm leaving." Because she wouldn't have this conversation with him unless he was sober.

Or at least not getting drunker.

Nine minutes and fifty-eight seconds later, Neil sat down beside her in the lobby, leaving a respectable distance between them. His eyes were still rimmed in brandy-overload and his movements were jerky, but he'd shaved and put on a shirt and pants that barely carried the scent of his pity party. "Hi," he said.

Anna sat as tall as she could without standing up. "You divorced me," she said without preamble. "You insulted me in front of our friends, you broke my heart, and then you left me here. You don't get back into my life. Not yesterday, not today, not *ever*."

His left cheek twitched like it always had when he was agitated. "I made a mistake."

"And now I've made a life. *Without* you. You don't get a second chance, Neil."

"I just—" His head dipped to his knees. "I'm lost, Anna. I haven't been on time for anything since I left. I can't find stuff. I don't know when I should book tickets to go home and see my parents for the holidays. I just don't know."

She'd been down too many times the last few months to take pleasure in kicking him. Seeing him broken was like staring back at herself right after he left, and she felt for him.

But he'd walked away from her. As they said down here, she could fix broke, but she couldn't fix stupid. "Welcome to adulthood."

She stood.

"Anna." He reached a hand out, a pitiful offering from a man she'd given so much to. "I can do better by you."

She caught sight of Kaci and Lance across the reception area. Two wonderful people she never would've met if Neil hadn't abandoned her and who had introduced her to others she was blessed to call friends. She looked down at her ex one last time. "I have a good life," she said.

And this time, she did the walking away, and he did the not-following.

Chapter Nineteen

She did less climbing of the ladder and more hopping rung to rung.
—The Temptress of Pecan Lane, *by Mae Daniels*

MONDAY MORNING, Rex sputtered his normal protest, but Anna couldn't stop smiling.

Until Jules popped in. "Hey, I need new RR—holy hell, what happened to you?"

Anna fingered the bruise on her cheek. "Next time you're at a wedding where the bride's bouquet is made of lollipops, run."

Jules reached for Anna's ruler in her desk organizer, but stepped back and gnawed on her thumbnail instead. "Nice wedding otherwise?"

"Yeah."

"See anybody I know?"

Anna froze. Had Jules helped Neil? *Why?*

They stared at each other. Jules didn't blink. Anna's fingers tightened on Rex's mouse. "I don't think so," she finally said. "How was your weekend?"

Jules held her gaze a moment longer.

As if she were calling Anna a liar.

Jules opened her mouth, but heat surged through Anna's

cheeks. "You know what?" Anna said. "I *did* see somebody you know. And I'm having a hard time figuring out how he knew where to find me."

A guilty flush crept up Jules's neck. Her eyes hardened. "You trying to say something?"

"I'm saying it would've been a shame if my ex-husband made scenes at *two* of my friends' weddings this year," Anna bit out. "Why would you do that?"

"Do *that*? God, you act like getting back together with Neil would be horrible. How long did you mope that he was gone? How many times did we need to hold your crybaby hand over him? Did you ever think I was trying to do you a favor?"

Anna's jaw dropped. "You want to mess with my head? Fine. Mess with my head. But leave my friends out of it. It's called a conscience, Jules. Get one."

The flush had reached Jules's ears and was sneaking up her cheeks. "You should be thanking me. Not like anybody else is interested in dating you and your problems."

"Tell that to my boyfriend." And even through her anger, she heard the squeal of triumph in her own voice. Maybe he was, maybe he wasn't, but she was sleeping with him and he'd asked her to lunch today. Close as she would get.

Jules's lip curled. "Enjoy it while it lasts." She thumped the door frame. "I need new RR-40s. If you want to keep your job." She left a lingering odor of pessimism and ugliness in Anna's cube.

Anna dug into her drawer for her can of Lysol. She shot a spray of disinfectant into the doorway.

And then she got back to work.

Because standing up for herself was fantastic, but it wouldn't pay the bills.

IT TOOK THREE DAYS for Louisa to get around to telling Mamie she'd found Jackson with a woman. Jackson knew that, because it took three days before Mamie called him. He was propped on his couch, eating reheated chicken and biscuits, still in his ABUs. He muted the game he still hadn't watched all the way through and took the call. "Yes, ma'am?"

"We need to halt the biscuit orders over here?" she asked.

He gave a grin and a head-shake. Radish settled her head back down on his foot. "My freezer's getting mighty full."

"You eating okay? Or are your new friend's biscuits that good?"

He paused the DVR and settled deeper into the couch. "Tell you a secret, Mamie?"

"Of course you can, sugarplum."

"She bakes pies."

Jackson almost felt the wind Mamie made when she sucked a breath in. "Better than your momma's?" she said with the same discreet tone another woman might've used to ask about plumbing problems.

"Told you it was a secret."

"Well, you bet your biscuits *I* won't say anything."

"Much obliged, Mamie."

"So when do I get to meet this girl?"

Jackson cleared his throat.

"Don't you be starting that, sugarplum," Mamie said. "You're old enough to know forever can work. Just because your daddy—"

"She's not interested in marrying a military man again," Jackson interrupted, because Mamie was the only person in the world who got to say a bad thing about his daddy, but that didn't mean he wanted to hear it. His daddy was the best man Jackson ever knew. If he wasn't man enough to keep Momma happy, Jackson didn't reckon that left him with much of a chance of ever doing any better.

Mamie cackled one of those deep, evil chuckles she got when she threw the kitchen sink at her hero. "Oh, sugarplum. Sounds like you found your perfect woman."

Yeah, and it left those biscuits feeling like IEDs in his belly.

They'd go off sometime, and when they did, it wouldn't be pretty.

Maybe he'd get lucky and they'd be duds. But seeing how much he was looking forward to seeing Anna Grace tomorrow night, lucky wasn't in his future.

Well, *that* kind of lucky was. Long-term lucky, probably not.

But her smile was worth the risk. They both knew the rules. "You taking notes, Mamie?"

"Notes? This here calls for firsthand research."

The thought of Mamie and Anna Grace teaming up against him should've made his blood run cold.

Put something warm in his veins instead. "Mamie—"

"Oh, don't go getting your bootlaces all knotted. I've been around the turnip truck a time or two. Know you gotta time these things right."

"And here I was fixing to ask how you were planning on fitting in a visit, what with your schedule. Don't know that this warrants missing a bowling night."

"Well then maybe you might could bring her on over so we can check out her form."

Radish lifted her head and gave a disgusted snort. Jackson couldn't blame her. He didn't need a mirror to know the goofy grin he was wearing didn't do any justice to his manhood. But he couldn't help it, not when he got to thinking about what Anna Grace would make of the Misses. "She's booked tighter than you, Mamie."

"Don't you worry about that, sugarplum. If I need to meet her, we got lots of time."

But after he'd hung up with Mamie, something bothered him.

And he had a pretty good feeling it was knowing that if he was picturing Anna Grace bowling with the old gals, he had a good case of being smitten.

THURSDAY NIGHT, Anna stepped out of the James Robert

chemistry building and into the night. The cooler air eased her swollen, exhausted brain back down to its normal size. She powered up her phone and headed for the parking lot. Wisps of mist danced through the streetlights. Disjointed conversations of her rapidly scattering classmates rolled over the asphalt. Anna's phone beeped with a text message notification.

The message put a giddy jog in her step.

Radish misses you.

Her shoulders scrunched in girly excitement. She thumbed a quick message back. *Such a sweetie. No wonder she and Enrique get along so well.*

When she pulled up in front of his house, he was tooling around with hunting gear in the garage. Radish watched him from her position sprawled across the floor. They both glanced up at her, and she couldn't decide which one had the biggest grin.

This wasn't permanent, but a warm welcome from a friend couldn't be bad for her.

She swung out of her car with her bag over her shoulder. "Getting packed?"

"About done." He tossed a camo duffel into the truck, dusted off his hands, and then pulled her in for a peck on the cheek. "Rest can wait. Tests good?"

"Passed one. Won't know about the other until next week."

"Feel good about it?"

"I'll let you know when I find my brains to think about it again."

His thumbs flicked over her ribs. "Looking for some stress relief?"

She leaned into him, inhaling the subtle hints of Old Spice. "I'm here, aren't I?"

"We'll get to that," he said on a chuckle. "Had a buddy over the other day. Said he wished his kitchen was clean as mine. Said he'd pay good."

Anna perked up. Organizing for cash? "Really?"

"Yeah, but don't you be getting any ideas about his drawers, you hear me?"

She laughed. "Yes, sir."

"Now then." He pulled her closer. "You're looking right pretty tonight."

And he was being right gentlemanly to say so, since there was no way it was true. She reached up to trace his ear. "You too."

He inhaled sharply, and his eyes went dark.

"So you like *that*." It was probably the most useful thing she'd learned all week.

"Not all I like."

Over her laughing protests, he swung her up over his shoulder, ordered Radish inside, and spent the next two hours making her brains completely unnecessary.

MONDAY MORNING, Anna fired up Rex then swung herself into the snack kitchen for coffee. Shirley turned from the sink and gave Anna a once-over.

Anna was humming.

"Good weekend?" Shirley asked. Her tone implied her real question. *Get laid?*

Anna stifled an irreverent smile. Not since Thursday. She'd spent the weekend studying, cleaning Walker's fish bowl, and getting paid to organize one of Jackson's old ROTC buddies' kitchen. But on the drive in this morning, she'd realized something.

She liked her life. "It was. Yours?"

"Too much time at soccer games, but it was nice. Classes going well?"

The one speed bump. She was doing well, but she wasn't enjoying them. She felt as if she were spitting out a bunch of *blah blah blahs* every time she took a quiz or test. But she was hitting the right *blah blahs*, because she was passing this semester. "Very."

"Good. I called Corporate and told them you're qualified on the equipment. They want you to start running tests."

Anna sucked in half of her bottom lip. This should've been good news. But— "Does Jules know?"

"She's out sick today. Order a couple of extra samples from storage so she can double-check you when she gets back."

The pot of coffee Shirley held suddenly looked like a big, black void, sucking all of Anna's happy feelings out her skin. Shirley might've been trying for her poker face, but her tone, the incline of her head, the way her eyes narrowed, Anna knew.

Shirley wanted Jules fired.

Anna couldn't deny her own feelings toward Jules had frosted like Minnesota in October, but she didn't want the guilt of being the catalyst that got someone fired.

She inhaled through her nose and moved to close a drawer that was sticking out. "Things have been improving," Anna hedged. Her suspicions about Jules and Neil aside, Jules *had* been more pleasant lately.

"Or she's hiding it better from you. Shit happens, kid. I'd rather work with someone who bakes pies through it. Been real impressed with you lately. Don't go screwing it up, putting misguided loyalty above taking care of yourself. Nice doesn't pay the bills."

Anna gulped back the bile making her feel as filthy as the coffee looked. She backed toward the door. "I'll get those extra samples ordered."

"Good decision, kid. Good decision."

JULES WAS BACK on Tuesday. She was so pale, she made the moon look tan and her cheekbones bordered on Cher sharp. But it was her subconscious gesture to her lower abdomen that made Anna's breath slip out in surprise.

Jules's eyes went as brittle as Anna's luck at weddings. "Problem?"

Anna shook her head. "Just remembered I have a quiz tonight. Feeling better?"

"Yep."

"How was your weekend?"

"Fine."

"How's Brad?"

"Fine." Her first *fine* sounded as fine as a flat tire. This one sounded as fine as cleaning up roadkill.

Anna stifled a sigh. "You talk to Shirley this morning?"

The wonky eyebrow made a rare appearance. "Now why would I want to ruin my perfectly good Monday morning?"

Oh, goody. Anna loved playing go-between as much as she loved having someone play with the days of the week. Her Tuesday, Jules's Monday. "She asked me to get a couple of extra samples and run them yesterday. Thought she might've mentioned it to you."

"Nope," Jules said. Her left nostril scrunched up in a sniff, but otherwise, she didn't seem to care one way or another. She ambled over to Anna's desk and plopped down at the edge, hands in her lap. "How'd it go?"

"Good," Anna said cautiously. "I have everything lined up for you to double-check, but nothing looked unusual or raised any flags."

"Great." Jules flicked her left thumb over her right fingernail, which was the only one that hadn't been already taken down to the quick. "Maybe after I'm done we can grab a late lunch."

They hadn't done lunch in months.

"Unless you have plans already," Jules said quickly.

"No plans. Lunch sounds great." Great for easing some guilt, anyway.

"Great," Jules said again. She slid off the desk. "Now quit goofing off and get back to work. Reports won't write themselves."

"Yes, ma'am."

Chapter Twenty

There were large fires and small fires, but the fire that burned inside him was the most dangerous fire of all.
—The Temptress of Pecan Lane, by Mae Daniels

ANNA WAS BUSIER than ever, but she had her full calendar color-coded and sticky-tabbed, she'd found her studying groove, Jules was mostly pleasant, and Anna managed to find some quality time for Kaci and her friends.

And Jackson was keeping her girly bits happy too.

The Friday after midterms, Anna rushed home after work to pack. Jackson arrived before she was done. Not that she minded. If she'd had to wait on him, she would've been mad about missing prime marshmallow roasting time.

But something was off. He walked stiffly through her door with a wrinkle in his forehead and no sign of his normal good humor. "Jackson? Are you okay?"

He shut the door with a definitive click. He cast a quick glance around the room, spun her against the wall next to her overflowing bookshelves, and kissed the bejeebers out of her. His hands slid up her shirt, his hard body, hard *everywhere*, trapped her against the wall with her purse hook poking her back. His leg pushed between hers, and she forgot all about campfires and marshmallows and sleeping naked with him in a sleeping bag.

That was hours away.

He was hot and hungry and ready *now*, and she was in a mood to oblige.

She pushed his flannel shirt out of the way and reached for the button on his jeans. He let out a primal growl, then cupped her rear end and tugged her closer.

Someone knocked at the door.

Jackson broke the kiss with another growl, this one more frustrated than turned on.

Anna blinked up at him, her chest rising and falling in time with his, neither of them all that steady. "Who's that?" she said.

"Hurricane Louisa just blew all my plans to hell."

His words filtered through the haze of lust obscuring her senses. She wanted to cry.

No naked sleeping bag time. Not with his baby sister within earshot.

But Jackson had said *hell*.

She bit back a giggle. He shot her an irritated look.

She couldn't stop her smile. "Does your momma know you cuss like that?"

"Don't you be getting on my list, Anna Grace." He flung the door open.

"What are y'all doing in here?" Louisa poked her head in. She gave Anna a once-over. "Ain't you packed yet?"

"Almost done."

Anna hadn't known Jackson even *had* blood pressure, but a vein in his neck throbbed so hard, he might need medical care before they got out of the apartment. "Is Radish coming?" she asked.

"She's waiting on your lazy butt out in the car," Louisa said.

"She eats that food, you're having sticks 'n leaves for dinner," Jackson said.

"Fine." Louisa dragged out the word to triple its normal syllables. "But hurry it up. I want to help build the fire."

She stalked back out. Jackson shut the door, then collapsed against it. "Couldn't leave her home," he said on a wince.

"Don't trust her, or feel guilty?"

"Both."

"She *is* legally an adult. What were you like when you were twenty-one?"

He shoved away from the door and into the kitchen to nudge her cooler with his foot. "Anna Grace, that's a three-point question."

On a laugh, she scooted around him and headed toward her bedroom. "Let me toss some flannel pajamas in my bag, and I'll be ready."

"Flannel pajamas." The last bits of hope evaporated from his voice. "You gonna go all independent on me if I take this cooler out to the car?"

"I suppose I can give you this one little show of macho." Her duffel bag lay open on her bed, ready for one last check. She pulled a pair of pajamas from her cold-weather drawer and turned to deposit them in her bag on top of three new Mae Daniels novels she'd snagged at his house last night. "Is it that bad? It's not like we were going to be alone."

"How about you let me know how those flannel pajamas are working for you in the morning."

She heard the distinct sounds of cooler handles groaning as they took on the weight of the ice and food packed inside, then footsteps toward the door. She was about to flip her duffel shut when something green and wiggly stuck its head out of the corner and leaped onto the bed.

Anna yelped. "Ohmigod!"

The lizard froze on the bed. Its throat pumped, and it trained one beady eye on her. Jackson flung himself into the room. "Anna?" The lizard dashed over the corner of her comforter and disappeared somewhere on the opposite side of the bed.

Anna sucked air through her nose. "Gecko."

She couldn't leave with a lizard on the loose. What if it stayed? What if it left lizard slime in her bed or it crawled in her underwear drawers?

She tried to rub the shiver out of her arms. Jackson took two steps around the bed, but she flung a hand out. "It's okay. I'll get it."

He pinned her with one of those *quit being an irritating female* looks she was seeing too often from a guy who was a friend with benefits, then continued around the bed and squatted. "Think he went under?"

Anna's toes squirmed inside her hiking boots. "If you hadn't come running in here, I could've grabbed him off the bed." She shuddered. Did lizards bite? What about their tails? Could that one drop his tail? She *so* didn't want to get stuck holding a lizard tail.

Did the tails still move after they detached?

Would there be blood?

Jackson peered over the side of the bed. "Probably looking for a warm place to hide. He'll find his way out if he gets hungry."

Hungry? Her gaze flew out to the gigantic brandy snifter on the counter beyond her bedroom door. "Walker," she whispered. Did lizards eat fish? Or swim?

"Walker?" Jackson asked.

"My fish." Anna dropped to her knees and squinted under the bed, but she couldn't detect any lizardly movements.

Jackson stared back at her from the other side. "You named your fish Walker?"

Still nothing lizardly. She reached into her nightstand and pulled out a flashlight, then trained it under the bed. "Long story. Not appropriate for a gentleman's ears."

He chuckled. "Got me there."

"Do you see it?"

"You quit shining that thing in my eyes, I might."

There was a knock on the door. "Hell-lllooo?" Louisa

yelled.

"Oh, there he goes!" Anna lunged and caught herself across the temple. The flashlight clattered away. Something heavy bumped the bed, and her mattress slid above her.

"Got it," Jackson said.

Anna rolled over. He winked at her on his way out. The lizard dangled from his fingers, and she swore the stupid thing blinked at her. "You stay right there, Anna Grace. Back in a minute to help you up."

If she could've reached a pillow, she would've thrown it at him.

Louisa poked her head in the bedroom. "What's going on?"

"Luggage malfunction." Anna pulled herself up. She tugged her hair to straighten her ponytail, then zipped her duffel up with the same efficiency she was using to slow her pulse.

"You guys making out?"

Jackson strolled back into the room and grabbed Anna's bag. "We're just friends. No making out."

Just friends? Who was he kidding? Louisa knew better.

Of course, they weren't much more than just friends, but still. Anna stalked after him. She'd *just friends* his ass off. "I can get my own bag."

"Shoot, Anna Grace, I haven't been this useful since that day we met."

He shuffled ahead of her, fast enough that she couldn't catch up. "I don't have problems like this when you're not around," she said.

"You saying you want me to leave you alone?"

The thought sent a pang through her heart, but she stomped it with her hiking boots and an irritated growl. "Why do you like to be so difficult?"

The full-force grin he tossed at her made her stomped heart flutter as if it had grown butterfly wings. "Too easy, Anna Grace." Her duffel over his shoulder, he snagged the cooler too. "We all ready, or you need to give your fish some counseling on account of his near-traumatic experience?"

The betta fish banged his face into the glass. Anna gave the bowl a little finger stroke, and Walker's blue gills flared out.

"That fish has issues," Louisa said.

"He's a good fish." Anna dropped a couple of fish flakes into the bowl, gave it another little tap, then grabbed her tent and followed Jackson and Louisa. Radish leaned her head out the truck window. She looked happy as a puppy in a field of rawhide bones.

While Jackson had his hands full, putting Anna's stuff in the bed, she took advantage of the opportunity to open her own door. Radish leaned off her seat to nose Anna's cheek. Anna scratched her ears. "Hey, pretty girl."

Louisa boosted herself into the backseat with the dog. A minute later Jackson climbed in. "Y'all ready?"

"Been ready," Louisa said. "Let's go make a campfire."

"You didn't tell her?" Anna murmured. Kaci had cancelled her classes for the day, and she and Lance had been out at the campsite since noon. Odds were good the fire had been going since 12:03.

She'd known Jackson had a devious streak, but his evil chuckle and the glint in his eyes sparked some sympathy for Louisa. "Anna Grace, you think you might could talk Louisa through that algebra homework she's been whining about not understanding?"

Louisa heaved a sigh. "It's gonna be a long ride, isn't it?"

"You bet your x-squared." Anna twisted in her seat to face the younger girl. "Bet you a marshmallow I can explain it better than Jackson."

Louisa straightened. She met Anna's gaze for a long minute, then pulled up a backpack. "You're on."

Jackson squeezed Anna's knee. She settled her hand over his, and got down to the dirty business of talking math while he pulled on an old Bama cap and pointed the truck toward a little spot of land Kaci had borrowed for them for the weekend.

CAMPING WASN'T HUNTING, but Jackson loved sitting in front of a roaring campfire under a full moon next to a pretty lady. Even Louisa wasn't irritating him so much, though it looked like Radish wanted earplugs. Anna was being a right good sport about it all.

Come to think of it, she was a right good sport about everything. Right down to his getting in her way when she was putting her tent together.

He bet the fire was driving her crazy too, all those logs stacked up in the haphazard way that made a campfire good. But she was doing a good job hiding it as she rotated her marshmallow the perfect distance over the coals to get a nice, even brown over a gooey center.

His groin got tight thinking about her gooey center, but with his sister three feet away on his other side, he'd have to burn all his own marshmallows if he didn't want to embarrass any of them.

"They don't," Anna said beside him.

"Hm?"

"The logs. They don't bother me."

He rubbed his chin. Now he *knew* he hadn't said that out loud. "I was thinking about your marshmallow."

"Not doing either of us any favors with *that* tonight."

It wasn't funny, but he chuckled anyway. Because maybe it was a tad bit funny.

His daddy would've thought so. *Anything worth having's worth working and waiting for*, he always said.

And suddenly Jackson was back at not funny. He shifted on the ground, looking past the fire to Louisa. He'd failed her in passing that lesson along.

He didn't much care for failing at anything.

He didn't much care for the thoughts he was getting about his sister lately either.

He reached around Anna, and he might've accidentally on purpose bumped her arm that was holding her marshmallow so steady. He also accidentally on purpose sniffed in that pretty scent of her hair longer than he meant to while he grabbed the bag of marshmallows.

Because those were the only marshmallows he'd be getting tonight. "Don't suppose you brought any pie?" he said softly.

"Pie?" Kaci said from Anna's other side. "You brought pie, sugar?"

Anna held up a smoking marshmallow. That pout was cute as all get-out on her. "Burnt-marshmallow-on-a-stick pie," she said. "It was almost perfect too."

"I'll fix one up for you," Jackson said.

Mostly because he felt bad hers got ruined. Some too because it would irritate her.

And irritate her it did. Her eyes glowed bright as the fire. "You need to worry about your own marshmallows."

He flashed her a grin he didn't feel. She was a special lady. Starting to sneak into places she didn't have any business being, making him believe he *did* need to be worried about his marshmallows. Mamie said he had a way of making women think it was their idea when they finally broke up with him, but she also said she planned to live to see him get his comeuppance.

He wasn't real happy with the idea of Mamie getting her final wish, but darned if Anna's frown didn't flip upside down when she took the stick he handed her. He had to swallow twice before he found the teasing note she'd expect. "You're a softie, Anna Grace."

"Only because I know you'll make it up to me later."

He blew out a slow breath. She hadn't taken too well to being just his friend. But Mamie had mentioned that Louisa was taking up with a boy, one who was old enough he should've had a degree and a real job instead of four more semesters ahead of him. Jackson wasn't about to be a bad example for her.

Never mind he already was.

But if Anna was willing to be miffed, it was a sacrifice he was willing to make. Provided it was only a little miffed.

Because he wasn't ready to push her away yet. He still liked her within arm's reach. "You sure you don't need me to show you how to hold that stick?"

"Again with the worrying about your own."

Half of his blood drained due south. "Killing me here, Anna Grace."

"This friend thing was *your* idea."

"Here. Do one for me." Louisa shoved her stick at him. "I like it a little burnt."

Turned out, Anna could roll her eyes out loud too. He stuck the marshmallow into the fire then cut a glance toward her. If she'd made any faces, they were gone now. She rotated her new marshmallow and scratched Radish's head with her other hand. Radish opened one eye, and Jackson could've sworn his dog silently called him a dummy.

A little too much female bonding going on around this campfire for his comfort. Didn't usually mind being outnumbered, but then, he prided himself on knowing when to skedaddle away from the girls before they started getting too womanish. But that wood on the fire wasn't the only thing burning tonight. Problem was, he couldn't decide if it was Louisa's brain from thinking so hard on the way up here, or something else entirely.

"I said a *little* burnt," Louisa shrieked.

Jackson lifted the blistered marshmallow and blew out the flames. Over the crackling of the campfire, he heard Anna chuckle softly. "If you want it done right," she said.

That was a challenge if he ever heard one. He shoved the stick back at Louisa. "You go on and show me how to do it."

He picked up another stick and put a marshmallow on it, eyed the way Anna Grace's marshmallow was toasting nice and even, and propped his own stick the right distance from the flames.

"That's not how," Louisa said. She stuck her marshmallow into the coals. A shower of sparks exploded.

Radish jumped. Anna yanked her stick away from the

sparks, and her marshmallow flew right off the end of the stick. Jackson lost sight of it once it cleared Louisa's head.

"Dammit," Anna muttered.

Jackson sucked his cheeks in. He silently handed over his stick.

"Now that's a good marshmallow," Louisa declared with her mouth full.

"Think Anna Grace likes 'em gooey on the inside," Jackson said.

"That right, Anna Grace?"

"Just Anna, please. And yes, I do. Hot, sticky, and melted on the inside, nice and toasty on the outside."

There went the other half of Jackson's blood. He propped himself back on his hands to keep from going too light-headed. "Fits you perfect," he said, and he almost sounded like his brain cells weren't operating on a lack of oxygen.

She cut her eyes away from her stick. "I'm toasty?"

"Uh-oh," Kaci said.

Lance chuckled like a man who'd said his fair share of stupid things.

"In all the good ways," Jackson said.

"What do you know about her gooey insides?" Louisa asked.

Darned if Anna's cheeks weren't suddenly glowing bright as the fire. He couldn't deny that he liked that polite side of her.

"Gotta have a gooey heart inside to put all that time into helping you with your homework," Jackson said.

He liked that about her.

Liked it a lot.

Anna's stick wobbled in the fire. She yanked it up, not so hard this time.

"Sure you don't want me to do that for you? Ain't looking so steady, Anna Grace."

"I'm gonna put you on a stick and roast you."

Might've sounded like a threat to a weaker man, but

Jackson liked those husky undertones.

"If you two are planning on making out, you're gonna have to do it in the truck, because I'm not sleeping in a dirty tent," Louisa said.

"No making out," Anna said crisply. "We're just *friends.*"

"Friends who do the naked hibbity-jibbity," Louisa said.

Jackson shoved a marshmallow stick at her. "You talk to Momma that way?"

"Where are y'all keeping the graham crackers and chocolate?"

Jackson gestured across the fire. "Picnic table." When Louisa stood, he shifted closer to Anna and nudged his nose against her cheek. "Might could lose her in the creek tomorrow."

She brushed a marshmallow kiss over his lips. "No, you couldn't."

"Awful tempted."

He felt her smile. "I could though," she said.

Kissing Anna was always sweet with the right sprinkling of spice, but with melted sugar hot on her tongue, she was taking his mind and his body places he couldn't stay.

Twigs snapped. He forced himself to pull away. Clouds were rolling in, dampening the moonlight. When Louisa settled back next to him, Lance and Kaci stood. Lance mentioned a walk down by the creek, and Jackson's hope for his own moonlit excursion squished into the dirt like Anna's launched marshmallow.

Anna paused between marshmallows to rub her bare arms before trading her empty stick for the new one Jackson had waiting. He stood, gave his pants a dust, and headed for the truck. A minute later, he dropped his favorite Bama sweatshirt into Anna's lap.

She made to hand it back to him but her nose twitched. She gave the shirt a sniff, then stretched it over her head. "Thank you," she said in that same husky, sleepy way she used late at night when they were tangled up in his sheets.

Jackson's nerves coiled so tight between his legs, he wouldn't be able to stand up again tonight. Couldn't remember the last time he was jealous of a sweatshirt.

They all went quiet, Louisa burning and eating half the bag, Anna doing more roasting than eating, Jackson getting jealous of the marshmallows every time she put one in her mouth. Eventually he caught her yawning. "Giving up?" he asked.

She stretched her arms. "Mm-hmm."

Couldn't blame her. With the fresh night air, a full belly, and being all cozy by the fire, sleep was one of his top-five camping activities.

Sleeping curled up next to her would've been first, but with Hurricane Louisa here, he was plum out of luck.

Jackson stood and held out a hand. "C'mon, then, Anna Grace. Better get you to bed so you can't blame fatigue when I catch more fish than you tomorrow."

He helped Anna up, then his sister. He wrapped an arm around each of them and walked them to their tent across the campsite from Kaci and Lance's smaller tent. Radish trailed after them. "No pillow fights without me, understand?"

Louisa smacked him in the gut. "Dirty old man. I'm telling Momma."

Jackson chuckled. He gave Louisa a shoulder hug, then shooed her into the tent. She rolled her eyes out loud again, but she zipped herself inside.

He linked his hands around Anna's back and pulled her closer, because not kissing her was about to drive him mad. He wanted to strip her naked in front of the campfire and see where else she tasted like marshmallows, but he couldn't do that discreetly.

Radish nudged between them, and he reluctantly let her go.

"We'll go for a walk tomorrow night," he murmured.

She brushed her finger along the edge of his ear in silent agreement. "As long as you're not a sore loser when I catch more fish than you tomorrow."

"We'll see about that, Anna Grace."

She kissed his cheek, then disappeared into the tent. Jackson headed back to the fire, listening to the girls talk about him.

"Sorry I wrecked your plans," Louisa said. Her voice dripped with Southern honey, the kind that made it impossible to taste the poison underneath.

He started for the tent, but stopped himself. Some other Yankee girlfriend might've needed his interference, but this was Anna.

Sure enough, her voice came out gentle as a feather, picking her words as though she were looking for good peaches off a late August tree. "Um, did you steal all the fish out of the creek?"

"No."

That was his Anna, catching Louisa off guard. Jackson didn't have to see his sister to know she'd be wrinkling her brow and doing that *what in tarnation are you talking about* thing with her lips.

"And we have another three bags of marshmallows, and plenty of firewood," Anna continued. "And the tent doesn't leak, and I *love* campfire breakfasts. How would you have ruined that?"

"You know," Louisa said, a little less certain, a lot less sweet, "your time *alone*."

"With Kaci and Lance and Jackson? I can see them anytime."

Not between Uncle Sam's sending Jackson TDY and Anna's class schedule. It was nice of her to stay with Radish once or twice, but he couldn't deny he'd been jealous of his dog.

She thought she got enough time with him?

"I wish I'd had an opportunity to spend some more time with my big sister before she got married and had kids," Anna said. "It must be nice to have Jackson close by."

He blinked in the darkness, and he imagined Louisa was

doing the same thing.

He'd be darned. Anna Grace was playing right back.

"How old is she?" Louisa asked after a long silence.

"Five years older."

Jackson watched their silhouettes. Looked as if Anna was still wearing his sweatshirt.

Good.

"How many kids does she have?" Louisa asked.

"Three boys." Anna reached for something. "Wanna see pictures?"

Louisa scooted closer to Anna.

He'd never seen pictures of her nephews.

The two girls put their heads together, and Jackson felt an unfamiliar, uncomfortable swelling beneath his breastbone.

Anna was good for Louisa.

"He's really not into commitment." Louisa said it so quiet, Jackson almost missed it.

It was true, but when he saw Anna's shadow nod, and when he heard her answer, "That works for me," the swelling in his chest broadened up toward his shoulders and sunk into his gut, making his stomach feel every bit of the marshmallows he'd eaten.

But twigs snapped and leaves swished near the trail down to the creek, so Jackson took a deep breath to make his lungs squeeze his innards back into their proper places. The campfire didn't feel warm at all anymore.

"Girls go to bed?" Lance asked when he and Kaci appeared, hand in hand, happy and content and committed.

"Yep," Jackson said.

"Sugar, we'll watch the fire if you want to call it a night."

He was calling it something, but the right word wasn't *night*.

It was *lonely*.

Chapter Twenty-One

He'd always thought fishing was for catching fish, but that was before a woman hooked his heart.
—The Temptress of Pecan Lane, *by Mae Daniels*

SATURDAY DAWNED WITH perfect fishing weather. A little overcast with a breeze rippling the surface of the water. Anna could still smell the breakfast campfire. She'd eaten so many pancakes, they were filling in the space between her ribs.

She'd been out of bed before Louisa, which had given her the opportunity to use Jackson for nose- and finger-warming.

Kaci would've been proud of her for asking for help.

Jackson certainly had been.

But now everyone was up and about, poles in hand, casting on the bank of the creek.

Jackson slid up next to her. "You want me to bait that hook for you, Anna Grace?"

She just looked at him. He grinned. "No lizards, but worms are okay, huh?"

"Worms don't bleed on my carpet if their tails fall off."

He did that amused coughing thing. "Slime and dirt are okay, but no blood. Got it."

"We're camping. And fishing. I'm flexible."

"Well, you give a holler if you need some help."

If his dimples weren't so utterly irresistible, she would've considered wasting the time by being irritated.

And if Louisa hadn't been tapping her foot a few feet down, fishing pole weaving in the air, Anna would've considered asking the difference between lake and creek fishing. With so many lakes back home, she'd never had reason to fish in a creek.

"If she doesn't want help, I do," Louisa said.

Anna's jaw clenched. She retrieved a can of worms from the tackle box and made her way down the creek in search of the right place to bait her hook and cast.

The last time she'd been fishing, she was a teenager. But she still remembered how to hook the worms, and it took a practice cast or two, but soon she was comfortable with the rod and reel Lance and Kaci had loaned her.

They spent most of the morning wandering up and down the creek. The fish weren't biting. Might've had something to do with Kaci and Lance and Jackson's one-upping each other with more stories of their youth and all the laughter bouncing off the water. Louisa told a few stories of her own, but she couldn't compete with the three musketeers.

From its perch in the ocean-blue sky, the sun shone down over the massive oak and pine trees and glinted off the creek waves. Louisa wandered closer to Anna until they had to watch for each other when casting and reeling in. Anna would've moved farther, but a rocky outcropping of clay and tree roots blocked her way.

Jackson was on Louisa's other side, down far enough to cast without hitting anyone, close enough to rebait Louisa's hook on demand.

Louisa's attitude annoyed Anna, even though she shouldn't have had an opinion one way or another about how Jackson humored his sister's helplessness. Just because Louisa was still young enough to have the luxury of time to decide what she wanted to do with her life didn't make her *bad*. If Anna could've gone back to twenty-one, she would've done a few things differently. Not married Neil. Experimented with classes in other degree programs to make sure chemistry was her true love.

Most days she was happy enough with her goals, but the schedule was a drag sometimes. Especially during some of the more boring lectures.

Anna cast with a frustrated grunt and turned her reel.

According to Louisa, *all* college lectures were boring. So maybe Anna's problem wasn't jealousy. Maybe it was simply that Louisa had a bad attitude that Jackson kept humoring.

If he wanted to treat his sister like a spoiled princess, that was his business. They weren't in a *real* relationship. She had no right to care.

Something tugged at her line.

Anna snapped to attention. She adjusted the reel. Tension bent the tip of her pole.

"Got something there?" Jackson asked.

"Think so." Anna kept reeling. Whatever she'd hooked was putting up a massive fight. "Feels like a nice one."

Louisa backed away and gave her room.

"You go, sugar," Kaci said. "Bring him in."

The fish thrashed to the surface. Anna laughed. "Got you now." It pulled and tugged, but Anna held steady, and soon she dangled the fish out of the water. Its sleek silver body curved in a C when it wasn't making its last-ditch efforts to escape.

"Hang on, big guy." Anna reached for it, but bumped hands with Jackson. Ornery man. "I've got it."

"Gonna take forever to get that fish stink off your hands," Jackson said. He batted her hands away with a calculated twinkle in his eyes. "Besides, he might bleed. I got this one for you. He'll be good all fried up for dinner."

Anna swung the pole so the fish was out of reach. "Catch and release. We've got food for dinner."

Jackson hooked the edge of her pole and swung it back. "No fun in that."

The fish flopped and twisted on the end of the line, gills

flaring, eyes big and fishlike. Creek water flung off it.

"Catch and release," Anna insisted. "Would you let go? I've got this."

She tugged the pole again, and the fish swung wide.

Right into Louisa's face.

She ducked too late. "Oh, gross! Get it off! Get it away! Gross gross gross! *Ew!*" She scrubbed at her face, shrieking.

"Ohmigod!" Anna gasped. "I'm so sorry."

Jackson's eyes flared wide. "Okay, Lou-Lou?"

Anna floundered to snatch the fish. She unhooked him and tossed him back. Kaci and Lance trotted over.

Louisa was in the midst of a fit that would've made Kaci's momma proud. "How could you do that?" she wailed. "A fish touched me. On my *face*. Ew, ew, *ew!*"

"Gonna live, Lou-Lou," Jackson said. He pulled off his T-shirt and handed it to her.

She swiped it over her fish-slime-infested skin. "God, I can't smell anything but fish." She gave Anna the stink-eye. "*This* is why you let the menfolk do man-things. So we *ladies* don't get smacked in the face with a fish."

Anna's face burned, but worse, her chest felt as if it had been rolled in fishing line and was now being tugged tighter and tighter, as if she were the one dangling naked on a hook for all her friends to see.

She hadn't done anything wrong. Not on purpose.

A roar of displeasure erupted in her veins, and she felt her nose flare. "You'll go hunting. You'll shoot an animal. But you can't touch a fish?"

Louisa channeled an air of Southern belle outrage even while scrubbing her nostrils. "Touching's for boys."

The line around Anna's chest squeezed tighter, cutting into her breathing space. She quaked with an energy she hadn't expected and didn't understand. "Seriously?"

"And dead squirrels and deer don't smack me right in the kisser like Moby Fish."

Anna's jaw ached. "It's just river water."

"It's just *gross*, and I shouldn't have to touch dead things."

"Sugar, down here, our mommas teach us the value of being helpless sometimes," Kaci said to Anna.

"Sometimes." Anna gripped the handle of the fishing pole so hard, she was probably leaving dents in the hard plastic. "When does *sometimes* turn into a complete inability to take responsibility for yourself and your actions? When does *sometimes* cripple your chances at being able to hold a real job and pay your own bills and survive on your own?"

Louisa's eyes snapped. "Honey, that's why we go fishing for men."

Jackson stepped between them, wariness and something else Anna had never seen darkening his eyes. "Pipe down, Louisa. Think you're gonna make it."

"I—"

Kaci cut her off. "Anna, sugar, I'm pickled out with this fishing stuff. You got a book I could borrow?"

But Anna wasn't looking at her. She was too busy having a staring contest with Jackson, and she didn't like the *quit picking on my sister* message.

Sure, she would've expected the same from Beth, but Anna wasn't the spoiled rotten brat Louisa was.

Jackson's eyebrows knit closer together. *You better quit talking now* came silently from his pursed lips, like he didn't appreciate her assessment of his sister.

"It *is* what men are for," Louisa said. "Russ won't give me a job, so I'll just get married and have babies and let my husband take care of me. Nothing wrong with that. It's what Momma did and what her momma did before her, and it's what I'll do."

Anna's heart ached. It ached for Louisa's ignorance, it ached for the wedge splintering her good thing with Jackson, but mostly, it ached for herself. "Yeah, works great, right up until it's over."

Kaci tugged Anna's arm, and this time, Anna looked away from Jackson.

"She's young, sugar," Kaci said. She steered Anna back to

the campsite. "Give her time."

"Won't matter if he leaves me in a ditch with six babies," Louisa called. "Russ and Jackson will take care of me."

Anna wrenched herself out of Kaci's grasp and spun back toward Louisa. "And forty years from now, do you want to be the person Russ and Jackson took care of, or do you want to be the person who left a mark on the world?"

"That's enough." The quiet warning in Jackson's voice sent a chill down Anna's spine. His eyes had gone completely dark, his disapproval directed square at her. The only message she got now was *get the hell out of my business.*

Her eyes stung. "Apparently not. You're not doing her any favors, you know."

Anna wasn't doing herself any favors either.

IT TOOK LOUISA near about three-point-two minutes to quit her hollering once Anna and Kaci were out of earshot. Lance had apparently gotten a boost of intelligence through getting hitched, because he'd tucked tail and followed the women.

Once Louisa finished with her say, she returned Jackson's shirt and grabbed her fishing pole.

Which meant it was time for Jackson to do something he wished he'd been smart enough to do over the summer.

He blocked her rod so she couldn't cast. "I won't," he said.

She channeled Momma's favorite disapproving blink. One long, two short, followed by another pointed long. "You won't what?"

He had to swallow to get the words halfway out his mouth, because it went against everything his daddy had ever taught him, but he had to say it. "I won't take care of you."

Her lips parted. Her left eyebrow crinkled in the center. "What did you say?"

"I won't take care of you," he repeated. He felt like his lungs had turned into glaciers, freezing the air inside him, inching outward, crushing his other organs, but he channeled one of his own favorite parental expressions, the one his daddy had always used whenever Jackson disappointed him. "Only person in this world responsible for you is you. You want to fall back on Russ, you go right ahead. But until you start trying to make your life better for you, until you start taking school seriously and looking for a job, don't expect me to come around and pick up the pieces."

Her mouth formed a perfect O. Her shoulders went back, and she tried to do that fourteen-feet-tall thing Anna Grace had mastered. Jackson widened his stance and narrowed his eyes.

She faltered. "Yeah, well, it's easy for you." She poked him in the chest, right on his tiger paw. "You had Daddy."

His blood roared. He clenched his teeth against it. Yeah, he'd had Daddy. But Louisa hadn't been lacking in support. Killed him to admit it, what with all that Russ and Momma would've put Daddy through if he hadn't been in that accident, but Russ had made sure Louisa didn't want for anything. And it killed Jackson to admit maybe Momma had done something Anna Grace would've scoffed at—she'd gotten married to take care of her family when Daddy wasn't there to provide anymore.

"Life's what you make of it," Jackson said. "What it looks like here, you're making a mess of yours. Nobody to blame but yourself. You want to be a grown-up, we'll hang out. You want to be a baby, go on home and get yourself a nursemaid."

Tarnation. Not the tears.

And the chin wobble.

Jackson yanked his T-shirt back on. He hated when girls cried.

Hated it worse when he made them, but he was pretty good at avoiding that.

Usually.

"You've never liked me," Louisa said.

Jackson blew out a sigh. He'd asked for this. "That's not true."

"Then why didn't you ever come home?"

He regarded her suspiciously. He felt like a worthless yahoo for making her cry, but she'd had a lot of years to perfect the *poor me* act. He was a sucker for believing the trembling lip and big old teardrops, but she was the only sister he'd ever have. "Wasn't about you."

"And you always stay with Mamie and then rub it in my face that she likes you better than me."

She'd crossed the line there. Mamie didn't play favorites.

But he hadn't heard tell of many times she'd taken Louisa out bowling with her like she'd done when Jackson was little.

"Momma and Russ did Daddy wrong, but y'all took it out on me," Louisa said. She sniffled. "And now you're back home, but you're spending all your time with *Anna*. I could've been with Stone all weekend, but instead, I'm here. Maybe I wanted to go camping with you all by yourself. You ever think of that, you big lug-head?"

Considering Jackson knew good and well she didn't like hunting, camping hadn't crossed his mind as an activity she would've liked for much more than the marshmallows and the chance to make Jackson miserable. "Too far, Lou-Lou," he warned.

She shrugged. "Worth a try. You're being mean."

"Not mean to tell you what you need to hear," he said, but he had to force it, because he didn't want to hurt her. Didn't like feeling like an old man either. "Time I was your age, I had a job lined up and I was putting everything I had into doing my best every day. Like Daddy taught me to."

"Daddy raised you better than to go to Alabama."

"Daddy raised me better than to let you grow up worthless."

Louisa's eyes started their heavenward supplication, but Jackson nudged her foot. "You're not worthless," he said. "But you're working on it. Gotta pull yourself together, Louisa. Get your grades up. Work at something for once."

"You're a jerk," she said.

And then she spun and was gone, headed away from him, away from camp, and away from the creek.

Well, tarnation again.

He was working on being useless himself.

Not much a man could do after that but sit himself right back down and wait for it all to blow over.

Took two hours. Two long hours of sitting with his dog, flinging a halfhearted line into the creek, debating with himself over the wisdom of going to talk to Anna, but eventually Louisa showed back up, looking for all the world like nothing was wrong. "I'm hungry," she said, "so I'm gonna go up to camp and get myself some food."

Still felt like dangerous territory there, but he went with her.

And when they returned to camp, Jackson realized he had another problem.

"Is that a label on the fire pit?" Louisa asked.

Kaci and Lance were polishing off some cold fried chicken at the picnic table. From what Jackson could tell, the only thing *not* labeled were their foreheads. Anna was nowhere in sight.

"Plum tuckered herself out." Kaci nodded at the tent. She dropped her voice to a stage whisper. "Strained her thumb doing all that typing, then her label maker overheated. Good thing it was her spare."

"Weirdo," Louisa said.

Jackson glowered at her. She stumbled back a step. "Um, lunch. I'm hungry."

"Might want to take yours back down to the creek," Lance said to Jackson. He seemed to only half-imply that Jackson might get some make-up nookie. The other half warned he might want to dig out some Kevlar instead.

"Yep, you go on," Kaci said. "We'll keep a good eye on baby sister here."

Louisa opened her mouth, but twin looks of *don't do it* from Kaci and Lance had her snapping her trap back shut. She shoved a couple of bags at Jackson. "Chicken and biscuits?"

The vortex of festering, seething indignation surrounding the tent gave Jackson the impression he wouldn't be having any milk to go with those biscuits today. Probably not anytime this week.

Maybe even this century.

This was the normal part of a relationship where he should've been glad she had an excuse to give him what-for so he could pull his dumb redneck routine, wish her well, and let her walk away liking or disliking him as she saw fit.

Instead, an old burning sensation flared up in that dark, hidden place deep in his gut that tended to show only when he'd lost something.

Like his daddy.

He was having too much fun with Anna to lose her now.

Yeah. Fun. It was all about the fun. And there was his daddy's chuckle rattling around inside his head again, but this time, it had a wry twist to it, the kind Daddy used to make when he was watching Jackson dig himself deeper and deeper in a mud pit.

Jackson looked back at the angry-woman force field surrounding the tent.

It wasn't a mud pit this time. It was a whole stinking acre of quicksand, and he was right in the plum middle without a line.

He tucked his lunch under his arm, and went back to the creek.

Because he needed to do some festering of his own. Took a danged idiot to muck up his own rules this good.

Time to get back in touch with the rocket scientist.

Chapter Twenty-Two

Her smarts and her heart were rarely in agreement.
—The Temptress of Pecan Lane, *by Mae Daniels*

ANNA HADN'T REALIZED she fell asleep until someone woke her by unzipping the door. She squeezed her eyes shut and drew a hesitant breath. Lemons.

Not Old Spice.

She should've been glad. Because lemons meant the owner of the crap that had exploded all over the tent was back, and if she wanted to fight about Anna labeling and putting it all away, then Anna was ready to fight.

Old Spice would've meant she had to face big brother and find out if she got to continue deluding herself about this thing with him being a casual fling. Her relationship with Jackson was glorious because they didn't have hard stuff. The hard stuff took work, and since neither of them were in this long-term, there was no reason to work out big problems.

So why did she feel as though she'd dove headfirst into an icy river of self-examination and swam across it to commitment territory?

And why did Jackson's being upset scare her more than getting attached?

The other sleeping bag rustled. Anna held her body still until Louisa's breathing evened out.

After several minutes of no movement, Anna cautiously rolled over and peered at the other girl.

Her mass of curls spilled out over the sleeping bag. The back of her Auburn sweatshirt showcased the regular rise and fall of her ribs. Anna snuck off her own sleeping bag and crept to the door. She unzipped it one tooth at a time until she could squeeze out. The campsite was empty, though there was some movement in Lance and Kaci's tent. There was also a note on the picnic table, right above its shiny new "Picnic Table" label. Her cheeks flushed. She absently rubbed her sore thumb.

Maybe she'd gone overboard.

The note from Kaci told her they were taking afternoon camp naps but that Jackson was down at the creek.

The mere sight of his name on paper made her pulse pitter-patter. She squeezed her eyes shut and sucked in a breath for courage, then crunched over the scattered leaves and dried pine needles to see about her—whatever he was.

She found Jackson reclining against a hill. Radish snoozed at his feet. She stepped toward them. Both of them looked up.

Her hands hung awkwardly at her side. She didn't know what she was supposed to say. Jackson seemed more wary than irritated.

Obviously he'd seen the labels.

He patted the ground next to him. "Still mad, Anna Grace?"

She plopped down and stared out at the creek. The wispy clouds of this morning had blown out, and darker, more sinister clouds were slowly rolling in. "It's not any of my business," she said.

When he didn't answer, she risked a look at him. "But I have a hard time believing she's related to you, as dumb as she acts."

He brushed a hand over her back. Some of Anna's tight muscles unlocked. They didn't open, but they were unlocked. "Not everybody's built like you," he said, but his tone was more matter-of-fact than accusatory.

She rolled her lower lip into her mouth. "She doesn't have to be like me," she finally said, "but what happens if she gets married and moves halfway across the country, and something happens to you and the rest of your family, then she gets divorced or widowed and has kids to take care of and no way to support them because everyone always took care of everything for her?"

"Little extreme there, don't you think?"

"I'm sorry, have we met?"

He chuckled. A few more muscles clicked loose. He slipped his hand under her shirt, his fingers doing nothing more wicked than resting on her skin, and different muscles tingled in that oh-so-good way. "I know I give you trouble about not letting me do things for myself," she said, "but I do appreciate your gentlemanly side. It makes you special. Even if sometimes I want to beat you over the head and tell you girls aren't helpless."

He angled his leg against hers, nudged closer with his shoulder. "Takes a remarkable woman to stand up to life like you're doing. Got a lot of respect for that myself." He nipped at her shoulder. "Turns me on, if we're being honest."

Her breath hitched. She wanted to say more, but she didn't want to break the connection with him. She leaned into him. "I didn't mean to hit her in the face with a fish."

It started with a chuckle, but soon he was laughing so hard she worried he'd use up all his good energy before they finished this quasi-making-up thing.

But then she pictured that fish landing square in the middle of Louisa's shocked face, and soon she was laughing too.

He pulled her to his side and chuckled into her neck. "Ah, Anna Grace."

"Bet she doesn't crash any more camping trips."

"Nah, that'd take a dead squirrel tucked up in her sleeping bag."

At the speculative look on his face, Anna gave him a friendly shove. "Not in my tent, buster."

He pulled her in for a kiss, then tugged her up on top of him. "No?"

"Nuh-uh."

He threaded his fingers through her hair, holding her close while he did that thing with his mouth that he did so well. She shifted to straddle him better and felt his erection throb in response. "We shouldn't."

"Nobody comin' this way."

"But it's dirty."

The grin that lit his face told her that was the exact wrong thing to say.

"They'll all know," Anna said.

"Darlin', they already know." He suckled her earlobe and slipped a hand beneath her waistband.

She gasped and arched into his hand. "We don't have—"

"Back pocket."

"But—"

His hand inched lower. "Anna Grace. Hush." He sealed his mouth over hers and did things with his fingers that she was convinced no Southern gentlemen should know, but which she was infinitely grateful to him for knowing anyway. Soon, she was bare-assed for all the fish in the river to see, and, most surprising of all, she didn't mind a bit.

Because she was with Jackson, and he knew her, and he knew her body, and he handled both with the right amount of care and attention. Because he was Jackson, and that was what he did.

And if she was lucky, he'd keep doing it for a long, long time.

WHEN JACKSON BROUGHT Anna and Radish back up to camp, Kaci and Louisa were setting logs on the fire while Lance fetched more wood. The girls both looked up and grinned.

Kaci in a grown-up, good-for-you way, Louisa in a want-to-be-grown-up way he didn't like on his sister. Louisa lifted a pointed eyebrow at Anna and tugged her hair. Anna's cheeks flushed. She lifted her hand as if she were going to brush something incriminating out of her hair, but Jackson caught it. "No, you don't."

Louisa wrinkled her nose at him. He sent her another one of Daddy's looks.

The wrinkled nose morphed into a full-on irritated pout. "Where you been? I'm hungry."

Jackson started toward the coolers, before he checked himself. "Food's right there. You want some, help cook it."

Kaci lit the fire. It wasn't as hot as the one picking up in Louisa's face. She tromped across to the cooler, picked out a cheese stick, then plopped down in a lawn chair, one leg dangling over the arm. If she could've turned that smoke from her silent temper fit into poison and put it in his fried chicken, he suspected she would've.

Wasn't easy to remind himself she was old enough to be self-sufficient.

"Progress," Anna murmured. She squeezed his fingers then went to help Kaci pull good old-fashioned foil packs out of the coolers.

Making up might not've been the smart thing to do, but not making up with Anna was impossible.

He didn't much care to think about why.

After the ladies set the food out, Lance and Jackson put it in the right place over the fire. Louisa simmered down, and the tension slowly left the campsite. Everyone chattered away about safe topics.

They all settled in to eat dinner, Jackson flanked by Louisa and Anna, Lance and Kaci across the fire. Lance twisted the tops off two beers, then handed one to Kaci. "Heard you guys scored tickets to the Alabama-Auburn game," he said to Jackson.

"Four of 'em," Louisa said proudly.

"Craig's getting one," Jackson said.

Louisa almost toppled her chair into the fire. "Nuh-uh."

Jackson speared a potato and avoided looking at her for fear her eyes had turned into the lost ark, capable of turning him to ash if he looked too close. "Said he wanted to go."

He shot a glance at Anna to avoid the smoke of displeasure shooting out Louisa's aura. Anna Grace looked as if she were absorbing a couple new Southern insults.

"Guess you picked your date then," Louisa said.

Jackson's left ear twitched at the honey in her tone.

He grabbed for his water bottle. It made an ominous crackling noise. "Guess so."

"Well, good," she said. "I'm taking Anna Grace."

His head whipped around so fast it shifted the flow of the campfire smoke. He rolled his foot, trying to ground himself so the electric currents of disbelief would flow back through the earth down to hell, where they belonged, and quit making his heart stutter all irregular and panicky.

"Just Anna's fine," Anna said breezily.

"Well, *just Anna*, you wanna come to the Auburn-Alabama game with me?" Louisa said.

Kaci made a weird choking noise. Anna wasn't saying anything, and she might've been three feet behind him, but he could've sworn he felt her heart tripping in time with his.

He didn't want to take a gander on whether it was because she wanted to meet his momma, or because the thought turned her into a yellow-livered Yankee. But Louisa had put the invitation out there, and he'd do a lot of things for Anna, but he wouldn't insult anyone—not Anna, not Louisa, not his family—by taking it back.

But he had an easy out. Thank sweet baby Jesus for the timing of the Iron Bowl. "Anna Grace, you going home for Thanksgiving?" he said.

"Oh, no, you don't," Kaci hollered. "She's making our pies."

Well, this was as tidy as a palmetto bug in a cat's paw, now wasn't it? He forced himself to look at Anna. "You staying here?"

Wasn't that something he should've known? There was a reason he didn't date women during hunting season.

She shrugged. It irritated him that he couldn't read the semi-panicked expression in her eyes. Panicked he'd withdraw Louisa's invitation, or panicked he wouldn't?

Didn't help he couldn't decide himself.

"Finals are two weeks later." Her eyes shifted. *That* one he got. She was still hiding from family. "I'm taking some extra time at Christmas instead."

His daddy was having a full-out rolling-on-the-ground laughing fit up there in Jackson's head. Warm dampness broke out on his forehead. That usually happened only three miles into a five-mile run.

"So you could come on over for the game," Louisa said. "It's only a little drive on up to Auburn. Not like you gotta go all the way to the devil's stomping grounds."

Jackson was starting to understand what blood pressure felt like.

"I really need to do well on my finals," Anna said. She looked as though she wanted a new label maker, and Jackson's sympathy for her overrode his sympathy for himself. This wasn't her fight, but she was stuck in the middle all the same. Stuck in the middle with Louisa and Momma and Russ.

He had a sudden image of taking Anna out with Mamie and the girls. The pressure in his throat eased up.

Lot of pressure, matter of fact. Anna Grace would love the girls. And when she figured out who Mamie was—he grinned. Yeah, that would be worth taking a girl home for the first time since high school. "Break might be good for you," he said to her.

She looked at him like the campfire had smoked his brains. Probably had.

"Still owe you from that old redneck golf game," Jackson said, willfully ignoring the way her eyes went round as a UFO.

"Tell you what, I'll drive on over and pick you up so you can study in the car."

Her ears wiggled as though she were working on swallowing something too big. "I wouldn't know who to cheer for."

"That's a dumb problem," Louisa said. "We'll get you all dressed up in orange and blue soon as we aren't outnumbered."

"Shoot, sugar, Ole Miss's gonna kick all their asses in the end," Kaci said cheerfully. "You ever been to a real football game?"

"I went to a Big Ten school." Anna Grace pulled herself up, but it was only about nine feet instead of her normal fourteen. "*And* I've seen the Vikings and the Bears play."

She said it so earnestly, as though it meant something, that Jackson choked back a laugh. Louisa wasn't as kind, but Lance and Kaci made a good show of taking her serious.

"So you're in?" Louisa said after she got over her giggle fit.

Anna held Jackson's gaze for a short eternity, as if he was supposed to give her the right answer, and darned if it didn't feel great to finally have something she needed from him.

But when the thought made him grin, her pretty mouth narrowed tighter than he imagined she would've liked to be gripping her label maker. An answer to a challenge flared up in those doe eyes. "Sure," she said. "Sounds fun."

"You bet your Big Ten it will be," Louisa said. She rubbed her hands together. "I got a feeling nobody'll forget this one for a long, long time."

It was more than a feeling.

It was an inevitability.

Chapter Twenty-Three

She'd learned to ask beyond what she needed, but he'd yet to learn to provide only what was asked.
—The Temptress of Pecan Lane, *by Mae Daniels*

JULES WAS OFF AGAIN. Her sunken cheeks and eye bags had moderately improved, but she was arriving later and later, working some weekends to catch up. And Anna had had to correct a few notes and color-codings.

The color-coding was normal, but the notes?

Freaky, that's what it was.

Not that Jules responded to any inquiries about her health and happiness with anything other than, "Life's a beach."

So when she asked Anna to lunch the next Thursday, looking as if she wanted to talk, Anna cancelled her lunch date with Jackson and went with Jules to the food court at the BX on base.

Neither of them were authorized to shop at the BX anymore, since Anna's divorce and Brad's separation from the Air Force, but contractors were allowed to eat at the food court. Jules wanted a Philly cheesesteak, so they climbed into Jules's car and headed out for Charley's. Their base access badges from work got them through the gate.

Anna didn't have a reason to visit base often. Being

surrounded by uniforms again felt odd. Jules didn't seem to notice much of anything around them. She was fixated on watching the girl behind the counter fry her steak. Even when they sat to eat by the soda fountains, Jules barely looked around. She downed the sandwich, then asked if she could have Anna's fries.

"Sure." Anna slid them over. A prickle went up her nape.

A good kind of prickle.

The my-boyfriend-is-watching-me kind of prickle.

Not that he was her boyfriend. Exactly. Yada yada. He stood with a couple of uniformed guys near the Robin Hood counter, giving her a half-smile.

The *I see you too but you're too busy for me and can make it up to me later* kind of half-smile.

And how could she not half-smile a *you bet your britches I will* half-smile back at that?

Jules cleared her throat. "So, how was your divorce lawyer?" She shoveled another handful of fries into her mouth and eyed the rest of Anna's sandwich as though she'd be asking for it next.

As if she hadn't just used the word *divorce* as casually as if they were talking about a mechanic and a tire rotation.

"Jules?" Anna's lips went rubbery, her cheeks paralyzed, her eyebrows so high she'd nearly given herself a permanent face-lift.

"Seriously, if this is going to get touchy-feely, forget I asked. You gonna eat your sandwich?"

Anna doubted she'd want to eat anything the rest of the day, and she regretted what she'd already ingested. She slid the paper box across the table.

"It's not working out between me and Brad," Jules said. If it hadn't been for the twitch in her cheek and the catch in her voice, barely noticeable between her inhalation of two fistfuls of fries, Anna might have believed her.

"God, I could eat a horse." Jules glanced at the next table over. A master sergeant was cleaning away an unfinished box of Burger King chicken tenders. Anna's stomach rolled over. She hadn't seen anyone lust after chicken like that since Beth hit her second trimester with Jacob.

"Jules—"

"Have you ever dipped fries in a milkshake? Because, oh. My. God. Better than an orgasm." The wonky eyebrow appeared. "Tells you something, doesn't it? Giggidy my ass."

Anna's face screwed up like she'd bit a lemon. She didn't need *that* mental image. She scrubbed her tongue over the roof of her mouth, swallowed hard, then put on her best poker face. "Have you two had counseling?"

"Counseling's for fucking losers," Jules said.

Out of the corner of her eye, Anna tracked Jackson moving her way. She gave a subtle head shake. He stopped.

"You've had some major life changes this year," Anna said delicately. Brad still wasn't working, but Jules had been tight-lipped with any other information. "Lots of stress. Are you sure divorce is the right answer?"

"It put you better off, didn't it?"

Anna's phone dinged a text message alert. "It put me different." She glanced at her phone even though she knew what it was.

Here if you need me.

"See?" Jules said. "Better off."

No, not better off. Jackson had an expiration date. "Temporary reprieve."

"Suppose it doesn't matter how good your lawyer was. Brad won't get off his ass long enough to fight me." Jules straightened. "Hel-*lo*. Hottie checking us out." She winked and waved.

And Jackson, happy-go-lucky, grin-at-anyone Jackson, didn't crack the barest hint of a smile.

"This repeal of don't-ask-don't-tell is seriously hurting the uniform hotness factor," Jules said. "God, I want a milkshake."

"Does Brad know you're pregnant?"

Jules went from slightly irritated to radiating pissed-off

anger in half the time it would've taken her to down a large shake, which was probably three nanoseconds. "Are you calling me fat?"

Anna held up a hand, more to stop Jackson than to make peace with Jules.

Jackson dropped into an empty seat at the end of a long row of tables.

Jules kept talking. "I could take you to human resources for that. The workplace isn't supposed to be hostile. What a woman does with her own body is nobody else's damn business."

"I'm asking as your friend."

"Well, who asked you to be my friend?"

Neil had.

A couple lifetimes ago, back when it had been Jules doing Anna the favor.

Anna stood. "Shirley had a good lawyer. Talk to her."

"Where are you going? You have to work this afternoon."

"I'll get a ride."

Jules flounced away. "Don't be late," she snapped.

Anna's phone dinged again. Jackson was slouched as much as he ever slouched in uniform, phone in hand, watching her.

She didn't check the message, but gave him a single nod. A minute later, he was walking her out to his truck.

"Thanks," she said. She rubbed her arms over her jacket. But her teeth chattered and the quivering in her stomach had nothing to do with hunger.

"Looked like a big mess."

"Makes my divorce look like a prance through the daisies."

He slid an arm around her shoulders. "Not too glad he hurt you, but I appreciate that the idiot gave me a chance to get to know you."

"You just want to get laid."

"Anna Grace, that's no way for a proper young lady to talk."

"Can I ask you something?"

"Yep."

"If one of your troops was having personal problems, what would you do?"

They stopped at his truck. He gave her the wary eye. "You know someone needing some counseling?"

"He separated over the summer." She brushed a strand of hair from her eyes. "But he's not doing well."

Jackson handed her his phone. "Name and address, if you've got it."

"Forget who you're talking to?" she asked with as much cheek as she could muster.

"Never, Anna Grace." He pressed a kiss to her forehead, right there, in uniform and everything, then boosted her up into the truck. "Thought you needed reminding."

She needed reminding all right.

Or, more appropriately, her heart needed reminding.

This one had an expiration date.

MAMIE WAS RIGHT. He'd met someone, and she'd kicked him in the collard greens. That was the only explanation he had for calling his commander to ask for a personal afternoon so he could kick a guy in the tulips because a woman asked him to.

Not that he was that up front with his commander. He'd told the colonel he needed to be a good wingman.

He swung by home, gave Radish some bonus attention, and changed out of uniform. Then he drove a couple of miles up the road to the address Anna had given him in the land of the cookie-cutters, the ones ostentatious enough to compare to Russ's Confederate mausoleum.

Anna had been sparse with the details. Today, anyway. She'd told him enough about her friend at work the past couple of months for him to fill in a few pieces.

Friend's husband lost a brother to the war, fell to pieces. Never a Southern gentleman, but a real something else now.

Grief was a bitch.

Anna Grace's words, not Jackson's.

The house was a big brick number with an arch over the front door, oversize front windows looking out on the lawn, and fancy landscaping in the middle of the block.

A big oil stain smeared the driveway. A motorbike was sprawled half on the grass. Two garden gnomes sat in the center of the yard, one tilted, the other modified to give the street the finger.

Jackson blew out a resigned breath and pulled himself out of the truck. Only took a minute to get to the door and ring the doorbell.

But he had to stand there ringing the doorbell for fifteen minutes before a chubby guy with bloodshot eyes and two-day-stupor breath answered. "What the hell?"

"Brad Hutchinson?"

"Yeah? What the fuck's it to you?"

"Rodney sent me."

The guy's face blanched. "Rodney's dead, motherfucker."

He shoved the door. Jackson shouldered into it. "You dead? 'Cuz Rodney ain't too happy with sacrificing his life so you could piss your own away."

The guy came out swinging.

Criminy.

Jackson ducked, then rolled his neck. He didn't want to do it this way, but didn't look like he had a choice. He turned to face Brad. Brad got his bearing, let out a feral growl, and charged.

His shoulder rammed Jackson's chest. The impact made Jackson stagger backward into the house. Took some of his wind out of him, but it was the sucker-punch to his kidney that made him mad.

He flipped Brad off, then stepped back. "Feel better?" Jackson asked. He winced, gingerly touched his back, wary eyes on Brad.

Anna Grace owed him for this one.

"Motherfucker," Brad said again. He rolled to his feet, fist flying.

Jackson thought about taking it again.

But self-preservation won out. He hauled off and socked the guy in the jaw.

Brad landed in the foyer with a thud. His stomach jiggled beneath his stained T-shirt.

"*Now* you feel better?"

The lug blinked at him. His eyes went shiny. "Fucker. Rodney *did* send you." He pressed his palms into his eye sockets. His shoulders shook and he drew in a series of soggy, ragged breaths that took Jackson on a trip down memory lane to the night he'd lost his father.

Jackson let himself into the house and kicked the door shut. He slouched against the wall out of Brad's reach, staring down at his own hands until the other man was spent.

"Who the fuck are you?" Brad asked again, this time without the charming venom.

"Friend of a friend." Jackson reached for his phone. He winced at the ache in his lower back. Moving would be a pain in the turnips for a few days. "You need help."

"Yeah, I need friends with the balls to tell me that to my face instead of sending pussies like you."

Jackson cut him a look over his phone's browser. "Can't imagine why they don't want to talk to you."

"Part of my charm, dude."

"Your wife like it?" There was the number he was looking for.

The silence from the gelatinous mass of man on the floor made Jackson look up.

"You know my wife?" Brad said.

"Haven't had the pleasure."

"Obviously, if you think it'd be a pleasure."

Jackson took his attention back to the phone. "Catholic, Baptist, Lutheran, Jewish, or other?" If Brad were still in, it would be an easy call to his First Shirt. But since he wasn't, Jackson was turning to the chaplains.

"Atheist, bitch." Brad gingerly fingered his jaw. "Fuckin' A, dude. You a Marine?"

"Haven't had that pleasure either."

"Fucking hit like one."

Jackson scrolled through his options one more time, then closed his eyes and hit the screen.

Looked like he was dialing the number for the Catholic chaplain's office.

The way Brad's eyes were getting shiny again, Jackson figured the checkout guy at the BX would do for someone to talk to, but Anna said he needed help. Said his wife needed help too, but Jackson was more qualified right where he was.

Got the impression from Anna that helping Brad would help his wife anyway.

Real nice example of solid forever marriage here.

Jackson popped the phone to his ear and listened to it ring. "You ready to man-up and talk to someone about this, or do I have to hit you again?" Jackson asked.

"I don't need to talk to some fucking—"

Jackson moved to slug him, and Brad shut up.

But only for a second.

"Can't make me talk," he said with a scowl.

"You owe it to Rodney to keep living, man."

And thank sweet baby Jesus, Brad wasn't a big enough man to argue with that one.

LATER THAT NIGHT, much, much later, flopped out on his own couch with Radish, Jackson had a pounding headache, an empty stomach, and a throbbing in his lower back.

Wasn't as young as he used to be.

But Brad had thanked him for being a—well, something his momma hadn't raised him to be, but something he occasionally had to be nonetheless, being male and all. And the chaplain—Father Bob, he said his name was—had thanked Jackson for making the call. Said all the right things about not leaving fellow airmen to suffer alone, insisted he'd stay until the wife got home, talk to both of them. Brad promised not to hit the chaplain, who insisted he could take it even if Brad tried. And Jackson had managed to get through the whole thing without dropping his name, so hopefully Anna wouldn't get any flack for interfering.

Speaking of Anna—he glanced at the clock. Just 8:43. She'd still be in class.

If it didn't hurt to move, he might've been a big old baby and asked her to come fry him up some chicken. Guaranteed to rile her up and get her into his house fast as nobody's business, even if he didn't get fried chicken.

Might play up the pity card to get an answer to that age-old question: Could she make biscuits or not? His supply was drying up since Mamie'd told the Misses he was seeing someone.

A timid knock pulled him out of his stupor. Now 8:44. Early for Anna, but maybe it was his lucky night. "It's open," he hollered.

The latch clicked. Anna peeked in. "Coffee and cookies?"

Never thought he was the loving type, but she was making it look damn easy.

That whole broken kidney thing notwithstanding. "You're an angel, Anna Grace."

She disappeared, then bumped her way through the door, coffee carrier in one hand, cookie bag in the other, a backpack, purse, and overnight bag all draped over her shoulders.

He should've gotten up to help her.

Those angel wing eyebrows scrunched together over her cute nose. "Are you okay?"

"Long as I don't move."

He wasn't for certain, but she might've gone a shade pale. The coffee wobbled in her hands.

He might've let out a pathetic, unmanly whimper. But if it was pathetic, only Radish thought so, and that was only because she didn't understand he probably saved a guy's life today. Took one for the team.

Anna Grace kneeled by his side. "Where does it hurt?"

His stomach growled.

They both looked at it. "Yeah, there for one," he said, and he sounded danged philosophical, if he did say so himself.

He'd never seen her doe eyes so big, though he didn't mind the way they kept roaming up and down his body. She checked him out, smoothed her hands over his skin, poked him here and there. "Have a cookie. Where else does it hurt? Did you two fight? Please tell me you didn't fight. I didn't mean for you to fight. Can you walk? I'm so sorry." She fell silent, her mouth a perfect little O. But then—"Oh, no. What does Brad look like? You were going to say it, weren't you? *Should've seen the other guy.* Good Lord. *Why* do men always solve everything with their fists?"

"Anna Grace," he said around a mouthful of oatmeal raisin cookie.

She stopped her inspection of his legs, which would've been enjoyable if she'd lingered more near the top and center instead of poking at his knees, which kinda tickled. Her head cocked and her eyes narrowed.

Yeah, she knew what he was talking about. "That's my girl."

If her eyes got any narrower, she'd be glaring at him through her eyelids. "How much pain medication are you on?"

"None." He drew a hand through her hair—always so soft and silky—then brushed his thumb over her ear. Her pupils dilated. He caught a scent of intrigued woman.

His intrigued woman.

"Might could use a little vitamin I if you're gonna get ideas though," he said.

And wouldn't you know she popped a little bottle of ibuprofen out of her purse. "Regular or flight-doc strength?"

God bless that idiot ex-husband of hers for teaching her the ins and outs of the Air Force medical system. "Flight doc."

She shook four pills into his hand and then gave him his

coffee. Mocha latte, double on the mocha.

She knew his favorite.

"I bribed the barista," she said. "And I'll poke harder if you don't tell me what happened this afternoon."

She looked like she would, too.

"We sorted it out like men," he said, not all that wisely, since he couldn't move to get out of the way of her jab to his shoulder.

Wasn't quick enough to catch her hand either.

Maybe he should've thought about seeing a doctor himself.

"Don't suppose you're up for baking biscuits tonight?"

"Are they going to be okay?" Anna asked, and he knew she wasn't asking about biscuits.

Not any biscuits he wanted to know about, anyway.

He lifted his arm and beckoned her closer. Once he had his nose buried in her hair, felt her hand on his chest, he told her as much as he could without breaking the unspoken man code.

And because she was Anna, she didn't press it.

And because she was Anna, she offered to thank him right proper for his service.

And because she was Anna, when he asked her to be careful around his kidneys, she did him one better.

She made his whole body feel better.

So better, he thought she might've found a missing piece of his soul.

Mamie was right. His collard greens were toast, and he was pretty sure Anna Grace had labeled his turnips.

And he didn't mind a lick.

JULES WASN'T AT work Friday.

She wasn't in Saturday either, which both surprised Anna and gave her some hope.

Jackson was out hunting. Anna was sad not to spend the weekend making sure he was okay, but relieved that they were still on the I-have-my-own-life end of the dating spectrum.

Not that working on a Saturday qualified her as having a life.

But with Jules out so much lately, Anna was catching up for Jules's catching up. They both needed the job security, so Anna declined Kaci's suggestion to practice Thanksgiving pies while Lance put in a Saturday at his squadron. Because Anna had work to do.

Her classes were dragging this semester, so she was glad to have an excuse to come in and double-check the color coordination on files from the last couple of weeks. She needed everything sorted for the October report, which *had* to go out Tuesday despite missing a few key points from Jules. Anna was comfortable running tests on her own, though the newness had worn off, taking the excitement with it. But she still enjoyed the filing.

Compared to school, it was fun.

But not as fun as spending Sunday organizing a kitchen for one of Lance's new lieutenants. Anna couldn't believe they paid her to sort and file their lives. She enjoyed the extra boost to her bank account, especially with Christmas coming, even if she felt guilty about the lost study time. It was hard to keep her heart in biochemistry when her label maker was humming.

Jules finally came back Tuesday morning. She brought a gush of chilly air more appropriate for a Minnesota January than a Georgia November, but she stopped in Anna's cube to hop on the desk and screw with Anna's organizer. "Why didn't you and Neil do counseling?" she asked.

Anna blew out a breath she'd been holding since Thursday. "He was a prick."

It was true.

Her ex-husband was a prick. She laughed, then shrugged. "I don't think he ever loved me. I think he loved what I could do for his life."

Jules chewed on the cap of Anna's favorite orange highlighter. "Did you love him?"

"Yes."

"Martyr."

Anna shrugged. "I did. But I loved myself too, and I couldn't love me for both of us. So when he decided enough was enough, I realized I could keep loving me for both of us, or I could love me for me."

"You are truly sickening."

"It's a gift."

Jules plunked the highlighter into the small space reserved for the staple remover. The marker clattered to the floor. She dropped her gaze. "Brad wants counseling. He's—well, frankly, I think some fucked-up version of Rodney's ghost came to pay him a visit, and now he's found Buddha or some shit like that."

"Brad's good for you, Jules."

Jules shoved her shoulder. "Shut up, Pollyanna."

"The Brad you married? He's good for you. You should do it."

"I know."

"You should do it for him too."

Jules scrambled off the desk. She grabbed the highlighter, then plopped it back in its place.

Not just in the highlighter container, but between the yellow and pink highlighters, so it was as close to rainbow order as possible.

Anna put a hand to her throat. "Ohmigod, Jules, I think I might cry."

Jules smacked her shoulder again, but she was smiling when she left Anna's cube.

Chapter Twenty-Four

She'd learned the ways of her new home, but she had yet to master them. And that was the critical difference.
—The Temptress of Pecan Lane, *by Mae Daniels*

THE DAY AFTER Thanksgiving, Anna's phone woke her at o-dark-early. She fumbled for it, heart clenching in her chest, and had a double-panic when she saw her sister's cell number. She answered it in a rush. "Beth?"

"Hey, Anna-banana."

Anna heard bells and a mass of voices in the background. She blew out a breath and draped a hand over her chest while her pulse fluttered back to normal.

"Mom and I are in Nordstrom, and we saw the *cutest* reindeer sweatshirt," Beth said. "What size are you wearing these days?"

"Happy Black Friday, sweetheart," her mom called through the phone.

The thundering in Anna's heart slowed to a trot. "I don't need a reindeer sweatshirt."

"But you know how much the boys love to give you sweatshirts for Christmas!"

She didn't have to be there to know Beth was muffling her

snickers in the sleeve of whatever gaudy sweatshirt their mother had picked.

Anna sighed. "My blender broke last week. Maybe they could get me a new one instead. I could tell them I was gonna make me up some squirrel soup with it."

The silence stretched between them, broken only by the bells and the crush of other shopping noises.

"Mom says you sound Southern," Beth said.

"I—crap."

"Somebody's been spending too much time with her boyfriend," Beth said in the singsong voice she used on her younger patients.

It would've been in her family's best interest for her to deny the boyfriend part. To let them think this was a crazy post-divorce fling. To prepare them for when she and Jackson split ways.

Because it would happen.

Eventually. When he got orders.

Even though it'd hurt like tearing off a Band-Aid.

Or maybe like being run over by a herd of rabid elephants on steroids. But she'd survive. Because that was what she did. She survived.

"How's work?" Beth asked.

Okay, she eeked by. But she did it on her own, and that was what counted. "Busy. Haven't seen much of anyone between getting ready for finals and working some overtime. But Kaci and Lance put on a nice Thanksgiving dinner yesterday. How was the Vaughns' annual snow-blow extravaganza?"

While Anna considered getting out of bed, Beth launched into a story about her in-laws' traditional Thanksgiving snowmobile run, and the danger in which they put her poor fourteen-year-old baby boy by letting him ride along.

But Jackson wouldn't be here for several hours—heaven forbid she be allowed to drive two hours to his family's house by herself—and she'd stayed up studying after getting home from Kaci and Lance's.

For her first post-divorce holiday, it hadn't been bad. Kaci could, in fact, cook a decent turkey, and the homemade macaroni and cheese had been unbelievable.

She'd missed her own family though.

"Maybe you want to go snowmobiling at Christmas?" Beth said.

Anna stared at her dark ceiling. She'd never gone before. Neil thought it was too dangerous.

Jackson probably would too, but he'd trust her to make up her own mind.

"Anna? You still awake?"

"Yeah. Kind of. Snowmobiling sounds fun."

"Great. I'll tell Tony's parents to save a run for us girls. When are you leaving for your football game?"

"Around noon."

"Well, get some studying done. I cannot *wait* to hear about this guy's family."

Something suspiciously similar to nerves rolled Anna's stomach into an icy ball of fear. "I'm a little afraid of his mother," Anna said. "Despite what you might think, I'm pretty sure I don't talk Southern enough for her."

Beth laughed. "Think of all the fun you'll have telling me everything afterward."

Yep. Fun. As long as she could concentrate on having fun, and not worrying whether she was wearing the wrong color shirt, or saying the wrong thing, or being too Yankee, or accidentally insulting anyone, it would be a blast.

TURNED OUT THE THEORY of Jackson's taking Anna Grace home to meet his family and the reality of it were two different kinds of fried chicken.

The theory had thick, crunchy skin and a juicy inside, a high meat-to-bone ratio. She was a special friend and his sister liked her enough to invite her to a football game that set him on the outs with his whole family every year.

The reality was a mite bit moldy. He hadn't been able to brush his teeth long or hard enough this morning to get the taste of dread out of his mouth.

Momma had had that look yesterday. Louisa had an entirely different one, as she'd spent three-quarters of the turkey dinner talking about *Just Anna this* and *Just Anna that*.

Every time Louisa said Anna's name, Momma ground her teeth. She kept her smile fixed and her tone pleasant as honey, but Jackson still heard the grating teeth.

It'd been so bad poor Radish had tucked her stub of a tail between her legs and hid in the mud room until Jackson brought her leftovers.

So when Jackson pulled up to Anna's apartment half an hour early Friday morning, he thought maybe hanging out here all weekend was a better plan.

When he'd take a woman over being in the stadium for the Iron Bowl, he *knew* he was in trouble.

Especially since he'd told Mamie he might bring Anna by for bowling after dinner.

Big trouble. Big, *big* trouble.

But Anna opened her door, looking sleepy and stressed out and happy to see him, and he'd never been so glad for trouble. "Anna Grace, you look like you need a break."

She grabbed a fistful of his third favorite Bama T-shirt—the first two packed away for the both of them tomorrow—and hauled him inside. He went right along, grinning as big as his old spaniel in a field of squirrels.

When they finally hit the road, Jackson was feeling a lot less stressed. Anna was wearing one of his favorite smiles—the kind she used only when she looked at him. But even when she looked away, when her brain might've taken her to thoughts of homework or work or her family or any number of things he hadn't figured out yet about her, her lips tipped up like she had a secret. It made his chest feel all cozy, as though the outside world were cold and windy and snowy, but his heart was wrapped up in one of Mamie's old quilts in front of a fire in that place he'd rented the year he spent at Minot in North Dakota.

Wasn't even dreading going back into the Confederate mausoleum again today, not with his spunky Yankee by his side.

The drive flew by with her chatting about whatever popped into her head, fiddling with the radio, nodding off and wheezing out a soft snore, and jerking back awake with that cute wide-eyed panic that she might've missed something. Jackson almost missed the turn off the backcountry highway to head into Auburn proper.

He took the long way, which could've meant he toured every street in Auburn before heading toward the iron arches guarding the house Momma had married into. Instead, he picked one specific street between the airport and the university.

They drew up to a split-level brick home halfway up the block. Jackson slowed the truck. Anna had gone quiet.

Probably thought this was it.

Should've been it.

"Grew up there," he said, flicking a finger at the old place. Had a lot of fun there too. Learned how to be a man he hoped his daddy would've been proud of there.

Wasn't sure he was doing everything right, but he was trying.

Anna's worry lines smoothed out. She gave him another of those secret smiles. "Looks like a nice place to grow up." She leaned into him, her hair smelling all sweet and Annalike, and pointed. "Is that the tree you tried to fly out of?"

Leave it to Anna Grace to remember the good ones. "That's her."

"Which branch?"

The old oak was bigger than she'd been back in the day, but the branch in question wasn't there anymore. "See that big lump about a third of the way to the branches?"

"Aw, it's gone?"

"It, ah, didn't survive my growing up." And he could still remember his daddy's face when Jackson had to explain how the second-largest branch on the whole tree had happened to splinter off on a thick, lazy, stagnant July afternoon: Irritation fighting with amusement, fear of Momma's reaction outweighing everything else. *How you planning on telling your momma you broke her favorite tree?* Jackson couldn't have been older than thirteen when it happened, but he could still see his daddy standing there on the driveway, rubbing his chin, eyes twinkling, choking on something. Pollen, he'd said, but it was only one of a handful of times Jackson ever heard his daddy talk about allergies.

Must've been a sight, Daddy had said.

Jackson shifted a glance back at Anna Grace.

His daddy would've gotten a kick out of that sight too.

"This another story not fit for my delicate Yankee ears?" she teased. But the soft brush of her fingers over his hand, the way she tilted her head so her eyes went all soft, he knew what she was really asking.

If it was his to keep, or if it was his to share.

He gestured to the tree again. "Reckon you could say I watched too much Road Runner and Wile E. Coyote as a kid."

"Oh, dear." Her cheeks split into his second-favorite kind of Anna Grace grin. Her eyebrows gave him a *go on* wiggle.

He flipped his hand up and gave her fingers a squeeze. "Rigged my momma's favorite old perfume bottle as a homemade bottle rocket. Didn't exactly misfire, but it didn't go where it was supposed to either." He'd been a hell of a kid. Wonder his daddy hadn't had a heart attack before Jackson hit his teen years. "Didn't help I filled the whole bottle with fuel."

Her eyes narrowed in that amused, suspicious way she had about her whenever he told some of his more heart-attack-inducing stories. "I don't want to know what you used as fuel, do I?"

"I ever tell you about my momma's family's upstanding

reputation in the moonshine industry?"

Her lips parted, her eyes still scrunchy around the edges. "Really?"

"Yes, ma'am. Henry Ford should've hired him some rednecks. Course, then you might not have a job here, but there's a reason they say it's like drinking gasoline."

She stared at him one heartbeat longer, then tipped her head and laughed.

Right good sound, Anna Grace laughing.

He hoped she found the Confederate mausoleum as amusing. They couldn't sit all afternoon parked across from what should've still been home, and he'd promised Momma they'd have dinner at the compound tonight.

Had to, what with how she'd channeled General Lee when issuing the invitation.

So eventually he pulled away from the curb, the gnawing in his gut serving as his own personal radar as to how close they were. Anna got quiet too. Looked as though she wished she had a label maker within reach, but whenever she caught him stealing a glance, she gave him a courageous smile.

He pulled through the wrought-iron arch and onto the freshly repaved drive beneath a canopy of old oaks and magnolias. Her knee jiggled. Jackson gave it a squeeze. "Okay, Anna Grace?"

"I don't like being the only Yankee in a room."

She hadn't seen the inside yet. "Between you and me, there's two of us who've lived north of the Mason-Dixon Line."

The house came into view. She went so pale, he saw the shadow of the veins in her neck, and they were hopping faster than the drum of the motor in his truck. "Is there anything I should know before we go in?" she asked.

Probably a lot, but too late now.

Wasn't sure he was brave enough to open up about all of it anyway. "Going chicken on me?" he teased.

"If your momma scares you, I don't hold out much hope for myself."

"She'll lady your boots off," Jackson said. He hit her with his best disarming smile, even though he wanted to pound his foot on the gas and get away from the negative gravitational pull of the house. "Don't reckon you studied that Officers' Wives Handbook to figure out how to use your silverware at dinner tonight."

She hitched one side of her mouth up. Looked as if she were trying to make it reach those wide doe eyes. "Get on my bad side, and I won't wear that sweatshirt in the backseat you think I don't know about to the game tomorrow."

He chuckled. "All right, Anna Grace. I'll behave myself. And I promise, on my honor as a gentleman, to defend you and your Yankee ways against all those suspicious looks and backhanded compliments you might be walking into."

He pocketed his keys, then stared at the house. Three stories tall, as wide as a football field is long, white so bright he could almost see colors in it, columns holding up the overhang over the front door.

Everything Southern grandeur was supposed to be on the outside, everything hell was supposed to be on the inside.

Anna was watching him. He made his face blank. "Ready?"

She put soft fingers to his cheek and pressed a kiss to his mouth.

Never knew it could feel so good to not be alone. "Don't you be trying that at the dinner table unless you're looking to get on my momma's bad side," he said, but his voice was huskier than he meant it to be.

"Only after I thank her for raising you to chase ants out of ladies' cars."

Couldn't help but smile at her gumption. "And don't forget pulling ladies out of garbage cans. That one there's my favorite."

"Bring that up again and no more pie for you."

He laughed, because he had to enjoy it while he could.

ANNA COULDN'T DECIDE which was worse, being underdressed to meet Jackson's momma in a house that reeked of old Southern money and elegance, or the fact that he hadn't warned her his momma lived in a house that reeked of old Southern money and elegance.

Jackson opened the door, a massive oak number taller than any door Anna had ever seen north of the Mason-Dixon Line. He led her inside, hand comfortably at the small of her back. She contemplated asking if she should take her shoes off, but he didn't seem to think anything of tramping across the gleaming wood floor, so she went along through the high-ceilinged foyer and into a grand living room. Paintings of battle scenes, complete with Confederate flags, gray-uniformed officers thrusting sabers on horseback, and 1860s-style cannons, dominated the walls.

That tingling on Anna's scalp might've been a little bit of sweat.

The couches were all dark leather with brass adornments. They were beautiful, but looked as cozy as a log in a bear's den. Anna suspected that if she dared to sit and prop up her feet on the spotless glass coffee table, its metal legs would morph into jaws and politely chomp off her lower extremities.

With barely a pause, Jackson nudged her through the next doorway. The dining room table was set and ready for a meal fit to serve a king and his entourage. Or, more likely, given the blue and white table runner lined with silver stars, General Lee and his top dozen advisers. A buffet and hutch with intricately painted china stood on one wall. On another wall, a huge picture window overlooked the lush yard where Radish was happily basking in the sun. So much for that fleeting thought that maybe his momma just worked here. Beyond the yard were more woods, separating the house from any suggestion of neighbors.

She cut a glance up at Jackson. He'd retreated into his blank mask.

Maybe she could fake a Southern accent all weekend.

A couple of old silver plates rattled in an ornate curio cabinet as they passed into the kitchen. At least, Anna thought it was the plates.

It could've been her feet quaking in her shoes, or her bones rattling out of their sockets.

The kitchen was brightly lit and large enough to support a whole cooking crew. The smell of money and opulence overpowered whatever was cooking on the stove. An average-height, curvy woman was chopping something green on a wooden block on the massive island in the center of the room.

Her skin was smooth and clear, lipstick perfect, light-brown curly hair tamed in an elegant yet simple bun. The shrewdness in her light eyes and the way she held her shoulders back told Anna that this was a woman who'd experienced life and was still coming out on top.

If Anna had had a kid who had done half what Jackson claimed, she would have wrinkles and gray hair.

Not Jackson's momma. She looked as though she'd gather a Confederate army of her own before she'd allow anything so plebian as age to sully her appearance.

Anna gulped.

Jackson let go of Anna long enough to greet his momma with a kiss to the cheek. Before he could make introductions, his momma wiped her hand on her simple white apron and then extended it to Anna. "Welcome, my dear. I'm Deb. Louisa has told me so much about you. How was your drive?"

Her hands were smooth and warm, and her accent was softer and less pronounced than her children's, but still there.

"Very nice, thank you." Much to Anna's amazement, her voice didn't wobble with the fear that her Yankee breath would tarnish the silver. Nor did it hint that she noticed Deb had said Louisa talked about her, rather than Jackson.

And why would he? They weren't committed or anything.

Anna recognized the twitch of his momma's lips, but her gray steel gaze was silently conducting an inquisition. Anna wanted to blurt her birthday, parents' and sister's names, high school and college GPAs, and the situation surrounding her first marriage and divorce.

Instead, she reminded herself that she had asked to meet this woman, and this would probably be the only time she ever disgraced the house with her Yankee presence. But she had to force a smile. "Is there anything I can do to help with dinner?"

"Oh, no, dear. You're our guest." She picked her knife up and resumed chopping. Efficiently. With a little bit too much verve.

"Louisa around?" Jackson asked.

"She's at Stone's, but she'll be back for dinner. Craig and Maura are bringing the girls over. Would you please go hang out the swings? Such a nice day today."

"Yes, ma'am." He nudged Anna, but an *I didn't excuse you both* look from his momma stopped them.

"Anna, dear," she said, authority dripping through the Southern in her words, "can I get you something to drink?"

A muscle in Jackson's neck visibly tightened.

Uh-oh. "Oh, no thank you. I'm good." Anna angled closer to him.

"I made a pitcher of sweet tea."

It was a struggle, but Anna kept her nose from wrinkling.

She could've sworn his momma saw it. The older woman seemed to take particular delight in Anna's lack of appreciation for the nectar of the Southern gods. "I hope you like stewed okra," Deb said. "We're positively swimming in it. Had such a good season last year, we'll be eating it out of the freezer for months."

Anna had gotten divorced and ended up in Confederate Alabama hell.

"Do sit down," Jackson's momma ordered. "Make yourself comfortable. Jackson can handle the swing."

"Sure can, but I promised Anna here a trip down the slide." Jackson's drawl flared, but not in the comfortable telling-stories-with-Lance-and-Kaci kind of way. Nope, this was his fake redneck act. "Wouldn't be right gentlemanly of me to not show her a good time."

Something shuttered closed in his momma's eyes, but she aimed a lip smile at Anna. "We'll chat over dinner."

"That'll be nice," Anna said.

Jackson led her out the back door to the massive acres of green lawn, where Radish greeted them both with sloppy dog kisses. Outside, his tension faded until he was back to his easygoing, blood-pressure-free self. He snagged a couple of swings from a shed attached to the house, then led her around to the side of the yard, beyond his momma's view from the kitchen window, where a gargantuan wooden play fort dominated the ground.

That slide *did* look like fun.

A lot more fun than staying with his momma in the kitchen.

If she'd had aspirations of being his long-term, permanent girlfriend, she might've asked about his relationship with his momma. But she was here as Louisa's guest for a football game tomorrow, not as the woman Jackson was sleeping with, so she didn't ask.

And he didn't offer.

But he did show her a good time on the play fort, fully clothed and G-rated and everything.

"We're not staying here tonight," Jackson said while he pushed her on a swing.

She looked back at him. "No?"

"Didn't want the Confederate mausoleum giving you nightmares of General Lee attacking you in your sleep." He gave her a crooked grin, and soon she was laughing so hard she had to stop the swing.

Jackson came around to sit on the ground in front of her, that crooked grin getting wider, the orneriness in his eyes lighting his entire face. "Gotta be honest here, Anna Grace. I ain't been allowed to sleep here since I defected to the Union. Real sticking point in the family. Should've warned you. Knew the okra would be thrown down."

"Oh, look, he's smiling," a female voice suddenly said.

Anna choked back her laughter. Jackson stayed loose and relaxed. He climbed to his feet and helped her out of the swing. A small family approached. "Friendlies?" Anna said.

Jackson chuckled. "Yes, ma'am."

He seemed happy enough to introduce her to his stepbrother and his family. Craig was tall and lanky, with a plain face and somber manner of speaking, not at all what Anna expected out of a guy who'd once helped Jackson make an airplane motored by his momma's vacuum engine. Maura was bubbly and pleasantly round, with lips that stretched in a perpetual smile. Their girls were three and one, and they were as much fun as Anna's nephews had been at that age. While she and Maura and the girls played, Jackson and Craig caught up with hunting and fishing and work stories.

But soon Deb called everyone to dinner, and they went inside. The smell of meatloaf and mashed potatoes, and unfortunately, stewed okra, covered the stifling scents of pride and prestige.

Louisa had arrived and was waiting at the table. Anna was introduced to Russ, Jackson's stepfather, and found him to be a somewhat more relaxed version of his son, and surprisingly pleasant given her knowledge that Jackson didn't care much for him. Obviously a story there.

None of her business.

Dinner was accompanied by painfully polite but nonetheless enlightening conversation. Anna hadn't realized that Jackson's stepfather was the fourth-generation president and owner of Whipple PeachNuts, the largest chain of tourist-stop peach and pecan stands in the southeast. Every new tidbit about Jackson and his family made Anna's eyebrows inch up, and every quarter-inch of raised brows on Anna's part seemed to result in smug satisfaction on Deb's part.

Despite the pleasant top conversation, the underlying tensions were choking her. Even the mystery ingredient making the collard greens about the best vegetable Anna had eaten without ketchup in decades couldn't ease her discomfort, nor did Jackson's pointedly passing the stewed okra.

But at least nothing was truly personal for Anna.

That, apparently, was reserved for the course between dinner and dessert.

One by one, everyone finished their food. Russ, Deb, Craig, and Maura lined their silverware in the middle of their plates and pushed them back discreetly. Maura settled her older girl's plate as well, then produced a wet wipe for the baby's face.

Jackson left his silverware skewed across his plate, but wasn't as dismissive of table manners as his sister, who leaned her elbows on the table. At some invisible signal, Craig picked up his and Maura's plates. Jackson took his and Anna's.

"I can—" she started, but stopped herself.

For the first time since they'd come inside, she caught an amused gleam in Jackson's eye. "Thank you, Anna Grace."

He and Craig disappeared into the kitchen. Deb dabbed at her mouth with her napkin, tucked it back onto her lap, smiled pleasantly, and tilted forward. "Maura, dear, do you remember the Fillmounts?"

Anna put her hands in her lap and ignored the crick in her shoulders from sitting erect for the last forty-five minutes.

Maura's face crinkled, then her omnipresent smile beamed larger. "Oh, yes! That lovely couple from down the street. They gave us the nicest set of matching crystal frames for our wedding."

"Mm, that's them," Deb said. "They're getting divorced."

Anna shivered against a sudden case of prickles on the back of her neck and knees that reminded her of Riverdancing fire ants.

"Oh, no," Maura said.

"Wasn't he her second husband?" Louisa said.

Make that Riverdancing on speed.

"Mm-hmm. So sad, but of course, not so surprising." Deb

turned that conversational smile to Anna. "She cheated on her first husband too, bless her heart."

Anna made a noncommittal kind of noise.

"Divorce is so sad, don't you agree, Anna dear?"

Something clinked in the kitchen, but it had nothing on the panic crashing through Anna's core.

Deb knew.

She knew Anna was divorced, and she knew her son could do a lot better than a divorced, undereducated Yankee.

And she wanted to make sure Anna knew it too.

What Anna wouldn't have given for her label maker. There wasn't even anything to straighten in front of her. The stars on the table runner were symmetrically sewn. Anna had left no crumbs to straighten on the tablecloth, and she would've bet the freaking grains of wood beneath it were evenly spaced too.

She tried to match Deb's pleasant expression, but suspected she looked like the collard greens had given her food poisoning instead. So she tried a lighthearted laugh.

Which came out about as pleasant as a chicken choking on the carcass of its first cousin. She cleared her throat and went back to the food poisoning look.

Was divorce *sad*? Deb certainly had the Southern way of understating things down pat. "Well, of course." Anna tried the choking chicken sound again and winced. "But really, can you imagine the alternative? That'd be a lot of dead husbands."

Too late, she realized she was the only one laughing at her bad joke.

Deb snatched her water. The intricate diamonds of the crystal goblet cast unsteady prisms on the walls. Russ shot her one of those concerned husband looks, the kind that spoke of history and private stories and understanding of moods and hot buttons.

Louisa's face went pale. Her eyes were a blue question mark of hurt, wavering between her mother and Anna.

Maura gaped at all of them.

Jackson shot back into the room, somehow managing to

make what classified as a breakneck pace for him seem like a casual stroll through a pecan grove. He settled into the seat beside Anna and gave her knee a soft squeeze. "Awful nice of you to let Craig out for the game tomorrow," he said to Maura.

Her perpetual smile wobbled. "He's earned it."

Russ cleared his throat. "Heard there's a petition going around our homeowners' association to lower the speed limit. You got a homeowners' association over there in Georgia, Jackson?"

"Sure do," Jackson drawled. His thumb brushed Anna's leg, while his drawl went past comfortable to somebody's-getting-rednecked. "Had to take down that there Ford I had up on blocks in my front yard. Fines were more'n I paid for the old piece of junk in the first place."

The groove between Deb's eyes grew deeper with every word he spoke. Russ's jaw tightened.

Anna struggled for her voice. "Those collard greens are the best I've had since I moved down south," she said. She tried to smile at Deb. "You must have a secret ingredient."

"Are you divorced?" Louisa said.

"Louisa," Jackson said on a low growl.

Anna put her hand over his. She was who she was, and her past was what it was. "Yes."

Louisa was the only one at the table who seemed surprised. "For real?"

"Yes."

The younger girl's chin shifted back and forth. "But you don't have any kids."

"No."

"Well, that's a relief."

Anna tensed. Jackson jerked in his seat. Louisa let out a yelp. She glared at him, but he cut her off with a curt, "Enough."

"Craig says he got a great spot for tailgating tomorrow," Maura said. "Getting out after the game should be a cinch."

"He always did have luck with parking lots," Russ said.

Were they kidding? It was like watching an elephant and a

tiger fighting the Civil War right there on the dining room table, and they were talking about *parking?*

No wonder Jackson didn't talk much about his family.

Louisa got another one of those gleams in her eye. The kind that normal people got when they were about to slip a snowball down their sister's back in sub-zero temperatures.

The kind that made Anna wonder—again—if she should've declined the invitation to come this weekend.

"Momma says marry the first time for love, the second time for money." Louisa's face shone with a pompous arrogance she was entirely too young to properly manage.

But, unfortunately, she was entirely rich enough to try anyway, and she was sitting in a chair that probably cost Anna's monthly salary, and she was implying that Anna was only here because she, too, wanted a chunk of Russ's wallet.

The thought sparked a fuse Anna hadn't realized she possessed. Her temper rocketed into the stratosphere as if it were attached to Neil's iPod and retainer. Anna savored the flight, narrowing in on her target, burning, building to her climax, and smiled sweetly through the flames spewing from her mouth. "Well, bless her heart."

And then everything exploded in a silent, slow-motion shower of embers, burning out the last bits of her anger as they hit the frosty air, as if she were watching the fireworks from far away and hadn't heard the boom yet.

Deb's lip curled. Her breasts rose, shoulders bouncing back. Her hand fluttered to her chest.

Louisa choked on something akin to a laugh-gasp.

Maura's hand flew to her lips.

Even good ol' General Lee scowled from his perch of honor in a decorative plate on the wall.

Russ's mustache twitched. He discreetly coughed into a napkin. Bless *his* heart.

And then the boom hit.

Her chair jerked out from beneath her.

It would be a long walk back to Georgia.

Chapter Twenty-Five

*He hadn't known he was sitting on the fence until
he toppled over onto the wrong side, only to
discover what was wrong had been right all along.*
—The Temptress of Pecan Lane, by Mae Daniels

JACKSON COULD COUNT on one finger the number of times he'd been furious with his momma.

He was still deciding whether he added another finger to that count, but at the moment, his primary mission was getting himself and Anna Grace out of that house.

He was on his feet hauling Anna out of her seat fast as he could manage, given the way he was choking back a snort of laughter the likes of which this dining room hadn't seen since before the Yankees won the war. "Great dinner," he said. "Promised Mamie we'd meet her for bowling, and golly gee, wouldja lookit the time."

Momma's eyes narrowed into slits. "But I made sweet potato pie."

"Might could have some for breakfast instead." He tugged on Anna Grace's arm to get her to move. She wouldn't look at him, but he recognized the slump of her shoulders and the tilt of her head. Reminded him of the day he'd first laid eyes on her. Made him angrier than a rabid armadillo that his momma and sister would hurt her. "Night, y'all."

Anna's feet finally moved in the right direction. He let up his grip on her arm and instead steered her by the shoulders through the house and into the cool evening.

He barely made it down the front steps before he swung her against him. Tears glittered in her eyes.

"Jackson, I—"

He sealed his mouth over hers, gripped her waist and hauled her close until they were chest-to-chest, stomach-to-stomach, knee-to-knee. And he kissed her.

And kissed her.

And kissed her until she wrapped her arms around his neck and kissed him back, her tears touching his cheeks, her hold on him so tight his lungs couldn't breathe, but he didn't feel that they needed to, because he didn't need the oxygen.

He just needed Anna.

He kissed the wet trails down her face, threaded his fingers through her soft hair, cradled her close. "Ah, Anna Grace," he murmured, "you are one magnificent woman."

She pushed her hair off her forehead with a shaky hand. "I just insulted your mother."

Sweet Lord, she had. She'd done it good too. Shouldn't have been funny, a Yankee insulting his momma in her own home, but Momma'd started it, thinking he'd bring home any woman who couldn't hold her own, Yankee or not.

Anna Grace, he'd decided, could hold her own with the devil if she had to.

The laughter welled up inside him again. This time, he didn't try to hold it back. "Darlin', you did it right good for a Yankee."

"I need to go apologize."

"Oh, no, ma'am." His fingers flexed at her waist. "You go on and let her stew on that for a night. You do whatever you need to in the morning, but tonight, you go on and let her stew."

"But—"

"Trust me on this one." He cradled her closer. "Besides, we got somewhere better to be."

"Promise?"

"Yes, ma'am."

And he felt only a mite bad that she probably expected somewhere quiet and alone.

But when he pulled into the parking lot of Mamie's favorite bowling alley, Anna Grace looked at him as though he'd sprouted his own Confederate cap. "You were serious." Her voice broke.

He almost shifted the truck back into gear.

But this was the closest he'd get to introducing her to his daddy. "Five minutes," he said. "You still want to go after five minutes, we'll go."

She looked at the building, then back to him, a silent plea in her eyes.

"Trust me?" He brushed his thumb over her ear and followed it with a kiss.

She scrunched her eyes closed, then blew out a sigh. "Five minutes."

He checked his watch. "Ready?"

"Don't push your luck."

But she climbed out of the truck. He had three minutes and forty-three seconds left when he spotted Mamie's crew. Took another thirty-three seconds to pass the eight lanes to get to them.

Miss Dolly saw him first.

Then she saw Anna. Her eyes went wide, and she tilted her head at Mamie. "You didn't tell us Jackson was bringing a friend tonight."

Mamie's head popped up from where she was lacing her designer bowling shoes. "You're late, sugarplum." She frowned. "What's this? You make this poor girl go to dinner at that old house? Ophelia, get this poor thing a Coke. You like root beer, sweetie pie? Jackson, what did your momma do?"

Anna Grace still had that wary, shell-shocked look about

her. He squeezed her hand. "She tried that old nobody's-good-enough-for-my-baby thing, but don't you worry none. Anna Grace here blessed her heart and set her straight."

Anna's cheeks went all sweet and embarrassed. Mamie wrapped her in a hug. "Don't you be worrying none about Deb." The top of Mamie's tightly rolled hair barely hit Anna's shoulder, but she patted Anna's back and said all the right Mamie things, and he felt the tension leaving Anna as much as if it'd been his own.

Miss Ophelia dove back into the pit with a root beer. "Hope y'all don't mind sharing," she said with a wink. "They're plum short on cups tonight. Y'all done introductions yet? I wanna meet this girl who got our Jackson's attention without a single biscuit to her name. Lots of disappointed mommas in these here parts over you," she said to Anna, who was looking on the mend.

And he still had a minute and a half left.

"Did you really bless Deb's heart?" Miss Dolly asked.

Anna looked to Jackson. He grinned at her, and one of her own popped back up. "Right there at the dinner table," Anna said.

"Oh, listen to her," Miss Flo said. "I love a good Northern accent. Isn't that precious?"

"Ask her to say 'about,'" Jackson said.

Miss Dolly clapped her hands. "She's Canadian!"

"Minnesotan," Anna said.

"Sugarplum, anything north of Kentucky's all Canada to us," Mamie said. "You bowl? We got us two lanes tonight."

He saw the moment realization hit Anna Grace. She blinked at Mamie. A smile hovered on her lips, then her eyes went wide, darting between Jackson and Mamie, her lips mouthing something that might could've been *She's Mae Daniels.*

Anna squinted at Mamie one last time. Her cheeks flamed up and she turned an accusing glare on Jackson. "Are you *kidding* me?"

"Oh, Lordy," Miss Ophelia said. "Rabid fan alert, lane six."

"But I *like* her," Miss Dolly said.

"Would all y'all hush up," Miss Flo said. "She didn't know."

Jackson tucked his hands in his pockets and stepped back before Anna Grace decided to deck him with something stronger than a heart blessin'. "That's about five minutes," he said.

A squawk flew out of her pretty mouth. "We can't leave *now*."

When he grinned, she scowled. "You're on my list, Jackson Davis. On. My. List."

Couldn't think of anywhere else he'd rather be.

"Aw, sweetie pie, don't be holding it against him if he don't like to talk about family," Mamie said. "You seen the rest of it yourself tonight."

And his Anna Grace, who could face down a hundred Confederate generals and leave them all standing in their underpants, got all flustered in front of Mamie. "I've been borrowing all your books from him," she said. "I can't read them fast enough. I've lost study time for you."

Mamie winked. "I know, sweetie pie. Jackson told me. Told me more about you than he probably thinks he has, matter of fact. Now, we gonna bowl or not? Jackson hasn't mentioned if you're any good on the lanes."

"Afraid to find out after she wiped me out in redneck golf," he said.

When her eyes narrowed in that determined sort of way, he got a little kick in the gut.

So *that* was why Lance was always throwing games for Kaci.

"How about we find out the old-fashioned way?" Anna Grace said.

"You got a right good way with plans, Anna Grace."

They rented shoes and settled in for an evening with Mamie and the Misses, who treated Anna to the finest hospitality this side of the Alabama-Georgia border. Whether

Anna Grace rightfully kicked his rump on the bowling lane, well, that was between him and God.

And Mamie, he'd reckon.

Mamie cornered him during one of Anna's last throws. He was lounging in the pit, watching Anna Grace's hips swing as she approached the lane, her arm hanging lower than it had when they started. She was getting tired.

Mamie gave an evil chuckle. "You got it bad, sugarplum."

"Yes, ma'am." No sense in denying it. He'd fallen off the turnip truck and right into a pasture of love-patties.

Eight pins toppled at the end of Anna's lane. She stomped her foot. When she spun back to wait for her ball, her face screwed up with gritty determination. Adorable woman.

"Your daddy would've liked her."

"Been thinking that a lot lately."

Miss Ophelia stepped up next to Anna. The two of them talked angles of attack for the split she had to tackle. If ever there was a woman who could knock those pins down with sheer willpower, it was his Anna Grace.

"I'm no expert on love outside the pages of a book," Mamie said, "but seems to me the best husbands and fathers are the ones who can look at all the downsides and hardships of love, but decide to love somebody anyway."

"Military life's rough on families."

Mamie tsked at him. "You're halfway through your career. Day's coming when the military can't be your family anymore."

Anna picked up the bowling ball and stared at the pins. Looking at how to put them in their places.

He wondered where she thought she'd fit once she was done with school.

"Never understood why Daddy wasn't enough for Momma," he said. "Best man I ever knew, and he couldn't keep her happy."

"She wasn't the one he was supposed to make happy." Mamie's voice was soft, but it echoed in his head louder than all the bowling pins in the building. "You think your daddy'd be happy knowing you found somebody you want to make smile every day the rest of your life, but you were too chicken to go for it? Sugarplum, they got married for you. Now I ain't ever pushed it, because I thought you'd be doing better finding a nice girl from back home, but a girl who makes you look like that don't come round all that often."

Anna Grace balanced the ball in her hands, her head cocked so her hair brushed her shoulders. She did that hip-swinging thing and drew up to the lane. Her arm dropped, the ball swung back, then she yanked it forward and let it go so smooth it barely made a sound on the slick surface of the lane.

"What if I'm not enough for her?" he said.

Mamie patted his knee. "That's not a question the likes of me can answer for you, sugarplum."

Anna's ball connected with the outside edge of the first pin. It shot sideways into the second pin, knocking it down and picking up a spare.

He jumped into the air, fists pumping and hollering. Anna spun around, laughing, arms high. "Yes!"

Jackson met her halfway. He wrapped her in a hug and spun her around. "Beautiful, Anna Grace."

"I know." Her big, infectious grin glowed brighter than the score board. "And I can bowl too."

Sure could.

She'd bowled him right over.

JACKSON WAS QUIET on the drive to the hotel. Anna's exuberance over the night slowly faded.

This meeting-the-family thing had a flavor of commitment to it.

And it tasted more like strawberry shortcake than stewed okra.

Not good.

They checked into the hotel. Jackson insisted, of course, on carrying her bags. But he didn't claim his momma'd have his hide if he didn't. The clerk greeted him by name, though the happy twang in her voice dropped when she spotted Anna. Still, she gave him a wink and an upgrade.

Apparently he'd been serious about not staying at the mausoleum.

Up in the room, Jackson gave her a *let's have a talk* look. A heart-in-his-eyes, contemplating-the-L-word kind of look.

Also not good.

Anna stumbled back a step. "Does an upgrade mean a whirlpool tub? Because I think that's the only thing I miss about my old life."

He humored her with a half-grin. "Yep."

She stopped short of declaring the tub a good reason to love him, and instead swallowed so quick she choked on her own spit. "Great." She had to get close to him to claim her bag, so she gave him a peck on the cheek and a forced smile. "You're a peach."

He ruffled her hair, then flopped back on the bed with the remote and flipped on a commentary on the history of the Alabama-Auburn rivalry. "My life mission is complete."

Except a week ago he would've asked if he could join her in the tub, and tonight he let her go alone.

Maybe he didn't like baths. Too cramped or slippery or hot or something.

But given what he could do in that little space of his shower—nope, definitely something else.

She almost turned around, asked if he was okay.

But there was that commitment taste again.

So she went in the bathroom and turned on the faucet, but she left the door cracked.

Just in case.

Her heart would hate her when this went sour before his expiration date. But she couldn't move for a man again.

Start school over. Find a new job. Leave her friends. She knew how many hours he put in at work. The higher he went up in rank, the less time he'd be home.

The thought of living that life with Jackson, of hating that life with Jackson, made her lungs choke as if the steamy water from the tap were filling them instead of the tub. Her pulse echoed a long-forgotten plea.

Don't hurt me, don't hurt me, don't hurt me.

And who was to say that pensive expression he'd been wearing half the night had anything to do with her?

Who was to say he'd changed his mind about commitment?

Who was to say she was worthy of his love?

Or if she was, for how long? They had lust, but did they have anything else?

Would she ever have anything else?

She filled the tub and killed the overhead lights. The glow off the hair dryer light illuminated the room softly. But despite the hot water shooting out the jets, she shivered.

"Anna Grace?" Jackson knocked at the door. "Okay in there?"

Definitely not. Not if the mere sound of his voice stilled her internal earthquake. "Mm-hmm. Pruney goodness."

"Need help getting your back?"

She needed help with a lot more than her back.

Concern knitted his brows together. Stubble darkened his cheeks. She felt a pull of interest low in her belly.

She was already in toes over tomatoes. Wasn't as though letting him closer would change anything.

And he *was* exceptionally talented at helping with her body parts. "I wouldn't want to take you away from your pre-game coverage."

He slipped into the room and took a seat on the floor beside the tub. His gaze darted at the foamy water. "Thinking about other coverage right now."

The dark heat in his eyes made her want things she had no business wanting, and no chance of ever having.

She dropped her head against the cool surface of the tub and ignored that voice in her head warning her to keep her mouth shut. "What are we doing?" she whispered.

His hand brushed her hair. "Whatever comes natural."

She peeked at him from beneath lowered lashes. His eyes were big and dark in the low light, watching her watch him. "You think it's that simple?"

His fingers inched lower, brushed her ear, then her neck, and her shivers morphed from fear to anticipation.

"Ain't much simple in life." Even in a low volume, his voice rumbled off the walls.

"But you think we are?"

His lips twitched, but it seemed more habitual than intentional. His eyes were too serious to pull off the smile. "Started that way."

"This isn't going to end well."

"You ending it tonight?"

The correct answer was yes. Get out before she got in any deeper. Before she spent more time with his family, before she missed the sound of Radish snoring on the floor beside her, before those secret looks and private touches went from I'm-into-you to the full-blown I-love-you.

Because no doubt that's where things were headed. No matter how much she liked him, no matter how easy they usually were, he wasn't in the long-term plan.

His fingers had stopped moving. Like her, he seemed to be holding his breath, waiting for her answer. The jets in the tub bubbled away, the warm water buffering her body from the realities of the world outside. "No," she finally said.

"Right glad to hear that." He cupped her nape and brushed a kiss over her jaw. He drew back, inhaled deep and parted his lips to speak, but Anna pulled him in for another kiss before he could spoil the moment.

Whether they had one or a hundred moments left, she intended to savor every last one.

His hand slid beneath the water to caress her breast. Her breathing hitched, her heart thumped, her blood crashed. Her better judgment slipped away, replaced with her body's instinctive craving.

She traced his ears, enjoying the little shudder that wound its way through his body. *That* was easy.

She licked his lower lip, thrilling at the soft texture above the sandpaper feel of his chin. *That* was easy.

She let him tip her lower in the tub, glide his hand down her belly, between her thighs. His fingers expertly coaxed her into a haze of frenzied arousal while he continued to kiss her jaw, whisper sweet nothings, nip at her shoulders, her lips, making her forget the world outside their bodies existed.

So, *so* easy.

She whimpered, thrust her hips against his hand until she exploded in a mass of satisfied, overheated cells. And when she could breathe steady again, she hooked a hand around his neck and held on tight as her wobbly arms would let her. "Is there anything you *don't* do well?"

"Probably, but I don't much care to find out what it is."

She tugged at his shirt. "Water's nice and warm if you want to come in."

He tossed his clothes on top of her neatly folded ones before she had time to process the fact that he'd slipped out of her arms. When he slid into the tub, condom in hand, the water nearly sloshed over the side. When Anna crawled over to straddle him, it actually did.

"Making a mess there, Anna Grace."

"I'll let you clean it up later."

He chuckled. "That there's progress."

"Wanna see a little more?"

He cupped her rear end and pulled her closer. "Always."

Twenty minutes later, the water was cooling, and Anna was catching her breath and leaning on Jackson's wet chest. It rose beneath her. She smiled, anticipating another comment on her progress.

Instead, his voice came out quiet and a little rough. "Momma married Russ two months after my daddy died."

Anna went completely still. "Oh," she whispered.

"They were best friends, my daddy and Russ. Collected all

that Confederate stuff together. Went hunting every fall. I went with 'em once I was old enough. Craig too. After Russ got divorced, Momma invited him over every holiday."

The jets had long since quit running. The small room was silent save for Jackson's voice. "My daddy was my hero. Taught me everything I know about being a man. If he couldn't keep his marriage together, if my daddy couldn't do it—nobody could. Worked his tail off doing everything he could to make her happy, and it still wasn't enough."

Anna twisted her head and pressed a kiss over his tattoo. His wet fingers tangled in her half-damp hair. "Taught me to treat her the same," he said quietly, "but after she married Russ, she wasn't the same. Not to me. Not when I realized what she'd done."

"How old were you?" she asked.

"Summer before my senior year," he said. "I was gonna go to Auburn. Follow in the old man's shoes, play ball, make him proud. Couldn't much afford it, but I knew I had the brains to get a good job and work it off after."

A shiver wracked his body. Goosebumps pebbled his skin. If she could've squeezed him tighter, she would've.

"When Momma married Russ, he moved us into the mausoleum, took all of Daddy's stuff like it was his own, like that's what Daddy would've wanted. Offered to pay my tuition. Give me a job at the family business. Take care of things. Like I was following his footsteps instead of my daddy's. I told him to go to hell and applied to Bama."

"Pretty extreme," Anna murmured.

"Best thing I could've done. Got my head screwed back on straight, found something bigger than me worth working for. Might not be able to fly the jets, but I can't imagine working for anyone else. The Force, it's family."

A familiar ache pricked at her chest. She knew better than to fall for a uniform.

She did.

But another part of her ached too.

The part that couldn't help but sympathize with Deb. Had she been right to marry her husband's best friend two months after his death? That wasn't Anna's business.

But choosing happiness, taking a chance at love again, that was something Anna envied.

She envied that Kaci had found it, she envied that Jules was looking for it with Brad, and she envied that Deb had been brave enough to risk her relationship with her son to go after what she wanted.

"Does she still love him?" she whispered.

Jackson's hand stilled on her head. His chest rose beneath her once, twice, then once more, his heart beating out a strong, steady rhythm. "Never paid it much attention."

"It's not always people's fault if they get it wrong the first time." Her voice was so soft in her own ears she wasn't sure she'd said it out loud.

But when his grip tightened around her, she knew he'd heard. "My daddy was ten times the man your ex is."

She squeezed him back. "I know. I can tell."

His fingers went back to toying with her hair, his breath cool against her damp skin. "Not sure I've done my duty in showing Louisa."

Anna's eyes burned. A full-body shiver racked her to the core. She could feel that L-word creeping through her subconscious, looking for a crack to sneak through, to burst out to the forefront of her mind, out her mouth, out every pore in her skin.

But it couldn't. She wouldn't let it. She had to get through tonight, get through tomorrow, and then she had finals and work. Whatever this was tonight, it would fade. They'd go back to being friends who liked to be naked together, nothing more.

"Guess it's time for me to clean up that mess, huh, Anna Grace?" He reached for a towel, but she stopped him.

"Give her time." Her teeth chattered. Jackson reached for the towels again.

Anna stopped him once again. "No more money. No more

tickets. Just your time. She'll see. She'll see you, and she'll see him through you."

Jackson hauled her out of the tub and wrapped a rough white towel around her body. "Got some experience there, Anna Grace?" He rubbed her arms with a second towel.

"When Beth got married and had babies... I just wanted some time."

He smiled at her with those beautiful eyes, those perfect lips, and she realized it was still what she wanted.

Just a little more time.

Chapter Twenty-Six

She'd traveled far but still had hills to conquer.
—The Temptress of Pecan Lane, by Mae Daniels

ANNA WAS SLEEPING so deeply Saturday morning, her lashes didn't flutter a wink when Jackson nudged her. He dug through the drawers for a notepad and a pen, wincing every time a hinge squeaked, but she kept right on sleeping.

He left a note on his pillow and slipped out of the hotel, phone in his pocket in case she woke up and didn't see the note, then headed for Louisa's place.

He had to bang three times on the door of the old manor she and three of her girlfriends rented before she yanked the door open, bleary-eyed in her pajama pants and a white tank top he wouldn't have let her wear in public. "What?" Her lip curled out. "Not all of us keep military hours."

He handed her a slip of paper. "You owe Anna an apology."

Louisa's hair fell in her face when she looked down at the note. "What's this?"

"Cost of your ticket."

He didn't know hair could spontaneously combust, but the temper that shot through Louisa left the tips of her curls smoking. "Excuse you?"

He angled himself in the doorway so he was blocking her chest from view of any passing cars and caught a whiff of something that reminded him of his granddaddy's moonshine. It put his own temper on a short fuse. "You disrespected a guest in Momma's house. *Your* guest. You know what Daddy would've done to you? You're lucky you can walk today. You want to go to that game, find a way to pay for yourself. You got four hours."

And even though Daddy would've whipped *his* hide for it, Jackson turned his back on Louisa's shocked expression and took himself back to the hotel.

For the first time since coming home, Jackson was finally doing right by her.

ANNA HAD JUST FINISHED reading Jackson's note when the hotel door clicked open. She swiped her hair out of her eyes, and an unfamiliar ache in her shoulder made her wince.

Jackson grinned at her. "Feeling that game last night?"

She didn't bother giving him a dirty look. Because her stomach was growling and he had paper bags in one hand and a box with two to-go cups in the other, and the scents of biscuits and bacon and coffee wafted into the room.

There she was again, holding back a declaration of undying love.

He plopped on the bed. "Looks like you might need some feeding."

She gave him a playful shove with her left arm.

But she let him help her eat.

Because he liked to reward progress.

Eventually they headed out for game-day activities. But first, Anna insisted that Jackson take her to the Confederate mausoleum so she could apologize to his mother.

He gave in to that a mite bit too easily.

Jackson's jaw took on a mulish set when his gaze landed on Louisa's car. He saw Anna into the house, then angled toward a side doorway she hadn't noticed last night. "Okay for a bit, Anna Grace?"

"Any place I should stay out of?"

He flashed a grin that didn't reach his eyes. "No, ma'am. Not you."

"Thanks."

He pressed a kiss to her temple, then disappeared. Anna heard the distinct sound of stairs creaking. She guessed he was going in search of Louisa.

Which meant Anna had to search somebody out too.

Deb was in the kitchen, wiping down the sink and humming a tune Anna didn't recognize. Anna paused at the island and cleared her throat.

Deb's shoulders hitched, but she flicked them down and turned. "Good morning."

"I owe you an apology," Anna said. "I'm not from round here, but I've lived here long enough to know when I've crossed a line, and I'm sorry."

Deb's lips set in a thin line. Her chin wavered, and her gaze shifted away. "I wasn't entirely fair to you." She looked down at the dishrag she was twisting, folded it in thirds, and laid it across the sink. "Jackson's never brought home a girlfriend."

Anna tried to swallow, but it felt as if she had sawdust in her mouth. "Louisa invited me."

"If he didn't want you here, you wouldn't be here."

"Regardless, you don't need to worry about me."

Deb merely lifted a well-groomed and spectacularly colored eyebrow.

"I was married to the military once," Anna said. "I have no intentions of doing it again."

"My son knows this?"

Anna flashed a wry smile. "It's why we get along so well."

Deb turned and picked up her dishrag again. "Y'all go on and keep saying that, but when you realize you're lying to yourselves, it's going to hurt. And I don't like seeing my children hurt."

Of course Momma Deb wouldn't. What mother would? But after the year Anna'd had, she did have some appreciation for what came out of the aftermath of hurting.

Not that she'd offer her opinion to Momma Deb.

She stepped back. "We met over an ant infestation in my car. Jackson wouldn't let me help clean up my own mess, because he told me you'd have his hide if he left a lady in distress. Even a divorced, undereducated, messy Yankee lady."

Deb's face was turned, but Anna saw the plump of her cheek when her lips curved softly upward. "He's a good man."

"One of the best," Anna agreed. "Thank you." She left Deb in the kitchen, found the most comfortable looking spot on the rocks that were the living room furniture, pulled her school notes out of her purse, and sat down to wait for tailgating time.

JACKSON FOUND LOUISA digging a piggy bank out from under a loose floorboard in her old closet.

"I ain't ready for you yet," she said without turning around, the pout evident in her voice.

She'd moved out of the mausoleum when she started college, but Jackson hadn't been around enough all the years before that to know if the butterflies fluttering around the walls and the lacy curtains were original to Louisa's time in the room, or if they'd been added as a special touch for overnights when Craig and Maura's girls came. The Power Rangers bedspread, he knew, was all Louisa.

He made himself comfortable in the doorway and checked his watch to make sure he didn't leave Anna Grace alone too long. She could handle herself, but that wasn't the point. "Been thinking about some stuff."

"So?"

"So got to reckoning you don't do well in school because you don't know what you want to be."

"*So?*" Louisa's shoulders bunched so high they blocked her

eardrums.

But Jackson kept talking anyway. "*So* it's my job to help LTs figure out their career path. Reckon I might be able to help you too."

She gave the piggy one last tug. It sprang free, and sent her skidding back on her rump. She gave him the same suspicious eye Momma was probably aiming at Anna Grace right about now. Louisa pulled herself up, dusted her jeans, hiked the piggy under her arm like a football, and crossed the room. "Yeah, well, I don't want your help." She shoved the pig at him. "Here. Now where's my ticket?"

He ignored the pig. "How's your engine running?"

"Slicker'n Momma's gravy down your gullet. Where's. My. Ticket?" She poked him in the chest with each word.

He went on and let her. "Craig said you've been filtering the oil yourself."

"What, now girls can't pump their own gas? New millennium, dummy. Girls can do anything they want."

"You ever looked into Auburn's environmental engineering program?"

Her eyes went wide. She punched him in the arm. "Shut up. You don't get to walk around here like you're somebody. You don't get a say in my life. You don't care about me."

She was wrong, and he was pretty sure she was being a melodramatic female—perfection, indeed—but her opinion sliced him deep. "You're too old to be a brat."

"That what your Anna Grace calls me?"

Well, color him slow on the uptake. She was *jealous*. "You get me twice as much as she does, but she appreciates it three times more than you."

Her lips curled into a snide kind of sneer, the kind that usually preceded a slimy comment from a drunkard in a bar. He cut her off. "Never thought I'd meet a Yankee with better manners than my own sister. You go on and nurse your mad all day if you want. I'm gonna go enjoy a beautiful football game."

He plunked the piggy bank on the burnished oak dresser, then headed for the back stairs, half surprised, half relieved Louisa didn't follow him.

When he got to the kitchen, Momma was alone, but he could smell Anna's shampoo lingering in the air.

That scent stayed with a man.

She had a couple of views on how the world worked that were sticking with him too. Including one or two about his family. She'd been good for him that way.

Momma looked up at him with sad eyes that seemed to be going around the female population in his life. Her mouth settled in a grim line, and she went back to the pot she was washing. "Sweet potato pie's all gone."

"Do you love Russ?"

The pan slipped. Water and suds splattered the counter. She fumbled for a towel, her cheeks taking on a stain, her hands shaking. She twisted her face to him, but before their gazes connected, she dropped her chin and pointed her nose at the mess. "Yes." Her voice was soft but laced with steel, answering both the question he'd asked, and the one that had always lingered between them.

Do you love Russ more than you loved Daddy?

But he'd never asked.

He'd never asked, because he hadn't wanted to know. Hadn't wanted to believe that this woman who'd stood shoulder to shoulder with Daddy—keeping Jackson straight, raising him to understand and appreciate the value of a clean house, of a good meal, of the backbone of a family—could have loved another man more than she'd loved his daddy.

Maybe loved another man more than she loved her own son.

"Does he make you happy?"

He'd never asked her that before either.

Never considered it part of the equation.

But she was more than just his momma. She had her own life as much as he had his, and Daddy was gone, and Momma

being happy or unhappy wouldn't change that.
She might as well be happy.
She *should* be happy.
Her shoulders trembled. She made a quick swipe at her cheek with the back of her hand. When she looked up at him, her nose matched her cheeks. Her chin wobbled. Her shiny eyes asked what would've been the world to him at seventeen.

At thirty-three, he realized it was long past time to give her his blessing to have her own life, and to enjoy it.

He felt as if one of those biscuits he'd had for breakfast was stuck in his throat, another one lodged up against his heart. "Reckon he's done more right by you than I have."

"Oh, Jackson."

And suddenly she was hugging him with all her might, smelling like blackberries and biscuits, and he felt about six years old again, letting her titanium strength crush all the bad and turn it into hope and peace and an innocent belief in the good of the world. "My sweet baby boy," she whispered. "You've always done as right as you could. Never could've asked for more."

The back door banged shut. Jackson broke away from Momma. Russ stopped in the threshold.

He looked between them, mustache twitching, then settled his gaze on Jackson. "Wish your sister had your good taste in dates."

Momma's cheeks and nose flushed deeper.

Another door shut in a different part of the house. Jackson heard a squeal, followed by a barely-past-puberty drawl.

Momma and Russ heaved a sigh as one.

And that's when Anna started talking.

The shading dropped right out of Momma's cheeks. Russ flinched like the Yankee accent hurt his ears, and they both started past Jackson.

"Don't trust Anna Grace to take care of the boyfriend?" Jackson drawled.

"Well, he ain't from our South, but he ain't from her North

either," Russ said on a wince.

Jackson reckoned that was good enough reason to check things out himself.

Before the three of them hit the living room, Anna's voice had gone past cheerful to what he would've classified as joyous in any other woman.

He knew Anna Grace well enough by now, though, to know that whatever she was saying, she was doing it with a special kind of devilish delight. "I *love* your tattoo. Did you design that?"

The fleabag molesting Louisa came into view. He tossed his stringy bangs back and looked down his nose at Anna. "It's henna." His voice came out nasal and a little high-pitched, as if puberty had slightly missed its mark.

Russ was right. The guy talked as though he didn't have a geographic home. Not one in the good old U-S-of-A.

Maybe not even in this whole world.

"He paints them on himself," Louisa said. After one look in the doorway where Momma, Russ, and Jackson were gathered, she seemed to make an effort to not look at them. And she snuggled up right closer under the boy's arm.

Anna grabbed the loser's other wrist and tugged at his sleeve. "Oh, wow, are there more?"

Amidst all Louisa's not-looking in Jackson's direction, she jiggled a foot, gnawed on her lower lip.

Her yahoo boyfriend yanked his arm out of Anna's reach, and Jackson discovered his stepfather was good for something more than making his momma happy.

He was good for being a brick wall keeping Jackson from showing the little peon the importance of good manners.

Anna Grace seemed completely unfazed. "So you guys met at school? What are you studying?"

"He's still deciding," Louisa said, the note of pride in her voice making Jackson want to wince. "He can't be boxed in, you know?"

Anna Grace made her doe eyes fake-wide and heaved a

sigh Kaci would've admired. "That's so awesome," she said. "I mean, to be young and carefree, the world still your oyster, having fun, experimenting. If I'd done that in college, I never would've ended up divorced halfway across the country, still figuring out how to support myself, you know? You guys are so lucky."

Louisa's smug my-boyfriend-makes-my-parents-twitch gleam looked seemed to be coming down with food poisoning.

"But I'm glad I didn't do what my sister did," Anna continued. She gave a fake laugh that sounded so funny in Jackson's ears, he had to step back into the dining room for fear Louisa'd catch on to the joke. "She had three kids by the time she was your age. Can you imagine? I mean, that's something people shouldn't do until they're like thirty-five, right? And you don't want to know what daycare cost when she finally went to college." Her voice dropped, like she was pretending she didn't know Momma and Russ were still standing in the doorway with gaping jaws. "Hope you use protection. Double-or-nothing, I always say. Have you ever *touched* baby poop? Oh. My. God. But enough about that. Stone, you must know some awesome art festivals. Jackson and I would *love* to go. We should double-date sometime."

Russ retreated from the doorway, mustache twitching.

"Yep," he said, "right smart for a Yankee."

Jackson cleared his throat, pretended he was in uniform about to face a flight of LTs fresh off their commissioning, and stepped back into the doorway. He gave Momma a gentle elbow nudge. She clapped her mouth shut.

Anna Grace turned on the couch, grinning as if she were the one fighting that battle up there on the wall, and winning. "Oh, Jackson! There you are. Have you meet Louisa's boyfriend? He's an *artist*. Isn't that cool?"

Louisa was pale, like maybe it was already the fourth quarter and her beloved Tigers were staring at the backside of a scoreboard they couldn't flip right.

"World needs art," Jackson said.

Anna's brow twitched at him. Anna Grace code for *you're welcome, now don't be an ass*.

Her words, not his.

"We should all go check out a museum sometime," he said. He followed Anna's lead and kept a straight face, but it hurt to keep his cheeks from showing his amusement.

Louisa drew herself up, falling way short of Anna's fourteen-feet-tall even sitting down, and wrinkled her nose at Jackson. "Stone has an extra ticket. I'm going with him. I hope under the circumstances, you'll make sure Anna's comfortable at the game."

"My pleasure. Anna tell you about the biofuels project she's working on?"

Yep, that was definitely Louisa's best I-hate-you face. Jackson ignored it and held out a hand to the *ar-teest*. "Stone. Nice to meet finally you. Hope you make sure Louisa's comfortable at the game, given the circumstances."

The kid had a limp grip that left Jackson moderately unworried about the state of his baby sister's innocence. His gaze flicked to Jackson's shirt. "Hope you don't get beat up."

"Ain't too worried."

Anna Grace's foot tapped. Jackson let the kid's hand go, and Louisa promptly wrapped herself back around the yahoo's arm. "Maybe we'll see you there," she said. She looked down at Anna, and her composure faltered. "Nice to see you today, Just Anna."

"You too, sugar."

Louisa dragged the loser out the front door. Momma heaved another big old sigh. "Your grandmother must've loved her," she said with a nod toward Anna.

Jackson couldn't answer.

Couldn't talk through laughing.

Chapter Twenty-Seven

It took him years to find love, minutes to discover loving and being loved were not one in the same.
—The Temptress of Pecan Lane, *by Mae Daniels*

DESPITE ANNA'S FEARS that she was entirely too attached to Jackson, she found herself humming at work Monday morning.

Until she realized Jules had mis-color-coded half of the work she did over the long weekend.

The re-color-coding didn't bother Anna. Days like this restored her faith in her job. Not that she didn't *like* her job. Exactly. She appreciated the paycheck. The tuition assistance. The security.

But it wasn't *fun*.

Nor was thinking about how Jules worked all weekend. If Jules had been at work, she wouldn't have had the good family time she and Brad needed. They'd looked good together lately too. Jules had announced her pregnancy. She was gaining weight, glowing even.

Being nice.

But when she dragged herself in to work Monday morning, she plopped up on Anna's desk, skewing the calendar, and started rearranging the desk organizer. "Enjoy meeting the parents?" she asked Anna.

"Not really, but his grandmother's cool. How about you? Nice Thanksgiving?"

"Brad made nice with his parents this weekend. Got too touchy-feely, so I came in here."

"But otherwise good?"

Jules plunked the staple remover into the Post-it Note holder. "I ate too much. Don't suppose you have leftover pie?"

"Nope. Sorry."

"And here I thought we were friends." She slid off the desk, but she was as smiley as she used to be, which wasn't very smiley for most people but looked positively psychotically happy on Jules. "Quit goofing off. We've got work to do."

"Yes, your holy maternity-ness," Anna said.

And Jules—irritable, screwed up, snarky Jules—laughed.

FOR THE FIRST TIME in almost two years, Jackson was hunting.

Alone.

That made him one happy hunter.

Or it should've.

The weather was perfect. A bit on the crisp side, overcast skies, wind carrying the chirp of the fall birds. He was snug and alert in a prime deer-watching spot.

Hunting heaven.

But the first time a deer wandered past his blind, Jackson picked up his rifle quiet-like, got his shot lined up, put his finger to the trigger...

And couldn't do it.

Because he practically saw Anna Grace looking at him with her own doe eyes, and he heard Louisa chattering away about how after her best friend from kindergarten showed her Bambi, she used to lie awake at night and cry for Bambi and his mother.

Son of a biscuit.

He was lonely. Didn't even have Radish here to keep him

company, since she tended to scare off the creatures.

He lowered the rifle and grunted. The doe bounded off.

Going home wouldn't much help the lonely since Anna Grace was organizing. That was his fault. He needed to keep his trap shut about having a girlfriend who'd put a guy's kitchen away for fun.

But maybe Mamie was around. He waffled a minute or two, but soon, he was packing it in and heading up to Auburn.

He'd been worried about bothering Mamie this early, but she was sitting on her porch with a guest.

A guest who probably needed her time more than Jackson did. But they waved at him, so he pulled over and joined them for a cup of sweet tea. "Morning, ladies."

"Well, now, sugarplum, isn't this a nice surprise." Mamie moved to stand, but Jackson gave her a head shake. She reclined in her flowery wicker chair. "Louisa here was telling me how she broke up with some silly boy who thought she was going to fund his art."

"Right sorry to hear that," Jackson said. The Louisa look of death told him she saw the party he was having inside over *that* bit of news. He snagged a glass from Mamie's tray and propped himself up on the top step. Hadn't heard much from either of them since the game last Saturday.

Louisa pulled her legs up beneath her. Her death look faded behind mild speculation. "Mamie says Just Anna kicked your butt in bowling."

"Sure did. Wouldn't cross her in redneck golf neither."

"Are you going to marry her?"

Jackson almost dropped his glass. "Ain't you a little young to be talking about marriage?"

"Not yours, old man."

Maybe he should've stayed hunting.

It was cool out there in the woods. Unlike the heat that was growing under his camo here. "Not everybody's meant to get married."

She snorted into her tea. Mamie hid a grin behind her

glass.

"Military life's hard on a family," he said, even though he didn't have to justify anything to these two busybodies.

But maybe he needed to justify it to himself. Because much as he didn't want to stop seeing Anna, the thought of being responsible a hundred percent of the time for someone other than himself—worrying about what would happen to her if he got deployed, if he got shot, if he got killed—it near about choked him.

The thought of packing her up and taking her with him next time he got orders, that wasn't so bad. But knowing what she'd leave behind, the life she built for herself on her own, her independence, her schooling, her job... she'd blossomed, his Anna Grace had.

She knew well as he did that every assignment had a different feel, a different flow. Never knew if he'd have a ten-minute or hour-long commute. If he'd be on the road all the time or home for dinner every night. If he'd be able to plan vacations in advance or have to ask his family to roll with whatever the job threw at him.

She'd signed up for that life once, and she'd made it clear she wouldn't do it again.

Shouldn't have to do it again. She was making her life for herself this time, and good on her for it.

Wasn't right of him to ask her to choose between her career and his.

So he'd enjoy her as long as he could, and deal with the pain later.

Louisa rocked back in her chair. "Sounds like you're making excuses for not taking responsibility for yourself. Ain't nobody gonna give you what you want in life. You gotta get out there and do it for yourself."

Jackson blinked at her.

Then had to blink again.

"She hear herself?" he asked Mamie.

"Just the words, sugarplum. She'll figure out what they

mean later."

Louisa wrinkled her nose. "Why are you here? Me and Mamie were having us a girls' day."

Jackson sighed and got to his feet. "Just passing through."

Just passing through, wishing he were back in Georgia with Anna, even if all he did was bring her food and something to drink while she was putting some other guy's kitchen to rights. Awful sad state of affairs to his way of thinking.

So was settling on spending the rest of the day working on making more rights with Momma and Russ, but it did them all some good, or so he reckoned.

TWO WEEKS AFTER Thanksgiving, Anna took her biochemistry final. It was her last class commitment until next year. When her feet hit the sidewalk in the darkening evening outside the James Robert chemistry building, she drew in a breath of temporary freedom.

Her brain had melted into some new form of organic matter, but she was done.

Done.

Until her molecular spectroscopy class started in January.

The thought made her molecules radiate as excitedly as an ice cube's. Two semesters down, nine more to go. She was so tired.

Plus she had two more certifications to slog through at work.

Tonight, though, she'd earned a late dinner at Jackson's house. When she arrived, he had chicken baking, potatoes boiling, and salads already made. He was washing dishes while Radish snored beneath the table. She greeted him with a kiss on the cheek.

"Hey, there, pretty lady."

"I'm impressed," she told him with a smile.

"Suppose you earned it." He dried his hands, then brushed a thumb over her cheek. "Talked to Louisa. She offered to wash your car if you'll talk to her about biofuels."

Work and school. Yuck. But if it helped Louisa figure out what she wanted to be, Anna was in. "Sure."

"How'd that test go?"

"It's over."

She poked at the potatoes. Jackson shooed her away. "Sit. Look like you're fit to pass out."

She would've argued, but if he was brave enough to tell her she looked bad, she'd sit. She scratched Radish's ears, said hi to Enrique in the corner, then plopped down at the table to watch the show part of dinner. "My adviser says I might be able to test out of organic chemistry," she said over a yawn.

"If studying for the test doesn't kill you first."

If it hadn't been for the affection in his voice, she might've been offended. "Gotta do what I've gotta do."

He carried the potatoes to the sink. "Still think chemistry's your thing?"

Yuck again. "You betcha."

Through the steam coming off the potatoes, he pinned her with a look. "I know you're a busy lady, Anna Grace, but you can stop now and again to ask if you're doing what makes you happy."

His washing machine buzzed in his mud room. "Don't you touch anything," he warned. "Be right back."

Anna snitched a slice of red pepper off her salad. She was tired, but was she tired of school and her program, or just tired?

If she weren't working forty hours a week, would she still feel that knot of dread every time she faced the drive to James Robert? What if her classes were closer to work and home? The quality of her education was top-notch. And the homework only seemed worse because she was rusty at studying. Plus, she was already tired from work by the time—

"Son of a biscuit!" Jackson yelped.

Anna shot out of her seat behind Radish and darted to the laundry room. "Jackson? Everything okay?"

He eyed a spot on the floor. His chest was heaving in that coming-down-from-a-fright kind of way. He held out a hand. "Hold on there."

Radish growled low in her throat. She pointed at the intruder on the baseboard.

"Dal-gurn thing jumped out of the washer," Jackson said.

Anna clamped a hand over her mouth, but the snicker had to go somewhere. It came out in an unladylike snort.

Jackson's lips twitched too. "Get it, girl," he said to Radish.

The dog sniffed the little green lizard. It wove drunkenly toward the garage door. Radish growled again. The lizard opened its jaws as if it could take on something a lot bigger than an old spaniel.

Radish whimpered and cowered down on the tile floor.

Anna clapped her other hand over her mouth too, and she snorted again.

"You women," Jackson said. "Always afraid of a little lizard."

The lizard misstepped and tumbled off the wall. Radish inched closer to it. The poor thing darted for the safety of a clothes basket, and Radish skittered back.

Jackson choked on a laugh.

Anna whimpered from holding it in, but soon they were both laughing so hard Anna had to lean against the wall while Jackson clutched his stomach. The lizard stumbled about like somebody had spiked its dinner, and it snapped at Radish, who alternated between cowering and growling until the little green guy disappeared beneath the washing machine.

Jackson wiped his eyes. He blew out a contented laugh and grabbed Anna by the waist. "I love you."

"I lo—" Anna caught the word before it made it over her vocal chords. Her heart drummed on her rib cage, her lungs seemed to fill with thick, wet clay, but it didn't change the truth.

She did. She loved him.

She would've driven all the way out to his house to spend

five minutes with him on a work night, simply to give him a hug and a kiss and listen to him *Anna Grace* her.

She would've baked him a hundred pies every time he threw a redneck golf game for her.

She would've given up her job and school and independence for him.

All she wanted was to know he'd love her forever.

But he wouldn't. They worked because they didn't want forever. They worked because they didn't need forever. They worked because they didn't believe in forever.

Except she did.

She needed the promise of forever along with the promise he'd let her be her own independent woman, but his cheeks and lips were taking on the green hue of a confirmed bachelor being shackled with the ol' ball and chain.

Her perfect, neat, scheduled and labeled world ripped to pieces like a calendar in a shredder. The laughter caught in her throat came out as a hysterical sob. "I have to go."

"Anna."

He gripped her tighter, but she pushed back until he let go.

"Anna, wait."

"No. No." She snatched her bag out of his bedroom. "I can't do this. I can't."

"I'm not asking you to. Wait. Listen."

The desperation in his voice tore at something bigger than her job, bigger than school, bigger than her life. But she stumbled through the kitchen, blinked through tears, and counted the steps to the front door, to her regularly scheduled life.

"Anna. Please."

She had a hand on the door knob. Two strides out the door, then across the porch, down those steps, around the cute little curved sidewalk to her car on the driveway three paces away from where she'd seen her first live armadillo, and she'd be free.

Empty.

But free.

And alone.

She hadn't had to think about alone for a while. That was a hole her fish couldn't fill. She slowly swiveled back to face him.

A deep groove wrinkled between his eyes. His lips turned low as she'd ever seen them. He reached for her, then shoved both hands in his pockets and went up on the balls of his feet. "I'm not good at this, Anna Grace. I don't know what it means, and I won't pretend I have all the answers, but I love you." The husky note in his voice, the longing, the uncertainty, it was all so un-Jacksonlike.

But it wasn't something she could fix. "For how long?" she asked.

He blinked. "How long?"

"When does it expire? When do you get tired of me?" She didn't mean to shriek, but once she got going, she couldn't stop. "When does my label maker start giving you heartburn, and my calendar and my plans and my *life* not fit into yours anymore? What happens when you get orders? What if I get a job in Minnesota? Or California? Or—or—I don't know, Iceland? What then?"

Radish whimpered and covered her nose with her paw.

Jackson stiffened. "I'm not him, Anna."

"No, you're not," she agreed. "But you don't believe in forever either."

"I believe in you."

He reached for her. She backed away and grabbed the door handle. "Please stop making this worse. I have to take care of myself. You can't do it for me."

He ducked his head. "More to life than work and school, Anna Grace."

"I have friends and I have family. That's enough."

"Never pegged you for an "enough" type of woman."

Her tears threatened to spill over. It wasn't enough.

Not by a long shot.

"You're a good man," she whispered, "but I can't do this

anymore. I'm sorry."

And she turned and fled the man she wished she'd met first.

IN HIS ELEVEN YEARS in the service, Jackson couldn't think of another day he hadn't been all there at work. He walked around the office, talked to his program managers, briefed the colonel, but he felt like his arms and legs and chest were empty tubes on strings being tugged by someone else.

The colonel suggested he take the afternoon off.

He wondered if Brad would be around to give him some payback. Instead, he texted Lance about lunch.

Should've specified he meant *alone*.

"Oh, sugar, you went and fell in the L-word, didn't you?" Kaci clucked the minute the honeymooners arrived at the Mexican dive just off Gellings. Her eyes went wide, and she paused without leaving room for Lance to scoot into the booth after her. "You didn't hurt my Anna, did you? Lance, kick his ass."

Lance flashed a cocky grin that went too well with his flight suit. "Man's kicking his own ass, Kace."

"If you dumped her—"

Jackson held his hands up. He tried to explain, but the words were rolling in his stomach like one of Radish's rawhide bones.

The problem with spitting out *I want to marry her* was that his mouth wasn't wired to put those sounds all together like that.

If he couldn't say it, could he do it?

Didn't much matter if she didn't want him, did it?

"Got it bad, man," Lance said. "Could marry her."

Kaci slugged him in the chest, eliciting an *oomph*. "You hush on up," she said. "You know how many schools that girl's been to without finishing a degree?"

Lance dug into the chips and salsa on the table. "Internet

age, babe."

"Not for lab work," Kaci said.

Lance pointed a chip at Jackson. "If you marry her, you can transfer your GI bill to her."

Yeah, Jackson had thought of that himself sometime between Anna's fleeing his house as though her pants were on fire and that darkest part of the night where the loneliness had taken him down an unmanly road. The very act of scrounging in his mind for a way to keep her told him he was swimming in a creek he hadn't checked for cottonmouths.

Jackson stared at his hands. "She likes to work. Likes to earn it herself."

"Being married to the military's earning it," Lance said. Jackson felt Kaci nodding her agreement. "She could go full-time, let Uncle Sam pay for it. Could finish up a degree before you get orders."

"And then have to find a new job when we move. Take a chance we end up somewhere that doesn't have need of fuels specialists and chemical engineers, and then she'd start all over again." His throat was getting thick, his voice clogged up.

There was an easier answer.

He could get out of the service.

A shiver thrust through his shoulders and rocketed down his spine. Felt as if his life were ripping in two.

He could have Anna. He could have the Air Force. Couldn't have both.

The bench across from him squeaked. Kaci shooed Lance out of the booth. "You deal with Major Heartbreak here," she said. "If she's looking half as bad as he is, she's gonna need a friend too."

Jackson opened his mouth. *Tell her I said hi. Tell her I love her.*

Tell her I'm sorry.

None of them fit.

"She knows, sugar," Kaci said.

And when she gave his hand a squeeze, he felt like she was

using a Band-Aid to hold an earthquake together.

She sashayed out the door.

"So," Lance said, "want to get shitfaced?"

"Will it help?"

"No, but it'll give you a reason to look like that."

Jackson grunted. Lance ordered eight burritos and three bags of chips and salsa to go. The two of them loaded up in Jackson's truck.

"Class Six," Lance said. "My treat. Merry Christmas."

Jackson didn't figure the Class Six had anything that would touch his granddaddy's moonshine, but he didn't share *that* with anybody, so he pointed the truck to base.

"And then," Lance said, sliding on his aviator sunglasses, "you can help me figure out how to tell Kaci I'm getting deployed."

Maybe they'd need that moonshine after all.

Chapter Twenty-Eight

She loved him for who he was and what he did until who he was and what he did made her hate him.
—The Temptress of Pecan Lane, *by Mae Daniels*

ANNA SPENT THE weekend after finals at work. Her throat was raw, the skin around her nose so brittle she'd had to buy a tub of Vaseline. But there was filing and re-color-coding to do, and she'd promised Jules she'd run a few tests.

Beat staying home watching Walker bang his little fish face on the side of the brandy snifter. Fish apparently didn't appreciate *The Wedding Singer*.

Besides, she'd relabeled the kitchen *and* bathroom cabinets already. She needed something else to organize.

She started with the tests. Get the boring stuff out of the way first. Then she dove into the files, and the next thing she knew, nine hours and eight years' worth of samples had passed. She drove home, warmed up a serving of hot dish, squirted it with ketchup, and ate it over a *Buffy the Vampire Slayer* marathon.

Walker still didn't approve.

But she wasn't in the mood for another Mae Daniels book.

She wasn't even in the mood for ketchup shots.

"Relax," she said to the fish, her voice as clear as if she were talking through water herself. "You don't have enough blood for the vamps."

She fell asleep on the couch, and Sunday morning she went back to work. Corporate *had* asked for all the older data to be re-color-coded, they just hadn't specified a time line.

With school out and having to break up with Jackson—her heart squeezed out a few more tears, dripping acid down to her stomach—now seemed like the right time.

Kaci brought her dinner Sunday night. Anna draped a cloth over Walker's snifter and put on *The Wedding Singer* while they shared a pizza. When the rapping granny came on screen, Kaci developed a case of the sniffles.

Anna blinked her own tenderized eyelids to peer at her friend. "Kaci?"

"He's leaving me," Kaci said.

She exploded in a beautiful mass of tears.

Anna tossed her pizza on the ground and wrapped her friend in a hug. "What happened?"

It was hard to get the whole story through the broken bits of words Kaci spit out between heaving gasps and sobs, but eventually Anna recognized *deploy* and *months*.

"Oh, honey, he'll come back." Anna's heart broke for her friend's fears and her own love, who wasn't coming back.

She was an idiot for letting herself get that involved.

"But I'll *miss* him," Kaci sobbed. "And what if—"

"Oh, no, ma'am," Anna interrupted. "No what ifs."

Kaci elbowed her. "What if you leave me too?" she finished with a dramatic flair.

A week ago, Anna would've laughed. Today she felt her own case of the sniffles coming on.

What if she moved home? Away from Kaci, away from her independence, away from this crazy beautiful life she'd made for herself?

And what if she were never as happy again?

"I want my mommy," Anna suddenly whimpered.

And she did. She wanted to go home to her mom and her dad, to Beth and Tony and the boys, to her family who missed her and loved her and who still might not accept that she was the first divorced Jensen in the history of the Jensens, but who had to love her anyway, because that's what family did.

"Don't you dare leave over Christmas and not come back," Kaci said. "I need you here. You hear me, sugar? Don't you take the easy way out on me now."

Anna managed a hiccup that could've passed as a laugh. "There's nothing easy about my parents' couch."

"Oh, sugar." Kaci dabbed at her eyes. "That's the best news I've heard all day."

They spent the rest of the night alternately crying and laughing. By the time Kaci left, Anna was absolutely positive she didn't have a single emotion left in her body.

But then Jules called in sick Monday morning.

And Shirley came tearing through the lab hollering about certifying the last shipment from EFA Inc., their newest vendor. Anna lost her temper and yelled back that it hadn't been delivered yet, and Shirley told her to find it anyway. Not even the paperwork with the backup printout from the samples inventory database could convince her.

So Anna spent the day in a stupor, tired of the lab, tired of running tests, tired of her life. She found the paperwork Jules had misfiled and had a sample delivered from the storage tanks, then set everything up to run the test in the morning. She'd delivered the final results of the day to Shirley's office when she noticed something wrong in Jules's cube.

One of the stacks of magazines had fallen over, which was situation normal.

But the sample container tucked in the corner behind the magazines wasn't.

"Dammit, Jules," she muttered.

Sure enough, it was the missing sample from this morning.

Now she had two samples. Great.

Anna grit her teeth and carried it to the samples storage

locker.

But then she thought about having another row with Shirley tomorrow when the tests hadn't been run. She heaved a sigh, went to grab her protective gear again, and suited up to run the analysis.

Three full runs later, Anna felt as though she'd swallowed the stuff. Her stomach burned with a nauseous twinge that went beyond *I'm going to be sick* and straight to *this must be hell*.

Because the container was labeled 50/50 HRT biofuel, delivered Friday, from EFA Inc., but the contents were most definitely *not*.

Not in the container from Jules's cube.

Not in the container that the field had trucked in today and that had been waiting all weekend for clearance to go into storage.

But those two containers matched perfectly.

Anna stumbled back to the storage locker. Her heart wanted to quit, and the air in the lab was too heavy to breathe. She'd used the fume hood properly and nothing smelled out of the ordinary, but the knowledge that something was very, very wrong made her throat and her tongue and her nasal passages swell with panic.

She flung open the storage locker, scanning last month's inventory until she found the previous sample from EFA, Inc.

It tested wrong too.

Completely at odds with the data in the inventory system.

She'd run a test wrong, she'd missed a step, she'd added a wrong test solution, the timing was wrong.

She'd done something wrong.

Because the other option was that the problem wasn't in the testing but in the fuel, the fuel *labeled and approved* by Jules, the fuel cleared for use in the planes she could hear flying overhead and cleared to be stored in the same tanks as the other biofuel.

Anna wrenched her coat off and fled the lab.

She needed fresh air.
She needed to think.
She needed to call Shirley. But most of all, she needed a minute to breathe.

According to her lab results, it was the last minute she would have for a very, very long time.

What she *didn't* need was the heart-stoppingly handsome Southern gentleman leaning against her car, sweet spaniel at his feet.

He straightened when she stopped. "Anna Grace?"

And there it was. Just her name, but it said so much. *Are you okay? What's wrong? Let me fix it for you.*

"No," she said.

He watched her as he would a wounded coyote. He didn't so much as twitch, but she felt him circling her, sniffing, looking for a way in. "Just wanted to talk."

Anna reached across herself to rub her stiff shoulders. She wanted to go home, run a hot shower, and crawl into bed.

Looked like neither of them would be getting what they wanted tonight. "I can't."

Radish whined.

And suddenly Anna had more tears. Because she should've been able to talk to him. Because she needed to shut the door between them, but all it took was a whisper from him to keep it open. The backs of her eyes prickled. A lump grew in her sore, achy throat. "Please. I can't tonight." Because he couldn't fix this for her.

She wanted him to, though. She wanted to hand him the test results and Shirley's number, let him call her and let them fix it.

He stood there, watching her. Waiting to be asked.

She didn't move.

Neither did he.

At length, he looked past her to the building. "Work troubles?"

She squeezed her eyes shut and rubbed at her temples.

"My samples aren't coming out right."

He straightened. "How not right?"

"It's just the samples from one company. The rest are fine."

"How not right, Anna Grace?" he repeated.

Her whole body sagged. "The baselines are wrong."

"It's not JP8? Not an authorized HRJ?"

And this time she heard it.

She wasn't talking to quasi-boyfriend Jackson.

She was talking to Major Jackson Beauregard Davis, officer of the United States Air Force, sworn to protect and defend the United States of America with his life.

He stood tall, legs wide, arms over his chest, glaring at her as if she were an airman just out of basic who'd forgotten how to lace up her boots.

"I think it's contaminated," she said, not because Major Davis intimidated her, but because she needed to talk through this to figure out how she was going to tell Shirley.

"With what?"

"I don't know."

"Is it flying?"

"I—" She stopped, looked up at a set of blinking lights far off in the sky.

"*Is it flying?*"

Jules had been clearing the fuel for months.

Last month's shipment had gone to base two weeks ago.

The shipment with contaminated biofuel was on base, in their tanks, fueling their cargo planes.

Her windpipes were choking her, her body turning against her. "Yes."

He uttered something he *definitely* hadn't learned in his momma's house, then yanked his phone out.

He pointed with it up at the lights. "That could be Lance."

She felt the blood drain from her face.

And then he was dialing a number, half-turned away from her, but every word he said echoed like shattered crystal in her eardrums. "Colonel, we've got a problem." He cut a glance back at Anna and cursed again. "Gonna need OSI and whoever can ground the fleet fastest."

Anna's legs wobbled. Her knees melted to liquid balls between bones that couldn't have been any stronger than spun sugar. Her hands shook so badly she could barely grip her own phone. But she had to call Shirley.

Anna would probably lose her job, lose her tuition assistance, lose her apartment, and have to move home with her parents.

She'd already lost all shot at finding any more happiness with Jackson.

Because not only had he just told her loud and clear his job came before her, he'd also told her he didn't trust her to solve the problem herself.

And he'd done it by calling to report her to the Air Force's internal version of the FBI.

JACKSON COULDN'T DECIDE which was worse, explaining to the colonel that every military aircraft in the state of Georgia needed to be grounded until their fuel could be evaluated and cleared, or watching Anna lose that battle she was fighting against herself.

Seared his heart when she turned her back to him. He knew it killed her to let him see her hurt and scared.

Pretty much killed him that he had to do it, but if there was a problem with the jet fuel, his *only* concern needed to be getting those birds on the ground.

Might've been some good in that too, since truth was, she didn't want to love him back. If she wanted to make a criminal case out of his taking charge here, he'd go on and let her. Even if the thought made his heart flop around like that fish that smacked Louisa in the face. Catch and release with Anna Grace, it was.

The colonel hung up soon as he had a grasp on the

situation. Jackson kept his eyes trained on the C-130 lights. Wasn't surprised when his phone rang with an unfamiliar base number.

It was gonna be a long night.

Anna retreated to the lab door, waiting for her boss, he assumed. Couldn't see much of her, huddled as she was out of the light, but a single headlight lit her up good halfway through his call with OSI.

The C-130 banked, then leveled off, its lights getting bigger on approach. He blew out relief he didn't know he was waiting for.

If the tests had been *that* bad, Anna would've insisted on the grounding herself.

But she hadn't argued when he'd suggested it, so knowing tonight's missions were being recalled gave him some peace.

The big guy climbing off the motorcycle next to Anna's car didn't.

"Brad?" Anna straightened beside the building. "What are you doing here?"

The OSI officer was still talking, so Jackson kept listening, answering "Yes, ma'am" and "No ma'am" as appropriate. Yes, ma'am, he was there at Rockwood Mineral Corporation now. No, ma'am, the lab tech wasn't a flight risk. Yes, ma'am, she said the contaminated fuel was in the air.

Lance was a damn good pilot. So were his buddies. They'd see it in the cockpit if something were wrong.

Didn't mean it wasn't a risk though.

"You seen Jules?" Brad said. "She didn't come home from work."

Anna went so pale she turned white. "She called in sick today."

"Excuse me, ma'am," Jackson interrupted the OSI agent. "Got another name for you."

He looked at Anna.

Her eyes went shiny.

"What the fuck's he doing here?" Brad said slowly. "Aw,

shit. That was *you*?"

Jackson hit the mute button on his phone. "Need her name, Anna. Title too."

"What. The fuck," Brad said.

Jackson unmuted his phone. "Thinking you need to hurry, ma'am. About to get ugly over here." He handed Anna the phone. "Tell her."

Anna went about her business telling the OSI officer that Jules had falsely cleared contaminated fuel for use, while Brad stood by gaping in denial. Jackson stood between the two of them, Radish at his feet, and waited for the rest of the fallout.

But after Anna's boss, Jackson's boss, the OSI agents, and half the base security forces arrived, after they'd all been separated and interviewed and talked past exhaustion, after they'd been cleared to go home for what was left of the night—with instructions to speak to no one, including each other, about this until further notice—Jackson still felt as if he were hanging.

This was worse than when Daddy died. Because when Daddy died, it was the end. Over. He'd gone through all the stages of grief, repeating denial a couple of times before he came to terms with facing the rest of his life without the best man he'd ever known. But tonight, when Anna was gone before Jackson and Radish were cleared to leave, he knew as long as she was out there, making the most of her life without him, there wouldn't be any closure for his heart.

Chapter Twenty-Nine

And they made beautiful biscuits together.
—The Temptress of Pecan Lane, *by Mae Daniels*

ANNA SPENT THE rest of the week on administrative leave. Kaci popped in daily. Anna's mother, bless her heart, flew in midweek.

OSI had told her not to leave town until their investigation was complete. She had no idea how long that would be.

Shirley had been furious, but she'd swung by as well. "We should've been the ones to report this," she said Thursday afternoon at Anna's little dining area table.

She might as well have impaled Anna's heart with that damn angel pin she was wearing again.

"You shouldn't have put her in this situation in the first place," Anna's mother said. She was in the kitchen, whipping up a batch of maple bacon chocolate chip cookies while she supervised Shirley's visit. "What kind of screening do you do on your employees anyway?"

Anna shot her mother a shushing look, but Mom was impervious.

A case of the blushes and knee-shakes interrupted Shirley's usual implacable calm. "Todd did some digging on EFA, Inc. Looks like it was a front to sell off rejected 20/80 biofuel." Shirley paused. "Jules found them for us."

Anna hadn't thought she had any chunks of heart left in her chest, but another piece crumbled off and bounced down her left lung to shatter against her liver.

"She was getting better," Anna said.

"She was getting filthy rich." Shirley's knee stilled. The floor stopped shaking. "That much money would make anyone better. They found her last night trying to cross into Canada."

"Does Brad know?"

"No idea."

There was a banging at the door. Kaci flung herself in. "Hey, sugar. Y'all having a party without me?" She gave Shirley an appraising glance, flicked a friendly finger-wave at Anna's mom, then plopped down in the nearest empty seat. "You treat her good, you hear me?" she said to Shirley. "Only thing Anna's ever done wrong is work too hard to take care of herself."

"You betcha," Mom said.

Shirley stood. "I expect things should wrap up quick with Jules in custody. We'll call when you're cleared to come back to work."

The thought of going back to work didn't inspire Anna with the happiness it should've.

The lab was so far away, that crazy place where she'd desperately tried to define herself after her marriage failed.

Instead, it felt like some mystical, fake place of bad memories.

Then she remembered meeting Jackson in the parking lot, and the smell of the cookies made her nauseous.

And that was before Kaci slid a familiar-looking envelope onto the table. "Messenger duty again," she said with an uncertain smile.

Anna was teary-eyed before she broke the seal. Mom paused to hover over her shoulder.

"You want to be alone?" Kaci asked.

Anna shook her head. What she wanted was to have gone

home over Thanksgiving and not come back.

Would've been easier that way. For once, easier sounded better than right.

The message was simple.

Anna Grace,

I will always believe in you.

Love,
Jackson

P.S. Turns out that was *Radish snoring. Sorry for—you know.*

Kaci squeezed her hand. "He's not doing too good, sugar. Misses you a lot. Sad, what with him not moving for at least a couple years."

"That'll make it easier." Anna swiped at her eyes. "How about I go burn my school books and dedicate my brain to science now? They can figure out what kind of mutant gene makes me want to continually sacrifice my ability to take care of myself by marrying men who only want someone to put their life in order every time they move."

"It's okay to not want him, sugar, but don't lie to yourself about why."

"You love this one?" Mom asked.

More prickles attacked her eyelids. Her mom still thought Neil might come over for Christmas dinner.

Wouldn't that be fun.

"Doesn't matter." Anna dabbed at her nose. "He called OSI on me."

"Sugar, he didn't call on you, he called *for* you. And I'm right glad he did, because Lance was supposed to be flying that night. I'da had to beat you silly if you let my husband get on a plane with bad fuel."

Yeah, Anna hadn't had any heart palpitations over *that* the last few nights either.

"The news last night said the military doesn't think the fuel would've caused long-term problems," Mom said. "It wasn't done to bring planes down."

Anna wanted to kick her. Kaci's lips went bloodred against the sudden pale of her face.

"We don't put those words in the same sentences around pilots' wives," Anna hissed at her mother.

"Well, it wasn't," Mom insisted.

"I vote we strap *her* to a firecracker," Anna grumbled.

Kaci rubbed some color back into her cheeks. "You gonna blow up all Jackson's notes?"

Anna snatched the newest one off the table and shoved it in her pocket.

Kaci chuckled. "Guess that answers the love question, now doesn't it?"

ANNA GOT THE CALL late Sunday that she'd been cleared to go back to work Tuesday, two weeks before Christmas, one week before she was due to leave for home. Jules had confessed and was supposedly working on a plea deal.

The OSI agent recommended that Anna stay clear of any further contact with her.

The agent didn't say anything about Brad though. So Monday afternoon, Anna had a late lunch with him.

"You sent that guy to beat me up," Brad said over his boat of sushi.

"I asked him to do what he would've done for a fellow airman." Anna's appetite was as nonexistent as it had been following her divorce, but she forced herself to eat some edamame. The salt stung her lips. She liked it. Not as if her lips would feel anything else ever again.

"I'm gonna try to get custody of the kid," Brad said. "Got an interview later this week."

"So you and Jules...?"

He didn't meet her eyes. Couldn't or wouldn't, she didn't know. "Turns out we've both got some growing up to do. Don't think we're looking for the same things."

"I'm sorry," she said.

He lifted a massive shoulder. "Shit happens." His eyes shifted to her, then away again. "She said to tell you she was sorry. She wanted to be able to take care of the baby. When— you know. Because I was a worthless shit for a while there."

Back in Minnesota, apologies were met with *Aw, it's okay, you betcha*. Here, Anna supposed blessing Jules's heart would be mild. "As long as you put half as much effort into fatherhood as you did into being a shit, I think you'll be fine," Anna said.

The staff at the small restaurant swished around them, seating other customers and delivering food, while Anna and Brad ate in silence.

"Appreciate you sending that wake-up call," Brad said finally.

"You and Jules were good friends to me and Neil when we got here. I couldn't not do something."

"Your friend did more than Neil would've. Don't think he deserved you."

He looked as if he wanted to say more, but Anna brushed it off. "It is what it is."

"Think you'll marry this guy?"

And now she felt as though the salt had settled in her eyes. "No." She blinked rapidly.

"Dude. Might want to talk to somebody about that."

Anna sucked back the sad and tilted her head at him. "You still seeing somebody?"

"Yeah, but he's not my type. Maybe I should find a girl shrink. Baby's gonna need a momma. Giggidy."

He grinned, and Anna laughed.

If Brad could go through losing his brother *and* his wife and survive, she reckoned she could keep trudging too.

"IF *I* WERE WRITING your story," Mamie said, "you'd sacrifice a whole lot more than your dignity to get her back."

Jackson thought about dropping the phone down the garbage disposal. "Great plan, Mamie, but sad truth is, she doesn't want anything from me. Not my help, not my paycheck, not my dignity."

Most perfect woman God ever created.

Except she didn't want his love either.

He scrubbed his fork. Hadn't much felt like eating tonight, but he'd done it anyway. Seemed like something that would've been on Anna Grace's schedule for him.

"Maybe it's time you figure out what she needs instead of what she wants." The sound of pins getting bowled over echoed through the phone.

"Anything she needs, she goes out and gets for herself." He dried the fork, then dropped it into his silverware drawer, right in the spot in his silverware holder labeled *forks*.

"Maybe she doesn't know what she needs. Flo, you go on and pass me by. Still gonna kick your hiney even without this frame." Mamie lowered her voice again. "So tell me, sugarplum, you want to be her hero?"

He didn't answer.

He was too busy trying to piece together how he was supposed to be smarter than Anna Grace to figure out what she didn't know she needed.

Conundrum, that's what it was.

"If you can't say yes to that, I reckon you ain't cut out to be that hero she needs."

He was thinking she might be right about that. Chapped him in places he didn't like being chapped. "What's she need, Mamie?"

"What do you need?"

More pins *plink-plunked*. Jackson felt like the whole bowling alley was lined up in his chest, the old Misses taking shots at knocking down his heart. "I need her to love me back," he said, sounding as pathetic and unmanly as every man in love he'd ever met.

"Oh, sugarplum, she does. You trust old Mamie on this one. She does."

"Not so sure about that."

"Ophelia, this boy ain't got the sense God gave a plucked rooster when it comes to women. You go on and give him a talkin' to before he breaks my heart."

Jackson went back to the sink of soapy water. Miss O's deep voice came on the line. "How far'd your mamie get with you, hon?"

"'Bout run me up the wall talking in riddles."

"Alrighty, then, listen on up. Miss O's gonna tell you a secret."

If she gave him her recipe for Miss O's Magic Mallow-bomb shots, he might have to accidentally on purpose drop his phone in the water. "Hanging on your every word, Miss O."

"You want her, you make her number one. Above your dog, above your job, above yourself. You can do that, you're worthy of her. If not, you don't love her enough to keep on bothering her. That clear enough for you, honey pie?"

It was clear.

He didn't know whether it helped, but it was clear.

THE RMC BUILDING was cold. Not heater-not-running-right cold. With the unseasonably warm December, the heater wasn't necessary.

It was more like an unwelcome chilly, and Anna couldn't tell where the chill was coming from.

Could've been the odd looks that she may or may not have imagined from her coworkers as she walked to Shirley's office at 7:56 A.M.

Could've been the steel-blue walls, walls that two weeks ago had been a warm, welcoming shade that soothed Anna's soul but today threatened to suck her joy meter empty.

Or it could've been fear.

Plain, simple fear that no matter what she did, no matter how hard she worked on this contract, the government might terminate her own contract in as few as three short months.

What incentive would RMC have to find her a new position in the company?

What incentive would Corporate have to keep this branch open?

How would she finish her damn degree and get a stupid technical job *then*?

"Get on in here," Shirley said from her doorway. "Got a lot of work to do, and not enough lifetimes to do it in."

Anna followed her into the office and took a seat on the edge of a prettier-than-it-was-comfortable guest chair. She pulled her cardigan tighter around herself.

"Congratulations, you're our new lead analyst. Gonna have to stay in school, have to continue with the certification series, but Corporate's approved your promotion." Shirley dumped a stack of papers at the edge of her desk. "All the resumes from the last six months. Pick out four or five you like, and we'll interview them for your assistant."

"My—wait, *what*?"

"Assistant. We need somebody to do your old job when you take over the vacant analyst position."

It was stupid, immature, and really, *really* stupid, but Anna's chin trembled.

Then her core quaked, a rumble that emanated from her midsection and bounced through her chest like Rex's motherboard on a Monday morning.

"There a problem?" Shirley said.

Anna licked her lips.

Of course there wasn't a problem. "A promotion?"

"With a pay raise. A *big* one."

A pay raise. Comfort. Temporarily more security.

But—*God*, this was stupid—but—"Will I still do the filing?"

Shirley peered at her.

She pulled her glasses off, wiped them, pushed them back

up her long nose, and peered harder. "No," she said, enunciating the word so Anna heard at least six letters and eight syllables of highly uncomplimentary opinions aimed toward her person.

But it didn't matter, because she was being offered a promotion. She'd proved her technical worth and her loyalty to the company, and she was in a position to convince the customer that she ran a lab as sound and smooth as the best damn lab analysts in the entire country. The experience would look fabulous on her resume after she finished her degree and started job-hunting. This was a gift from the heavens, a karmic high-five for all that she'd endured since the moment she set foot in the great state of Georgia. And she was honored to have the opportunity to serve her country while she taught someone else—someone fresh and green and eager—how to keep the paperwork of a laboratory in good working order.

She was the luckiest woman on the face of the professional and technical worlds.

And she would tell Shirley so as soon as she could get oxygen past that red *remove before flight* tab blocking the flow of air through her throat.

"You *do* want the job," Shirley said.

Anna's lungs and nose and air passages snapped back into rhythm.

She forced an overly bright smile, nodded, opened her mouth, and said—

"I quit."

Shirley blinked.

So did Anna.

And then she gasped, felt her eyelids stretch so wide her eyeballs bulged and her vision crossed. She ordered her tongue to take the words back, to correct that erroneous statement.

It came out stronger. "I. Quit."

And instead of feeling the earth quake and tremble beneath her, instead of being struck down by a sucker punch of God's laughter delivered through a lightning bolt, instead of imploding with a panic attack of epic proportions, Anna closed her eyes, inhaled the stale office air twinged with a hint of Shirley's pre-workday smoke, and smiled a real smile.

Her chest expanded, free and clear and *free*, wide-open to a new world of possibilities.

"Oh my God," Anna said on a laugh. "I really do. I quit."

Quit the job, quit the expectations, quit feeling the weight of everyone else's disappointments in her failures.

"You have lost your ever-loving mind," Shirley said.

But there was something else there.

Admiration.

A tad bit of jealousy.

And, yeah, a lot of *this one's gone loony* too, but it was beneath the good stuff.

"You bet your ketchup-drenched fried Twinkies I have," Anna said.

She grinned wider and laughed again.

She was free.

FREEDOM, IT TURNED OUT, didn't come with a recipe for biscuits.

But Kaci was happy to share her momma's recipe, her tub of bacon grease, *and* her old cast-iron skillet, along with an offer to blow up Anna's separation paperwork whenever RMC got around to delivering it.

And the bills for those classes she'd taken.

But she'd refused alimony from Neil in exchange for their modest savings, so all was not lost.

She flashed a wide grin at the mess on her countertop. Bowls and spoons and pans littered the dirty surface. She slid on spilled flour, but she didn't stop to wipe it up. She had better things to do than clean her kitchen.

As soon as that timer dinged.

Someone knocked on her door.

Banged, really. Repeatedly.

Probably her landlord to kick her out after he found out she'd quit her job.

She eyed the timer. Forty-five seconds. She'd give the landlord her notice, and then she'd get on with getting on with her life.

She hoped.

One way or another, she wouldn't be staying here.

But it wasn't her landlord on the other side of the door. Her heart launched a thousand butterflies into her chest. *"Oh!"*

"Anna. Don't go." Jackson was disheveled, his uniform blouse crooked, his eyes wide and pleading. He touched a finger to her lips. "Listen a minute, okay?"

This wasn't the plan. She was supposed to find him.

But she was working on being flexible, so she nodded, all those butterflies in her chest making her ribs tingle like her lips beneath his finger.

"I owe Uncle Sam about another year and a half. Always figured I'd retire nine years on and then get to figuring out what I want to be when I grow up. But the last few months, I've been what I want to be, I just didn't know it. But I know now. I want to be yours."

The oven timer beeped. Anna tried to pull in a breath, but those butterflies were tickling her lungs. Her eyes went misty.

"I love you, Anna Grace," Jackson said. "You wanna go to Iceland, I'll go to Iceland. Darlin', I'd go live in an igloo if it's what makes you happy. You go on and tell me what you want, and I'm gonna go on and do it."

A whimpery laugh slipped through her lips.

Wonderful man.

Crazy, wonderful, perfect man.

The oven timer beeped again. "I quit my job," she said.

Confusion skittered over his features. "Kaci said you got—" He stopped. His jaw went slack. "Son of a biscuit. She got me good."

Anna's breath hitched. If he couldn't play hero, did he still want her?

A familiar old grin flashed. "We'll find you a new one. A better one. Whatever you want to do, we'll make it work for you. Just don't go." He engulfed her in a full body hug, stroking her arms, her back, rubbing his jaw in her hair. "Don't leave me, Anna Grace. You and me, we're just getting started. Thirty years from now, I want to be rocking on our front porch with you, watching our grandbabies, smelling that fancy shampoo you like to use, laughing and talking and loving you."

"Grandbabies?"

"Babies and grandbabies and great grandbabies. And I'll buy you enough label makers that you can stamp labels on every single one of them."

Oh.

Oh, yes.

He was worth every painful moment of this year. Every moment of her first time as an Air Force wife.

Every moment of her life.

"You need to stop talking," she said, "before you make me burn your biscuits."

His eyebrows knit together. He sniffed the air. "Biscuits?"

She smoothed a hand over his blouse, then flicked open the top button. "I wouldn't have left without offering you my biscuits."

His delicious chuckle sent a shiver through her bones. "Thought you figured out I'm a pie man."

His fingers went to work doing wicked things to the back of her neck. He was solid and safe and more dependable than she'd known she could possibly want. She didn't care that the biscuits were burning, because he had six more buttons that needed undoing, plus the rest of his uniform to get through.

She pulled back to look into those wonderful, crinkled cobalt eyes while still working at his buttons. "I love you."

"I love you. Pies and burnt biscuits and label maker and all."

"You love my label maker?" Her voice cracked.

"You bet your biscuits."

She grabbed *his* biscuits and gave them a squeeze.

Still solid and perfect as ever.

So was his mouth when he kissed her.

Slow and thorough and perfect.

The man didn't just love her. He loved her good. She wrapped herself around him and kissed him and loved him back until they fell against the wall for support.

"Been thinking," he said into her neck, "we could find you a job with that label maker."

She knew. She'd been researching professional organizing while she baked, and already had a color-coded binder started. Best part was, it was a mobile career. It'd take a while to build up her reputation, to draw a regular, decent salary, but she didn't plan on doing it alone. "Have I mentioned I love you?"

His eyes went soft and smoky. "I love your independence."

"I love how you take care of me."

His arms tightened. "I mean it, Anna Grace. If anything ever happened to me, I know you're gonna be able to take care of things."

The oven timer beeped again. "I need to take care of your biscuits."

The rich sound of his laughter washed over her and enveloped her in bliss. "Darlin', we got the rest of our lives for making biscuits."

"Just biscuits?"

He swooped her up into his arms. "Biscuits. And pies. And stewed okra."

She laid her head against his shoulder and let out a leaky laugh.

"And corn bread," he said. "We haven't talked about your corn bread yet. You make corn bread?"

She pressed a kiss to his jaw. "Three-point question."

"You're asking for trouble, Anna Grace."

"And you're going to love every minute of it."

"Yes, ma'am."

And he loved her so much, he even buttered her burnt biscuits.

Epilogue

OF ALL HIS ASSIGNMENTS, Jackson hadn't thought of any of them as *home*. They'd merely been assignments, temporary places to do what he'd always thought he did best, Radish at his side. But Gellings?

Gellings felt like home.

He was willing to lay odds it wasn't the house or the base, though.

It was his domestic Anna Grace frying up some chicken in the kitchen while Radish watched from under the table. Or maybe it was his brilliant Anna Grace putting the world in order, one house at a time, building up a reputation for herself. Probably, too, his beautiful Anna Grace growing his baby while she went on about her business making sure his world stayed put to rights.

He was one lucky son of a gun to come home to this every night.

He slid up behind his wife at the stove, put one hand to her belly that had started to swell, and pressed a kiss to her cheek. "'Bout to burn those biscuits again, Anna Grace."

"Oh!" She swatted him away, snagged a hot pad, and rescued the biscuits from the oven.

They both stared at the smoking cast iron skillet on the counter.

Jackson smothered a grin. "Probably the oven's off again."

She gave him a look that could've come only from two and a half years of asking her favorite and not-so-favorite Southern women for their biscuit recipes. "Do you know *anyone* willing to tell me the *real* recipe for these stupid things?"

"Probably not, darlin'."

"Then you can tell 'em all I'm fixin' to feed you canned biscuits the rest of your life." She looked at the stove and gave a girly shriek. The fried chicken was smoking now too.

Jackson snagged a plate and spread a couple of paper towels on it, then eased up next to her. "How about you let me finish up for you?"

He swallowed a chuckle at her *I do it myself* face, but then her doe eyes went all soft and a smile sweet as summer rain crossed her lips. "I'm in trouble if this is a boy, aren't I?"

"You bet your pie, Anna Grace."

She laughed while she heaped fried chicken onto the plate.

He waited until she'd turned the stove off and stepped over to the fridge. He knew his wife loved him more than he ever would've thought possible, but he also knew better than to spring potentially unhappy surprises on any woman while she was standing next to hot oil. "Think I might could get you a real biscuit recipe," he said.

She plopped a Tupperware bowl full of potato salad onto the counter. "How's that?"

"'Bout the same way I got you my momma's sweet potato pie recipe."

Her face went ghost white before she'd finished her surprised gasp.

"Not deploying," he said quickly. He gave her belly a soft rub, then pulled her close. She'd handled his last deployment as only Anna Grace could, and he knew she'd pull through another one strong and steady as ever if she had to. But he'd move heaven and earth before he'd leave her to deliver their baby alone. "Cross my heart, Anna Grace, ain't no way I'm letting you meet our little one by yourself."

Her fingers flicked at the top button on his uniform blouse.

"PCS orders?"

"To the Pentagon," he said into her hair. "Got word about an hour ago."

And he'd be lying if he said he didn't felt a little itchy in his ABUs, worrying how she'd take the news. She'd done real good for herself setting up her business. Starting to get more work than she could handle on her own, baby or no baby.

She straightened, eyes darting about the kitchen.

Then toward the bedroom.

Up to the ceiling, then to the living room.

Plotting the packing, if he knew his Anna Grace.

Amazing woman.

"Okay, Anna Grace?" They both knew what he was asking her to give up.

She flashed a brilliant smile. "Jackson Davis, you don't think I haven't planned for this, do you? I thought you knew me better than that."

Huh.

Maybe he wasn't always as smart as he thought.

She laughed, and he found himself chuckling too. "I love you, you know that?" he said.

"That's also part of the plan. Let's eat. Baby's hungry."

He'd do anything she wanted. Because like his momma said, there was a lot of perfection in his Anna Grace.

About The Author

Jamie Farrell writes humorous contemporary romance. She believes love and laughter are two of the most powerful forces in the universe.

A native Midwesterner, Jamie has lived in the South the majority of her adult life. When she's not writing, she and her military hero husband are busy raising three hilariously unpredictable children.

For more information on Jamie and her books, visit her online at JamieFarrellBooks.com.

Made in the USA
Charleston, SC
29 November 2015